"I won't go easy on you." Truth. He couldn't. Not if he was going to be rid of her. Maybe it was unfair of him to want her kicked out because he was attracted to her. Didn't matter. She was rich. She'd get over it.

"Go easy on me? Why, Agent Mean, I'd be disappointed if you did."

"All right. Let's see what you've got."

"Oh. Okay." Eyes gleaming, she lifted her tank and bra. "I've got thirty-six C's."

The male trainees might have whistled, the females might have gasped. Hector couldn't be sure because he lost focus of everything but those perfect breasts. Honest to God, his thoughts derailed, his nerve endings going white-hot throughout his body.

Rose-colored nipples, beaded and ripe for sucking. She had no tan lines, was the same sweet cream and honey all over. And she was closing the distance between them, tempting him, daring him. Totally within reach.

He flexed his fingers; he wanted to reach.

She double tapped him in the mouth so hard he was spitting blood as he fell. Stars winked through his line of vision before he landed. And then, when he hit, his skull cracking against the ground, the stars vanished and thick black cobwebs took their place.

Lights. Out.

*Turn the page to read praise for Gena Showalter and her bestselling novels of danger and desire . . .*

## Also by Gena Showalter

# GENA SHOWALTER

# DARK TASTE OF RAPTURE

Pocket STAR Books
New York   London   Toronto   Sydney   New Delhi

Pocket Star Books
A Division of Simon & Schuster, Inc.
1230 Avenue of the Americas
New York, NY 10020

This book is a work of fiction. Names, characters, places, and incidents either are products of the author's imagination or are used fictitiously. Any resemblance to actual events or locales or persons, living or dead, is entirely coincidental.

First Pocket Star Books paperback edition September 2011

POCKET STAR BOOKS and colophon are registered trademarks of Simon & Schuster, Inc.

For information about special discounts for bulk purchases, please contact Simon & Schuster Special Sales at 1-866-506-1949 or business@simonandschuster.com.

The Simon & Schuster Speakers Bureau can bring authors to your live event. For more information or to book an event, contact the Simon & Schuster Speakers Bureau at 1-866-248-3049 or visit our website at www.simonspeakers.com.

Cover design by Lisa Litwack
Illustration by Cliff Nielsen

Manufactured in the United States of America

10  9  8  7  6  5  4  3  2  1

ISBN 978-1-4391-7578-1
ISBN 978-1-4391-7580-4 (ebook)

*To my amazing editor Lauren McKenna, who saw the diamond in the rough, then helped me see it, too!*

*To the fabulous Louise Burke and all the wonderful folks at Pocket, for the support and enthusiasm (and such a gorgeous cover)!*

*To the awesome Megan McKeever, for helping me out any time I came a-calling!*

*And to the adorable pocket rocket Jill Monroe, for the pep talks!*

*And to the incomparable Kresley Cole for the love.*

# Acknowledgments

To you, my readers, for falling in love with Noelle and asking for her story!

# Prologue

❧

TWO MEN STOOD IN the middle of a shadowed, barren field. Both were human. One was tall, muscled, with dark hair and a busted-up face. His syn-cotton shirt was torn, his jeans dirty, and his boots scuffed. There were telltale weapon bulges under his arms, at his wrists, and at his ankles.

Clearly, he was the bodyguard.

The other wore a perfectly tailored silk business suit, his Italian loafers freshly polished. His sun-kissed hair was expensively coiffed, and the only bulge he sported was the one in his pocket, where he kept his wallet.

Clearly, he was the money.

Acrid wind shrieked as if someone had cranked a hard rock song on a radio, dancing thick dirt granules in every direction, Money radiated impatience mixed with glee—until two other men materialized a few feet away, and the impatience vanished.

The newcomers had appeared in a blink, without walking a single step: a white-haired Arcadian—an otherworlder with the ability to teleport, among other things—and another human, this one wearing a suit as well, only his was ill-fitting and made from a cheap synthetic fiber.

The human's arms were cuffed behind his back. He smelled of pungent fear and urine. Poor bastard must have pissed himself.

Without a word, the Arcadian pushed the trembling male to his knees.

*Night's about to get interesting.*

The rust-colored sky appeared swollen, the storm-drenched clouds ready to burst. In the center, the sun was a hemorrhaging hook of gold, offering only a fraction of light. That hardly mattered to the witness. From high in the gnarled trees surrounding the field, his gaze cut through the gloom as easily as a knife through flesh.

"You think you can encroach on *my* territory?" Money snarled down at the kneeler. Another gust of wind created that perfect background music.

"N—no. I just . . . I . . . I'm so sorry. I never meant . . ."

"You never meant to offer New Chicago's elite prettier girls? Better prices?"

"No. No. You have to believe me. I only thought . . . hoped . . ."

"You thought . . . hoped . . ." Money sneered. No question, he was a man used to getting what he wanted, when he wanted it. He held out his hand, and Bodyguard smacked the butt of a pyre-gun onto his palm. "Well, your thoughts and hopes just got you killed."

"No!" Kneeler sobbed like a baby. "Please! Don't do this. I'll leave New Chicago. I won't ever come back. I swear!"

Money nodded to the Arcadian, who jerked his T-shirt over his head and stuffed the material in Kneeler's mouth. Kneeler shook his head, perhaps to dislodge the cloth, perhaps to attempt another plea for mercy.

Either way, he failed.

"You were right, you know," Money said, smug now. "You won't ever come back." A blaze of yellow light erupted from the barrel of the gun, arrowing out and nailing Kneeler in his chest.

A muffled scream of agony pierced the air. As Kneeler toppled to the ground, twitching, dying as his organs fried to a crisp, Money returned the gun to Bodyguard and wiped his hands in a job well done.

# One

---

TRAINEE AFTER TRAINEE EMERGED from the auto-bus. Some were in their late teens and had just graduated from AIR High, but most were in their early twenties, male, and obviously overwhelmed by the line of instructors watching unabashedly as they carried their bags to their new digs: a rundown, luxuries-are-a-thing-of-the-past bunkhouse in the middle of an isolated valley.

Isolated, and ugly. There was dirt, dirt, and more dirt, with the occasional knotted, naked tree to spice things up. Only thing that wasn't a complete eyesore was the obstacle course woven throughout the entire mile-long stretch, with its tall but thin brick walls, elevated beams, and manmade holes and pools, but by the end of the day, everyone here would hate the course so much they'd want to burn it down and dance on the ashes rather than look at it.

The few females to disembark, well, they were in their early twenties, too, and just as overwhelmed. Except for the last two. They just appeared eager.

Poor, dumb kids. They'd learn.

Thirteen years ago, Agent Hector Dean had ridden in that bus himself. Everyone on it had been yelled at, demoralized, and slapped around, all in an effort to weed out the pussies. What those two girls didn't know but should? The yelling, the demoralizing, and the slapping were just precursors for what was to come.

Poor, dumb, about-to-be-traumatized kids.

Hector didn't have to check the roster to learn the identities of his eager beavers. He'd memorized the stats of all twenty-nine recruits, and recognized the pair from their photos. Ava Sans and Noelle Tremain.

Ava, a twenty-three-year-old fluff of femininity who was barely five nothing in a pair of heels. She had curly brown hair and chocolate brown eyes. Cute in a Sunday school teacher kind of way. Which was ironic. She had a rap sheet with more pages than the Bible.

She'd grown up in Whore's Corner, the poorest part of New Chicago, with a drugged-out mother and more stepfathers than fingers. Hector could relate. Not about the multiple dads, he'd just had the one, and a fucking terrible one who'd enjoyed watching his young sons prize-fight, but about the drugged-out mom living in Whore's Corner.

The WC was where Hector had been born, chewed up, spit out, and reformed into the man—or weapon— he was today.

*Moving on.*

Noelle, also twenty-three years old, though she was a tall, reed-slender slice of elegance, with lighter brown hair that was straight as a board, and eyes of the lightest gray. The product of old money, she'd grown up in the wealthiest part of town, in a giant-ass mansion, with doting servants to attend her every whim.

Hector could not relate.

She was as lovely as a cameo, and appeared to be as untouchable as a goddess. Which was also ironic. She might have a shorter rap sheet than Ava—most likely because her money had *bought* her a cleaner file—but every one of her arrests had stemmed from touching someone. Violently.

He didn't mind admitting he'd been somewhat impressed with her before he'd seen her. A former delinquent himself, he knew the gals and guys who'd get down and dirty when necessary, uncaring whether they were hurt—or worse—always made the best agents.

Now he had to reevaluate. She looked like a tasty after-dinner treat ready to throw a tantrum over *everything*, not a potential badass.

He watched as she stretched her shoulders, her white T-shirt pulling tight over the plump rise of her breasts, the golden sun lancing down and worshipping flawless skin that somehow boasted a post-orgasmic flush. Hector stopped caring about relating and realized he wanted to do a little touching of his own.

Oh, hell, no. Attraction wasn't something he allowed himself to feel, even in the smallest degree. Touching wasn't something he allowed himself to do, ever. The one and only girlfriend he'd had, he'd accidentally killed.

Goddamn mutant arms, he thought with a snarl. Strong emotion literally fired them up, atomizing both into some kind of hot, molten steel that burned through bodies, ripped out organs, and hell, destroyed *anything*. Even a woman he only wanted to pleasure. So, lesson learned. He and females were not a good mix.

Friend and fellow agent Dallas Gutierrez stood on Hector's right and moaned as if in pain. "Sweet damn, but those legs are long enough to wrap around me like a pretzel. And God, I love pretzels. Anyone know when we break for lunch?"

"That's my cousin, dickwad," Agent Jaxon Tremain said from Hector's left. Had Whacky Jacky been next to Dallas, he would have drilled his knuckles into the guy's bicep. "Watch your mouth."

"By *watch my mouth* do you mean I should invite your cuz back to my place for a game of Hide the Magic Wand, or my new personal fave, Puff on the Magic Dragon?" Dallas asked conversationally. "And I know what you're thinking. I'm really into wizardry these days. Well, you're right."

Hector gave a rusty bark of laughter. He hadn't observed Dallas in this good a mood in a long time.

A low growl escaped Jaxon. "I meant I'd scoop out your liver with a spoon, you idiot!"

"Sterling silver or plastic?" Hector asked. In their line of work, details were important. Besides, he liked being part of their banter. Considering the fact that his work friends were his only friends, and he rarely socialized after hours, this kind of thing made him feel connected, like a part of the team.

*Team*. Something he'd never thought to be a part of,

as dangerous as he was, but collaboration was a very important part of AIR. Sometimes the only thing that saved your neck was the man guarding your back.

Dallas groused, "I remember the days when you were actually nice."

So did Hector. Once upon a time, Jaxon had been so by-the-book he could have *been* the book. Then he'd met his wife, Mishka, and the pretty little assassin had somehow infected him with asshole-itis.

Jaxon liked to say she'd helped him accept his "true self." And he actually said it with pride and affection, rather than revulsion, as if being yanked out of the shithead closet was a good thing.

*No one* was pulling Hector out, and that was that. He was the way he was for a valid, life-saving reason, and that reason wasn't ever going to change. Therefore, neither was he.

"You won't be remembering anything," Jaxon said on a rumbling breath, "if you say one more goddamn word about my—"

"Jaxy!"

The argument must have drawn Noelle's attention because she clapped her hands and twirled. Then, with a carefree laugh, she tossed her overstuffed duffel at Ava, raced across the distance, and flung herself into Jaxon's open arms.

Clapping? Twirling? *Seriously?* Maybe her record was exaggerated rather than cleaned, because damn, in that moment, the little-girl innocence radiating off her was astounding.

Sadly, that wasn't the turn-off it should have been.

With those lush breasts and right side of dangerous curves, she was still one hundred percent woman.

*Don't go there.* AIR was his life, saving innocents his only goal. He'd spent a good portion of his childhood locked in a cage, and had been forced to listen as his only brother was beaten to death. He never wanted anyone else to suffer that kind of tragedy. More than that, he never wanted to *cause* another tragedy.

Noelle, no matter how hot, was off limits. During camp, and forever after.

"I missed you." As she pulled back to look Jaxon over, she giggled like they were all at a sleepover and pillow fighting. Giggled, yeah, but there were hints of smoke in her voice. The naughty kind that made him think of sex. "You get handsomer—more handsome? Whatever! You're prettier every time I see you."

"You, too, honey," Jaxon said. "You, too."

"Just for that, I'm willing to forgive you for not calling, writing, or letting me crash at your place when I was being chased by the law."

The agent chucked her under the chin. "You're supposed to be *aiding* the law, Elle."

Elle. The nickname didn't fit her. It was too cutesy. Which, he supposed, *should* have fit the china doll in front of him. Actually, it did fit, except for those hints of smoke.

"Oh, I'll aid the law, all right," she said with a flare of determination. "Just as soon as I'm given a badge."

Hector did his best to cut off his snort. He failed. As if she would last through a single week of training.

Before seeing her live and in person, he would

have bet she'd soar to the top of her class. *After* seeing her live and in person . . . not just no, but *are you fucking kidding me* no. Whether she was truly violent or just a poser, no one he knew wanted a partner like her.

Those silvery-gray eyes flipped in his direction, narrowed briefly, swept up and down his body, as if seeing past his clothes and memorizing every detail. Then she looked away, dismissing him as if she'd found him to be substandard.

All right, then. She didn't find him attractive. *Good.* That's actually what he preferred, because it saved him from having to deal with unwanted advances. In fact, he kept his head shaved to a glossy shine for just that reason. He was a man willing to do *anything* to discourage feminine attention.

Because yeah, females could be vanity hounds and most preferred their dates to have hair. Black, blond, red, it didn't matter, as long as the locks were thick and lustrous. And here was a news flash for little Miss Giggles: when he allowed his to grow, it was dark brown, nearly jet, with hints of gold and worthy of a fucking lion.

Not that he was feeling defensive or anything.

Besides, even if he'd had hair, Noelle wouldn't have wanted him. Most females found him a little too intimidating to speak to, much less someone to consider hooking up with. And soft, pretty girl Noelle had to like soft, pretty boys. That's just the way the world worked.

"Ava," Jaxon said to the Sunday school cutie who'd

just ambled over to their group. Her duffel, as well as Noelle's, sagged from her arms, weighing her down. "Good to see you again."

"Yeah, you, too." She returned the nod, curls bobbing around her face.

So. Ava and Noelle were friends. And long enough for the shorter girl to have met members of Noelle's extended family. Interesting. With their vastly different backgrounds, Hector never would have paired them.

Then again, Noelle enjoyed treating Ava like a servant. And Ava took it.

Huh. Why were they here again?

Ava leaned over to Noelle and whispered, "Are you *meaning* to sound like such a douche?"

Noelle winked at her.

If Hector hadn't been so focused on the pair, he would have missed the byplay. Now his attention sharpened. So . . . there were times Noelle *didn't* sound like a douche?

Could the bubblehead thing be an act, then? If so, what was her purpose? And why hadn't Jaxon, her blood kin, recognized the difference?

That last question had Hector shaking his head, dismissing his suspicions. Jaxon was sharp, one of the best and most observant agents out there, and he would know his own cousin better than a friend/servant would.

Dallas cleared his throat, the universal sign for make-the-damn-introductions-already.

Jaw clenched, Jaxon made them. Dallas first, then

Hector. No one tried to shake anyone's hand, thank God, but at least Ava met his gaze. Noelle peered somewhere over his shoulder. *After* pinching Dallas's cheek as if he were the sweetest toddler she'd ever seen.

Stupid shit enjoyed the fondling, giving her a high-wattage grin of encouragement.

"You both know I can't show you preferential treatment while you're here," Jaxon said, uneasy. His scarred face paled in the sunlight, becoming almost waxen. "Right?"

"Of course we do." Finally removing her attention from Dallas, Noelle patted the top of Jaxon's head with the sugary tolerance usually reserved for the brain damaged. "But that's okay, because everyone else will."

Uh, that would be another are-you-kidding-no. *No one* got preferential treatment in this shit box.

Hector was kicking things off this first week, and would then hand the reins of control over to Dallas, who would run things for a week before handing the reins to Jaxon for *his* week. Jaxon would then hand the reins to Ghost, as well as a female agent named Phoenix for their hell week. Then, Ghost and Phoenix would return the reins to Hector, and he'd have to endure another seven days.

He'd make damn sure Ghost and Phoenix knew these two were to be ridden harder than everyone else.

*Ridden . . . harder . . .*

Damn. Now he was Freuding himself. Arm-wise, that was the first sign of trouble.

Dallas he didn't have to worry about. Boy would know what to do. It was the principle of the thing and all.

"I can guarantee you'll get the gold star treatment from me," Dallas said, bombing Hector's expectations into oblivion. "After you answer a question for me. Do you like pretzels?"

Ava rolled her eyes and muttered something unintelligible under her breath.

"Oh my God, yes!" Noelle's grin was all white teeth and that damn innocence. "I love pretzels! They're just so yummalicious."

*Yummalicious?*

"I'm so glad you said that," Dallas began. "Because—"

Jaxon reached around Hector and slugged Dallas in the jaw.

"Ow! What was that for?" the agent grumbled, rubbing the already swelling area.

"Just be happy I don't have a spoon." The scowl wiped from Jaxon's face as he gave Noelle his full concentration. "Don't pay him any attention. Just . . . go get settled, honey. Orientation starts in an hour." He gave her a gentle push in the direction she was supposed to go.

Noelle stopped at Ava's side and slung her arm over the girl's shoulders. "All right. We'll go. We know you guys have important stuff to do. I just want to say thank you. You've done your best to make us feel welcome, and we're just so grateful."

Were those tears in her eyes? Shit. They were. Deep

down, he'd *known* she was a crier. How pathetic. And even disappointing.

"Take your bag already," Ava snipped at her. "It's, like, two hundred pounds heavier than mine."

"Impossible. I merely brought the essentials. Clothes, my favorite boots, face cream, makeup, a few books to read, a couple cans of caviar, lingerie, and my coffeepot. Plus a few other things a girl like me just can't live without but can't mention in mixed company because it would be indelicate. You know, because they're *sexual*." There at the end, she whispered, the hints of smoke blending with echoes of midnight.

Worse, at "lingerie," Hector and Dallas had stood a little straighter. At "sexual," they'd moaned. Jaxon punched them both in the back of the head.

Hector always ignored his attractions, yeah, but come on. Now images of the elegant Noelle wearing a trashy, barely-there scrap of lace and a take-a-bite-out-of-me grin were seared into his brain.

And wouldn't you know it? His arms began to burn, his hands to itch. The second and third signs of trouble.

If this kept up, his arms would begin to glow and the tattoos etched from his shoulders to his fingertips would crackle. The final *oh, shit* signs that meant he was nearly too late to stop the ensuing carnage, that his skin, muscle, and bone were about to mutate into fiery mist and melt everything he touched. A transition that would last several hours, until the heat finally lost steam and died down.

Problem was, he couldn't masturbate his sexual desires away because he'd fry off his cock. And he couldn't take pills because they scrambled his cognitive process, preventing him from solving his cases.

So, when sexual frustration became too much for him and his arms, he called a hooker for a blow job. That way, the girl stayed on her knees, mostly out of reach, and he got off without having to worry about torching an entire town.

Another problem made itself known. He couldn't— wouldn't—call Happy Endings while he was here. That would mix the secret, seedier side of his personal life with the crucial business side, and he would *never* do that. AIR was the one pure thing in his life; he refused to taint it. For any reason.

"I think I just heard someone groan from inside the bag." Ava shouted the words as she fumbled with the zipper. "You have a body in here, don't you? Well, you're not framing me again, and that's that."

Noelle stepped away from her, palms up and out. "Darling, just carry the thing already. You've been whining about needing to step up your exercise program for a long time, and I've decided to help you. You're welcome, by the way."

"I never asked—oh!" Ava stomped a foot. "I'm going to murder you in your sleep."

Noelle gasped, intense waves of hurt wafting from her. "I can't believe you just threatened me like that. I . . . need a moment to collect myself. Excuse me, everyone." Sniffling, she walked away. Without taking her bag.

Frowning, Hector rubbed at the abrupt ache in his chest. What the hell? He actually cared that she'd been threatened?

Ava followed after her friend, dragging both bags and mumbling under her breath about taking douchieness too far.

The three agents watched them go. Each for a different reason, Hector was sure. Jaxon, to make sure they entered the bunkhouse without any trouble. Dallas, to see his pretzel's perfect ass sway, and Hector because he just couldn't seem to stop himself.

"Girls' bunk is upstairs, honey," Jaxon called. "There's an entrance to the right, so you won't have to go through the guys' area."

"Oh, thanks," Noelle returned without looking back—and without moving to the right.

Funny, there hadn't been a trace of hurt remaining in her tone.

Ava finally managed to unload Noelle's stuff—by drop-kicking it into the girl's path and causing her to stumble. Laughing, now free of her burden, Ava darted ahead of her. When Noelle righted herself, she swept up the nylon and raced forward, too, chuckling all the way. No more baby giggles for her, but a grown woman's amusement.

The change was startling, but understandable. She must have been nervous around them.

At the last moment, she shoved past Ava and reached the door to their new home first. The two disappeared from view.

O-kay, then. His final impression? Take the "yum-

malicious" then add the giggles, multiply the clueless-
ness and the split-second change of emotion, subtract
the chuckling and the wink, and you most likely had
a recipe for dumb as a box of rocks. Pretty as a cameo,
yeah, that hadn't changed, but she was still dumb as a
box of rocks.

No doubt about it now. Her record was exaggerated. Kinda like when the scrawny kid in class paid the
bully to protect him. At the moment, Hector wasn't
even sure Noelle Tremain could fight off a piece of
lint.

"How many strings did you have to pull to get her
here?" he asked Jaxon.

The guy sighed, all kinds of weariness bubbling in
the undertone. "Too many."

Thought so. "And why does someone like her want
to do this?" AIR agents worked long hours, made gruesome discoveries, and constantly waded through the
darkest dredges of humanity. All of which had been
lifesaving for Hector, but rich, pampered Noelle didn't
need any saving.

"She said something about putting her kung fu skills
to good use." Jaxon shook his head at the ridiculous-
ness of his words. "I laughed, so she finally admitted
the truth. That she wants a chance to carry a badge and
tell people what to do, then shoot them if they disobey
her."

That, Hector believed. "You are such a sucker."

Good news was, there weren't enough strings *anyone*
could pull if she screwed up. And she would. Probably
before orientation ended.

The thought of never looking at that pretty face again caused an ache of . . . something to smolder in his chest. The same ache he'd experienced when she'd reacted to Ava's threat.

He ignored that something, whatever it was, with the same determination he usually ignored his lusts.

*I'll have you gone by the end of the day, Tremain. Guaranteed.*

# Two

NOELLE THREW HER DUFFEL—WHICH was filled only with necessary clothes and shoes—on the squeaky regulation twin rollaway and looked around. Honestly? This sucked sweaty donkey balls.

A hovel, that's what her new living quarters were. Peeling paint on the walls, a dirty concrete floor. No windows. No desks. No compusoles. Just a row of tiny beds and won't-hold-anything nightstands, with a layer of dust coating the air. So . . . borderline-poverty basics, she thought with a grimace.

How would she survive?

There were only three essentials in Noelle's life. Ava, money, and comfort. In that order. Ava was her rock, her coconspirator, and her biggest supporter. But she couldn't wrap Ava around her like a mink to ward off the slight chill in the air. Not again. And her truckloads of money were (supposedly) off limits while she was here. That meant comfort had a big fat "denied" stamp over it.

For the next three months, at least. That's how long

she was required to stay here. But the worst part? When those three torturous months were up, she *still* wouldn't be considered an AIR agent. Not until someone within the organization finally deemed her worthy enough to carry a badge.

*Yeah, good luck with that.* No one besides Ava had ever before deemed Noelle worthy of anything—except therapy. Her parents had claimed to love her and her dad *had* sought to protect her, but she'd never been . . . enough. Not for either of them.

*Can't you do anything right?* How many times had her father shouted that little gem? In fact, he'd been dead for years, but every so often she would swear he was yelling at her from the grave.

*Are you really that stupid, Noelle Jade?* Then and now, that was her mother's favorite phrase. And tossing in her middle name for that extra demoralizing affect? Priceless.

*God, Noelle, when are you going to grow up?* That delightful query came courtesy of her three older brothers every time a news station blasted a story about something she'd done.

Corban Blue, the first, last, and only real boyfriend/relationship she'd taken a chance on, had insisted on picking out her clothes, telling her how to wear her hair and what to say. And yet, she'd stayed with him for a little over a year, proving her mother right. How stupid *was* she?

Only when Corban had demanded she cut Ava from her life had she dumped him. That very day, actually. Hell, that very minute.

The moment the door had closed on his ass, Noelle had realized she had never really loved him, that she'd just hoped someone would . . . want her, she supposed. Someone who would at last admire and respect her, even in the smallest way, beyond her looks and money. Someone who would fill the void inside her. That hollow, hungry place that had never known a moment of satisfaction.

A void carved from anger, frustration, and bitterness. A wound that never quite healed, sometimes flared up, but always poisoned her sense of self. Her hands fisted at her sides.

Well, not this time. If AIR didn't want her, she'd start her own agency and offer them a little competition in the bagging and tagging of predatory otherworlders' business. Wasn't like she truly *wanted* to be an agent. But Ava did, she reminded herself, and what Ava wanted, Ava got. So, never mind on the new agency. Noelle was doing this, one way or another.

"Remind me why we're excited to be here again," she said to Ava, needing the pep talk after the award-winning performance she'd had to put on for the Three Blind Mice outside.

"We're going to make a difference, fight injustice, blah blah blah."

"The *blah blah blah* part sounds familiar, but I'm still mostly drawing a blank."

"Well, do you remember the part about getting to carry a weapon and hurt people legally?"

"Ah. Now it's coming back to me." But seriously.

Starve her, beat her, sleep deprive her, but don't take away her feather down comforter. Or her genuine wool rug. Or her servants. God, what she wouldn't give to have a servant fetching and carrying for her this very second.

"How sweet is this?" Ava spun like a ballerina on crack, her arms splayed. "It's perfect, just perfect."

"Are you retarded? This place is a dump," another agent-in-training said as she folded her shirts and jeans and placed them in the nightstand next to her bed.

The bed next to Noelle's.

First, no one but Noelle was allowed to speak to Ava like that. Ever. She loved Ava more than she loved herself. Maybe because Ava was the one person in the world she trusted. The one person in the world who always told her the truth, straight up, nothing held back. The one person in the world who thought Noelle was perfect, just the way she was.

Second, it was important to establish a prison-like hierarchy right from the beginning. That way, no one would dare try to shank them.

A quick twist and kick on Noelle's part and the girl's nylon went skidding across the floor, panties flying in every direction. Another kick, and the girl followed. "Say something like that to her again, and your balls will take the same path as you and your underwear. Feel me?"

"Noelle, my love," Ava said in a sing-song voice, balancing *her* bag on the now vacant bed. "I think the person in question is female."

"Oh, my bad. I'm so sorry," she told the girl with the same saccharine sweetness she'd used on the guys. Her hand fluttered up to her heart, baby bird delicate. "I thought you were a dude. It's the mustache. That'll fool me every time."

Huffing and puffing, the "person in question" jumped to her feet. "Just what are you gonna cut my balls with, bitch? They frisked you same as they frisked me. You got nothin'."

Question of the day: was now the time to reveal the switchblade she'd smuggled in?

Nah, she thought next. The girl was a crier. On the bus, the black and very gorgeous instructor, Ghost, had gotten in her face and called her a carbon-based waste of space, and her freaking bottom lip had quivered.

Talk about humiliating to watch. Noelle hadn't cried since her father paid his medical staff to fry her nerve endings and destroy her pain receptors *while she was still awake,* and she sure as shit wasn't going to cry when someone called her silly names.

And okay, her dad had done the unthinkable to safeguard her from ever being tortured by others, but that didn't change the facts. At twelve, she'd been strapped to a gurney and cut open like a melon.

All because she'd been abducted a few weeks before, her captors wanting to cash in on her ransom. To prove how serious they were, they'd sent her parents video of her being beaten, screaming from the pain and begging for help. So, when her dad had gotten her back, he'd gone a little nutso.

That little receptor-frying procedure had taken endless, torture-filled days, with needles shoved into her tendons, muscles, and sometimes even drilled into her bones. Days of having what seemed to be acid and broken glass poured straight into her bloodstream.

Anytime she'd passed out, the doctors had woken her up with chemical injections to the heart. Adrenaline, and crap like that. She'd had to tell them when something hurt, after all, so they'd know where to concentrate their efforts.

Well, everything had hurt. Until the very end, when she'd stopped feeling anything at all.

"Just going to stand there, coward?" the girl huffed at her.

Coward? Oh, hell, no. Noelle was a lot of things—spoiled, sometimes cruel and clueless, always gorgeous—but never a coward. She had survived a hell most people would only ever have nightmares about.

*If you flash metal, the first thing she'll do is run. The second is tattle.*

Was that enough to get Noelle kicked out?

Ava must have known she was thinking about risking it because her friend, who knew her better than anyone else in the world, whipped her cell phone from her pocket, pressed a few buttons, leaned over, and said, "Lookie, Noelle. Lookie at what Ava's got," to distract her.

"As if that'll—ohhh, a pretty!" A holophoto of Noelle had crystallized above the small device.

Usually Ava only snapped her picture when she was

at her worst. Black eye—boom, there was Ava. Hangover morning—Ava again. Nasty cold—hello, darling Ava. But in this one, Noelle was leaning against a doorjamb, hands stuffed in her pockets, her expression far away, as if she were lost in thought.

"When did you take this?" she asked, unable to find the memory herself.

"A few months ago."

"And you're just now showing me? Harsh, Ava. So harsh."

"Hello, I'm talking to you," Mustache Girl snarled.

*I'll call her MG for short,* she mused, before saying to Ava, "I look so smart. I bet I was pondering nuclear physics. Or maybe quantum mechanics. Oh, oh, I know. Paradox theory."

"Nah. I'd just asked you if you'd eaten my granola bar."

MG gave up waiting for a response and wandered away to find a new rollaway.

"Send it to me." Noelle rubbed her hands together. "That's gonna be my new screen saver. For reals."

The photo disappeared, and Ava stashed the phone back in her pocket. "I'll send it to you the day you share the butterscotch candies you're having delivered here."

Always the negotiator, her Ava. "Sorry, darling, but I'm not—ah, wait. I feel you, oh, devious one." Butterscotch was Ava's biggest weakness. "I'll have them here by the end of the week, you just wait and see." Making her friend happy was one of her top priorities in life. "Until then . . ." Where had their conversation left off before they were so rudely interrupted? Oh, yeah. "*Are* you retarded? This place is a dump."

"Uh, you forget. I've lived in worse."

True. They'd met in junior high, when Noelle had been acting out to prove her parents' disapproval meant nothing to her and had (allegedly) burned her former boarding school to the ground. Ava had been desperate to lose her drunken mom's attention, as well as the attention of the nasty men her mom had allowed to parade through their trailer.

They'd needed each other, and so they had clung to each other. Hell, they still did. There was nothing Noelle wouldn't do for her beloved Ava. Commit murder? Sure, why not. Only thing to figure out was where to hide the body. Lie, cheat, steal? Done, done, and done. Eagerly, happily. Ava was the best thing that had ever happened to her, and Noelle took care of what was hers.

And yeah, they razzed each other. A lot. Matching "dim wits" with little Ava, as Noelle's brothers used to say, was *fun*. Torturing her was even more fun. But at the end of the day, if anyone else even looked at Ava funny, Noelle went lethally insane.

Speaking of funny looks. "Did you see the way that Hector guy eyed me up and down, as if I belonged in a scientific studies magazine for newly discovered fungus?"

"Yeah, but did you see his muscles?" Ava threw MG's forgotten wardrobe over her shoulder before unpacking her own.

"How could I miss them? His I've-tasted-human-heart-and-liked-it black T-shirt was strained to the point of lunacy."

"Vocab lesson time. You mean lewdness. As in, indecent."

"Stuff your lesson. I meant lunacy. As in crazy. One glance and my brain short-circuited." Short-circuited with the urge to touch, the desire to lick, the need to claim.

None of which she understood! Claim? Not in this lifetime.

He wasn't her usual type. He was tall, tattooed, and bald, with the cruelest frown she'd ever seen. Oh, she liked 'em tall, but tattooed? No. Try refined. Bald? Even peaches sported fur.

Although he wasn't bald from age or genetics. A shadow of stubble had covered his scalp, proof his roots were there and thriving. So, obviously, he shaved. But who shaved on purpose? And why?

She'd almost asked him. Only thing that stopped her was the suspicion he would ignore her. Because the entire time she'd stood there, trying not to notice him but noticing him anyway, he'd had her under that microscope for fungi—and clearly found her the worst of the lot. Honest to God, that frown of his had made her shudder. Or shiver. She wasn't sure which. But there was no denying something about him appealed to her.

His eyes were an intense gold and utterly piercing, the rest of his features all kinds of intimidating. From the hard slash of his dark brows, to the blade of his nose, to the aggressive slant of his lips. Throw in the rough angle of his chin, and you had a visual definition for hardass.

And okay, okay, a beautiful visual, at that, with the kind of rugged sex appeal one might find in a survivalist. Which . . . come to think of it, was a favorite fantasy of Noelle's.

She'd often imagined herself alone in the mountains, some kind of hungry animal chasing her down. Survivalist Guy jumped from the shadows and saved the day. Then he turned to face her, shirtless, sweaty, kind of grungy, his pants ripped and stained with the creature's blood and gore, and he refused to wait for her to thank him. He just backed her up against a tree and plundered the living hell out of her mouth.

Sweet heaven. A definite shiver this time.

*You don't go for hardasses in real life, remember?*

Yeah, but Hector had such wide shoulders. And even as tall as she was, he'd towered over her. He'd dwarfed her, really. Made her feel small . . . feminine. She liked feeling small and feminine, she realized.

"Okay, time's up," Ava said. "I gave you a chance, but you didn't take it. So, I call dibs!"

Damn it.

Noelle was *not* disappointed. If one of them called dibs on a guy, the other had to back off. Besties before testes, and all that. So, no touching, no licking, and no claiming Hector for herself.

"Fine, but I've got dibs on Dallas." Rather than unpack—surely someone would eventually do that for her—she jumped on her mattress. Dust plumped from the stiff syn-cotton covers, making her cough, scowl.

Maybe when she phoned for those candies, she'd request a maid. One maid. AIR could not deny her such an indispensable part of life, a service as necessary as breathing. Not if she had her attorney threaten them. Food for thought.

"Dallas." Ava closed her nightstand drawer and rigged a lock on the handle to keep people like MG out of her stuff. "Good choice. He's a gorgeous one."

And he was more Noelle's type. Tall, dark, and pretty. Although there'd been a serial-killer vibe in his electric blues. Something that could explain why she wasn't as drawn to him as she was to Hector.

Even though Hector gave off the same vibe.

So, okay, there was a flaw in her logic. Big deal. She wasn't admitting to an attraction to Hector. Not aloud, at least. One, he clearly wasn't interested in her. And well, reason number two kinda fell back on reason number one. Being with a man who did not absolutely, utterly adore her would screw with her hard-won self-esteem and mess her up inside.

She'd start trying to prove herself worthy of him. Like baking him a cake after his terrible day at work, when she and kitchens were long-time enemies. Or pretending not to care when he blew her off or forgot her birthday. Or attending parties with her family when she'd rather have her skin peeled from her bones, just because that's what good girls did.

Noelle was done with that kind of thing. Done with trying to be something other than what she was. If a guy couldn't see the treasure underneath the smart mouth, he didn't deserve her.

*And I* am *a treasure, damn it.* Right?

Ava finished her chore and snuggled up beside Noelle on the bed. "So tell me. What was all that lame-assed giggling about? And the couldn't-find-my-brain-if-given-a-map-and-a-shovel stupidity?"

"And the laziness," she said, being helpful. As always. Automatically Noelle rolled to her side and tucked her hands under her cheek. This was how the two of them had spent many a night during their childhood. Lying side by side, chatting for hours.

Those were her favorite memories. Nothing she'd said had ever shocked or disgusted Ava.

"Please." Ava rolled her eyes. "You're always lazy. That's just part of your charm."

And one of her more intelligent traits, if she did say so herself. Why do something for yourself when plenty of people wanted—and needed—to be paid to do it for you?

*God, I'm* such *a giver.*

"Oh, and the next time you want to go the master-slave route," Ava said, "I need at least a month's warning to work on my biceps."

"Consider this your warning. I want to go the master-slave route for the rest of our lives."

A snort. "Did I mention that I loved the pretend hurt over my death threat? Classic!"

"What I can say? I totally missed my calling as the best actress in the world."

A calling she'd missed because she'd never actually planned to work.

Noelle would have gladly financed Ava's entire life

of leisure, saving her friend—and herself—from ever having to get a job. But Ava actually enjoyed earning her own way, so Noelle always went along for the ride.

They'd worked in a bakery, at a used car lot, inside a makeup factory, and as interns at her brother's law firm. Sad truth was, Noelle would rather toil herself into an early grave than be without her best friend.

*Codependency, thy name is Noelle.* Did she care? God, no. She just loved Ava.

"So?" Ava prompted. "What gives?"

Noelle pushed out a breath. "Well, you know my family has always viewed me as a useless doll." Not just her immediate family, but her cousins, aunts, and uncles, and anyone else associated with the Tremain name. They fed off each other, delighting in sharing humiliating stories about the things she'd done and said.

"Useless, but so beautiful." Ava nodded. "Yeah. Continue."

She beamed. "I *knew* you thought I was hot."

"Dude. If you had a penis, I'd freaking marry you."

A genuine chuckle left her. "Anyway, I was just giving Jaxon a taste of what he expected."

"Lesbos," MG muttered as she walked past them, heading toward the . . . enzyme showers.

"Tranny," Ava threw at her.

Ugh. Group showers. Sure, you could remain fully clothed in an enzyme stall, and the dry mist would even clean your shoes, but Noelle preferred to strip and sing in private.

At home, she bathed in water. The real deal, which was hugely expensive, but she didn't care. There was something so soothing about the patter of liquid against porcelain, the spray of hot water against skin, the enveloping, invigorating steam that filled your nose, your lungs.

Ava snuggled closer. "What else?"

"Plus," Noelle continued as if there'd never been a lag in the conversation, "I thought it'd be prudent to lower Hector and Dallas's expectations. You know, start at the bottom and fly our way up." Thereby making it easier to prove themselves.

*What's this? Trying to prove yourself already? Tsk, tsk.*

AIR wasn't a potential boyfriend. She could make an allowance, but only this once. And only because Ava wanted this so badly.

"Normally I'd agree with your methods," Ava said, "but we kinda need their support if we're going to pass this thing."

"Oh, we'll more than pass. We'll *crush* this place."

Delicate fingers smoothed the hair from her brow. "You're right. We're too awesome to do anything less. Plus, we've got good old-fashioned lust on our side. I think Dallas was imagining your body twined around his like a pretzel. Hence his asinine question about pretzels and Jaxon's swift retaliation."

"Nah, Dally was just showing off in front of his friends. Which is why I went with *Oh, my God,* as if I really thought he meant the food, but afterward, I felt like I should have brought it down a notch and said *OMG.*"

The corners of Ava's mouth twitched with her amusement. "Would have been priceless, and I would have broken a few ribs from laughing. As it was, I just peed a little."

"And the other guys? How'd they react?" *Not too obvious, not too eager.* "I was too entrenched in my role to notice."

"Jaxon was embarrassed by you. Sorry. And Hector was disapproving."

*No disappointment. You knew they felt that way.*

Had Jaxon told Hector embarrassing stories about her before her arrival? she wondered suddenly. Was that why Hector had frowned at her the moment she'd stepped off the bus?

Her cheeks heated as she imagined exactly what Jaxon could have shared. The time she'd interrupted a dinner party her parents had thrown, walking through the dining room in only a bikini, giving an elderly gent a heart attack. All because earlier that day her father had said, "You want better grades, buy them. You don't have what it takes to earn them on your own and I'm sick and tired of being embarrassed by your lackluster performance," and she'd hoped to punish him.

Or the time she'd filmed a bit part as a murdered waitress in *Chucky's Evil Twin*, just to embarrass her elitist mother. Another punishment. The week before, Madam Tremain, as Ava sometimes liked to call her, had asked all her friends to send their single sons Noelle's way so that she'd stop "digging through the trash for her dates."

"My math could be off here," Ava went on, "but I'm

pretty sure all three guys thought you'd been dropped on your head one hundred and seven times."

Noelle gave another chuckle, a common occurrence in Ava's presence. "Teaching them better is gonna make this experience," *delicious, exciting, thrilling,* "halfway tolerable."

# Three

**N**OELLE HAD LIVED THROUGH orientation.

She also had lived through the first round of drills. And the second . . . third . . . and fourth—no thanks to her instructor. Hector Dean had it out for her, for real, demanding she run faster, climb higher, and shoot straighter than anyone else.

Whenever he felt she wasn't giving something her all, which was all the damn time, he yelled at her.

Usually that kind of thing pissed her off and sent her spiraling—either with anger or frustration, causing her to act out. Instead, she truly found herself running faster, climbing higher, and shooting straighter.

Trying to prove herself to him—and not just for Ava's benefit either. For her own. Just like she'd done with her parents and Corban. And yet, this time around, the experiences filled her with a weird blend of happiness and sadness. Happiness because she was succeeding, sadness because Hector didn't seem to care.

*Why am I never good enough?*

Well, whatever. She wasn't going to ponder that mystery again, and she wasn't going think about AIR or Hector. Wasn't going to consider how good he always smelled. Like fresh laundry and a storm-drenched sky. Wasn't going to remember the way his eyes glittered like amber when someone—namely her—pricked his ire. Or the way the swirling tattoos on his arms flexed erotically, highlighting the thick muscles underneath, whenever he moved. Or the strange way her blood heated every time she looked at him.

She'd go insane. With rage. Yes, rage, and not an insatiable urge to fling herself against him and slide her tongue into his mouth. Ava had called dibs, after all. Not that Ava had done anything about it. There'd been no time for flirtation, and at the end of each day, everyone was too exhausted to do anything but collapse into bed.

Not Noelle, though. Not tonight. She deserved a break. From Hector, from exercise . . . from her own tormenting thoughts. Plus, Ava wanted those butterscotch candies and Noelle hadn't yet found a way to have them delivered.

That changed *now*.

Having peeked at (*cough* stolen *cough*) the week's schedule, she knew the agents planned to let the recruits sleep the entire night. A first—and a one-time-only thing. A reward of sorts for Ava setting a camp record at target practice. Go Ava! The little tyrant had hit her mark every damn time, no matter the angle she'd stood, and even when they'd blindfolded her.

*That's my girl.* So, while Noelle's peers snoozed and

snored, and while the agents zoned out in front of a plasma screen, she snuck out of camp.

Midweek, she'd found an escape hatch on premises. Her dad had been an intelligence agent for the government as well as a businessman, and he'd taught her that Plan B's were a necessity. So, while it was smart of AIR to have a place for trainees to go if otherworlders attacked, they should have hidden it better than underneath the back porch of the trainee bunk, with only a thin layer of dirt covering the lid.

Why not just hang a sign overhead that flashed the words *Party Through Here*.

Noelle had to shimmy underneath the wooden porch slats, streaking her bare arms and legs with the dirt, and ended up inhaling a mouthful of granules, but . . . *Worth it*. No one had used the thing in years, as proven by the rusty hinges. The air inside was musty and coated with dust.

Fortunately, the long, narrow tunnel had everlasting bulbs posted on the rounded ceiling, providing a well-lit path for anyone who walked. Or . . . drove? Hells yeah! There were three small go-carts lined up and ready to shoot into action.

*I must have died and gone to heaven.* Noelle climbed into the car at the head of the line. Voice activation and thumbprint ID had been disabled. Probably because the AIR agents who came to camp varied greatly. So all she had to do was turn the key already resting in the ignition.

The engine roared to life loudly, making her cringe and pray no one inside the overhead bunk heard. She waited a moment, expecting someone to peel back the lid, but . . . no.

Grinning, she pressed the gas, and *boom*, shot into motion, speeding down the tunnel, twisting, turning, the blasts of air lifting her hair from her shoulders and winding the strands together.

*Take that, Hector Dean*. Not that she was thinking about him.

Exhilaration pumped through her blood. She'd so needed this, every fiber of her being crying out for something that would fulfill her and quench the constant hunger for more. In fact, she would have to find a way to win another night off. Ava had to see this.

Even better, Ava had to race her.

Twenty minutes later the tunnel ended abruptly. A wall of brick with a dilapidated wooden staircase hanging in the center loomed ahead. Noelle slammed on the brakes, barely missing a lethal smash. She laughed out loud. *Fun*.

After shutting off the car, she climbed the steps, picked the lock of the new hatch, and shoved the heavy metal aside. Cool night wind blustered as she peeked out. Two graffiti-covered buildings at her sides. They were several yards apart, with a dark abandoned alley in the center, leading straight to—

New Chicago's Main.

*Rock on*.

She climbed the last step and shimmed to a stand, then closed the lid and gaped. Wow. Anyone who walked this alley would see cracked concrete, nothing more.

Urgency riding her, she grabbed the lipstick from her pocket—a girl had to be prepared for anything—and marked the rim, then tossed the now-contaminated gloss in a nearby trash bin.

Her exit strategy taken care of, Noelle practically skipped from the alley. She made sure to note the shops. One a twenty-four-hour photo. The other an abandoned, crumbling crack house. *Quaint.*

She also made a mental note to inquire about buying both buildings. She could fix the alley, maybe turn it into a garden-type area, then run goods and services through the tunnel at her discretion.

What a day!

Cars whizzed along the road. Bikes and scooters, too. Despite the late hour, crowds had yet to thin on this poorer side of town. Humans and otherworlders traipsed the sidewalks, talking, laughing, shopping. She spotted a few Arcadians, the race known for white hair that couldn't be dyed, the ability to teleport, and in some cases, the ability to use mind control.

A group of Terans, a very cat-like species, with pointed ears, spotted skin, and feline grace. One Mec, tall and thin, with skin that glowed different colors with different emotions. And two Deleseans, with six arms and azure skin that kind of reminded her of whale blubber.

*One day I'll be policing these people.* A surreal thought. Noelle had always been the troublemaker. So, arresting others for breaking the law? Kinda seemed wrong.

Maybe that's why Hector kept pushing her so intently. Maybe he doubted her capability and integrity, as she'd first assumed, and thought to mold her into something better.

*You don't need improvement.*

*And you're not thinking about him.*

Deep breath in, filled with the scents of corn dogs—her mouth watered—car exhaust and perfumes, as well as faint traces of dirt and . . . other things. Towering lamps lined the streets, and the shop signs pulsed. *Live Nude Girls. World's Best Coffee.* A Toys R Us right beside a Hooters. The moon was full, a shining beacon of gold.

"Hey, darlin'," someone called. "How much for an hour?"

*He better not be talking to me.*

"Hey, you, in the red shorts. I'll take whatever you're selling, no matter the price."

*Yep. Me.* The only clothes she'd had were for working out. Right now she sported a red tank and matching too-tight shorts. Streaked by dirt as she was, she probably looked like she spent a lot of time on her knees and back. Plus, her hair was tangled, as if someone had plowed their fingers through one too many times.

Someone had, of course, but that someone was her.

Noelle didn't bother searching for the guy, just threw a finger in the direction of his voice and kept walking.

"Bitch!"

His friends snickered.

Yeah, yeah. Took her fifteen minutes, but she finally found a candy store. A bell chimed above the door when she entered. Ava would flip out of her mind

when Noelle presented her with a butterscotch breakfast in bed.

Stray thought: Who served Hector breakfast in bed?

Noelle's teeth ground together sharply. The answer
didn't matter. Hector was her instructor, nothing more.
Not once had he ever acted as if he found her attractive.

"Can I help you?" the guy behind the counter asked.

She sized him up with a single glance. Human. Late
forties. Comb-over, sugar gut. He wore a white apron
and earned major points for cleanliness.

The store itself was small, with three display cases
and nothing in the way of furniture. Definitely needed
a new business manager. There were no couches for
customers to sit on so they could chat and eat more
and more of the candy. No tables offering samples and
free alcohol to encourage unwise spending, as she was
used to.

"What do you have in the butterscotch depart-
ment?" she asked.

"Not much." He thumped a finger on the glass at
his right, just above a plate of what looked to be fudge
squares. "Just these."

"I'll take them."

One of his brows winged into a stray lock falling
down his forehead. "One or—"

"All."

Cash signs practically glowing in his eyes, he got to
work, wrapping the squares individually and stacking
them carefully in a small box.

The bell over the door gave another chime. The

server glanced up, said, "I'll be with—" then snapped his mouth closed and gulped with apprehension. His bloated cheeks paled. "Uh, just a second, please."

Robber? Thug? Noelle spun around—and came face-to-face with her tormentor.

Hector Dean stood in the doorway, wearing a black T-shirt that molded to his muscles and black slacks that hugged his thighs indecently. He scowled over at her, his golden eyes glittered brightly. His arms were folded over his chest, and his legs braced apart, as if he meant to leap into an attack at any moment.

Oh . . . shit.

# Four

———❦———

"NOELLE," HE SAID TIGHTLY, his voice full of gravel.

"Hector." What did it say about her that she was *aroused* rather than scared? He looked capable of murder, his hard features cold and merciless, but damn if he wasn't sexy as all hell.

Maybe because he wasn't yelling at her.

Yet.

"What do you think you're doing?" he demanded.

"Buying a few sweet treats." Her heart sped into a too-swift rhythm. *I will not come on to him.* "How did you find me?"

"Should I, uh, call the cops?" the server said from behind her.

"He *is* a cop," she mumbled.

Frost appeared in Hector's eyes, a snowstorm of menace. "You think AIR doesn't monitor that tunnel? You think they'd place a hatch in town and not watch it? You were tailed the second you hit the alley, and I was notified."

The crack house, she thought. Stupid, stupid, stupid.

Why hadn't she considered the possibility of cameras and alarms? Had she *wanted* to be caught? And why hadn't she sensed the tail?

"That'll be, uh, twenty-one seventy," the server said now.

The frost thickened in Hector's eyes, his spine stiffened.

Nibbling on her bottom lip, she dug her ultra-thin money card from her pocket, flashed it in front of the scanner and added a twenty-dollar tip.

A bright smile full of yellowing teeth. "Thank you, thank you so much."

"Welcome." She grabbed the box and returned her attention to Hector.

He hadn't moved from his command post at the entrance, probably assuming she wouldn't try to fight her way out, or that she would plead for mercy he wouldn't show. As if! She raised her chin. "You kicking me out of the program or what?"

*If he does, I will have failed Ava.* Her stomach somersaulted, acid tumbling around like clothes in an enzyme washer. *I can't fail Ava.*

He popped his jaw before reaching back and shoving open the door. With a tilt of his chin, he motioned her out. Well, well. He must not want a witness to what would happen next.

The acid burned a path up her chest. Still, Noelle strapped an imaginary iron rod to her back and marched into the night. She didn't look back to be sure Hector followed, and she didn't wait for him, either. She headed back the same way she'd come, not bothering to move out of the way as pedestrians approached; she simply barreled past them.

The streetlamps suddenly seemed too bright, the roaring car engines and inane chatter too loud.

Hector caught up with her quickly enough, his booted feet stomping into the concrete. "I take my job seriously, you know," he began.

O-kay. Not the direction she'd anticipated. "Why?"

A crackling pause. "Did you really just ask me *why?*"

"Yes." Not to be facetious or anything, but because she was curious about him.

"I stop predatory aliens from hurting others," he gritted out. "I save lives."

*And didn't that just make him even sexier?* she thought with a wistful sigh.

"Why do you want to be an agent?" he asked. "And don't give me that bullshit about wanting to shoot people legally."

So Jaxon *had* told him about that.

Hector went on, "I believed it before, but I've seen the way you push yourself."

He'd seen—and been impressed? She wouldn't get her hopes up on that front. "To be honest, I just want to spent more time with Ava." No reason to lie. If AIR had decided to can her, she would be canned, no matter what she said.

A beat of silence. Most likely her bluntness had stunned him. That happened a lot. With her family, her friends, everyone but Ava. "Well," he finally said, "your reason sucks, and it won't get you anywhere."

"Why would a girl like me want or need to get anywhere?" she asked, only the slightest trace of bitterness escaping.

"Don't do that."

"Do what?"

"That *girl like me* crap. You've got determination and drive, and you should be proud of it, not masking it with sarcasm."

Hector Dean had just . . . praised her. She was dreaming. She had to be dreaming. "Are you saying I'd . . . make a good agent?"

Another beat of silence, as if he had to gather his thoughts. And that was answer enough, wasn't it.

*Knew better than to ask.* Also, good thing she hadn't gotten her hopes up.

"I'm saying you need to think long and hard about whether or not you're right for this," he said. "It's hard and it's dirty."

Even as she fought the urge to punch him in the face for implying she couldn't handle something like that, she forced her voice to go low and husky. "Hmm, hard and dirty. Just how I like my sex."

He tripped over nothing and, scowling, hurried to right himself. "A few weeks ago, we found a storage unit with three otherworlder females trapped inside. They had been taken as prisoners, were malnourished, and near death. Is that something you can handle?"

Yeah, she could. She could handle anything. Rather than answer him, however, she asked a question of her own. "What happened to them?"

"We set them free, got them medical care. Now they're on the mend, both mentally and physically."

Ire rose on behalf of the females. "You catch whoever put them there?"

"Not yet, but we will."

The words held a promise, a vow to avenge the weak.
His sexiness factor jacked up a few more notches, and
she shivered. "You really love your job. I mean, you
more than take it seriously."

"Of course." He sound astonished that she'd think
otherwise. "It's my life," he added.

Like Ava was hers. Fancy that—they had something in common. Both of them cared about something more than they cared about themselves. *I will not
admire him.*

They turned a corner. A split second later, Hector slammed his shoulder into hers, shoving her into
a shadowed brick wall in an abandoned alley. Gasping in astonishment, the touch catching her off guard,
she lost her hold on the candy box. *Splat.* The bottom
busted and the contents spilled out onto dirty concrete.

Oh, gross. There went Ava's surprise.

"Hey! That was uncalled for, you—"

A growling Hector got in her face, putting them
nose-to-nose. He glared down at her as the heat of
his breath fanned against her, caressing her despite his
obvious anger. "You *should* be kicked out for this little
adventure. If I had my way, you *would* be kicked out,
effective immediately."

*And I should knee you in the balls.* "I didn't do anything wrong," she snapped, keeping her knee to herself.
She hadn't been this close to a man in a long time. And
that the one so close to her was Hector, a brute who

shouldn't appeal to her but did . . . her stomach fluttered with hot flames of arousal. Her nipples tightened beneath the fabric of her bra, abrading deliciously.

He pressed closer to her, caging her completely.

Suddenly she had trouble catching her breath. Her gaze lowered to his mouth, and her survivalist fantasy came roaring back to life. Just then, Hector was the epitome of danger, a man who saved the day and demanded his due. A man who took what he wanted, damn the consequences.

What would he taste like? How would his strong body feel moving on—in—hers?

His pupils flared, black overshadowing gold. Had she somehow given her thoughts away?

"You disobeyed orders, Noelle. You put the entire camp in jeopardy. How is that not doing anything wrong?"

A spark of anger ignited, burning away the fear of being found out, but somehow increasing the arousal. "I get the order thing, but how did I jeopardize the camp?" *I want to bite him. Claw him.* The good kind of biting and clawing.

"What if an enemy had seen you exit that hatch? He could next blow up the buildings around it, then sneak through the tunnel, no one the wiser, everyone too consumed with the outside chaos. Should I go on?"

The anger drained, a guilty flush heating her cheeks. *I want* him *to bite and claw* me. "You're right. I'm sorry," she said, and she meant it.

He slapped his hands at her temples, and pressed the rest of the way in, his lower body brushing against hers. For the second time in her life, she felt small and feminine. "You play the role of airhead damn well, but I've got your number now, honey."

Panic momentarily overshadowed her desire and guilt. "And what's my number?" He couldn't know. He just couldn't. She didn't *want* him to know. "One eight hundred LOVE BUNNY?"

She'd always taken a perverse kind of pleasure in throwing fuel on the *she's so silly* expectation. And yes, that pleasure was a double-edged sword because no one ever saw the real Noelle. No one ever experienced pride for her or in her. No one ever laughed with her. Always they laughed *at* her.

Time and time again, she could have proven everyone wrong, could have laughed at *them*. One thought had always stopped her: What if they didn't like the real Noelle, either?

What if Hector had learned all about her, as he claimed, but found her lacking anyway?

"The others think you lucked out tonight," he said on a ragged exhalation, "but in all the years of camp, you're the only trainee to ever successfully sneak away. I think you knew to look for that hatch. I think you knew exactly what you were doing."

He suspected, but he didn't know. Part of her was relieved. The other part of her was disappointed. "Poor Hector, thinking he's right when he's so obviously wrong. Didn't Jaxon tell you all about my life choices? About how childish I am. How frivolous. *Of course* I didn't know what I was doing. I dropped a bracelet and crawled to get it." A high-pitched giggle. "*That's* how I found the hatch."

His eyelids slitted, the long length of his lashes fusing together. Such pretty lashes, she mused. Better suited for a woman, and yet, they were gorgeous on him. Perfect.

"Jaxon didn't tell us shit. We like to form our own opinions. And you didn't bring any bracelets to camp. Try again."

Double shocker. Jaxon had kept his mouth closed, and Hector had noticed her lack of jewelry. That meant he'd paid attention, studied her. *I just plain want him. Really, truly want him.*

"My big, bad instructor thinks he's got me all figured out, huh?" She'd meant to taunt him. The huskiness of her voice merely revealed a lingering craving for him. She'd probably been on low simmer for him since the moment she'd met him.

Probably? Ha! She just hadn't recognized the signs properly. Now . . . there was no denying what she felt.

*Ava would want me to have him,* she told herself. *Dibs or no dibs.*

"Whatever you're thinking," he snapped, "stop."

The truth slipped from her on a whisper, a deliberate provocation. "Stop thinking about what we could be doing right now? Stop waiting for you to bend down and feed me your tongue?"

"Shit," he cursed quietly, punching the wall with a hard fist. Dust plumed. "Don't talk like that."

"Like what?" *Hector . . . close . . . tongue . . .* Unable to stop herself, Noelle blatantly arched her hips and rubbed her core against him. A moan left her. Sweet insanity, he had an erection.

"Like I'm already inside you." A groan—but he didn't pull away from her.

"Well, if you don't want to be, all you have to do is resist me," she taunted. *Have to kiss him* . . . She slid her hands up his chest, his muscles jolting in greeting. Heat radiated from him, wrapping around her. Still he didn't pull away. "Are you scared I might get to you?"

His breath shallowed, sawing in and out of his nose, and *his* gaze lowered to *her* mouth. "Scared," he parroted, as though in a trance.

Doubtful. Nothing would scare the intractable Hector, she would bet. "Give me a taste, then, and we'll both walk away happy," she said, licking her lips, playing along. "There's nothing scary about that."

"A taste, yes."

They met in the middle. The moment of contact, the gentle tasting she'd imagined spun out of control. Swept up on a tide of sensation, she ate at his mouth, sucked on his tongue. He flavor was as decadent as his scent, fresh, wild, and stormy, passion spiced with apples.

Though he seemed as wrapped up in the moment as she was, the flicks of his tongue were hesitant at first. But when he decided to go all in, he really went all in. He became the aggressor, taking over, dominating.

He kicked her legs apart and held her up, off her feet, using his lower body to press her into the wall. Her nails scraped along the stubble on his jaw, then his scalp, angling his head for better, deeper contact.

He growled at her, demanding she accept his domination. She liked that. The muscles in his neck pulled tight just before he arced away from her, letting her slide, slide. Then he slammed forward and pushed his thick erection between the vee of her legs once more, this time as forcefully as he could, catching her before her feet could touch the ground.

She trembled violently, gasped, utterly lost in him. Lost in the electric connection.

He arched back and slammed forward again, then again, forcing his cock against her with so much vigor she though he might break the thing in half. Either he liked things rough, or was too wrapped in his own desire to care about any injury to his shaft. Naughty girl that she was, she liked that, too.

Knowing Hector wanted her as fervently as she wanted him caused the ache inside her to intensify, and moisture to dampen her panties. *More, need more.* She climbed him like a mountain, winding her legs around his waist, making the rub between them constant.

"More!" she commanded.

Another slam, and she nearly erupted. The sensation . . . so strong . . . so wonderfully overwhelming.

"Noelle. Yes, more."

"Please." Her nails dug deeper into his scalp as she kissed him with all the passion trapped inside her. Passion she'd long denied herself. Passion she hadn't known she was capable of feeling.

"More," he repeated, the word slurred. He bit at her lips, nibbling. "I need more of you."

"Yes, please. I—"

A car honked, jolting them both. Panting, Hector

jerked up his head. He peered down at her, comprehension and horror dawning in his eyes. Why horror? She tried to kiss him again, to help him forget whatever troubled him, but he turned away.

"Down," he barked.

"Hector, I—"

Again she was cut off. "Down, Noelle. Now."

Little chips of ice joined the fire in her blood, cooling her down. The moment her feet hit the pavement, he leapt away from her as if she were toxic, ensuring no part of them touched. Her knees were weak and nearly buckled, but she managed to remain upright.

She looked him over. His expression was now chiseled from granite, his jaw clenched, his lips swollen. His erection, gone. And there was a faint blue glow emanating from both of his arms. Arms he quickly hid behind his back.

She must have been mistaken. Surely he hadn't glowed. No time to reason things out, though. As she inhaled, she caught the scent of burning cotton and frowned. A swift scan, and she realized her tank had been singed at the straps. Her brow furrowed in confusion. How had that happened?

"You're not being kicked out," Hector rasped. "You've excelled at every exercise, and for that, Mia Snow thinks you've earned a second chance. You won't get another."

Mia Snow thought. Not Hector. "Thank you," she replied with only the barest tremor.

"Don't thank me. Thank Mia."

He wasn't going to say anything about what had just

gone down between them—and what had *almost* gone down. Had it not been for that honk, they would have kept going, would have had sex right here, against the wall.

His rejection, when she still trembled with need for him, cut deeply. He didn't like her, was probably ashamed about kissing her. Probably? Try definitely. That horror . . .

Despite her money, he probably thought she wasn't good enough for him. That she was flighty, selfish, and stupid, after all. *You pander to that mind-set. You can't blame him.*

*I've got your number,* he'd said. As she'd suspected, he hadn't really.

"You've got two hours to make it back to camp. The tunnel's been locked, so you'll just have to hoof it the long way," he said. "Which means you're going to need every second of those two hours. I'd get started if I were you. And Noelle?" he added before she could take a step. "Don't sneak out again, and don't ever—*ever*—kiss or touch me."

"Then don't kiss or touch me back," she snapped.

"*And don't play this game with me,*" he shouted. "Understand?" He didn't wait for her reply but stomped away.

"Ava," Noelle whispered, shaking her friend awake. The bunkhouse was dark as hell, and Noelle was drenched in sweat and dirt, but she didn't want to take a shower until she'd spoken to her friend.

Ava bolted upright, reaching for the razor she kept under her pillow. Then she paused, caught her breath. Her glassy gaze cleared. "Noelle?"

"I kissed Hector." A murmur of longing, pain, and anger.

A delicate hand scrubbed over Ava's face. "What?"

"I kissed Hector, even though you had dibs." *And now I think I hate him.*

After he'd stalked out of the alley, he'd climbed into a nearby car. He'd followed her back to camp. As she'd run. The entire freaking way. Not once had he checked on her, offered her something to drink, or taken pity on her and allowed her to catch a ride with a stranger.

"First taste is free. You'll have to buy the second one. So . . . how was it?" Ava asked, falling back on her mattress. Only curiosity filled her tone.

"Let's just say I did you a favor. He's *such* a bastard."

"Did he not finish what he started?"

"Worse. He told me to never, ever kiss or touch him again, as if I'm toxic."

"Want me to kill him for you?"

See? This was why she loved Ava so damn much. "Nah. Let's just torture him a little."

"If by *a little* you mean until he's writhing and screaming for mercy, I'm in!"

# *Five*

---

GOD HAVE MERCY. IF Hector died of a massive coronary this morning, Noelle Tremain would be at fault. He had to be closing in on the number of erections one man could experience—and ignore—in a single week before he just up and died.

Hector wasn't the only one suffering with unrequited lust, either. Every man in the area watched her with differing levels of arousal. And that didn't piss him off; he'd simply woken up in a bad mood. Again.

He wasn't getting any sleep. Not before their bone-melting kiss, and certainly not after. Every night he dreamed about her. About kissing and touching her, and that only deepened his need for her, the ever-growing obsession. Because he kept thinking that while he'd rolled his tongue against hers, he hadn't cupped her breasts, or felt her nipples bead under his palm. Hadn't delved his fingers deep into her wet, dripping sex.

And he never could.

But now he wanted to do those things more than he wanted to breathe.

So what had started out as a small attraction was now a full-blown case of the must-fucks.

That ended today.

Hopefully.

If this was what happened in seven days, imagine what would happen in fourteen. Then twenty-eight. And, God forbid, fifty-six.

He couldn't. Not without sweating.

He never should have gone near her that night, but she'd peered up at him with such defiance, he'd practically wrapped himself around her in a bid to intimidate her. At least that's what he'd told himself. All while drinking her in, luxuriating in the sparkle in her eyes, the sultriness of her scent, the feminine curves of her body.

And the kiss? He had no excuse for that. It was the stupidest thing he'd ever done. He'd known it then, and he really knew it now. Especially since his desire to have her had been so consuming, his arms had fired up and *he hadn't freaking cared.*

He'd burned her shirt, had nearly burned her skin, risking her safety, his own. Even his freedom.

No one at AIR knew what he could do, and that's the way he wanted it to stay. Because if anyone ever found out, they'd either lock him up and toss the key or feed him the barrel of a .22. And he would deserve it!

Even still, he would never allow anyone to lock him away. He'd spent most of his childhood in a four-by-four cage, laughed at, starved, bruised and broken after being forced to fight other disposable kids, time and time again.

Most had been picked up off the streets, but some, like him, had parents looking for a quick buck. Parents who'd pit their own children against each other, while adult men and women bet on the winner and the condition of the loser.

Hector had worked hard to free himself, and had had to kill a lot of people along the way. Something he did not regret. His life might not be fun or easy, but he made his own choices. Made a difference in the world. Helped those who suffered as he once had. He had purpose.

Thankfully, Noelle hadn't noticed the glow. Had she, she would have said something. She wasn't the type to remain mute. About anything.

*You're good to go, but if you keep this thought process up, you won't be. Concentrate on the here and now. On what matters.* Anything but that kiss.

The trainees had been roused from their beds less than ten minutes ago. 'Course, they'd only gotten two hours of shuteye before that, so most were dead on their feet. Once the horn blasted, signaling it was time to rise and shine, they'd had five minutes to dress, do whatever they needed to do, and line up outside.

Noelle had emerged in the tiniest, tightest pair of pink shorts he'd ever seen, and an equally tight white tank top. She should have looked like any other female in the camp, but he could see the curve of her ass, and goddamn. *No one* else in the entire freaking world had an ass like hers. Toned, curved, perfect. Biteable.

*Don't go there.*

Her hair was anchored in a ponytail on top of her

head, and the length swung back and forth, back and forth with every perky step she took. Perky steps that bordered on lascivious because of the red lace winding up her combat boots.

*Yeah. That's why.*

Her face was scrubbed clean of makeup, giving her a fresh, dewy appearance. And with the rising sun behind her, framing her with golds, oranges, and pinks, she was every man's fantasy come to sizzling life.

A fantasy. That's all she could ever be to him. So he'd just have to pretend he didn't notice that her nipples were hard from the cool, too-early morning air. Nipples he'd felt against his chest. And oh, sweet Jesus, there were goose bumps winding around the band of skin seductively revealed between the hem of her shirt and the waist of her shorts. Her navel dipped so exquisitely, it would be a playground for his tongue.

*Don't you dare go there, asshole.* A plea from a deeply rooted need to protect himself.

"Start running," he shouted to the twenty-four recruits remaining at the camp. Two had already dropped out due to injuries, two had been kicked out for finishing last, and one short, effeminate man with a thin mustache and a habit of sleeping in the female barracks had simply disappeared.

Shockingly, Noelle hadn't been among the out-for-the-counters. "And don't stop until you're told," he added. "You do, you go home."

The group shot into action so quickly their moans of not-this-again barely had time to register. Desperate for a distraction—one that would actually work—

Hector kicked into gear, determined to run this bitch of a course himself.

This was his last day here. At least until next month. Like the others, he was supposed to stay, but because of his ability, he'd gotten permission to leave campus the weeks he wasn't in charge. Not that his boss knew the truth.

When Hector first joined AIR, he'd lied about a medical condition. A skin disease that demanded his coworkers remain hands off, that he sometimes wear gloves, and sometimes, when "the agony" became too much, that he stay home. Most of them respected the first, all of them laughed about the second, and on rare occasions, a few of them brought him chicken noodle soup because of the third.

Now he had less than twelve hours until he adiosed, which meant he had twelve hours to get rid of Noelle. He should have fought Mia when she'd said, "Tremain snuck out? So what. I like a girl with initiative. She stays." Instead, he'd jumped in his car and burned rubber into the city to go and get her.

All the way there, he'd told himself she was too young for him. He'd told himself that screwing a trainee was unethical, but his mind had snagged on the word "screwing" and the rest had ceased to matter. He'd told himself that, if he ever talked her into bed, she would consider him such a bad lay, she'd laugh about their encounter for years to come, but his mind snagged on the words "lay" and "come," and he'd started plotting ways to taste her.

Shit.

Bottom line: she shouldn't have lasted this long.

Yeah, she was more intelligent than he'd first given her credit for, but you needed more than smarts to succeed at this job. How would she react at the scene of a gruesome murder? Vomit? Pass out? Probably both.

He'd cleared most of his cases before coming out here, and all of them had been bitches. Especially that last one. A human teenager had fought a Teran teenager, and neither had walked away, leaving a bloody mess. The Teran's claws had slashed the human into a thousand different Christmas ribbons. Then, knowing otherworlders were judged harshly and sometimes things like self-defense were forgotten, the Teran had killed himself rather than spend the rest of his life in AIR lockup.

Kids, man. Their murders and suicides affected Hector in a way nothing else ever had. They hadn't yet truly lived, and they didn't know there was something better out there.

Noelle had only ever been pampered. What did she know of pain and suffering?

And her arrests? He still wasn't buying. Not to that degree. If she lived through camp and somehow became an AIR agent, she'd be ripped to pieces on the streets. More than that, she would hinder whoever was unlucky enough to be paired with her. Guaranteed, she'd contaminate evidence and shit like that. Rules meant nothing to her.

Last night, she'd managed to smuggle in food—and not through the tunnel. Actually, he didn't know how she'd done it. She wasn't talking, and neither was anyone else. And because he couldn't prove any rules had been broken, Mia had once again put her foot down with a smug, "She stays!"

Hector never would have known about the contraband if not for Dallas, who was always hungry and had followed his nose like a hound. And Hector, thinking the shithead just wanted a peek at Noelle in the shower, had followed the agent. What he'd found: the trainees huddled together, ripping meat off chicken bones as if they were at the Last Supper.

That's what this fifteen-mile run was about. And why the trainees would be living outside for the next month.

Punishment was a bitch.

Still. Hector didn't think the location change would break Noelle. She'd say something excruciatingly optimistic like, *Camping is fun,* and twirl. So it was time to step up the torment. Time to . . . hurt her.

"I think I forgot to tell you good morning," she said as she passed him, that smoky voice tugging him back to the course. "So, allow me to remedy that. Good morning, Hector."

He almost tripped over his own goddamn feet. Honest to God, she'd said his name as if he were already inside her and thrusting. "That's Agent Dean to you," he snapped. Not with anger, as he should have, but with more of that crackling arousal.

Arm check. Slight burn, slight itch. No glow. He was okay. For now.

She sniffled as if her heart were currently in the process of breaking. "You're not going to wish me a good morning, too?"

"No, I'm not." *I hope your morning blows*. Mmm, blows. Shit. Damn. And a thousand other curse words. He needed to rewind, and try another thought. *I hope the rest of your day sucks*. Mmm, sucks. Damn it! "Now concentrate like a good little girl." A command to both of them. Because yes, he was more like a chick every second he spent with her.

"Sir, yes, sir." No more hurt in her tone.

Was she mocking him? Surely not.

The first lap had left a fine sheen of perspiration on her exposed skin, making her glisten erotically. Same with her friend, Ava, who kept pace at her side. But he didn't want to throw Ava on his bed and screw into her spinal cord.

*You don't want to do that to Noelle, either*. This kind of wanting was new to him, that was all. He'd deal. He'd overcome. He always did.

"Agent Mean, watch out for that—"

His boot slammed into something hard and immobile, and he barely managed to keep himself vertical.

"Rock," she finished. Her husky laugh echoed across the distance, sank past skin and into cells, fizzing like champagne. She'd moved several more feet ahead of him and didn't look back, that ponytail continuing to swing.

Mortifying.

"Have you forgotten the meaning of the word *dibs* again?" he heard Ava ask her.

Noelle cartwheeled as she replied. "Nope. I was just showing you how it's done."

Ava snorted. "How what's done? Annoying everyone to death?"

They had a strange relationship. More than boss/employee, as he'd first supposed. Exactly what they were to each other, however, he hadn't yet worked out. But he wasn't going to ponder it now. There were more important things to do. Like run everyone into the ground, himself included.

"Faster," he commanded.

They groaned, but obeyed.

Time ticked by.

More time ticked by.

Noelle never again bypassed him, but that was not the blessing it should have been. She remained just ahead of him, and he never lost sight of her. She moved like a panther. Sleek, fluid, effortless. And she never slowed. But then, he never did.

She always pushed herself harder than anyone else—except for him. *He* pushed her even harder, hoping to break her. So far, no luck.

Damn it. She *had* to be gone by the time he returned next month. His arms, his hands . . . yep, they really began to burn and itch. The ink had already faded a bit.

When he got home, he'd take a few days of personal leave and redo his tattoos. Somehow those Celtic symbols were the only thing that actually helped him. How they kept his ability under control for as long as they did, he didn't know. Just like he didn't know why he was like he was. No one else in his family had ever exhibited this kind of curse.

Plus, the ink was his gauge. The lighter it was, the

more of a danger he was. When there was nothing left, even God couldn't help him. Hector wouldn't just kill everyone around him; he'd inadvertently destroy entire buildings.

"He's trying to murder us," a trainee wheezed as he came up from the rear.

"After this, I'm going to murder myself," another rasped.

Hector glanced at the timer hanging from his neck. They'd been running three hours and thirty-two minutes. So he'd gone a tiny bit over the two and a half hours he'd intended. Babies.

He studied each one. They were drenched in sweat, even Noelle, and their steps were now dragging. Good. He would have liked to push them even harder, and hell, push himself since the jog hadn't yet done shit to his hormones, but there was more crap to do before he could take off, so the sooner he got started the better.

And the sooner he got himself under control, the sooner he could get back to work. A case would occupy his thoughts, keep him focused.

"All right," he shouted, halting in the middle of the dirt track. "Bring it in. And hustle."

All but Noelle and Ava obeyed. The twosome kept running.

What was this? National Test His Patience Day? "Now!" he roared.

"You didn't say stop," Noelle blasted back.

"Before," Ava panted, "you told us to run until you said stop."

They were right. *Smarter by the second.* His narrowed

gaze swept across the trainees around him. "What are you doing, standing around? I didn't say stop, did I?"

With a symphony of groans, they leapt back into action. He let them eke out another mile before saying the magic word. "Stop."

Every single one of them dropped where they were and sprawled on the hard, cool ground.

No mercy. "Did I say you could rest? Bring it in. And actually hustle this time."

He watched as they lumbered to their feet and closed the distance. 'Course, he watched Noelle a little more intently than the rest. Because she was soaked, her white tank and sports bra were see-through. He saw more than hard nipples. He saw color. Pink, perfect circles made for a man's tongue.

Scowling, Hector rubbed the building burn from his left arm. Time to take care of his problem once and for all.

# Six

———❧———

 ECTOR SPUN SLOWLY, SURVEYING each member
of the group forming a circle around him. Well,
every member but Noelle. Avoiding those nipples was
priority one. "So far, all you pussies have done is exercise. Time to change that."

He gripped the collar of his shirt and tugged. The
material swept over his head and dropped to the
ground. Someone might have gasped, but he couldn't
be sure. Next to go was the stopwatch. He rolled his
shoulders, stretching the muscles. The bones in his neck
popped as he turned his head left, right. Sweat formed
rivulets down his chest, and caught in the waistband of
his jogging shorts.

Another gasp, then a moan. A smoky moan. As if
Miss Noelle Tremain liked what she was seeing.

Shit. He wouldn't look; he fucking wouldn't look.

"You." He pointed to the guy some of the girls had
been caught sighing over. Johnny Deschanel. Dark
hair, dark eyes. Not quite as tall and muscled as Hector—who was?—but he was the closest in size and

perfect for the first demonstration. A demonstration that would, hopefully, scare the stubbornness right out of Noelle, saving him from having to take this to the limit. "Ass in the circle. We're doing hand-to-hand."

Cocky little bastard strutted despite his obvious fatigue.

Those with a modicum of training were always the easiest to flatten. They considered themselves experts, maybe because they'd actually managed to take down a few opponents in the outside world. Here, now, that experience was more of a hindrance. Johnny had no idea what someone with *a lot* of training could do to him.

But again, he'd learn.

"Attack me," Hector said to Johnny. He withdrew the thin newly designed asbestos gloves hanging from the back of his waistband and tugged the material over both of his hands. "Hit me, even once, and you and the rest of the trainees are free to do whatever you want for the rest of the day."

Excitement and resolve glittered in those dark eyes. But the guy didn't say anything, just nodded and dove for him.

Something Hector had foreseen. He merely stepped to the side, and Johnny soared past him, slamming into Ava with a *hmph*. Noelle took exception and kicked him off. What did surprise Hector was the way Johnny used the momentum to his advantage and popped to his feet. Smart. Wouldn't bring home the victory for him, but smart.

Having witnessed how quickly Hector could anticipate and react, Johnny chose a different route for his second go. He circled . . . circled . . . closing in. Moment he was within striking distance, he threw his fist into Hector's nose. Or tried to. Hector caught his hand and twisted, spinning him around and pinning his arm against his back.

The angle was awkward, painful, and mortifying, because there was nothing Johnny could do to escape without popping his shoulder from its socket.

Easier than anticipated, and somewhat disappointing. Hector hadn't gotten to break a single bone.

"What did he do wrong?" he asked the group. And yeah, maybe he was showing off a little. As Johnny squirmed, Hector's chest puffed up like a peacock's tail, all *look at me, look how strong I am.*

Noelle and Ava both raised their hands.

"Oh, I know. Me, me, pick me!"

"No, pick me! I'm righter. More right. Whatever, pick me!"

A few seconds later, they were attempting to lower the other one's arm.

Ignoring them, intending to explain the intricacies of his magnificence himself, he released Johnny and gave the guy a shove toward the open spot in the circle. "Have a seat."

Rather than obey, Johnny swung around with a growl, fist cocked and flying. Hector dodged, and threw a punch of his own. Johnny wasn't fast enough to dodge. *Contact.* The trainee went down like a stone in water, and just like that, it was lights out.

Hard fact: you put knuckles against cartilage, and knuckles would win every time.

"Lesson number one." Hector straightened, his arms falling to his sides. "The fight isn't over just because your opponent is. You can't use a pyre-gun to stun humans, and some otherworlders have somehow inoculated themselves and can move within seconds of being hit with the rays. Always make sure your target is really down and out. Example."

He kicked the unconscious Johnny in the stomach. Air whooshed from the guy's mouth, and his body jerked, but he didn't curl up to protect his vitals. All right, then. He was really down and out.

Someone clapped, whooped. Hector spun, eyes slitting. There was Dallas, in Johnny's old seat, pearl-white smile flashing against his deeply bronzed skin as his fist pumped toward the heavens.

"Taught him everything he knows," Dallas said. "Hector, I mean, not the one who got the nose job free of charge."

*I will not laugh.* "Take out the trash, would you, Dal?"

"Sure, sure." Dallas snapped to and was dragging Johnny out of the circle within seconds.

"So." Hector performed another spin. "Who's next?" He waited a few heartbeats of time. "Noelle?"

He nearly flattened her with the fierceness of his stare, their gazes locking together, clashing. Her starling gray against his crackling gold. He expected her to decline. Maybe to cower. She grinned the eager beaver grin he'd seen day one, and stood. All innocence, all playfulness, total contradiction.

Irritation—and surprise and more of that stupid arousal—twisted a knot in his gut.

"Don't kill him, Noelle," Ava cheered. "Just hurt him a little."

Noelle gave her friend a thumbs-up. The sun had finally found its place in the blue, blue sky, shining brightly, no clouds obstructing the brilliance. Her ponytail was plastered to her head, her cheeks flushed bright red, but damn it all, she'd never been prettier.

"I won't go easy on you." Truth. He couldn't. Not if he was going to be rid of her. And okay. Maybe he was wrong and she'd make a good agent one day. That determination of hers, if channeled properly, could take her places. And maybe it was unfair of him to want her kicked out because he was attracted to her. Didn't matter. She was rich. She'd get over it.

"Go easy on me? Why, Agent Mean, I'd be disappointed if you did."

He was not impressed.

"Same rules? Meaning, it's on like Donkey Kong, and we get a freebie if you're hit?" she asked.

He nodded. Donkey Kong? And goddamn it, her voice. That husky, smoky quality once again made everything she said suggestive and dirty. Like, *same rules* somehow became *inside me*.

So now he would have to give her everything he had *without* using his arms. The burning had cranked up a notch, the tattoos glowing through the material's pores. He prayed no one noticed. Or, if they did, that they assumed it was an optical illusion.

Not a farfetched thought, he told himself. As exhausted, hungry, and abused as they were, they'd believe anything. Surely.

Hopefully.

In a world where aliens walked among humans who did not yet accept them, discrimination was rampant. How much worse would that discrimination be for a horrendous genetic mutation? And that's what Hector was. He knew it. He'd researched the hell out of himself, his past, and his family, and that was the only explanation that made sense.

"*Soooo,* are you just going to stand there or what?" Noelle asked.

Shit. Distraction wasn't going to help his cause. "All right. Let's see what you've got."

"Oh. Okay." Eyes gleaming, she lifted her tank and bra. "I've got thirty-six C's."

The male trainees might have whistled, the females might have gasped. Hector couldn't be sure because he lost focus of them. Lost focus of everything but those perfect breasts. Honest to God, his thoughts derailed, his nerve endings going white-hot throughout his body.

Rose-colored nipples, beaded and ripe for sucking. She had no tan lines, was the same sweet cream and honey all over. And she was closing the distance between them, jiggling, those breasts staring at him, tempting him, daring him, almost within reach. Totally within reach.

He flexed his fingers; he wanted to reach.

She double tapped him in the mouth so hard he was spitting blood as he fell. Stars winked through his line of vision before he landed. And then, when he hit, his skull cracking against the same rock he'd tripped over, the stars vanished and thick black cobwebs took their place.

Night, night, Hector.

However long passed before he blinked open his eyes and saw a flame of white flashing over him, he wasn't sure. All he knew was that his temples throbbed and the stars had decided to do an encore.

More flashing.

Seriously, what was— Understanding dawned, and he growled with barely suppressed rage. The white flame was from a fucking camera phone. *Humiliating*.

Scowling, he grabbed the device and crushed it into multiple pieces.

A grinning Noelle bent down, looming over him and blocking the sun, becoming all he could see. "That's okay, Agent Mean. I'd already emailed myself a copy."

"Fuck me," he breathed, the words slurred past his rapidly swelling lips.

That grin brightened. "I can't. You're Ava's."

He was . . . Ava's? Wait. *What?*

"So," Noelle said, grinning slowly, wickedly. "Do you want to know where you went wrong now, or should I wait and tell you later?"

# Seven

❧

*E*IGHT-YEAR-OLD HECTOR BECKHAM GRIPPED *the bars of his cage and peered over at his ten-year-old brother, Dean. Dean lay in his own cage, not asleep but not moving either. He'd lost more weight. Bones protruded sharply on his bruised and dirty face, making him look like a skeleton with hair.*

*Hector probably looked just as bad. Why wouldn't he? All the other boys and girls around him did. Also like him and Dean, they were trapped in cages and utterly helpless.*

*There were twenty-six cages in total, some lined side by side, some stacked on top of each other. Old, rusty cages once used to contain dogs. But then, that's what they were. Dogs.*

*A week before every fight, they were all locked inside their new "home" and placed in this barn. That way, they were good and feral when they were released. They were purposely starved, even though that left them weak, because hunger made them do very bad things.*

*Plus, what better way to reward them for a job well done? Turn your friend's face into pulp, and earn a sandwich.*

*Yeah, Hector had made friends with most of the kids in here. After all, some of them had been doing this for over a year and they were the only ones who understood his pain—the only ones he could ever talk to about what happened. Come tomorrow, though, when the fights started up again, he'd forget he liked them and they'd forget they liked him.*

*Until it was over and all any of them would want to do was cry.*

What are you, a sissy? *his dad's voice suddenly screamed inside his head.*

*How many times had Hector heard that particular question? Too many to count. Not that he knew how to count. He'd never been to school, had never learned to read.*

*Well, he wouldn't cry tonight. Or tomorrow. He was better than that. And, well, he just didn't have the strength.*

*He hadn't been fed today, and the only thing he'd gotten yesterday was a single scoop of slop. He'd hated the bitter taste but he'd licked the bowl clean—because they were never given a spoon. Now his stomach was twisted into itself, no longer growling but burning. Burning so bad.*

*"Hector," Dean whispered.*

*Hector met his brother's gaze. Tonight their cages had been placed one in front of the other. "Yeah," he whispered back out of habit.*

*The Zoo Keeper—the man responsible for their "care"—had already done his nighttime check, so they didn't have to be quiet. Besides, kids were moaning and groaning all around them, some even sobbing. One girl was praying for someone to help her.*

*This was her first time in the cages, and Hector didn't have the heart to tell her that no one ever would.*

"Dad told me I have to kill the first person I fight this round," Dean said.

A sharp intake of breath. The smell of disgusting things filled his nose. From himself, from all the others. They were never taken out to go to the bathroom. "No." He shook his head, dirty hair scratching at his cheeks.

"He says I have to."

"No!" That's the one thing they'd never allowed themselves to do. Kill another kid. A kid in the same situation, locked away, forgotten when he was lucky, forced to fight for every scrap of food when he wasn't.

Dean's golden eyes—eyes so like his own—were grim. "You know what'll happen if I disobey him."

Yeah. Hector knew. A whipping far worse than anything they ever experienced inside the ring. "At least you won't feel guilty or hate yourself." Hector might cry sometimes after hurting another kid, but Dean shut down. He'd cut himself, and wouldn't speak for weeks. Not even to Hector.

If Dean delivered that final blow . . . he would never recover. Hector knew that, too.

He and Dean had tried running away together, but their dad had caught them two days later. At some point during the beating that followed, Dean had thrown himself over a blacked-out Hector, and gotten his arm broken for his daring. An arm Dean had had to treat himself. An arm that was still bent at an odd angle, six months later.

"Who are you fighting?" he asked.

Silence.

"Just . . . don't kill him, Dean. Please. I don't want you to suffer about it later."

*Again, silence.*

*"I'll do it, okay? I'll do the killing. Whoever I fight, I'll kill him, I promise. You just . . . don't. Okay?"*

*Silence.*

*Hector tried reaching his brother another way. He worked his arms through the bars, gripped Dean's cage door and shook.* Rattle, rattle. *"Listen to me. After this round, we'll run away."* Risking another beating had to be better than this. Living on the street *would be better than this. "This time, he won't find us. I won't let him."*

*"I just wanted you to know,"* Dean finally said, his voice low and emotionless.

*Hector spent the rest of the night telling his brother how wonderful things would be when they were on their own, but Dean never said another word. Then the sun was gleaming brightly in the sky, illuminating the crumbling barn filled with dirty cages, listless kids, and human waste.*

*Outside, Hector heard what seemed to be a thousand cars drive up, and even more doors slam. Footsteps shuffled. Carefree laughter drifted to his ears.*

*There was an arena set up in the surrounding field. The bleachers were always overflowing. Beer and popcorn would be sold. Just the thought of that popcorn made Hector's mouth water.*

*People would watch the fights, cheering and booing. That always set Hector's already raw nerves on edge. Why didn't they help? Why didn't they realize the cruelty of what they were doing? Watching? Why didn't they care?*

*His own mother used the money she made off his and Dean's fights to buy her drugs. Hector hated her for that. Why couldn't she love him? Why couldn't she love* Dean?

Dean was the best person in the whole world. Smart, kind, generous. A few times, Dean had pretended not to be hungry so that Hector could have his portion of slop. Hector was ashamed to admit he'd actually accepted once.

Fear shuddered through him when the Zoo Keeper strutted in a few minutes later.

It was time.

A short, squat man with thinning hair and a few missing teeth, the Zoo Keeper liked wearing overalls stained with blood his "animals" had spilled. Grinning with satisfaction, he rapped a stick against each of the cage doors.

"Rise and shine, my little mutts. Today's your day to shine. Or not." He chuckled cruelly. "We're gonna kick things off with a big bang this go-round."

He dropped the stick and grabbed two of the leashes hanging on the far wall—a pink one and a blue one—then he strode to Dean's cage. Fear intensifying, Hector sat up. His mind swam with dizziness, sharp lances of pain making him grimace.

Dean just lay there as the Zoo Keeper unlocked his cage. Hinges squeaked as the door opened. The pink collar was strapped around Dean's skinny neck, and Dean was jerked to the dirt-laden ground.

"Stand up, boy." Another jerk.

Dean dragged himself to his feet, swayed.

The Zoo Keeper tugged him forward—and stopped at the praying girl's cage.

Oh . . . God. Oh, no. "Dean," Hector said, his stomach threatening to heave, even though there was nothing inside it.

If Dean killed another boy, he'd hate himself and never get over it. But if he killed a girl . . .

*Dean didn't look in Hector's direction.*

*The Zoo Keeper wrapped the blue collar around the girl's neck, but she had enough steam to get herself out and to her feet without aid. She was Dean's height, with matted blond hair and eyes glassy with fear.*

*"Boys are never pitted against girls," Hector called, desperate to stop this. "Please, don't make him fight her. You have to—"*

*"I don't have to do shit, mutt." The Zoo Keeper tossed him a scowl that promised he'd suffer later. "Boys and girls didn't fight before. Now they do. And you'll keep your mouth shut from now on if you know what's good for you."*

*Hector's body began trembling as Dean was dragged away. What would happen? What would Dean do? He closed his eyes, fighting those sissy tears he'd told himself he wouldn't shed.*

*He knew the moment the fight started. The crowd erupted, people calling out instructions. Things like, "Rip his ear off!" And, "Punch her in the face!" All he could do was huddle in the corner of his cage and wait to learn the outcome.*

*And when he did—*

Hector's eyelids popped open.

Barely able to catch his breath as the dream receded, he realized he was drenched in sweat, his body seemingly on fire. He did a quick scan of his bedroom. He was alone. His thick, dark curtains were drawn, and the only light source was the azure pulsing from his arms.

His arms. Shit! He jackknifed to his feet and studied

both. The skin was raw from his determined scratching, the ink faded. Again.

Scowling, he looked over his bed. Despite his flame-retardant sheets, he'd left singe marks behind. *Have to control yourself better*. His heart drummed erratically against his ribs, his blood molten in his veins.

Hector hated dreaming about his childhood, but he especially hated that particular memory. *At least you didn't dream about what happened the next night*.

Shaky, he lumbered to his kitchen. His tattoo gun, ink, various other paraphernalia, and gauze rested on top of his kitchen table, where he also had papers about his past scattered.

Articles about people with unexplainable abilities that had nothing to do with otherworlders. Things like skin turning to stone, and bone to metal. Things like eyes that swirled and hypnotized and voices that enslaved. Then there were the papers concerning his mother and father's family trees. Hector came from poor, uneducated trash, and he'd even had to teach himself how to read and write.

*Another reason you shouldn't be with Noelle.*

The stray thought didn't exactly take him unaware. He'd thought about her the entire drive home yesterday. He'd thought about her while watching TV before bed. He'd thought about her when he'd fallen asleep. He was only surprised he hadn't dreamed about *her*.

Annnd . . . there was his hard-on. The stupid shit. Hector had developed a very bad habit. Think of Noelle, and become aroused. No matter where he was or what he was doing.

*You can't have her. Why is that so difficult to accept?*

To encourage that acceptance, he listed the reasons he needed to avoid her.

She had money.

He did not.

She was sophisticated.

He was not.

Actually, he was as rough and gruff as a man could be.

With the publicity a woman like her garnered combined with his soiled past—and present—they'd be headline news and none of it would be good. Mia had told him how the press had already phoned AIR about Noelle's enrollment, asking how she was doing at camp.

No matter what happened or how much digging was done, no one would learn about the violence of Hector's childhood. That, he'd buried and buried deep, ditching Beckham for his brother's name. But the hooker thing? Yeah. That information was only a phone call away.

And if he was caught "dating" Noelle, his sexual practices would stare at him from every newspaper and TV screen he encountered. No, thanks. The fact that *he* knew was bad enough.

Plus, what better way to lose someone like Noelle? *Not that you can ever have her.* Once she learned the truth about him, she wouldn't want him anyway. She'd stop looking at him as if they were alone and naked, the only thing keeping them apart a prayer that neither of them wanted answered.

A look he didn't trust. Girl was tricky. Big-time

tricky. A man would never know where he stood with her, what she was capable of, or what she truly wanted from him.

Not only was she was devious, but she was smarter than she appeared, tougher, a little bit cruel, and a whole lot prepared for whatever AIR threw at her. After the double tap she'd given him, there was no denying the truth: if something drastic wasn't done, she'd make it to the end of camp and he'd have to deal with her for the rest of his working life.

His hands fisted, the glow intensifying. *Damn it, stop thinking about her and fix your tatts.*

Hector plopped into a chair, sorted through his supplies, clipped the ink gun together. He'd been doing this so many years, it was second nature. Honestly, he could have done it with his eyes closed.

The little needle glided over his skin, creating the Celtic symbol for peace over and over again. Every so often he would have to stop to wipe away the blood, but soon the glow died. Unfortunately, the heat never did.

Shit. Until he at last released the darkest edges of his body's sexual needs, Hector realized, the tattoos wouldn't help him. Because clearly, his desire for Noelle had made him sensitive to all other emotions. Especially anger. Now he was like a bomb ready to blow.

So. No question, he'd reached the danger stage. The do-something-now-now-*now* level. Or suffer.

*You know what you have to do.*

Yeah, he did, and he'd get to that. Right now, he had

to finish his tatts. They might not help him now, but they'd help him later, after he'd *gotten to that*.

He'd discovered this method about a year before joining AIR. He'd been desperate, having tried meditation, and even keeping a freaking food journal on the off chance the problem stemmed from something he was eating. Then he'd read somewhere that once upon a time berserkers had tattooed themselves with images meant to keep themselves calm.

Hector had thought, *why not*, and had done the same. Though he'd quickly burned through the first round of ink, he'd liked the fact that he could judge his heat factor with a single visual sweep. So he'd tried again, peppering his arms with different symbols for peace. He'd soon learned the Celtic one lasted the longest, helped the most, and acted as the best guide.

So he'd been applying these ever since.

If any of his coworkers had ever noticed that the ink was sometimes light, sometime dark, or that the symbols sometimes linked in new places, they'd never said. He never let anyone study them, anyway, and everyone knew never to touch him.

When he finished, he cleaned both arms and applied antibiotic ointment. Tomorrow he'd have scabs, but whatever. He'd wear his gloves and no one at AIR would know.

Mia had a case for him, and he was excited to dive in. Five more otherworlder girls had been found in a warehouse. They were around the same age—late teens—though each was a different race and unable to speak English. They weren't as undernourished as the three before them, but they were just as traumatized.

Mia had brought in translators, but even still, the girls had given very few usable details. All they'd known was that they'd been home one moment and in the warehouse the next. Unfortunately they hadn't seen their captor—or didn't remember seeing him. Drugs could screw with anyone's memory, and they'd each had fresh track marks on their veins. Track marks they'd claimed to know nothing about.

They'd been trapped for three days, and no one had come for them. They'd beaten at the walls and screamed for help, but no one had heard them. Understandable.

After the human-alien war, the planet had been razed and nearly everything had to be rebuilt. Most buildings were now comprised of shield-armor, and most walls were soundproofed steel. Even in warehouses.

Great if your planet was going to war. Bad if you were a woman locked somewhere you didn't want to be.

Mia had found them only because she'd received an anonymous tip. The same way she'd found the others. Hector planned to do a little digging and learn what he could about Mr.—or Miss?—Anonymous.

He also planned to interview the girls and see if they'd remembering anything new—or had held anything back. He would try to be gentle, but his voice was gruff no matter what he said or what emotion he was going for, and his appearance alone usually scared the fairer sex.

Maybe that's what the girls needed, though. Maybe

they were still afraid of their captor(s). Maybe they needed to know an AIR agent could be just as frightening, and that someone like Hector would protect them with his life.

And he would. He had a weakness for the young and the damaged, and worked that type of case harder than any other. Which was why he had to be top shape tomorrow.

Determined, Hector made himself a sandwich and quickly inhaled every crumb, even though the thing was tasteless and settled like lead, then downed a glass of water. All right, then. He'd taken care of two needs. His arms and his hunger.

That left only one.

Biting the inside of his cheek, he picked up the phone and dialed Happy Endings.

# Eight

❦

*T*HE DOORBELL RANG.

Hector had been waiting for that shrill *ding dong* all morning. Having stayed up the rest of the night, unwilling to go back to bed and risk another dream, he'd had nothing to do but think of Noelle. Of her lips pressed against his, of her tongue battling his, of her body arching into his. Of her accepting him, just as he was. Of her needing him, all of him.

If ever there had been a woman created solely to tempt him, it was Noelle. Her beauty, her scent, her taste, her . . . everything. She appealed to him on every level.

Now he was like a junkie in need of a fix, worse off than before. He couldn't go to work on edge like this. And yet, he wished like hell he'd never made that call to Happy Endings.

*You want to accidentally hurt the otherworlders you're supposed to interview?*

No. He didn't.

*Ding dong.*

He stalked to the ID panel and gritted, "Open." The front door obeyed, metal sliding to the side, no longer separating inside from out.

Air laced with car exhaust, sunshine, and thick, cloying perfume drifted to him. He didn't look at his visitor's face; he didn't care what she looked like and actually preferred not to know. He looked at her arms. No track marks. He looked at the pulse at the base of her neck. Good, strong, and steady.

She wore a loose white blouse and a well-fitted black skirt, as if she were headed to the office rather than the bedroom.

His gaze moved beyond her. Bright sunlight glinted off the dark, nondescript sedan she'd parked in his driveway. He scanned the houses across the street from his. Tall but narrow, each was built with a different color of brick—from brown to gold and even purple— and packed closely together. None of his neighbors were outside. Even though they'd never be able to tell what the girl did for a living by her car or appearance, he was glad.

To his left was a dentist, and to his right a family of four. They'd be disgusted if they knew what went on behind his door. He was.

Hector moved aside and motioned the woman inside.

She soared past him without a word. So. She knew his MO. Either she'd been here before, or the girls who'd been here had talked and told her what he "liked." Zero communication, a straight shot to his guest room, a blow job, then a straight shot out.

"Close," he said and once again the door obeyed. He didn't turn around. Didn't follow the woman as she clicked and clacked down his hallway. He just stood there, looking around as if his home was new to him.

He had no holophotos, not of himself and certainly not of his family. He would have liked a few of Dean, if any had ever been taken or if Dean had still lived. They hadn't. He didn't.

There was no clutter. No vases, no colorful but useless bowls or other shit women seemed to like. Just the basics. A couch, a loveseat, and a coffee table. An entertainment bureau, and a few plaques for "heroic" behavior on the job.

The fabric on the furniture was synthetic and worn, the table cheap stone rather than real wood, and the TV as basic as electronics came. He didn't live here so much as exist here, flittering through between cases.

What would Noelle think of his stuff?

The answer didn't matter. Couldn't matter. *Why are you stalling? You're a menace. This is necessary.*

Necessary. How he hated that word. Hated how it took away his freedom of choice.

Why couldn't he be like every other man? Able to touch a woman, hell, even touch himself, without causing all kinds of devastation. Instead, he was a killer with undetachable weapons strapped to his body.

Rage at his own helplessness suddenly exploded through him, and he punched a hole in the living room wall. There was a spray of little rocks, some springing across the room, some just tumbling to the floor. His knuckles barely registered the sting.

*Calm down, idiot.* Anger had the same effect on his arms as sexual frustration. Combined, the two created a toxic mix of *oh shit.* He had to do this. He would do this.

Grinding his molars, he traced the lingering scent of that perfume to his guest room. He never let anyone into the master, never let anyone do anything to him in the living room or the kitchen, either. He didn't want to ever walk inside those rooms and think about this part of his life. Therefore, all sexual activity happened here.

The woman was already on her knees.

Per his specifications, she was still fully clothed and hadn't even bothered unbuttoning her collar.

He'd never had sex with a working girl, had never dared risk that kind of physical contact with one. Hell, he'd never had sex period. Not even with Kira, his one and only girlfriend. He'd killed her before they actually sealed—

*Stop that shit. Now.*

Hector threw a dark curtain over his thoughts. Out of habit, he checked the condition of his "nothing can burn through these, I swear!" gloves. A dark curse left him. Damn salesman. Hector should have known better. Even though he'd tattooed himself last night, several spots were already burned and ringed, the edges of those rings caked in soot. He even smelled of cinder.

Damn that Noelle.

And wouldn't you know it? Just as before, merely thinking her name got him hard as a goddamn steel pipe, desire overshadowing his lingering anger.

What was it about her that lit him up so completely? She was gorgeous, but so were other women. She was silly and violent, a little playful, a lot vengeful. Her only vulnerability, that he could see, was Ava.

What was Noelle doing right now? Causing trouble, he thought, and next found himself grinning.

The moment he realized what he was doing, he scowled. He'd never obsessed about a woman before. Always he'd been able to walk away. So why did simply thinking Noelle cause such a strong reaction?

"Should I . . ." The female in front of him motioned to his zipper. She must be in a hurry to get this done to have broken his no-communication rule.

"No. I will." But he didn't. He just stood there, as motionless as a statue. He wanted Noelle, yet he was going to allow another woman to put her mouth on him. A woman who didn't want him.

Guilt ate at him, the bites bigger than usual.

*You aren't locked in a cage. You aren't forced to harm other kids just to stay alive.* His life was good. He hunted predatory baddies for a living, helped prevent other kids from having a childhood as traumatic as his. So the fuck what if he paid a stranger to get him off while he craved someone else?

With shaky hands he unfastened the only button on his pants. Tendrils of smoke rose from the holes in his gloves. Shit. He had to do this quickly. He needed the release the hooker could give him, and soon, before he burned down his house with the two of them in it.

"You do the rest," he croaked, locking his arms behind his back. "And don't . . . don't talk anymore." He'd lose his erection, but his hormones wouldn't cool down.

She nodded, reached for him, and down went his zipper. Cold fingers moved his underwear out of the way and wrapped around the base of his shaft. His disgust with himself climbed.

As if she were part of a movie and someone had pushed the slow-motion button, he watched as she opened her mouth and inched toward his cock . . . closer . . . He clenched his teeth.

*What the fuck are you doing?* his better half screamed. *This is wrong, so wrong. There has to be another way.*

The answer was simple. He was surviving.

Closer . . .

Damn it, what if there *was* another way? He'd never tried to masturbate, had let fear stop him, but maybe he should have risked it. Maybe singeing off his cock would finally end his physical *and* mental torment.

Closer . . .

Sweat dripped from his temples, sliding down his cheeks. His legs vibrated with the strength needed to hold himself in place.

*Just get it over with!* the other part of him shouted. The part he knew, understood. *Until you do, you're dangerous. Operating on a hair trigger.*

That, too, was the truth.

What should he do? The two needs warred, both so fierce they threatened to pull him apart.

Closer . . .

*His entire body shaking.*

Closer . . .

*Heating.*

Closer still . . .

*Sweating, blistering.*

He jerked away, severing contact. The woman looked up at him, her eyes widening with confusion.

He couldn't do it. He just couldn't. This wasn't right. He wanted someone else, and if he couldn't have Noelle's mouth on him, he wouldn't have anyone's. That didn't change the fact that he needed relief, somehow, some way, but he'd deal with that as soon as the woman left.

"You have to go," he said. "I can't do this. I put the money on the nightstand. Please, just take it and go." He knew his voice lashed like a whip, but he couldn't help it. He hurt, he yearned. He was scared out of his goddamn mind about what he planned to do.

"I—"

"Please," he croaked. Finally he allowed himself to study her face. She was most likely in her early twenties, though life had not been kind to her. Had aged her beyond her years, with stress lines branching from her eyes and mouth. Her hair was bright red, too coarse to be real.

"I'm sorry you didn't want me," she said, but damn if there wasn't relief in her voice. She grabbed the money and strolled away, out of the house, a spring in her step.

# Nine

❧

$H$ECTOR WAITED UNTIL HE heard the front door snick closed before releasing the breath he'd been holding and carefully wrapping his hand around the base of his cock. He was going to masturbate, even if it killed him. And he was going to do it now, before he lost his nerve.

He could feel the burn his arm emitted through the fabric of his glove, but he didn't fry his shaft to a crisp and took heart.

*Do it.* Slowly up, slowly down, he stroked. Still no problems. He increased his speed. Up, down. The glide wasn't easy, but it wasn't bad, either. Up, down, faster and faster.

The glow brightened. The heat blazed. And yet, *still* no problems.

Relaxing, getting into it, he squeezed his thick, marble-hard shaft with a strength borrowed from his desperation. Up, down, up, down. No matter how excited he became, he never hurt himself—and yet orgasm eluded him.

*Come. On.* As much as he loved knowing he could do this, he wanted to reach the end. To know he'd be okay even then.

He tried softer strokes, then hard again, softer then harder. Harder still.

Nothing worked—until Noelle's image took shape in his mind. Tall, slim, her glossy brown hair hanging past her shoulders, the sun glittering behind her and forming a halo around her. Her eyes were languid, the lids at half-mast, those lovely gray irises becoming liquid silver as she traced them over his body. Her lush mouth was parted, as if she couldn't quite catch her breath. As if the sight of him had aroused her.

Next he saw her on his bed. She was naked, her nipples pink and beaded. Her stomach hollowed, and as he watched, enraptured, she dabbled her fingers around her navel, teasing herself—teasing him.

A moan escaped her as she arched her back and spread her legs wide. The curls between her legs were dark and glistening with her desire. So much desire. For him. Only him.

"Hector," she said, a prayer and a curse all at once. "I need you."

Yes, damn it, yes. He needed her, too. He imagined himself sinking inside this pliant, dream Noelle with a single thrust. Imagined the way she clutched him, hot and wet and so incredibly tight.

His cock loved the imagery as much as his mind, and his pleasure deepened. His strokes became jerky, but oh, shit, they felt good.

"Don't stop," she pleaded, all smoke and eagerness as her knees squeezed at his waist.

"No," he gritted. "Never."

"Yes, Hector, yes. Touch me. Please, touch me. I love it when you touch me."

Yeah, he thought again. He was going to touch her. Touch her everywhere. Was going to brand her, own her, become all that she knew, all that she wanted to know. Was even reaching for her . . .

His balls drew up tight, sensation ramping . . . ramping . . . Oh, hallelujah! He squeezed the head of his penis and jetted white-hot into his palm. Finally, finally, thank you God, finally.

When his shudders at last calmed, he simply stood there, sliding down from the high, the pleasure, and glorying in his success.

*His. Success.* The two words echoed inside his mind. He'd done it. He'd actually gotten himself off without hurting himself or anyone else.

It was a miracle. It was . . . his salvation. Whispers of excitement rushed through him. From this moment on, he could take care of himself. More words echoed. *He could actually take care of himself!*

His body must be immune to the heat and the atomizing. And damn, he should have realized that sooner. Felt stupid that he hadn't, and yet that still didn't dampen his joy.

Grinning, he walked into the hallway bathroom, tossed the gloves, washed up, and righted his clothing. The itching and burning in his arms had subdued completely. He was utterly calm, under control. It was like his slate had just been wiped clean. He felt wonderfully normal.

And now, any time his arms acted up, or his need became too much, he could take care of himself and feel this way again. He wouldn't have to call a hooker. He found himself laughing, the sound rusty.

He went to his bedroom and sat at the edge of his bed—such a terrible start to his day, with such a spectacular finish—then dialed Mia Snow, his bitch on wheels of a temporary boss. Jack Pagosa, his real boss, had taken a leave of absence for heart problems or some shit like that and had left Mia in charge of the New Chicago offices.

Truth be told, Hector had been a little surprised by Jack's choice. Mia was a good agent, one of the best, certainly, but Hector had been on staff just as long as she had, and had just as many arrests and kills. Same with Dallas. Hell, same with Ghost and Jaxon. And Jaxon was the most diplomatic of them all. Or rather, he used to be.

Probably didn't hurt that Snow was dating one of the most powerful men on Earth. An Arcadian who was as rich as Noelle, maybe richer, with the ability to move faster than the speed of light, control people with his mind, and predict the future.

Hector was a little envious of Kyrin's openness. The guy didn't care who knew about his origins or his powers. How nice would it be to have that kind of freedom? To just be who he was, unconcerned about anything else?

But Hector's abilities destroyed, caused pain, and

with pain came fear. Fear brought a whole new pot of problems to the table. Someone—probably multiple someones—would want to put him down to "protect" the innocent.

"This is Snow," she said five rings in.

"Hey. It's Hector." No preliminaries, just the facts. "Where are my girls being held?"

Breath crackled over the connection. "You beat me to the punch. I was just about to call you."

The tension in her voice distressed him. Mia wasn't touchy-feely by nature, and hardly anything threw her off her game. Took something major to upset her. "What's wrong?"

"They're missing."

"Missing?" His happiness vanished in an instant. His fingers squeezed the cell, nearly cracking the plastic. *Relax.* "Tell me."

"They were in the hospital, hooked to IVs, with guards at their doors. Doctor goes in to check on one, and she's gone. He thinks she left on her own, so he goes to the next room. She's gone. Same deal with the rest."

"Any witnesses?"

"No one. I'm sending a team to dust for prints, check for voice recordings, but . . ."

"You don't think you'll get anything." Recorders were set up strategically throughout the city, and because alien voices were so different from that of humans, in ways humans couldn't detect without the proper machinery, those recorders only picked up otherworlder conversations.

When you had a location and a time, pinpointing specific conversations was easy. However, otherworlders knew about the recorders and knew to commit their crimes quietly.

"Correct," Mia said. "I've already watched video feed and there was no one coming in or out of their room except the medical staff. And none of the staff wheeled anything out that was big enough to hold a body."

"The women could have fought whoever grabbed them. Maybe they said something during the struggle." They were alien, so their voices would have been recorded.

"I'll let you dig through the recordings."

"The hospital will be my first stop." For someone to grab the girls so quickly, so effortlessly, and without drawing a single bit of notice, teleportation had to be in play. "Any Arcadians working there?"

"A few, and I've already got men hunting their locations to pull them in for questioning."

They thought alike. "Good."

A lot of Arcadians could teleport, yes, but there were ways to prevent them from doing so. Like certain metals that were mined from other planets. Expensive as hell to acquire, and hard as hell to drag through one wormhole after another—the standard way to planet hop—but AIR HQ and all AIR vehicles were comprised of the necessary materials.

If you weren't near AIR or your vehicle, lasercuffs worked just as well. They weren't metal, but the light they produced bonded to skin, any kind of skin.

When an Arcadian was restrained that way, and he teleported, the bands would heat, just like Hector's arms, and his hands would literally melt off. Brutal, but necessary. AIR had to take precautions to protect the innocent.

"So here's a question," Hector said. "How did the abductor know the girls were in the hospital?"

"We aren't sure," she said. "Too many options. A chatty or even corrupt hospital employee. A chatty or corrupt friend of a hospital employee. The spread of idle gossip to the wrong people. An isotope tracker. Maybe one of the girls called someone, and that call was traced. We're checking the lines, but the other theories require more time to investigate."

His free hand fisted. "The MO for this abduction, as well as the other one, is similar. Therefore, it's safe to say that whoever took our first batch of girls took our second."

"I agree. And since the first one was yours, this one is all yours, as well," she said. "Wrap it up quick."

*I'll do my best.* He always did. "No anonymous tip to help us out this time?"

"Not yet."

"And we have no idea why the girls are being taken and locked away?" Made no sense, really. Why take them if you weren't going to use them in some way? Why starve them?

He'd studied pictures. Each girl was pretty, very pretty, and his first thought had been sex slaves. He'd busted a few whorehouses throughout the years. Otherworlder females were promised lodgings on Earth,

DARK TASTE OF RAPTURE

a job, whatever. So they came here expecting to start a new life.

They started a new life, all right. In some rich guy's bed. And that's if they were lucky. The unlucky ones were placed in those whorehouses, forced to service countless men and women each and every day.

But again, why take these girls and not put them to work right away?

"We don't," Mia said. "We hadn't gotten any other answers out of them. Not any we understood, anyway."

Very well. "After I finish at the hospital, I'll go over transcripts of what was said. Maybe I'll pick up on something."

"Sounds good."

"And, uh, Mia." Self-preservation rose. "I don't want to go back to camp."

"Why?"

"For personal reasons. And I swear to you, they're good reasons. Important. Life-threatening even."

A weary sigh. "I'll give you some time off, no prob. You rarely ask. And okay, sure, miss your second week at camp. I'll deal with Dallas's whining, as always. Because yes, he will complain about the injustice of someone taking a break without him."

Actually, Hector thought Dallas would be happy to have Noelle to himself, but whatever. He didn't care. He—

Smelled melting plastic and realized his hand had heated to the point of deep-frying in mere seconds. Despite his sexual release. What the hell? He was so jealous, so possessive, he immediately reacted to the thought of anyone else with Noelle?

He'd never had a woman, all to himself, and he—

Didn't need to be thinking that way. Breathing in and out, Hector forced a surge of calm. "Thanks," he said to hurry the conversation along. "I owe—"

"But you're going back to camp for the final month," she cut in, heartless as only she could be. "I value your opinion, and I need to know how the remaining trainees have progressed."

He didn't point out that Dallas could tell her. Or Jaxon. Or Ghost. Phoenix was the youngest and newest member of the team, so no one would care what she thought. "Okay. I'll go back." Maybe.

Hopefully, he wouldn't be thinking about Noelle every spare minute of every day. Hopefully, he wouldn't be thinking about her at all. But even if he was, he now had a method for dealing, he reminded himself.

"Good," Mia said. "Now get to work, Dean. Oh, and say hello to Noelle Tremain for me when you finally return to camp. I hear you guys are tight." Her laughter echoed over the line.

"Fucking Dallas," he muttered.

"Uh, no. Don't blame him for your infamy. There's a video of your KO, and it's all over the web. At least thirty people have emailed me a link. Congratulations, you're a star." *Click.*

Wonderful. Worldwide humiliation. Exactly what he'd needed.

Hector tossed his phone on his nightstand and

padded to his bathroom, where he hopped in the shower. The dry enzyme misting from the overhead and side spouts caused the plastic he'd melted to dissolve quickly.

Six weeks, he thought. Then he and Noelle would once again cross paths.

He had a feeling only one of them would survive. He wondered just who that would be.

# Ten

*H*E WAS BACK.

Noelle hadn't seen Hector since she'd laid him flat, oh, around six weeks ago.

Maybe she should have gone easier on him. Two little taps, though. Love taps, really, and he'd dropped as if he were the slowest gazelle in the pack and she the hungry lion who'd won rights to first bite. Then he'd collected himself, stood, and walked away without uttering a word.

In her defense, he'd kind of deserved it. Not just for the way he'd eyed her with such disgust the day they'd met—and had since admitted he'd been wrong about, she reminded herself—but because he'd knocked Johnny Deschanel on his ass and looked at Noelle, all *this is what's going to happen to you if you stay here.*

Well, she had stayed—but he hadn't.

She sat at the window cubby in the bunkhouse. Night had long since fallen, but the lamps surrounding the instructors' quarters provided the perfect spotlight.

Hector had just driven up in a sleek black Porsche, emerged without looking around, and carried a bag up the steps, finally disappearing from view.

She had *not* watched the way his pants pulled tight against his perfect, muscled ass with every step. And she had *not* thought of him while he'd been gone. Not more than a few hundred times.

And she *really* hadn't thought about the way he'd removed his T-shirt that day, revealing cord after cord of hard-won strength, tanned skin glistening with sweat, and a smattering of dark hair. Or how she'd gasped when she had first spied him, awed and aroused and aching to put her hands on him.

Something else she hadn't thought about: how his right arm had sported fewer tattoos and how, just before he'd tugged on his gloves, those tattoos had shimmered, softly glowing like they had that night in the alley.

She hadn't thought about why he glowed—optical illusion on her part? exposure to a toxic chemical on his? allergic reaction to alien cuisine? weird fluke of nature?—or how hot-off-the-streets sexy he was.

Yeah, uh, she really had to stop (not) thinking about him.

This attraction . . . she didn't understand it, didn't understand why his intensity fascinated her. Or why she'd missed him so damn badly. Or how he'd pepped her up while he was here. How he'd pushed and pushed and pushed, yet hadn't sent her into a frenzy of self-destruction.

Maybe because he didn't do it to malign her character. He did it to make her a better agent, someone who saved lives and protected those who couldn't protect themselves. He'd actually distracted her from her loneliness, making her forget all about that ever-gnawing void inside her. He'd given her purpose.

Or maybe the lack of sting was because he looked at her, really looked at her, as if she were a person worthy of his time and attention. And even though he'd shouted, he hadn't called her names.

For that reason, she'd abandoned her revenge plans for him. So he'd kissed her and rejected her. Wasn't a punch to that gorgeous mouth enough?

But again . . . why did she feel this way about him?

Sure, he was like no one she'd ever met before and he didn't care about making nice. He treated everyone with the same sense of cold detachment—except Noelle. With her, he barked orders and assumed she'd just comply. When he didn't get it, he physically forced the issue.

Sometimes he joked around with the other agents, and he was relaxed, casual. Yet still he radiated all kinds of ferocity, as if he couldn't quite lower his guard all the way. With anyone.

What would it take to relax him absolutely? What would *he* be like that way?

She'd never know, she was sure. Because . . . oh, God . . . she was going to talk to him and at last douse the chemistry sparking between them. Or at least, on her end. One conversation, and she could finally stop (not) thinking about him. She just knew it. He'd snarl, of course, and she'd remember how grumpy he was.

He'd tell her he wasn't interested, and she'd remember she wasn't into proving herself.

She tiptoed to Ava's bunk and sat at the edge of the mattress. "Ava," she whispered. No lights were shining over the bunk, no moonlight washing over the bed, but Noelle had been awake for the past hour and her eyes had long since adjusted to the darkness. "You up?"

"No," her friend whispered back, voice scratchy from slumber.

"Oh, good. Quick question. Let's say, hypothetically, that I snuck out." Walking over to the instructors' cabin wasn't a crime. For all they knew, she'd spotted something suspicious. But a girl never knew what the agents would decide to complain about.

*Can't get a third strike.* She did, and she doubted she'd be allowed to stay.

And now . . . now she really wanted to stay.

She finally understood what all the fuss was about. She was good at this.

Challenged. Intrigued. She thrived where others failed. And, if given a chance, she could make a difference in the world; she could save lives, destroy killers.

Having a goal was nice, and something she hadn't known she'd needed. But every day she felt a little more centered, a little more driven.

"Would you cover for me?" she asked, already knowing the answer. "I don't want any of the other trainees to know what I'm doing."

A big yawn, a total body stretch. "Did you get slapped upside the head today? *Of course* I'll cover for you."

"You're the best!"

"Do you need backup?"

"Nope." She had to do this on her own. She eased to a stand, the stupid mattress creaking.

Ava sat up, satin curls falling all around her face. "So where are you going?"

She couldn't lie to her friend. She wouldn't. "To see Hector Dean. He just arrived. I want to . . . talk to him." And a whole lot more, but she wouldn't do more, even if he begged. Definitely.

Maybe.

"You going to kill him?" Ava asked.

"Nah. I've decided to play nice."

Noelle had only been with two men. The first, a mistake in high school. The next day, the slimy bastard had told everyone at school how he'd popped her cherry. Within hours, she'd become a raging slut.

Of course, Ava had then popped his cherry red sports car into his parents' living room wall. Noelle still got all weepy when she remembered. *Such* a heroic gesture. A gesture that had marked Ava's very first arrest.

They'd celebrated by stealing *very* expensive champagne, and that had marked Noelle's.

The second guy, Corban, she'd chosen more carefully. Or so she'd thought. Even though he was an otherworlder, he'd come from a wealthy background. And even though he'd come from a wealthy background, he'd proven himself to be a warrior at heart. He hadn't chosen law enforcement or anything like that, but professional football.

They'd met at a cocktail party, and he'd come on strong. At first, he'd made her feel pretty. Special and accepted. When they began dating officially, however, that's when the criticism had started.

*A girlfriend of his would never* . . . . fill in the blank.

*A girlfriend of his had to* . . . fill in the blank.

Men were complications. Men were hassles. And though Noelle wanted to open herself up and take a chance—in theory—she hadn't yet.

Since the break-up, she had dated other guys. A lot of other guys. Always within the first hour, she found a thousand things wrong, and declined all invitations to go for a second round.

Strangely, she'd found a thousand things wrong with Hector, but she still wanted to see him. Again and again. Preferably naked.

"Noelle, you little hussy," Ava whispered. "Are you still with me?"

She shook herself back into the present. "Now I am, my darling—wait, do you prefer *little person, vertically challenged,* or *pocket rocket*?"

A grinning Ava reached up and patted her cheek with a bit too much force.

"Ow," she managed to quietly yelp.

"Oops, sorry. Sometimes I don't know my own strength. Now as I was saying. After the way Hector stared at your twins that day, I'm gonna pretend I never uttered the word *dibs*, but only for tonight. 'Cause you know, the first taste is free."

"So you've told me. This will be the second taste." *If* anything happened. Which it wouldn't.

Ava didn't miss a beat. "The first and second tastes are free. You want a third, you'll have to pay."

"I never doubted it." Noelle nibbled on her bottom lip. "If I'm not back by morning, send robo-cadaver dogs after my body. Hector's killed *me*."

"With pleasure?"

*I wish.* No, no, she didn't wish. They were going to chat, nothing more. "No, with a vengeance stick."

"Otherwise known as a penis?"

She had to smother her laughter with both hands.

"By the way," Ava said, "I'm rooting for you. Oh, and I have this strange feeling that you should check your phone for messages. See ya." She lay back down, but Noelle knew the girl wouldn't sleep. She'd listen and she'd wait, and if anyone woke up or came inside and noticed Noelle was missing, she'd take care of it.

Outside, Noelle jumped down the fire escape, landed in the dirt, the moonlit air cool as she pressed her back against the dilapidated bunkhouse wall. When no one sounded an alarm, she whipped out her phone. The new message? A photo of Noelle with her face scrunched up, about to sneeze.

Caption read: *Here's a true screen savor 4 U.*

*Little witch,* she thought with an inward laugh.

Storing her phone in her back pocket, she considered her options. The path from bunkhouse hell to instructor's paradise would take fifteen seconds, give or take a few depending on her hustle, and was completely illuminated. No one was outside, but if an agent were to walk past one of the many windows, she'd be spotted instantly.

No reason to worry about the trainees. Ava would tackle whoever wanted outside and perform a total knockout. Besides, after this morning's torture session, everyone was mentally and physically exhausted and more likely to die in their beds than get up to so much as pee.

Apparently the only way to learn how to interrogate your targets was to *be* interrogated. Also apparent, interrogation sometimes involved getting beaten to a pulp. Noelle's ribs had stopped her instructor's fist from slamming into the back of her chair, oh, about thirty times, and they were now probably cracked as hell.

Thanks to the nerve-frying procedure, those cracks hadn't and wouldn't bother her. Noelle wouldn't even know if she were dying. In fact, the only time she ever knew something was wrong was by the bruising—she had that in spades right now—or if she passed out from blood loss.

Her father had thought he was doing her a favor, and yeah, maybe he had, but the process had inadvertently destroyed some of her pleasure receptors, too. Now a guy had to really work to give her an orgasm.

Would Hector be able to give her an orgasm?

She didn't have to think about the answer. After that combustible kiss they'd shared, yeah. He would be able to give her one without trying.

*Don't think about that right now.* The mission was more important. Okay, so. She could either walk with purpose and risk enemy—aka instructor—capture and have to explain her presence, or crawl and risk damaging her ribs further, possibly cutting into her lungs and not knowing it until she woke up in a hospital bed. Also, she'd ruin her pretty cotton T-shirt that way.

She'd walk, she decided. The T-shirt was a gift from Ava and read *Good Girls Need Spankings Too.*

To her relieved surprise, no one spotted her and she reached the cabin without incident. Another surprise, the window closest to her was open, allowing fresh air inside and noise outside. She propped her arms on the pane and leaned in. Sounds, so many sounds. Laughter, cheering, taunting, curses, beer slurping, glasses tinkling together.

No wonder the agents hadn't paid any attention to possible infiltration. They surrounded a holoscreen and were watching a football game. Otherworlders had only been accepted into the NFL a few drafts ago, and no one had known what to make of that until after the first few games. Violence on the field had intensified, and so had the love of the fans.

Noelle had a profile view of everyone, and wow, Hector had the most wonderfully sloped nose, a little bump in the middle. Probably from being broken so many times. A girl could get ideas about that bump. Like kissing it all better.

"Damn, but Corban Blue is the best quarterback I've ever seen," Dallas said after finishing off his beer and grabbing another from the cooler beside him. "He's got an arm like a cannon. He throws and the ball just shoots to the receiver like it's on a string and being tugged."

Think of the past, and *boom,* it would fill your present.

Corban. An Arcadian with long white hair, eyes of the most brilliant violet, and the face of God's favorite angel. Would Dallas (*cough* Hector *cough*) be shocked to know Noelle had dated him? That she and Corban had practically lived together once upon a time? Something they'd managed to keep out of the media. An easy trick when you owned a lot of the media outlets in your city.

"We should recruit him," Hector said, slamming his glass into Dallas's in some kind of parody of a toast. What long lashes he had, fanning out like a peacock's tail feathers. "Imagine him tossing a target like that. With his perfect aim, he could have the body in the back of our cars without us ever having to take a step."

Dallas whistled. "Goddamn, Agent Meanie. I like the way your mind works. Noelle must not have damaged your brain as much as we feared."

Hector grinned. "Doctor asked me if I'd introed my face to the windshield of a Mack truck."

A grin. A freaking grin. And there were dimples in his cheeks. Noelle barely stopped a dreamy sigh from leaving her. Mostly relaxed, a lot amused, the tension drained from him, he was beyond gorgeous. His golden eyes were bright, his lips plumped and red rather than thinned with displeasure.

"She was some kind of lucky, getting the drop on you like that," Dallas said. "And you were some kind of stupid, letting her get the drop on you like that. She's a cream puff, man."

The urge to sigh vanished. She gnashed her teeth together. Maybe she shouldn't have thrown so much fuel on the I'm-so-stupid fire. They'd had weeks to uncover her intelligence, or what she liked to consider intelligence, yet only Hector had questioned his initial impression? Come on!

"Hey," Jaxon barked from the other side of the couch. "That's my cousin. Show some respect."

She noticed he didn't defend her smarts, the bastard.

"You didn't hear me say she has the IQ of a peanut, did you? *Anyway*." Blue eyes flipped back to Hector, and those strong shoulders lifted in a give-a-guy-a-break shrug.

"So she's still here?" Hector asked, and he sounded less than thrilled, if resolved.

This kept up, and her pretty white smile would be nothing but powder. Funny that when she came up in conversation, Hector's mood instantly soured. He'd just rejected her again, yet this time she hadn't had to say a single word to him.

"Yeah, and dude. Interrogation 101 was today, and you shoulda seen her." Dallas finished off his second beer and tossed the glass where he'd tossed the first. On the floor.

Hector scrubbed a hand across his scalp. "Who ran the op?" His tattoos. The ink was darker than it'd been before he'd left, and there were more swirling designs on both arms. Odd, but her mouth watered for a taste of them.

"None of us could bring ourselves to do it, to hit her, you know, so we called in the girls. Phoenix was already here, but Siren and Kitten came to help."

Phoenix, as delicate and fragile in appearance as

Ava, yet she was the one who'd stepped in at the last moment to finish pulverizing Noelle's ribcage. Siren was plain, average—until she opened her mouth. Girl had the voice of an angelic choir, and listening to her was embarrassingly orgasmic.

Kitten, despite her feline grace, was pretty in the same hardass way as Hector. Tattooed, intense, with no apparent softness.

"Let me guess," Hector said. "Kitten wanted a go at her first."

How had he known?

"Bingo. Kit asked her how she'd smuggled the maid in—the second time. Don't know if you were here for that. Anyway, Noelle said she'd used the tunnel. So Kit went off on this tangent about how, if Noelle had used the tunnel, none of us were alerted, yada yada, and roughed our girl Noelle up a bit. Noelle babbled about being willing to do anything to stop the abuse, even showing Kit her tits. Vulgar language out of that candy apple mouth and spoken in that I'm-already-in-bed-and-without-my-panties voice . . ." Dallas moaned, as if in pain.

"Hey," Jaxon growled again.

Hector gripped the arm of the couch, his knuckles bleaching. Then he stiffened and pried his fingers from the furniture. Breathing deeply, he settled his hands in his lap.

Such a strong reaction confused her, made her wonder what the hell was going on inside that head of his.

"You know what's really interesting, though," Dallas went on when he'd collected himself from the hormone high. "Even when Siren and Phoenix got in on the action, Noelle never cried. Never got winded or acted as if she were hurt in any way. I'll show you the video feed. This'll only be my eighteenth time to watch it."

"No!" Hector shouted, then more calmly added, "No, thanks. I'm too into the game, and I, uh, need something stronger than beer." He gave his bottle to a still-scowling Jaxon, pushed to a stand, and turned.

That's when he spotted her. His eyes widened, his nostrils flared, and the gold in his eyes blazed.

Oh, was she in trouble now.

# *Eleven*

NOELLE WAVED WITH ONLY the slightest hesitation, as if she wasn't reeling from the sight of him. As if she wasn't irritated for missing him all these many weeks while he wasn't even interested in watching her outsmart three of his coworkers.

Not that he would realize she'd outsmarted The Estrogen Brigade. Come on—use the tunnel again? Please. But because Noelle had offered a plausible explanation, Kitten had locked on that, never even considering there could have been another way. Same with the others.

Hector stood there a minute, popping his jaw. Rather than rat her out, as she halfway expected, he stalked from the living room, out the front door, and to her side.

He didn't speak as he grabbed her by the forearm—when had he pulled on gloves?—and tugged her away from the building.

Another shocker: he didn't haul her ass back to the bunkhouse.

Her heart drummed in her chest, and if she'd been a normal human being, that probably would have hurt the shit out of her battered ribs, was probably damaging her in ways she didn't know, but honestly? She didn't care. He smelled delicious, like he had that night in the alley, all earth and sky, fresh, wild, and untamable.

His skin was warm through the soft fabric, warmer than anyone else who'd ever touched her, and the intensity of that heat affected her, reaching those deadened receptors and forcing them to take notice.

After bypassing all of the lamps, he released her and rounded on her, getting in her face. He was scowling. She thought he was going to erupt into a tangent about sneaking from her quarters, but he merely stared down at her, silent.

She could still feel him, she mused, rubbing at her wrist.

He glanced down, paled. "Did I hurt you?"

"No."

He relaxed, but only for a second. "What the hell do you think you're doing, spying on us?" The gold in his eyes no longer blazed. They'd frosted over. "You should be in bed—I mean, you should be lying down, recovering."

He was so close, finally within reach. Every thread of her annoyance faded. She quivered with excitement. "I wasn't spying. I was eavesdropping." Was her voice as breathless to him as it was to her?

"There's a difference?" he asked, arching a brow.

"There has to be, since I was doing one and not the

other." She raised her chin, and the tips of their noses brushed.

Flickers of the blaze returned, melting some of the ice. He jerked backward, ensuring there would be no more contact. But he didn't stalk away, leaving her alone. He massaged his left hand up and down his right arm.

Was he glowing through the gloves? She couldn't quite tell.

"Your arms," she said.

His scowl returned. "I'm wearing glow-in-the-dark lotion. So what?"

He *was* glowing, then. He was also a liar. Glow-in-the-dark lotion possessed a very distinct odor—an odor that did not cling to him. Also, if your goal was to glow in the dark, why cover up when you succeeded?

*Ponder it later*. The answer didn't matter, anyway. He was Hector, beautiful, strong, intense Hector, and she was finally alone with him. No telling how long he would—or wouldn't—stick around.

"What kind of damage did Kitten do to you?" he suddenly demanded.

Was he simply curious, or did he actually care? "Well, I think I'm bleeding internally and I'll be lucky to live through the night, if that's what you're asking."

Horror bathed his features. "You're going to a medic. Now. Don't you dare think about protesting, either."

Chuckling, she dodged before he could clasp on to her. Or swoop her up, whichever he'd been planning. "No. I'm fine. Really." His show of concern delighted her. Meant he cared, as she'd hoped. Even if the caring was only for a subordinate. "She hit me a few times, but it's nothing I haven't experienced before."

He stood there, a muscle ticking in his jaw. "Before." A menacing growl. "Who hit you *before*?"

What would he do if she told him? Hurt the offenders in turn? God, she liked that idea. Liked the thought of him rampaging in her defense. Ava was the only one who'd ever had her back. "I've been in more fights than I can remember, so I'm afraid I can't give you any names."

A pause as he absorbed her claim, relaxed.

"Unless I'm in front of my computer, and open my People To One Day Destroy file," she added.

He shook his head in exasperation. "So. How did you do it?"

Confused now, she merely blinked up at him. "Do what?"

"Sneak in the maid. You didn't use the tunnel."

Her eyes widened. "How do you know? I totally could have."

He snapped his teeth at her. "How?"

She should lie. If he turned her in . . .

*He won't turn you in.*

*How do you know? You heard him with Dallas—she's still here, he said. He's had it out for you since the beginning and wants you gone.*

*He'll recognize my skill. He'll realize I'm an asset.*

Great, now she was talking to herself. "I overheard Dallas on the phone with you," she admitted, watching his expression. There was no flash of surprise or pride. No flash of anything. "You guys were talking about how an Arcadian had popped into several different hospital rooms, snagged a few ladies, and popped out with no one the wiser."

The ticking increased in speed. "Go on."

*I'm not disappointed.* "I have an Arcadian on my payroll and made a call."

Still he didn't react—but he did step closer to her. His night-wild scent enveloped her, seeping into her pores, forcing all of her thoughts on him—on getting even closer to him.

"Are you going to tattle on me?" she asked.

There were several beats of hesitation before he said, "No," the admission seeming to astonish him.

Relief cascaded through her. She wouldn't ask why. He might change his mind, the contrary brute. "So . . . any luck on your case?"

An abrupt shake of his head. He opened his mouth, and she suspected—hoped—he meant to tell her more about it, maybe even ask her opinion or thoughts, but he didn't.

"Where have you been?" she asked, putting them on the right track. "You were supposed to come back at the first of the month." Not that she'd asked around or anything.

"I was taking care of a few things." His eyelids narrowed to tiny slits. "And the *few things* aren't any of your business, so don't ask."

His lack of answer sent her mind into a tailspin. Had he been holed up with some skank he considered his intellectual equal? Working on that case and injured? Sick? "Do you want to know what I've been doing?" A husky note had entered her voice.

He stiffened. "I know what you've been doing. Causing trouble."

*Not. Disappointed.* The men in her life never took her seriously, so why should Hector be any different? Even though he saw a bit deeper than everyone else. "We've interacted so little, and yet you already know me so well. I'm impressed. Really."

He didn't take the bait. "Tell me something, Noelle." So seductively uttered, as if he were already in bed and crooking his finger at her. The change in him was breathtaking.

"All right," she managed without trembling. Much.

"What did you mean that day? When you said I was Ava's?"

"Oh, that." She waved a dismissive hand through the air. "Ava called dibs."

His brow did that arching thing again. "Explain."

"Short and sweet answer is, she gets to have sex with you and I don't." Was that a . . . pout in her voice? God, it was.

Breath hissed between Hector's teeth, all hint of seduction gone. "I won't be having sex with either of you."

Ouch. Such certainty on his part. That annoyed her so much, she forced herself to airily say, "Well, of course you won't be having sex with me. I just told you, I don't have dibs on you. I have dibs on someone else."

Silence. Heavy, oppressive silence.

"Who do you have dibs on?" he asked quietly. Savagely.

Jealously? "The very gorgeous Dallas. I just hope he

doesn't mind sharing me. I have an assembly line of men waiting for their turn with me."

One step, two, Hector closed the rest of the distance between them, in her face once more. "Have you slept with him?" Still he used that quiet tone. Quiet, yet somehow lethal, cutting. "Is that who you were waiting for at the cabin?"

She wasn't afraid of Hector, but she found herself backing away, anyway, until the cold brick-climbing wall stopped her. He was just so big, so masculine, unlike any man she'd ever met. She wasn't exactly sure how to handle him. And he hadn't responded to her lie about the assembly line.

He braced his hands beside her temples, effectively caging her in. God, she loved when he did that. Warm breath trekked down her cheeks, scented with mint. The lamps were a good distance away, yet she could see him perfectly, his face bathed in golds and whites.

"Noelle," he snapped. "Answer me."

"I thought you knew what I'd been up to. Therefore, you should know the answers to your questions already."

"Don't play. Talk."

He *was* jealous. The knowledge filled her with such joy, the truth instantly spilled out of her. "No to both. I was waiting for *you*."

Another round of silence, this one overflowing with promise. And yet his anger never faded.

"Let me give you a tip," he said in that cutting tone. "Sleep with your instructors, and lose the respect of your peers."

She ran her tongue over her lips, her own sense of

anger growing. "What makes you think I care about respect? I'm so dumb I wouldn't know the difference, anyway. Right?" Oops. Some of her bitterness had escaped.

"You're not dumb. You might be the smartest person I've ever met."

Shocking. "What makes you say that?"

"You continually convince people to believe what you want them to believe. That isn't accidental."

He so deserved a reward. She decided to press, to see how far he'd go with her. "What about one agent dating another agent, huh? Like, say, you and me. Is that acceptable?"

There. The reason she was here. She wanted to know where they stood, if the desire was mutual. He'd been jealous, yes, but you couldn't base a relationship on jealousy alone.

*Now you're thinking about doing the relationship thing with him?*

He glared down at her with an emotion she couldn't read. Something hot, though . . . not anger, not any longer. "You're not an agent."

"I will be." Truth. She would continue to work hard, to push herself, and one day she would carry a badge. Save lives.

"When you're an agent you can date whoever the hell you want," he said with a potent mix of hope and loathing. "Anyone except me. I don't date women, Noelle. Ever."

Her breaths came fast and shallow, yet every single one brushed her pebbled nipples against his chest. The friction speared lance after lance of pleasure through her. Hot, tingling, all-consuming.

"Men, then?" *No, please, no.*

"No."

*Thank God.*

"I don't date, period."

Oh. "Then . . ." She chewed on her bottom lip, pondering the dilemma he'd just created, but no answers were forthcoming. "What?" she managed to get out, unsure how to phrase her next question.

"What do I do when I need to get off?" he asked, even as he rubbed the hard, thick length of his erection between her legs, just as he'd done the last time they were in this position.

Was he doing that on purpose, urging her need for him higher, simply to leave her? Or, like her, was he acting on instinct?

Having trouble filling her lungs with oxygen, she nodded.

"I used to pay for it. Does that shock your privileged sensibilities? Offend you? And stop nibbling on your mouth." He leaned down and sank his own teeth into the sensitive tissue. Not enough to sting, just enough to stake a claim.

Oh, God. He was a biter. She really wished she hadn't learned that fact. No doubt she'd start fantasizing about those teeth claiming all of her.

*Claiming . . .*

*Have to . . . touch him . . .*

"No response?" he demanded.

She flattened her hands on his chest. His pectorals jumped up in response, flexing.

"Noelle." A snarl.

What had he asked? Oh, yeah. The prostitutes. "It confuses me." His intensity probably scared a lot of women away, but it would draw some, too. There was no reason for him to pay for what he wanted. "You kissed me, and I liked it. You shouldn't have to—"

Wait. He'd said *used to*, hadn't he? What did he do now?

"Too bad," he snapped. "I won't explain."

"Will you tell me if you liked kissing me?"

Such a tortured expression. "Yes. No. Damn it, it doesn't matter. We can't do it again."

Oh, really? "Challenge accepted," she purred, already rising on her tiptoes.

He opened his mouth, maybe to tell her off, maybe to welcome her inside, but either way, she rolled her tongue over his lips.

An agonized moan left him, and just like before the kiss immediately spun out of control. Their teeth banged together, and they both angled for deeper, better contact. He tasted sweet, decadent, and she thought she might already be addicted.

She gave him everything she had, feeding him kiss after kiss, conforming her body to his, kneading the muscles at his back. Pleasure rocketed through her, and she arced against him again and again, tossing fuel on her own need because, with every forward glide, her clitoris brushed against him.

This was far better than the first kiss, and that had been spectacular. But she knew more about him now. Wanted more of him. Had dreamed of this, night after night.

"Hector, touch me. Please." Knead her breasts, pinch her nipples. Give her more.

The rock wall behind her shook . . . shook . . .

"Hector. *Please*." She slid a hand down his chest, to the waist of his pants. So long and thick, his erection strained past the material, the tip already weeping for her. *Mine,* she thought. *This is mine.*

He wrenched his mouth away with a roar. "Damn it!" Still he ground that erection against her, and she closed her fingers around it as best she could. "I can't do this!"

His skin was like a lick of flame, blasting heat at her. Little beads of sweat broke out on her brow. She loved it, wanted more. Wanted it to be hotter. "Lift my shirt. Suck my nipples."

"Shit! Are you listening to me?" he snarled. "Do I have your full attention?"

"Yes." Yes, yes, yes. She could feel his heartbeat, pounding against her other palm.

"Good." The rubbing ceased abruptly, and she moaned. "I told you before not to seek me out. Now I'm telling you not to even speak to me. Not to even look at me. And I'll extend you the same courtesy. That's all I've ever wanted from you, Noelle." With that, he straightened, severing all contact, and walked away.

Walked *away from her*. Again.

He never glanced back.

What. The. Hell? She'd suspected, but . . .

Noelle rested against the wall, her knees weak, her blood on fire, with fury . . . with passion . . . She'd wanted his mouth on hers, taking, giving, ravaging.

She'd wanted to relearn his taste—and not just from his mouth—wanted to hear him groan as the pressure became too much for him, too.

And all along, he'd merely thought to prove a point. To humiliate her.

To force her into avoiding him.

Well, he'd get his wish, she thought. She wouldn't spend another moment craving him. She wouldn't even allow herself to think about him. They were done. Before they'd ever really started, they were done.

His loss.

Squaring her shoulders, determined, Noelle returned her weight to her feet. She spun, would have marched back to the bunk, but a thick waft of smoke, scented with burned syn-cotton and spiced with molten metal, danced in front of her face. She gazed around, searching for the source.

Not her this time, but the wall. Two perfect handprints had been burned into the brick. Big hands, a man's hands. Exactly where Hector had placed his.

Gulping, confused, she reached out and ran a finger over the indented stone. She hissed at the moment of contact. Though she didn't feel the sting, she knew the metal was hot enough to blister her skin.

So, the marks were fresh. But . . . how was that possible?

Her gaze returned to Hector. Or rather, to where he'd once been. He was gone now, no sign of him in the darkness. Was he . . . could he be an otherworlder capable of flaming objects with only a touch? Even though he appeared one hundred percent human?

Maybe. Many races possessed special abilities that their human counterparts did not. She'd always embraced those differences, and she would have embraced Hector's, if he'd given her a chance.

But he hadn't. By his own admission, he'd rather pay for sex from a nameless stranger than have Noelle for free. So, he would get his wish, she thought again. She would leave him alone.

A stray, torturous thought formed. One day they were going to have to work together, and she'd have to act cool, collected, as if this night had never transpired. And really, that should be easy to do. Ultimately, the men in her life *always* found something wrong with her. So, in that regard, Hector was no different than the rest. He'd simply been more upfront about it than the others.

*I'm fine. This is fine.* She'd suspected they wouldn't suit, and he'd proven her right. No big deal. Except her chin wobbled and her eyes blurred with tears. Shit. She never cried! Why here? Why now? Why over him?

The answer didn't matter. Like every time before, she stuffed her hurt deep inside and pasted an unconcerned smile on her face. She strolled back to the bunkhouse, to Ava, the only other constant in her life.

# Twelve

*H*URRY, HURRY, DAMN IT, *hurry.*

Though Noelle had only been an AIR agent for a few weeks, she already had one successful case under her belt. A case Ava was now engaged to marry, but whatever. Noelle couldn't think about that.

Her second case was currently sprinting down the wealthy side of Main.

Midday, on a nice, cool Saturday, the sidewalks were crowded with clueless shoppers and the other-worlder servants carrying their bags. The same species of otherworlders she'd spotted so long ago on the other side of town, only these were dressed in crisp, clean uniforms.

The shops were high end and pristine, the cafes sparkling with activity, their outside tables shielded by large umbrellas. This was the atmosphere she was used to. The perp busted through the crowds and toppled the tables, leaving chaos in his wake, forcing Noelle to push and shove her way after him, all while leaping over shattered glass, dropped purses, and slippery food.

Hector Dean was working this case, too. Not with her. Never that. In fact, they hadn't really spoken to each other since that night at camp. But Mia Snow, the new official head of AIR, had informed all agents to be on the alert for a white minivan with tinted windows.

Apparently, an anonymous tip had promised the van would be carrying three otherworlder females who'd been abducted from their homes. As that same anonymous tipster had never before been wrong, Mia had taken him—her?—seriously.

And ten minutes ago, Noelle had spotted the van and called in the plates.

Hector had barked over the radio: *This is mine, Tremain. Stay back, but maintain a visual. I'm on my way.*

As if.

Yeah, he was invested in the case. He'd worked it a year ago, but the whole thing had been iced when no new clues surfaced, the recovered girls vanished without a trace, and no other kidnappings occurred. (That they'd known of.) The tips had stopped, too. Then, two days ago that minivan info had come in, as if there'd never been a lag, and well, now things were back on.

*Have to beat him, have to beat him, damn it, have to beat him.*

The driver had realized she was on his tail, threw on the brakes, and abandoned the vehicle right there in the center of the road. There'd been no time to check on the women, so Noelle had sprinted after him while at the same time radioing in about the new development.

Agents were probably at the van now. Hector wouldn't have stopped there, though. A bruiser at heart, he would have followed the commotion and come after the driver. Like her.

*Have to beat him!*

Perp was a scrawny human in his mid thirties—and thereby unstunnable. He was also out of shape. Was now slowing, taking the corners with less vigor. No longer throwing stuff or people in her way. *I'll have him yet.*

Sweat poured down her back. Her muscles burned, the first sensation she'd had in months, and the bones in her legs vibrated every time she pounded a foot into the concrete. She was off the clock and not dressed for a street chase. Black leather halter, black leather pants, five-inch heel boots.

Plus, she had a killer hangover.

Ava's bachelorette party had roared all night long, and had still been going strong this morning.

Noelle increased her speed. Drew in closer . . . closer still . . . The guy rounded another corner. She stayed tight on his ass, practically stomping on his shadow. Another busy sidewalk came into view. He slammed into a pedestrian and flew backward—

Straight into Noelle.

Just the break she'd needed. She caught him with a *humph* and, using the momentum to her advantage, swung him around and slammed him into the side of a building. *Smack.*

Reacting on instinct, he threw back an elbow and knocked the air from her lungs. For a moment, she saw stars.

He tried to sprint off, but she kicked out a leg and tripped him. He toppled on his stomach.

"Bitch!" he spat, twisting around, going for a blade in an ankle sheath.

"I invented that move." Noelle kicked the weapon out of his hand, then kicked him in the face—knocking out a few of his teeth. He spat blood and attempted to crawl back, away from her.

With a muttered, "Oh, no you don't," she dove for him. Just before she hit, she reached for her own switchblade. Contact. She kneed him in the balls, making him howl with the intensity of the pain. Then she flicked her wrist, snapped the blade in place, and pressed the tip into his throat. Not enough to damage him, but enough to sting.

His struggles increased as panic hit his bloodstream, causing the knife to slide in deeper. Jolting upright, he head-butted her in the chin and she once again saw stars.

"Bastard," she spat, and tasted blood.

"Let . . . me . . . go," he gritted.

"Okay. Yeah, sure. I'll get right on that."

"I'll kill you!"

"After I kill you?" She hated being without her pyre-gun, but as she'd known she would be drinking last night, she'd left her piece at home.

"Fuck you!" he said on an explosion of breath, but he ultimately settled down.

"Good boy. First, a little warning. You run and you'll suffer. Second, I'm going to ask you a few questions and you're going to answer them. Or you'll suffer. Basically, just get used to the idea of suffering. First up.

Where were you taking those women?" Interrogations usually happened back at headquarters, but she wanted to throw the information at Hector and pretend it had been a breeze to acquire.

"Fuck you," he repeated, panting. "You can't hurt me. I'm human. I know my rights."

"Really?" Noelle slammed the palm of her free hand into the end of his nose, snapping the cartilage on impact.

Blood spurted from his nostrils. His scream nearly busted her eardrums.

"Let's try again," she said calmly. "Where were you taking those women?"

"Not scared of you." His trembling body belied the assertion. "Nothing you do will be worse than what he'll do."

*Should I be offended?* "Who's he, and what will he do?"

Realizing he'd said too much, the perp *really* panicked.

People formed a circle around them, gasping and contemplating what to do.

"—officers are on their way," she heard someone say.

"Dude! Out of my way, you're blocking my camera's view."

"I am a cop," she growled. "Everyone stay back, and shut the hell up."

They continued talking to each other.

"Cops are getting sexier by the day."

"Officer Hotness can ticket me anytime."

Okay, maybe she wouldn't chastise them for the chatter. They were highly observant.

As if he'd been frightened past his limits, her suspect's head lolled to the side, his body going lax. Noelle wasn't buying. She recalled Hector's lesson all too well. Always make sure unconsciousness had been achieved by delivering another blow.

Her guy could have easily gotten control of his panic, faked a pass-out, meaning to leap up and attack her the moment she let him go.

Rather than hit him, she jiggled his broken nose. No reaction. Still not taking any chances, she moved the blade tip to his belly, where his shirt rose above his pants, revealing a strip of flesh. "I've got a knife at your gut, so I'd be careful if I were you."

Warning issued, she balanced on her knees, intending to pat him down. Of course, that's when he erupted into motion. Yep. A fake-out. His determination must be great, to have ignored that jiggle.

The action caused her blade to slice his stomach, but he didn't seem to notice or care. Bleeding, he slid out from under her, jumped to his feet, and ran. Just ran.

"I am not chasing you!" Noelle jumped up, too, and tossed the knife. It whizzed through the air. The length embedded in the back of his calf, where he had just placed most of his weight, and he went down like a brick in water, screaming in agony. Heart thundering in her chest, she stomped over to him.

He'd cracked his cheek on the concrete when he landed, and a pool of crimson seeped from his mouth. He writhed, twisting, trying to reach the blade to remove it. Maybe she'd never gotten the mercy gene because she stepped on the hilt, digging the weapon even deeper.

Another howl rent the air.

"I told you not to run, asshole," she said. And damn it, she didn't have a pair of cuffs on her.

She bent down anyway and grabbed his wrists, pinning them behind his back and straddling his waist, so that her weight pinned him down. Tears leaked down his cheeks, joining the blood.

Gasps echoed behind her. Shuffling footsteps. The pounding of boots.

Noelle turned her head—and spotted Hector shoving his way through the crowd and stalking toward her. Big and muscled and so sexy her heart skipped a beat.

Puffing up, she said, "Bagged him," sounding so damn smug, he'd probably fume.

Dressed in his usual black shirt and slacks, he looked menacing and without a hint of warmth. As always. His tattoos looked different, though. The circles more jagged, the lines thicker. He'd grown his hair out, too. A Caesar cut, the messy, darkened strands adding an air of savagery to him.

Sweat glistened on his brow, dripped from his temples. He wiped the droplets away with the back of his hand, his golden gaze sweeping over her. His pupils expanded. "You okay?"

She'd heard his voice these past few months, of course. When he'd spoken to Dallas or Mia, or anyone else in AIR. But right now, with that gravelly timbre directed at her, she felt her body respond. Her blood heated, and her nipples tightened underneath the leather top.

*Oh, hell, no. Not going there again.* Lesson learned. No need for a repeat.

"Better than," she replied, and prayed she sounded breezy. She relayed everything the guy had said, and for a moment, Hector actually looked impressed. With her—or the info-hold-out perp? "Got a pair of cuffs on you?"

One of his brows shot into his hairline. "You chased him without a pair of cuffs?"

"Yes. Mine are still hanging from my bedposts."

No reaction. "What did you plan to do with him when you tackled him?"

"Duh. Exactly what I did. Hurt him until he caved."

Frowning, Hector reached behind him. Next he extended a pair of cuffs in her direction. She managed to take them without allowing her fingertips to brush over his skin.

In two point two seconds, she had the human bound, the laserbands wound around his wrists, lit up to a pretty gold—though not as pretty as Hector's eyes—and bonded to his skin.

And yet, still the guy writhed.

She said, "You pull at them too much, and you'll lose your hands. Or so I've heard. I'm more than willing to use you as a test subject and find out for real."

That got his attention. At long last, he stopped fighting.

*Did you see that, Hector? I won this round.* Noelle climbed off the perp, but kept a boot pressed into his shoulder blades to remind him that she was there. "Where's your car?" she asked Hector.

"Right there." He hitched his thumb to the street beside them, and sure enough, she spotted a standard AIR sedan.

"No Jag today?"

He didn't seem surprised that she knew he'd traded in the Porsche, even though they'd never run into each other outside of work. "No. I'm on the clock." His gaze swept over her a second time. Another flare of his pupils. "But you're not. Where have you been?"

"I was out on a date with my newest lover, the insatiable Don Carlos." She wanted to believe Hector liked what he saw, but . . . She'd gone that road with him before, hadn't she? A girl never forgot a burn like that.

"Don Carlos? Where'd you meet him? A romance novel?"

Her lips pursed. How had he known she was lying? "Do me a favor and carry the perp to your car," she said, ignoring his question.

A moment passed in silence, then he shook his head. "Bastard clipped your chin. He doesn't deserve a carry." As he spoke, he withdrew a pair of familiar gloves and slipped them on.

Her gaze immediately slid to his arms, and yep, for the third time in their acquaintance, she spotted that slight, barely noticeable azure glow. A glow that remained even after he donned the gloves, just above the top edge. She only detected it because she knew to look. And okay, because she was staring. Most people would probably think his tattoos were colored that way. She wasn't most people, and besides that, she had a picture of him seared into her memory. She had forgotten nothing about the way he was made, and always spotted any changes in his appearance.

She wished she knew what the glow meant, though. She'd even done some online research—because she'd been bored and not for any other reason—but had learned nothing.

Without looking at her, Hector closed the remaining distance, reached down, and hauled the guy to his feet, holding him by the scruff of his neck when his knees collapsed. Then he practically dragged the guy to the sedan, stuffing him in the backseat with as little finesse as possible, even letting his head bang into the top of the door.

Three other agents finally appeared on the scene, and they did crowd control, moving everyone back and out of the way, blocking off the pool of blood.

Hector faced her, still unwilling to peer into her eyes. "You want a ride to the station?"

No enthusiasm in his voice. Only dread.

*Why do you dislike me so much? What did I ever do to you?* Besides throw herself at him, time and time again.

"No, thanks," she forced herself to reply. "I've got people to do, and things to see. Besides, I abandoned my car a few blocks away. Behind our boy's." *Our.* Wrong word. Her heart skipped another beat.

An abrupt nod as his nostrils flared in—anger? "Mia and Dallas were there a few minutes ago, so . . ."

*So get lost,* he was saying. Bastard. "Next time put some hustle in your step and you might actually be first on the scene. Or maybe you couldn't help yourself. Old age is a bitch, I hear." Grinning as if she'd never been happier, she turned to walk away. One step, two. Three. Every inch farther away caused an ache to intensify in her chest.

"Noelle," Hector growled, stopping her. "You caught him, so you get to question him. I'll text you after medical's cleaned and bandaged him."

Without looking back, she responded, "Don't worry, I'll try to keep my blades to myself during the next round of my interrogation." She waited a moment, but he said nothing else, so she kicked back into motion. Totally *not* disappointed.

Soon as she rounded a corner and Hector couldn't see her, she lost her fake grin and hailed a cab, hauling ass back to the other scene. Mia and Dallas were still there, talking to witnesses. The pale, shaky girl Dallas was chatting up spotted Noelle and pointed.

"That's her."

Electric blues found her, and Dallas smiled in greeting. And yet that smile lacked any hint of amusement. Like Hector, he'd been careful to keep his distance from her these past few months. As if there were something toxic about her.

"She's one of the good ones," he said.

"Oh," the girl responded, clearly frustrated that she hadn't helped nail a suspect. And clearly hating on Noelle. Her eyes narrowed before she returned her attention to Dallas and placed a proprietary hand on his bicep. "As I was saying . . ."

There was her car, no worse for wear. She'd had the foresight to shut down the engine before diving outside, and someone would have had to know how to bypass her very extensive security system to start it up again.

"Noelle," a familiar voice called. "Wait up."

She stopped, and Mia Snow jogged to her side.

"How are the females?" Noelle asked her.

That petite face scrunched in anger. "My source said we'd find three, but we only found two. Not sure where the third is, but the other two were drugged, so they didn't know anything. They might have been pegged with a tracker, too. We're looking into it."

"Either of them speak English?"

"Just one. We sent both to New Chicago General with two agents in each ambulance and lasercuffs on the girls so they couldn't be teleported away. There will be two agents at their bedsides the entire time. Until they're well enough and we can move them into AIR HQ, where no one will be able to teleport them elsewhere, no matter what. This time, I *will* find out what the hell is going on with these abductions."

So much determination in such a tiny body, which reminded Noelle of Ava. A pang in her chest, razing that hollow place. "Let me know if there's anything I can do."

Mia nodded, dark bob swinging around her chin. "Hector texted me, told me what happened. You did well."

Pride unfurled wings and fluttered inside her. How pathetic was she, that she wanted to twirl a strand of hair around her finger and ask what, exactly, Hector had said? "I always do."

A snort. "Where are you headed now?"

"Home to shower." And most likely to replay every

change in Hector's expression, his every word, his every glance.

Yep. It was official. She was pathetic.

Mia gifted Noelle with one of her rare smiles. "See you at the wedding tomorrow, then."

"Don't remind me," she muttered.

Tomorrow her life changed forever. And not in a good way.

# Thirteen

*A*VA WAS LEAVING HER!

"Graduate Camp Hellhole—check," Noelle muttered. "Hired by AIR—check. Complete my first mission successfully—check. Kick Hector's ass at a foot race—check. Lose my best friend—check, check, fucking check, and scribble and crumble the notepad and slam it into the trash."

She leaned against the bathroom stall, clutching her two favorite men: a bottle of Jack and a bottle of Jim. She was trying not to cry. She hadn't felt this vulnerable since that terrible night at camp, when Hector had given her a figurative finger. Had thought she'd prepared herself for this life-changing moment last night, staying up to watch holo-vids of her and Ava.

Well, she wasn't prepared and never would be! Noelle banged the back of her head against the wall over and over. For once, she wished she could feel physical pain. A terrible, gut-wrenching pain. Anything to distract her.

Ava was about to marry her vampire boyfriend McKell, and Noelle would forever be alone.

*At least I look good,* she thought with a bitter laugh. As the maid of honor, Noelle wore a gorgeous red sheath dress that conformed to her curves. Spaghetti straps, a scooped neck that revealed ample cleavage. The material flowed to the floor, flirting with her amazing diamond-encrusted red stilettos.

Her hair was curled and now waved down her back, dancing with her every motion. Her makeup, perfectly applied. Her skin, glowing with health and vitality—or was that sickly dread?

Ava, her best friend, her only true friend, had fallen in love. Deep, abiding love.

Today Ava would abandon Noelle to tie herself to a vampire warrior.

Tonight Ava would give up the daylight and become a vampire herself.

Trying not to fall into a spiral of panic, failing, Noelle drained Jack and tossed the bottle in the toilet. Still trying not to fall into a spiral of panic, failing, she drained Jim and tossed the bottle in the toilet. She had to get herself under control. She couldn't let Ava see her like this.

This was Ava's day. Noelle would not ruin it. No matter how much she wished Ava would change her mind, tell McKell where he could stick his fangs, and sprint from the chapel. That way, things could return to normal. Just the two of them, kicking ass and forgetting names.

Alone, alone, alone. The word echoed through her mind, tormenting her.

Wasn't like she could call her mom and sob out all her problems. Madam Tremain disapproved of her more than ever.

*Isn't it enough that Jaxon has tarnished the Tremain name?* the blasted woman had sneered during their last phone conversation. Why couldn't Noelle act like a lady for once and do something with her life? Like charity work for one of their many causes?

No support from her brothers, either. She was more than welcome to silently sit on the board of Carter's firm. More than welcome to fly to Third World countries with Anthony and help the poor. More than welcome to seclude herself in Tyler's Italian villa while he partied.

As long as she stopped embarrassing everyone with her "wildness" and her "wayward mouth" and her "blue-collar job."

Wasn't it time she grew up?

A tear threatened to burn a path down her cheek, but she managed to blink it back. *Oh, Ava. I miss you already.* There would be no more ditching work to go shopping and have their nails done. No more midnight pillow fights. No more five-hour-long phone conversations about their hopes and dreams.

Fine. They hadn't done any of those things before, but now they wouldn't have the opportunity. Once Ava turned into a vampire, she would be unable to venture out during daylight hours without burning like deep-battered shrimp.

So Ava would only be doing night patrol for AIR. And yeah, okay, Noelle could change her schedule, too, and would, if AIR would let her, and they had better fucking let her, or she'd quit, even though she'd come to love the job. Even still, McKell would be the one with access to all of Ava's free time.

Time that had once belonged to Noelle.

Guilt was like acid in her veins, a disease without a cure. Ava was so happy. So damn happy, and here Noelle was, pouting about it. But too many things were changing all at once, and Noelle simply couldn't process everything.

A hard knock rattled the stall's door, and she yelped, straightened. The alcohol must have finally kicked in because the motion left her head swimming and her thoughts fogging. Good, that was good. The foggier she was, the happier she'd appear.

"Hey, Noelle, you in there?" Ava asked, concerned.

She could play this. No one would ever know the depths of her despair. Not even Ava. "Yes, rudeness, I am. Can't a girl do her business in private?"

"Not this girl, and not today. Finish and come tell me how gorgeous I look."

Yes, she could do that. Noelle leaned over and waved her hand over the motion sensor. The toilet flushed, Jack and Jim rattling together and refusing to go down. No matter. She squared her shoulders, pasted on her megawatt grin, and opened the door.

And there was Ava, her sweet Ava. "My God. You look gorgeous." Truth. Breath was actually catching in Noelle's throat, clogging the passage.

Ava beamed, love radiating from her, giving her burnished tan a melted cookies-and-cream sheen. Her curls framed her delicate face and tumbled past her shoulders. She wore a gown of golden silk, in a goddess cut, the material flowing all the way to six-inch hooker heels. The best part, though? A necklace made from human finger bones hung around her neck. A gift from McKell.

"*I* want to marry you," Noelle teased.

Ava was supposed to laugh, maybe twirl and demand more compliments. Instead, Ava cupped Noelle's cheeks, and peered deep into her eyes. "I love you. And really, McKell's just my starter husband. You know I despise commitment. I'll probably leave him before the honeymoon is over."

Hardly. Those two were forever, and all three of them knew it.

"I wouldn't do this if I thought I would lose you," Ava said, voice softening further. "You and me, we'll be together for eternity. Probably not in heaven, but we'll still be together. You know that, right? Tell me you know that."

Noelle held onto her smile. Barely. "I know that." And she did. But things *would* change, and more than they already had. One day Ava and McKell would have a kid. Or six. The way they went at it, they might have a baker's dozen. Ava would have a new family, one that did not include Noelle.

Aunts, even kick-ass aunts like Noelle would be, were merely an extension, rather than part of the whole. That's just the way things worked.

*Don't you dare cry!*

Where was her happily ever after? Where was her stand-by-you man? She hadn't been on a single date since leaving AIR training camp. There'd been offers, of course, but she'd been unable to feign interest.

Always she'd thought, *Where's Hector? What's he doing?* and flaked.

"Now," she said, performing a twirl of her own. A mistake. The dizziness magnified. When she stopped, two Avas watched her with more of that concern. "How do *I* look?"

Several moments ticked by in silence before determination overwhelmed the concern, and Ava smiled. Knowing the little witch as she did, Noelle knew her friend had just decided time would prove her right.

"You look amazing, and if one person, just one, says you look prettier than me, there's going to be a massacre after the vows are said."

"What if that someone is me? Because I'm just gonna say it. I do look prettier than you." She sighed, revealing only a hint of her wariness. "Maybe at your next wedding you'll manage to outshine me."

This time Ava laughed. "Shut up. I can get away with talking that way, but when McKell hears anyone else voice any kind of doubt, he lectures about what's his, his, *his*."

Yeah, there was no one more possessive than McKell.

Noelle experienced a slight pang of envy that none of the guys she'd dated throughout the years had ever tried to stake a claim on her. Corban might have demanded more of her time, but in the end, when she'd left him, he hadn't come after her, hadn't fought for her, and she'd realized he'd never really loved her either.

How could he? She'd never been the woman he'd wanted.

"So what are you doing in here?" Noelle asked. "Your ceremony starts—" she glanced at the clock on the wall "—five minutes ago. Oh, shit. I'm sorry!"

She'd been helping Ava with her hair, had felt the panic burning up her throat, and had fled into this bathroom under the guise of having to pee so badly she was ready to wet herself. Half an hour had passed.

The area was small, with two stalls, one sink, and no sitting area to check your makeup and chat. At least the walls were painted a pretty silver, none of the stone crumbling.

Ava should have sheer opulence, utter luxury, but she had flat-out refused to allow Noelle to pay for anything. Not that that had stopped Noelle from sneaking in a few improvements. Like, say, paying for the entire building to be refurbished in secret.

"I can't get married without my maid of honor at my side, so do me a favor and hustle that sweet ass of yours into the chapel."

"Yes, ma'am." Noelle jumped into motion, and Ava smacked the ass in question.

Out of the bathroom, through a narrow hallway with scarlet carpeting and glowing wall sconces she went. When she reached the main foyer, with faux wood tables pressed into the corners, and a chandelier dripping with glittering crystals, she paused.

There were the arching double doors that led to McKell. Though her stomach twisted with nausea, she held out her arm, waiting. Ava linked their fingers. Her skin was cold, a little clammy.

"Nervous?" Noelle asked. Beyond the entrance, she could hear the gentle strum of a harp, the delicate notes of a piano.

"A little," Ava admitted.

Some of the nausea eased. "I can get you out of here in five seconds flat and—"

Ava laughed. "I'm not having doubts, you dope. I love McKell, and he loves me, and I honestly can't live without him. I just hope I don't trip and fall. Or, do I have food in my teeth? I knew I shouldn't have eaten those strawberries."

"If you trip and fall, I'll point and laugh, but I'll also make sure your panties aren't showing. If you're wearing any, that is. But that's the worst that can happen, so your worry is kinda pointless. As for your teeth, they're perfect. Just like you."

The tension drained from Ava's grip, her temperature warming. "You're such a sap."

"Just for today." *I'm a big girl. I will survive this.* "So, are you ready to do this or what?"

Deep breath in, hold, hold, finally released. "Yes. I'm ready."

"Okay, then. Here we go." With that, Noelle kicked open the doors and escorted her best friend down the aisle.

A gasp swept over the crowd, and like a wave, they stood, one row after the other. McKell paced on the dais, his tux ripped at the collar, his tie sagging, as if he'd pulled them both a few times too many. He possessed hair the most luscious shade of indigo, pale skin and eyes of the purest violet.

He was a beautiful man, strong and muscled, toweringly tall, and he was utterly undone by the sight of his bride. He stilled, his gaze locking on Ava, his anxious expression changing to one of awe and reverence. He didn't care that everyone saw his reaction, either. He was too proud of his woman.

The little pang returned to Noelle's chest. McKell hadn't wanted a best man, or any groomsmen for that matter—none deserved the honor of standing next to him, he'd said—but all of AIR occupied the first few rows.

Noelle nodded to Mia, who looked gorgeous in blue. Beside Mia was her husband, Kyrin, a delicious Arcadian who reminded Noelle of Corban in appearance only. Same white hair, same lavender eyes, and skin the color of a winter storm. But Kyrin thought his woman was perfect and wouldn't change anything about her.

A movement at the corner of her eye had her glance shifting. Dallas had just reached up to tug on his earlobe. He realized she was watching him and smiled, but there was no amusement in the baring of those teeth. He'd been doing that a lot lately, like at yesterday's crime scene. Trying to appear nice and polite, but failing miserably. She had no idea why.

Her gaze slid away—and landed on Hector, who stood beside him.

Hector. He watched her intently, warily, as if she were a bomb about to detonate.

And he hadn't texted her yesterday, so she figured she'd done more damage to the perp than she'd thought.

Why, why, *why*, hadn't time and Hector's shitty attitude lessened his appeal, dissolved her fascination, and stopped the draw?

She really *hadn't* learned her lesson, had she?

He wore a dark pinstriped suit, and her heart fluttered at the sight of him. His eyes were shadowed, almost haunted—and they were glued to her face. As always, he was frowning.

So badly she wanted to catch a glimpse of his smile. A flash of those dimples, a peek at those straight, white teeth. Teeth he'd once used to bite her bottom lip. Some nights she imagined she still felt the sharp, luscious sting.

His head tilted to the side, his interest gliding from one of her features to another. Her brow, her eyes, her mouth, her chin. Either he was drinking her in, as she had just done to him, or he was fitting puzzle pieces together.

Could he see the pain behind her happy mask? No, surely not. He didn't know her well enough. Yeah, he saw deeper than any other man, but . . . . Only Ava saw the real Noelle, and Ava had no idea about the depths of her pain.

"Who gives this woman away?" a male voice suddenly boomed out.

Ava squeezed Noelle's hand, and she snapped to attention. Shit! They'd reached the end of the walkway, and she'd been twisted like Dallas's favorite sexual pretzel position, peering over her shoulder for God knew how long, staring at Hector.

Now there was silence. Such expectant silence.

"Uh . . . what now?" Her voice echoed from the steepled ceiling.

"Who gives this woman away?" the pastor repeated with the utmost patience, as if this kind of thing happened all the time.

Deep down, she wanted to shout "Not me! Never me! And no one else does, either!" but she didn't. Bile chugged up her throat again, threatening to spill over, but she managed to say, "Me. I do. In a minute," she added. "I haven't yet given my wedding present to the groom."

"What—" Ava began.

"Come here, you sexy morsel." She pulled an un-resisting, now laughing Ava in for a passionate kiss. That's how she and Ava had snared McKell, once a target of AIR but now the agency's biggest asset, after all. They'd distracted him with a girl-on-girl kiss before stunning him, and he'd loved every moment of it. In fact, he'd been pushing for another GOG PDA session for quite some time.

A few members of the crowd gasped. A few whooped. McKell reacted just as before, going taut with excitement. This was the only time he'd share "his woman," and only with Noelle. Anyone else tried this, and heads would roll.

When she felt they'd pushed the line of scandal to its limit, Noelle straightened and peered down at her bestie, whose smile was brighter than the sun. "You're welcome." Trembling, she placed Ava's hand in McKell's.

McKell's grin was just as bright.

"Shall we begin?" the pastor asked, some of his patience gone.

*This is it,* Noelle thought, sad for herself and blissfully happy for Ava all at once. *The beginning of the end.*

# Fourteen

‹›

SOMETHING WAS WRONG WITH Noelle. Big time. Hector had known it the moment he'd spotted her.

He remembered her as she'd been yesterday, so damn hot his mouth had watered for a taste of her. Black leather practically painted on her breasts, her flat stomach the tantalizing color of honey and cream, her legs painted with the same leather. He was certain no woman had ever rocked an outfit better. And yet there'd been a gleam of sadness in her eyes as she'd subdued her captive.

Still his cock had reacted instantly. So had his arms, proving she was as dangerous to his peace of mind now as she'd been before. Even when she'd insulted the shit out of him, calling him a slow old man, and lied through her teeth, he hadn't cooled down.

*I'm not old, damn it. I'm in my prime.*

Today's red dress—holy hell. A fantasy come to dazzling life, revving him up. But once again he noticed the sadness in her eyes. Only now it was amplified.

He sat in his pew and pretended to care about the ceremony while examining her. She was smiling prettily, but her cheeks were pale. She was smiling contentedly, but a line of tension creased her brow. She was smiling, but she was breaking his goddamn heart.

He didn't know how—he would have placed good odds on his not having a heart—and he didn't know why. All he knew was that he preferred her wild and silly and yeah, too smart for her own good.

After interacting with her yesterday, he'd craved more. Just a glance, something, anything, so he had finally broken down and watched her interrogation tape from camp. Not the one that had so enthralled Dallas, but the last one. The one Phoenix had overseen.

Hector had flinched every time Phoenix had slammed her fist into Noelle's midsection. But Noelle hadn't. Noelle had taken it and thrown out taunts.

Phoenix, who should have known better, had reacted, all emotion and no thought, allowing Noelle to lead her around on a leash. Hector had already realized Noelle was smart and tough, but that even he hadn't foreseen.

A clip played through his mind.

Phoenix: *You really think you're AIR material, huh? You think that pretty smile of yours is going to solve cases for you?*

Noelle: *Of course. Proof: when I walked into this room my smile solved the case of the mysteriously missing blond agent who only has half a brain.*

Punch.

Phoenix: *Do you like your brain slamming against your skull?*

Noelle: *More than anything.*

Punch.

Phoenix: *Think your smile will be as beautiful if I pop your front teeth?*

Noelle: *Oh, Agent . . . Blond Girl . . . Person. The fact that you'd find me so pretty even without my teeth is sweet, but you're not my type. I like my men with thinner mustaches.*

Brutal punch.

Phoenix: *How's my mustache looking now?*

Noelle: *Who cares? Caress me again. I liked it.*

Really brutal punch.

Hector had been so turned on by Noelle's attitude, his arms had glowed and he'd had to take care of himself. Twice.

Damn it, pushing Noelle away had been the stupidest, most intelligent thing he'd ever done.

After their second near miss that night at camp, he'd told Mia to take him off instructor duty or he'd quit AIR for good. Usually Mia didn't take ultimatums well, but in this, she'd caved. Maybe because she'd sensed his desperation.

Once he'd arrived home, he'd gotten himself under control. On his own. And he'd remained mellowed out, except for the few times he'd run into Noelle at HQ.

Other agents had flirted with her, and she had flirted back. But if she was dating anyone—seriously or otherwise, not counting the imaginary Don Carlos—he didn't know it. And he didn't like that he didn't know.

He didn't like the thought of her with someone else, in any capacity, either. Especially not the imaginary Don Carlos! And he knew the bastard was imaginary. Noelle's eyes took on a pearlescent sheen every time she lied, and they'd looked plucked straight from the sea when she had mentioned him.

Dallas used to flirt with her, but that had stopped a few weeks ago, after they'd all run into each other at a bar after hours. As if the pair had seen each other naked, but had argued and parted ways.

The thought alone enraged Hector. He flattened his hands on his thighs before he did something stupid. Like ask in the form of punching. The answer didn't matter. *Couldn't* matter.

Even as a teenager, with more hormones than brains, he'd known he was better off keeping females at a distance, and he'd succeeded. Until Kira. From the worst of the streets herself, she'd wanted, needed, a protector. Someone to keep her safe, to scare away anyone who thought to rape her. Someone to make sure she had a place to stay. So she'd charmed him and he'd fallen.

He'd tried to be careful with her. For a while, they'd kept things nice and easy. A kiss good night, a kiss hello. Then they'd graduated to a little heavy petting. His arms hadn't acted up too badly, and she'd hinted that she wanted to take things further, so he'd decided to go for it.

One night, as they made out, he'd stripped her, then stripped himself. His first skin-to-skin contact, and oh, had he been excited. The heat had intensified, but he hadn't realized how much. Until he'd reached up and cupped her breast. His arm had already atomized, so he'd gone through her and hit the mattress springs. She had died instantly, her heart rendered useless.

Seeing her like that . . . he'd never been the same. What little hope he'd carried for making a relationship work had gone up in flames with her. And to be honest, no one had ever tempted him to try again. Until Noelle. But . . .

His fear was simply too great, too deeply rooted. The fact that he craved her far more intently than he'd ever craved Kira only freaked him out more.

If he hurt her, burned her, he would never be able to forgive himself. Would never recover. That's why he'd done everything in his power to make Noelle hate him. Avoiding her at the office, making snide comments when they ran into each other.

Well, mission accomplished, he thought now.

Yesterday, they'd been all about the awkward polite. As if they'd never kissed. Never pressed their bodies together, straining, rubbing, both of them ready to explode.

"Be honest," Dallas whispered. "Are you imagining that red dress on your bedroom floor?"

He would not reply. Would not voice the words that would undermine his good intentions.

"Because I am," his friend admitted miserably.

He fucking would not reply. Not his agreement, and not a warning. What good would warning another man away do him? None, that's what. Hell, if anything, a warning would only make things worse for himself.

Dallas would expect him to act on his attraction.

And if he didn't, well, he'd open the door for Dallas to act on his.

"Don't be mad, but I can't seem to help myself. I want her."

Okay, so the door was already open. "Why would I be mad?" The words escaped loud, gravelly, and pissed as hell, drawing stares and a few hushes. Better question: how would he stop himself from ripping his friend's face off?

Noelle had called dibs on Dallas, which meant she was attracted to him. Wanted him in return. Would probably like being stripped by him, touched by him. Tasted by him.

If she hadn't been already.

He whispered fiercely, "Have you two . . . ?"

"No," Dallas answered, and he relaxed.

*Dallas* is *your friend.* Maybe Hector's only friend. Dallas knew about his arms. Hector had finally broken down and revealed all. While working a case together, Dallas had used a few unexplainable abilities of his own, moving faster than the eye could track, controlling people with his voice, shit like that.

Apparently Dallas was part otherworlder.

*I wish there were an explanation for me.* Though he'd kept searching, he'd found nothing. But he'd wanted Dallas to know there were others out there, that he wasn't alone with his differences, and Hector had never regretted sharing. They'd bonded over it, almost like brothers.

*And you can't kill your brother,* he reminded himself.

"And you two haven't?" Dallas asked.

"No."

"And you'd be okay if I . . . ?"

*No!* "Yes."

"Okay, good," Dallas said in that quiet voice. "That's good. I'm gonna go for it, then. Tonight. As long as you don't care."

"I . . . don't."

"Good, that's good," he repeated. "Bridesmaids can't help themselves, either. The romance, you know. Practically puts a bull's eye on their panties."

Another forceful breath, in and out, careful, measured, followed by another. Hector tried to release his growing tension with every exhalation. Suddenly his hands burned, itched, and both sensations spread up, up, all the way to his shoulders, until he knew the skin beneath his jacket was glowing.

This was very, very bad.

He jumped to his feet. The pastor stuttered to silence, and every head in the room turned his way, including Noelle's. He was careful to avoid her gaze as he stuffed his hands in his pockets, and shoved out of his row. Was that burning cloth he smelled? Despite the fact that he only ever wore fire-retardant clothing?

Without any kind of explanation, he stalked down the aisle and out of the chapel. Before he torched it and everyone in it to the ground.

# Fifteen

❧

WHO KNEW A WEDDING reception attended by stone-cold killers would prove to be the party of the century?

Noelle hid in a corner in back of the spacious ballroom, swathed in shadows, trying to take everything in. The walls were painted to look as if they'd been covered in pink lace. Glasses were clinking, conversations were raucous, and champagne and chocolate scented the air. Laughter abounded, as did the sucking sounds of a good kiss. A lot of people were getting down and dirty wherever they happened to be. A few down and dirtiers were even by the buffet table, rattling the dishes when gyrating hips met stone.

McKell had Ava on the dance floor, bumping and grinding and generally looking epileptic. So did everyone else on that floor, for that matter, moving to the hard, fast rock buzzing from strategically placed speakers. An elegant, twinkling teardrop chandelier winked over the seizers, highlighting their every blackmail-worthy nuance. She'd already done a little covert videoing from her cell, and planned to torture the agents for the rest of their lives.

"What are you doing over here all by your lonesome?" a male voice suddenly asked.

A flick of her gaze, and she realized Dallas had sidled up beside her. She'd have to pay better attention. Sensing a possible threat was necessary for her job, after all. Although Dallas didn't look threatening today. In his pristine suit, with his dark hair slicked back, his dark complexion flawless, and his electric eyes bright, he was handsome in a fallen angel kind of way, half innocence, half wicked temptation.

And he'd said something to her, she recalled. "I'm two-fisting drinks with dignity," she replied, toasting him with both of her nearly empty glasses. Her earlier buzz had already worn off, and she was looking for another.

His lips twitched, even as his gaze swept down the length of her, heating with desire.

Desire? Surely not. Not after the distant way he'd treated her lately.

"Darling," he said, "I hate to break it to you, but you lost your dignity the moment you walked down that aisle. In my mind, I already had you stripped."

So seductively uttered, so charmingly delivered, she found herself grinning with genuine amusement for the first time that day. "I do know how to rock a fantasy, don't I?"

The desire, or whatever it was, cranked up a notch, turning those vivid eyes into a kaleidoscope of differing shades of blue. "Please tell me that's not the only thing you rock."

A chuckle bubbled from her. "Tsk, tsk. I almost think you're flirting with me."

"If you *almost think* then I'm not doing a good enough job." His voice dropped a few octaves, going husky, layered with a needy rasp. "So, let me clear things up. I *am* flirting with you. Is it working?"

Her heart began to thud against her ribs. Not from arousal but from surprise and, well, quite frankly, unease. He was Hector's friend. So if he was flirting with her this heavily, he didn't think Hector would mind.

Hell, maybe Hector had even told him to go for it.

Her heart thudded harder, and she was disgusted with herself. Why did she care what Hector did, said? Or what he didn't do, didn't say?

She *didn't* care.

She wouldn't let herself care.

"No response?" Dallas asked silkily.

Oh, she had a response, all right. "Why now?" She drained one of her glasses, then the other, and handed them both to him. "First few months we knew each other, you treated me like a mischievous kid sister. Lately, I've been a diseased gutter rat."

He lifted one finger, the universal sign for one sec, and trotted off to set the glasses on a passing waiter's tray. When he returned, his hands were empty. Probably a wise thing, not plying her with more liquor. She'd start babbling about her kisses with Hector, her dreams about Hector.

Hector, Hector, Hector. Where the hell was he? Why had he stormed out of the chapel?

Dallas jumped back into the conversation as if he

couldn't wait another moment to engage her. "Let's just say there were complications, and leave it at that."

Intriguing. "Little known fact about me. I can't leave *anything* at that. So, staying with the topic. What were the complications and how do they no longer apply?"

One strong shoulder lifted in a deceptively casual shrug. "I won't tell you what they are, but I will tell you that they're diminishing in importance."

"Why?" Damn, but her curiosity was piqued in a huge way.

He released a wary sigh. "I'm certain I was wrong about one aspect of the— I was wrong, that's all. And don't you dare ask about what."

"About what were you wrong?"

"Huh-uh." Grinning like the imp he was, he shook his head, dark hair falling over his brow. "I'm not telling, and you can't make me. Not dressed, at least."

Clearly, he was an expert at flirting, and yet still she didn't soften toward him. "I took a class on interrogation, you know. There are ways to make a guy talk that involve a handful of thumb tacks and, drum roll, being fully clothed."

"Why don't you dance with me instead?" Not giving her time to protest, he twined their fingers and ushered her to the dance floor, where he stopped and drew her into the hard line of his body.

He must have cued the band, because the music instantly turned soft and slow. For a long while, they swayed, silent, each lost in thought. Hers: this was almost nice. He smelled good, like soap and the after-sweetness of a rainstorm. Heat radiated off him, enveloping her.

And yet, *still* no attraction.

Sighing, she flattened her hands on his chest and pushed. Just a little, just to achieve a few inches of distance. He pulled her back in, closer . . . closer . . . until their chests were flush.

"There, isn't this better?" he asked in that seductive tone, his breath fanning her cheek.

"Depends on what you're comparing it to. Better than a root canal? Yes. Better than a pedicure? No."

"Ouch. Harsh, Elle. Harsh."

"Honest." Elle. All the men in her life eventually called her Elle. A soft nickname for the soft girl they assumed her to be. Or rather, wanted her to be. Little wonder she longed to punch every one of them in the face when they used it.

Not that she'd ever admit the truth, however. Expressing your displeasure with something was tantamount to begging to be tortured by it.

Dallas's hand slid down her back and landed on the curve of her ass. His fingers splayed, covering as much ground as possible. "Besides the pedicure, what do you consider better than this?"

Where to begin? "Long walks on the beach, even if it's freezing outside. Good—or cheap—wine in front of a crackling hearth. Chicken noodle soup. But it has to be made from real chickens, and not that syn-shit, or I'll have to strike it from the list. A lukewarm bubble bath, a mediocre book, a—"

"Okay, okay. God," he said with a laugh. "You are hell on a guy's ego."

"Yours needing some stroking?"

"*Something* of mine needs stroking," he muttered, "but it's not my ego."

"Yeah, I can feel your something," she replied dryly. "Can you move that thing already? It's annoying."

"Annoyingly big, you mean."

"Define big."

Another warm, rich chuckle left him. "Fine. Give me a minute." He pulled back long enough to reach into his pants pocket. Her mouth fell open.

"I didn't mean—" She stopped. He was readjusting his erection in front of everyone!

Only he withdrew a pyre-gun, the crystal dull rather than sparking, indicating the safety was on, and stuffed the weapon in the waist of his slacks, behind him. Then he drew her back into his embrace.

"Now. Is *that* better?"

The shock had yet to leave her. "Now who's hell on an ego?" she grumbled, her cheeks just a bit hot.

"Then let's help each other out and revisit the whole stroking issue, hmm?"

Incorrigible sex fiend. And she wished, really and truly wished, she desired him. Even in the minutest amount. He was fun, funny, and probably a damn good lover.

"You know, Dallas," she said, straightening to gauge his reaction. "I have this friend . . ."

The light in his eyes expanded, only to be crushed a moment later as his pupils expanded, too, the black pulsing. Just as Hector's had done each time before they'd kissed, and then again yesterday when he'd eyed her black leather. "Is she a mild-mannered AIR agent by day and an insatiable nymphomaniac by night?"

Why wasn't Noelle attracted to him again? Because this shit was amusing. "Her name is Hope Van Der Pyke."

"And does she—wait." The pupils retreated to normal size, and he lost his glaze of excitement and desire. "What?"

"She's very pretty. Very wealthy. Kinda snobby, though. Anyway, you're exactly her type."

"Are you trying to set me up?" he said, nearly choking on the words. "With someone else? While I'm laying my best moves on you?"

"These are your best? Wait, never mind. Don't answer that. I'd just have to feel sorry for you. So, to answer *your* question, yeah. I am." His incredulity was adorable, and she couldn't help but twist the knife deeper. "Is there a problem?"

"But I saw . . . we're supposed to . . ."

One of her brows rose. This was more interesting by the moment. "We're supposed to what?"

A pause. Then a heated, "Fuck."

O-kay. "Do you mean that as a verb or a curse?"

"Both." He released her to run a hand down his face, once, twice, three times. With the first, he revealed confusion. With the second, anger, and with the third self-deprecation tinged with humor.

His arms returned to her waist, but there was no drawing her in. Not this time.

"Want to tell me what just happened?" she asked.

"No." Another grumble.

"Do it anyway before I show you the blades I'm carrying."

At least his humor intensified, his lips quirking at the corners. "Violent women really crank my chain."

"*Annnd,* not what I wanted to know."

"Forgive me," he said, fingers stroking up and down her spine. In reflex, she thought, rather than in a bid to arouse her. "This is just so new to me."

"What? Being let down gently?"

"Not that. You'll find this difficult to believe, I know, but I'm turned down flat all the time. I'm not sure why, either."

She snorted. She just couldn't help herself. "Yeah, that's a real mind puzzler."

"Hey. Is that sarcasm I detect?"

"Oh, Dallas," she said, reaching up to pat his cheek. "Somehow you have turned the blackest day of my life into one that's merely dark and gloomy. Thank you."

He frowned. "Blackest day? Why? You look happy to me."

Damn. She shouldn't have let that slip out. "What are you talking about? I am happy."

"But you just said . . . I just . . . Never mind. You'll only tax my poor, abused brain further. So, here's an admission for you, and an answer to one of your earlier questions. I saw this day . . . saw us . . . and we ended up in . . . Oh, never mind."

"Tell me."

"I—" The song ended, and his arms fell to his side,

severing contact. "Uh, I'm needed elsewhere, so I'll see you around, Noelle." Off Dallas raced, never once glancing back.

"Well, okay, then," Noelle muttered. Her gaze landed on Ava, who was peering up at McKell with utter adoration.

*I want that,* she thought.

Suddenly done with the party scene, and craving a minute alone, she took off in the opposite direction, heading for the back door. No one tried to stop her, and for that she was immensely grateful.

Outside, the parking lot was spread out around her. The sun was hidden behind dark, gray clouds, the air damp and cool. Closing her eyes, she leaned against the wall. She'd lived through the worst of the day. She could deal with anything else.

Right?

# Sixteen

❧

"DAMN IT," HECTOR CURSED when he spied Noelle.
He should have left the wedding and stayed
gone.

He'd left the wedding all right, but he hadn't made it
more than a mile from the chapel. Dallas's *I'm going for
it* had continued to ring inside his head, taunting him,
infuriating him. Then he'd thought about Noelle's red
dress on his friend's bedroom floor, resting beside a suit
other than his. He'd pictured two naked bodies straining
together on a mattress, had heard pleasure-filled moans.

He'd nearly destroyed the interior of his Jag as he
reprogrammed the chapel's address.

Once there, he hadn't gotten out, hadn't gone inside.
He'd remained in the car, in the parking lot, the tint on
his windows darkened to the highest setting so that no
one could see inside. He'd glared at the building, and
yes, he'd taken care of himself while imagining Noelle.
With *him*.

Finally he had calmed down, the burning in his
arms subsiding, the glow completely diminished.

The only thing that burned him now was humiliation and shame. That he'd done such a thing in a public place . . . his stomach rolled. At least he was out of the danger zone. Small comfort, considering he wasn't sure he'd stay out.

One of the agents inside the building was emailing pictures of the wedding reception to everyone in her address book, and not two minutes ago Hector had opened one of Dallas on the dance floor, his strong arms wrapped around Noelle. Noelle had been grinning up at him.

Only reason Hector hadn't stormed inside to rip them apart was that Noelle had still radiated so much sadness. Seeing her, his chest had ached unbearably.

He'd told himself to go home, that Dallas would work his magic and Noelle would fall under his spell. That the two of them would drive to the nearest hotel—they wouldn't be able to wait until they reached Dallas's apartment, because God knows, if the situation had been reversed, Hector wouldn't have been able to wait—and sleep together.

And once Noelle had slept with his friend, Hector would stop thinking about her. Stop dreaming of her. Stop craving her. Surely. He *needed* to stop. She was a thorn in his side, a torment to his soul, a sickness in need of a cure.

He could never be what she needed, never touch her the way she'd want. More than that, he wasn't good enough for her. Another man would make her happier. Far, far happier.

Yet he opened his car door, got out, and walked toward her anyway.

––––––––––––

Noelle heard the footsteps and opened her eyes, prepared to paste on a smile and wave whoever had intruded on her personal space inside. Then she spotted Hector, and straightened. A frown pulled at the corners of her lips. His presence was a surprise.

His big body was gorgeous, as always, but humming with tension.

His night-wild scent reached her before he did, waking every cell she possessed. Next she felt the heat of his body, electrifying her. And then he was there, just a few feet away. Within touching distance, the width of his shoulders practically engulfing her.

*Bad Noelle. No touching.* "What are you doing here?" she asked, not yet daring to met his gaze. She was too afraid of what she'd see. Irritation, maybe. Or maybe even nothing at all, as if she were meaningless.

"I'm cleaning my gun. What does it look like I'm doing?"

O-kay. The snotty attitude *wasn't* a surprise. "It looks like you're annoying me."

Still he didn't attempt an explanation. He just shrugged and said, "Well, *you* look beautiful." Grudgingly offered, as if the compliment had been yanked from his throat.

And yet that was the first time he'd ever said anything nice to her and she became wet. Just like that.

"Thanks," she muttered, fighting the arousal.

"Welcome."

Finally, she looked up.

Instantly her body reacted as if she'd just run a ten-mile marathon uphill. Her breath shallowed so much she was panting, her lungs refusing to fill. Her temperature went from melting to one hundred percent liquefied, her knees weakening, trembling.

Intense golden eyes narrowed down at her, long lashes nearly fused. Hard lips stretched tight over those perfect, bite-so-good teeth, the scowl most likely meant to intimidate her into silence. His chin angled stubbornly, and there was no sign of his dimple.

His tie was gone, his suit wrinkled and disheveled. His gloves, missing.

God, she'd never seen a more beautiful sight. And with those few inches of hair . . . wow. Beautiful wasn't a good enough description.

"You were sad a minute ago. And earlier." His head tilted to the side. "Why?"

A cold shower went through her veins. He didn't know. He couldn't. *At least he hasn't noticed your reaction to him.* Her beading nipples, her quivering belly. "What do you mean?"

"You're clearly upset about something."

He did. He knew. But *how* did he know? "I'm not upset."

"Bullshit."

How dare he call her on her lie! "This is my best friend's most special day and I have never, ever been happier—"

"—more miserable."

"—than I am right now."

"I can't believe you ever fooled me," he said, all

kinds of self-disgust in his tone. "You're a terrible liar."

How. Did. He. Know? Dallas hadn't. Ava had suspected, but even she hadn't realized the depths of Noelle's misery. Noelle was a master at hiding her emotions. She had to be. Otherwise her mother and brothers would have realized how they chipped at her self-esteem and launched a full-scale attack.

"What . . . what makes you think I'm lying to you?"

He rolled his eyes. "Like I'm really going to blurt out your tell."

She gaped up at him. "I don't have a tell."

"Whatever you need to believe to comfort yourself, sweetheart."

Sweetheart. He'd just called her sweetheart. He didn't mean it, though. Didn't see her that way, the way other guys saw her. But the funny thing? She liked that he'd said it. She'd known him a year, and he'd never once called anyone else by a nickname or endearment, even sarcastically. Still. Letting him get away with his attitude so wasn't happening. "You don't know me," she gritted.

"No," he said softly, suddenly more serious than she'd ever seen him. "I don't, do I?"

To Hector's astonishment, he was as desperate to learn about Noelle's life and her emotions as he was to have her underneath him. The latter was too dangerous, so he'd just have to settle for the first. "Do you feel like you're losing Ava or something? Is that why you're sad?"

A punch below the belt, maybe, but that was just his style. No mercy, and no prisoners. A motto he lived by. A motto life on the streets had drilled into his head.

Noelle crossed her arms over her chest, the fabric of her gown going taut, the pressure shoving her breasts together and creating the most delectable cleavage, but also hiding those beaded nipples he longed to tongue.

She snapped, "I've told you time and time again that I'm fine."

"Actually, you've told me twice. You're not fine, and sad girls aren't as much fun to play with, so start talking."

A lick of fire in her eyes, pursed lips. "Is that what you're doing? Playing with me? But Hector, darling, aren't sad girls what you're used to?"

Ouch. She hit below the belt, too, but then, he'd jumped right into that one, hadn't he.

He never should have told her about the hookers. None of his friends knew the truth. Not even Dallas. Hell, all of AIR probably thought he was gay. But he'd told Noelle in an effort to elicit her disgust. *And lookie. You got it. Shocker.*

"You better answer this, genius, or I'll kick your ass!" he heard Ava say before he could think up a reply. He frowned, panned the area. Ava was nowhere to be seen. "You better answer this, genius, or I'll kick your ass!"

With her left hand, Noelle held up her index finger in a bid for a second of privacy. With her right, she pulled a very slim cell from between her breasts.

Damn, that was sexy.

"I only have the ringer on for one person," she said

at the same time Ava threw out another, "You better answer this, genius, or I'll kick your ass!" Noelle added, "Ava stole my phone and programmed this as her personal ring tone. I liked it so much, I decided to use it for every call."

He snorted, though he was strangely charmed by her admission. She truly adored her friend. Every aspect of her friend, at that, even the bizarrely cruel streak both women seemed to possess. He was also strangely envious. He might tease the guys at work, but he wasn't comfortable enough with any of them to fool around. Again, not even Dallas.

"This better be important," she said into the receiver.

Jealousy flickered in his chest as her previous words sank in. She'd kept her ringer on for someone. A special someone obviously. His hands fisted.

"I told you no." Her gaze skidded away from him, allowing him to study her face more intently. Such a red, red mouth . . . He licked his lips, suddenly imagining ripping the phone away from her and giving her a hard, punishing kiss.

She smelled of something rich and heady, a perfume from the wilds of a jungle, as well as the stars in the heavens. His cells heated, his skin pulled tight against his bones. Nothing dangerous, not yet, allowing him to remain where he was.

And therein lay the danger.

He wanted her so badly, he might try and fool himself into thinking all was well so that he could have her. If he hurt Noelle, scarred her, marred her in any way, he truly would hate himself forever.

*You won't hurt her. You've kissed her twice. She'll be fine.*

He found himself reaching out to sift his fingers through her hair. Thankfully he caught himself in time. He scowled. Temptation was a dark, dark bastard.

*Mind out of gutter.* She needed support, not a pawing.

He attempted to listen to her whispered conversation, but couldn't make out more than "Forget it" and "I'm thinking about becoming a lesbian." That couldn't be right, though.

Bit by bit, those silver eyes frosted over. "Mother." She gave up trying to keep things quiet. "This is Ava's wedding. I told you I'd talk to you tomorrow. And for the record, I will tell you no about the set-up then, too." With that, she hung up, stored the phone, and glared at Hector as if everything were his fault.

Her mother. The jealousy vanished—even though the woman had been trying to set her up. Noelle had said no, at least, and would say no tomorrow.

"I can relate," he said. "My mother was . . ." A horrendous bitch. Trash. Utterly sadistic. "Persistent when she wanted something from me."

"Was?" The sharpest edge of her anger smoothed and just as she had the first day he'd met her, she suddenly appeared cool, aloof, and untouchable. Now, however, he knew she was none of those things.

"She's dead." *And I'm the one who killed her.*

"Sorry."

"Don't be. I'm not."

Their gazes locked in a long battle for domination.

A battle he didn't give his all. He was too busy enjoying her. She was a visual feast, and he couldn't help but gorge. Such lush femininity, ripe for the taking.

*Careful.*

"Why do you care what I'm feeling, anyway?" she grumbled, caving first.

Score one for him. Finally. He always felt out of sorts with her, as if he had never—could never—come out ahead. "I don't care." He said the words, an automatic response, but for once, he didn't mean them.

Her back straightened and her shoulders squared, a predator uncoiling for attack. "That was a very rude thing to say."

He was getting to her, cutting at her, and she needed that. Needed to drain the poison inside of her, whatever kind of poison it was. "I'm not apologizing for it." Unlike Dallas, Hector couldn't make her laugh. At least, he didn't think he could. He'd never tried to cheer a female up through humor. But he *could* help her, and maybe . . . maybe one day, when she looked back on this night, she'd remember him fondly.

Or not. "Oh, you darling man," she said with her sugar sweetness. "Your lips say *no* but your eyes say *I've never been sorrier for anything in my life.*"

*Will not laugh.* "Did you really think you and Ava would grow old together?" he asked, tossing enough disgust in his voice to piss *anyone* off. "That neither one of you would ever fall in love? Get married?"

Smoldering silence followed his words. She remained still—more predator than before. A wounded panther, ready to strike.

Whatever she dished, he could take. He *wanted* to take. To do something besides walk away from her—or watch her walk away from him. "McKell won her pretty quickly, didn't he? I mean, it only took him a few months to rip her from your side. That must mean she was ready to leave you, was probably tired of you."

Annnd here came the explosion. "She wasn't tired of me, you bastard! She will never be tired of me, just like I will never be tired of her. I'm her best friend, and she loves me. *She loves me.*"

Success, he thought, and oh, was it bittersweet. He did not like seeing Noelle so torn up. Did that stop him from continuing to push? No. "And you love her? Enough to miss her already?"

"Yes. Okay? Yes. Is that what you want to hear? I miss her so damn badly." Tears pooled in her eyes, a bone-deep hurt reflected there. "I love that she's happy, but I hate that I'm losing her. She's mine, not McKell's. *Mine.* I found her first, and I should get to . . . she should . . ." Her shoulders slumped.

"She should appreciate you better? Because you built her up, right? You made her what she is?"

The fire returned, swiftly burning through the hurt. "Hell, no! She built *me* up." Noelle thumped her chest, just over her heart. "She made me better. I was on a very dark path, and she became my light. I love her more than . . . more than . . ." She raised her chin. "I love her more than *anything*. I would bend over backward to help her bend *someone else* over backward! And I will always be there for her—if I've got nowhere better to be."

Maybe the hurt hadn't burned away. Maybe Hector had absorbed every last drop, because damn, his chest was doing that aching thing again. She was throwing out facts—her love—but mixing it with her pain—claiming she had somewhere better to be. A heartbreaking, amazing mix.

The tears sprang forth anew and cascaded down her cheeks in a white-hot stream. She wiped them away with a shaky hand, then stared down with shock at the wetness on her skin. "I'm crying. Shit! I'm crying. I never cry."

Yeah, and the sight of those tears nearly undid him the rest of the way. *Can't tug her close. Can't hold her.* "Why are you beating yourself up about your feelings?"

"Because," she sniffed, retreating into her stubborn shell.

"Don't make me rip the answer out of you. Why?" he insisted.

"Oh, all right." Another grumble. "I'll tell you, but only to save time. I can't wait to get away from you."

Hardly. If that were the case, she would have already left. Would have busted his lip with her fist and bolted.

The knowledge that she *wanted* to be here, with him . . . He remembered how she'd once begged so sweetly for him to kiss her. Just a taste, she'd said, luring him straight into temptation, unable to resist.

*Can't fucking hold her.*

"I'm beating myself up because I should only be happy for her," she whispered, each word dripping with shame. "I shouldn't be sad for myself."

"Just so you know, being both—happy for her and

sad for you—doesn't make you a bad person. It makes you human."

"I guess." How miserable she still sounded.

"Would you rather be a cold son of a bitch like me?"

She lifted her head. The first thing he noticed, her lashes were long, spiky, and wet. The second, she was a damn pretty crier. No swollen eyes or red, splotchy skin for this one. Just vulnerability and angel-soft loveliness.

"Why are you being so nice to me?" she asked in that soft tone. "You hate me."

Hate her? When he hungered for her more than he'd ever hungered for another? But then, he done everything in his power to shove her out of his life, hadn't he? And he needed to keep shoving.

If he stopped, gave in to her, the consequences would be everlasting.

Yeah. He should leave. Now. Should walk away. He was good at that, as he'd already proven. Instead, he gave her the words that might damn them both. "I don't hate you, Noelle. I fucking *crave* you."

# Seventeen

———◆———

SHOCK BOMBARDED NOELLE AS Hector's confession rang in her ears. He was breathing heavily, some dark emotion practically bursting through his skin. So badly she wanted to believe him.

Crave her? *Please.*

She studied his tortured expression. Pushing for answers here, now, wasn't wise anyway you sliced it. Public place, possible public humiliation. Did that stop her? Hell, no. "You can't—what you said can't be true. You wouldn't ignore me—"

A moment passed as he visibly fought for control. He rubbed a hand down his face, the skin on his palm normal, the ink dark. "I don't want to talk about this."

Too bad. "You brought it up. Also, you made me talk about my problems when I didn't want to." And he'd helped her in a way she could hardly believe. She felt lighter, more guilt leaving her by the second. "A year ago, you stomped all over me, told me never to speak to—"

"I know what I told you," he snapped, interrupting again. "I don't need a retelling."

"So why are you with me right now? Helping me with my problems? Telling me that you . . ."—her voice lowered to a barely audible rasp—"crave me." Why? The intensity of her need to know the answer staggered her.

How many nights had she pleasured herself while thinking of him? Now he was suggesting, in a round-about way of course, that he had done the same. That amazed her, delighted her. Truth or lie, though?

He looked over his shoulder, at his car, as if he longed to bolt.

"Oh, no, you don't." Scowling, she cupped his cheeks and forced his attention back to her. "You're staying right here and confessing."

His eyes narrowed to tiny slits, a glare that usually preceded multiple dark curses. Instead, he said, "I'll stay." Harsh, broken. "*If* we talk about something else."

Damn him. He meant it. Restrictions grated, big time. In fact, she would have left him in the dust on principle alone, but then he did the strangest thing. He leaned into her touch, rubbing his stubbled jaw against her palm, practically purring like a contented kitten.

Maybe he *did* crave her. But . . . but . . .

When he realized what he was doing, he went military straight and paled. He shook out of her hold, his eyes glazing fearfully, guiltily, then angrily.

He had liked the connection, but hadn't wanted to like it. Why? The question of the day, it seemed. Hell, the question of the year.

Whatever the answer, though, he wasn't yet ready to spill all and really would bail if she remained in pursuit. That fear . . . So she would drop the craving thing. For now. But, oh, God, hope swirled through her, a bright light in an endlessly dark void.

"So, uh, how have you been?" she asked, hands tingling where they'd touched him.

Now he arched a brow, losing his worry, guilt, and anger in a single instant. Relief descended. "Since yesterday?"

"No, smartass. Since . . ." *Our last kiss.* "All year."

"Good. You?"

"Same."

Awkward silence.

O-kay. Was this how it would always be between them? Either snipping and snapping at each other, on the road to kissing, or struggling for something to say? A fraction of the hope withered.

"How's our suspect, the van's driver?" she asked, deciding to talk shop rather than separating and ending on a bad note. There had to be more to their relationship than the snipping and silence. Right? He *craved* her.

A little color drained from his cheeks, and he rocked back on his heels. "I wasn't going to tell you until after the wedding, but . . ."

"What?"

"He killed himself."

"What! How? When?"

"At the hospital. Cyanide pill. Had one in a hidden pocket."

"Why would someone do that?"

Hector's strong shoulders lifted in a shrug. "Fear. You remember what he said, about the mysterious *he* hurting him worse than we ever could."

Yeah, but still. "You get any useful info out of him first?"

An abrupt shake of his head, the color returning to his cheeks and deepening with . . . shame? Probably. Hector took his job more seriously than most, and took his cases personally.

Noelle flattened her hand above his heart. The organ rushed up to meet her, the beat quickening. Hector didn't chastise her. "Wasn't your fault," she said, offering comfort. "And two women were saved from God knows what."

He gulped. His gaze met hers, the gold glittering, no hint of the frost he so often directed at her.

In an instant, her thought path changed course. From business straight back to the pleasure. She had her hand on him. He was close enough to kiss. And he craved her.

*Thought you weren't going to do this with him ever again?*

*Things change.* He craved her. She would never get tired of those words.

*You've forgotten the humiliation of his rejection, then?*

Argh! She despised these conversations with herself.

Dallas had amused her, but Hector . . . Hector tantalized her. He didn't tease, he snarled. He didn't flirt, he informed. His intensity was a constant brush against her nerve endings, awakening long forgotten parts of her body, working her into a frenzy.

"You know, the last two times we stood like this, we . . . did things," she reminded him huskily.

"Yeah," he croaked. "Never forgotten."

*Me, either.* "We should probably—" *Go our separate ways.* She tried to force the words out of her mouth, but they congested in her throat.

"Yeah," he repeated. He leaned closer, closer, probably seeing the pulse at the base of her neck speed out of rhythm. He hovered there, breathing her in, as if he wasn't sure what to do next.

Forget separating. She wanted more and took care of the rest, tracing her tongue along the seam of his lips. He moaned, but didn't open, so she turned her attention to *his* pulse, licking up the base of his neck. She loved the honey and almond flavor of his skin. Loved the—

Honey and almond.

Like a woman's body lotion.

Jealousy was like a thousand knives inside her. What he did—had done—wasn't her business. They weren't dating. He could do whatever the hell he wanted, with whomever the hell he wanted.

And yet, still Noelle felt her nails dig into his chest as she straightened. "Hector, I'm going to ask you a question and you're going to answer honestly or I swear to God I'll ensure you're never able to have children. Did you just have sex with someone?"

He stiffened, that flush of shame now so deeply rooted he might never get rid of it. "No, I did not have sex with anyone." Each word was carefully uttered, precisely measured, as if he didn't want to lie, but didn't want to admit the truth, either.

In his favor, he hadn't stated the obvious by pointing out that she had no right to pry into his love life.

"Did you make out with someone after leaving the chapel?" she asked. Every base would be covered before she allowed him to leave her.

"No."

"Kiss someone?"

"No." He pulled a pair of black gloves from his back pocket and tugged them on. "Let me make this interrogation easier and just admit that I haven't done anything with a woman, any woman, for a while. And before you ask," he added with barely a pause, "a while is a long time and no, I won't define a long time."

Well, all right, then. The potent mix of jealousy and fury drained the rest of the way.

"Are my testicles safe?" he asked, and damn if his lips weren't twitching as if he wanted to grin, those golden eyes sparkling.

*Irresistible man.* "For now." As relaxed as he suddenly was, now might be the perfect time to gain perspective and dig up some answers. Other than the ones he'd already denied her. "So, why did you storm out earlier?"

Lids narrowing, lashes fusing. "I didn't storm out. I simply made a hasty exit."

"Because your pants were on fire?" Wasn't that how the old song went?

"Something like that," he muttered.

Fighting an urge to draw him closer, she traced her fingers down the edge of his lapels, the material soft. He licked his lips.

Seeing his tongue ramped her up all over again. *You're so easy.* With him, yeah. She was. "You made me cry, Hector." Today, a year ago. But she didn't mention the past.

"I know," he replied, gruff. "But I'm not sorry. You needed it."

"Well, now you have to kiss me better."

Every muscle in Hector's body stiffened. Kiss her? "What about Don Carlos? Will he mind?"

"He has a very open mind."

*Exactly what I thought.* "No other boyfriends?"

"None."

Thank God. "I will kiss you, then," he croaked out, and it was a vow. "I'll make you better." He knew how he wanted to go about it, too. Strip her, spread her legs, push her against the wall, then touch and taste every inch of her. Knead her breasts, pinch her nipples, tongue her clit. Then pound his cock deep inside her, so deep she wouldn't walk for weeks.

What he'd allow himself to do was another story.

Running from this? Not an option. Her sweet scent was in his nose, her hand was on his chest. He'd leveled himself out only half an hour ago, wasn't in the danger zone. He could do this, have this.

A tremor moved through her. "You take too long. I'll help." Then she pressed their lips together and his thoughts totally and completely derailed.

*More.*

She tasted of champagne, female heat, and mint. He nearly brought his hands up to cup her jaw to angle her head for deeper access. *Don't touch, don't you dare touch.* Instead he pressed his gloved hands into the wall beside her and crowded her backward, until she couldn't move, was caged.

Their tongues rolled together, clashed. He operated on instinct, lust, and pent-up frustration. At no point was the kiss a gentle exploration. At all points, it was savage and hot and consuming, a rending of self, an unquenchable thirst. He wanted more, more, more, now, now, *now.*

*No. Slow it down, fool.* He had to remain distanced, had to keep himself under rigid control. But no matter what he told himself, he couldn't stop taking, giving, taking again. Taking everything she had, eating at her, desperate for her. To own her, possess her.

"Hector," she breathed. Her arms wound around his waist and she arched her lower body, grinding against him. A little moan escaped her, sliding down his throat and heating his every cell.

Her nipples were hard against his chest, rasping at his shirt. So badly he wanted to trace a path down the ridges of her spine and feel her ass. He pressed closer, instead, and she rubbed all the harder against the thick, swollen length of his cock.

At the first contact, she cried out and he groaned. "You feel so good, baby."

If he lifted her dress, opened his slacks, he could press into her wet, wet core—and she *was* wet, she had to be. Her need was palpable. What would it feel like to be surrounded by a woman? By this one, specifically? Warm and wet . . . tight.

*Amazing.* He could pound inside her, stretch her, pull out and start all over again.

He was rubbing against her madly, he realized, wringing deep, rich cries from her.

*Fuck! You're supposed to go slowly, you stupid asshole.*

Her fingers found their way to his scalp, skating through the strands of his hair. "Soft."

"Like?"

"Very much."

"I like *you*," he admitted. He liked every damn thing about her. Just then, he wasn't sure how he'd resisted her for so long. Always she was a drug, everything about her designed to lure him.

"I thought you didn't . . . do this . . . with agents," she said between kisses.

"I don't. Usually." Ever.

"So I'm special." A statement, not a question. "Because you crave me?"

One he couldn't deny. "Yes." Despite everything, she'd drawn him from glance one. A draw that had only grown stronger.

"I'm glad." She bit down on his bottom lip, the sting flaming his need, reminding him of when he'd bitten down on *her*. How her exquisite flavor had teased him, how he'd felt, for one stolen moment, that she was his, only his, that she belonged to him, body and soul.

Something he'd denied, even to himself. Until now, when he experienced that sense of ownership all over again.

He sucked on her tongue harder. Their teeth banged together, and even that he liked. Her hips continued to slowly gyrate against him, round and round, brushing against him, then leaving him panting for more, then brushing against him again.

Her fingers slid down his chest, to the waist of his pants, dug past the material, seeking his cock. They closed around him, and he hissed in a breath. Shit, he was going to lose it!

"The things you do to me," he rasped.

"So big," she breathed. "Mmm, Hector, I don't know if you'll be able to fit in me, but I can't wait to find out."

The first tingles sparked in his arms. Panic battered against his arousal, and he forced his arms to snap behind his back. "Stop. Just for a second. Please, Noelle." Begging? Shit. Yeah, he'd begged. "Just need . . . a moment. I have to calm down."

She stilled, licked at his lips one final time, as if she couldn't help herself, then lifted her head, her breath coming shallow and quick. Her mouth was red, swollen, and glossed with his taste. God, he liked that, liked knowing some part of him was on her, in her, that he was connected to her and she to him.

Her eyes were glassy with her arousal, her pupils blown and shadowing her irises. "Did I do something you didn't like?" Fingers loosening . . .

Wanting to moan at the loss, he shook his head. "I liked what you were doing too much."

"Oh." A blush stained her cheeks, or maybe a deeper flush of arousal. "*Oh.*" A slow, wicked grin spread, lighting her entire face as she clutched him tighter. "So by *stop* you actually meant *keep going?*"

He fought a laugh. Humor, when he was skirting the edge of danger. Such a thing should have been impossible, and would have been, with anyone else. Noelle's teasing spirit spoke to a part of him he'd never known. The mischievous child he'd never gotten to be.

"No. I just . . . I don't want to hurt you."

"You can't. Unless you leave me like this." She stroked up, down.

Another hiss of breath. "I *can* hurt you in other ways. Believe me, I really can."

Her brow furrowed with her confusion, and she straightened the rest of the way, removing her hand from his cock completely. He wanted to curse, but offered up a prayer of thanks instead. "How?" she asked.

Hinges squeaked, Mia Snow sticking her dark head out the door a second later. Her blue gaze scanned the area, then lightened when she spotted them. "There you are."

"What?" An unspoken *this better be a matter of life or death* coated Hector's voice as he angled his body away, hiding his erection and blocking her view of Noelle.

"Nice greeting, asshole," Mia snapped.

"Sorry," he muttered. *I am a calm, rational being.* "What do you want?"

With her, you never knew. Could be something easy, like being asked to go into work early the next day, or something slightly more difficult, like kicking your own ass into next week for some perceived slight.

"There's been a homicide. Dallas is having a meltdown about something, so I'm making you primary,"

Mia told him. "You need to head to the scene now, and have a look-see before local PD screws everything up."

Hector's gaze sought Noelle unbidden. She'd gotten herself under control, her expression blank, her breathing even. That she'd recovered so quickly, he didn't like. At all.

"Give me the details," he forced himself to say.

Mia spouted them off as if she were reading bullet points from a computer screen. When she finished, she added, "Oh, and take Tremain with you. You're going to need her."

# Eighteen

———⟡———

NOELLE TRIED TO RELAX in her seat. Hector had traded rides with Mia, taking her AIR standard issue, complete with uncomfortable syn-leather interior, a console perched between the driver and passenger seats, and dash-screens in place of a steering wheel and glove compartment. Clear shield armor separated front from back, so that naughty otherworlders couldn't attack with fists, teeth, or even mind control.

Noelle owned a garage full of cars, some made before the human-alien war nearly a century ago, and before the armor-modification had become customary. She much preferred the older models. What was more fun than cutting corners as if you were on rails, burning rubber, and spinning donuts without sensors to stop you from crashing?

Besides making out with Hector in a public place, that is. Again. After a year-long abstinence, as if no time had passed. Nothing, that's what.

Her blood *still* shimmered with desire. Her hand still ached from trying to fit all the way around him, his length so thick her fingertips hadn't come close to connecting.

Yet he appeared unaffected, all business.

She studied the harsh planes of his profile. He had a staring contest going with the road, ignoring her. Sensors covered the entire outside of this vehicle, so there was no reason to focus that steadily. The car maneuvered the streets on its own, slowing, stopping, and speeding up as necessary.

Well, she could do that, too. Noelle peered out the window. Soon they left the suburbs behind, with the cute houses and the cute families, inside eating dinner. They made their way toward the poorer part of the city. Cool air trickled from the vents, but nothing could override the scent of Hector that permeated the small front enclosure. Wild, earthy, and sweaty.

Every breath Noelle sucked in reminded her of what they had been doing before Mia interrupted—eating each other's faces.

Both times before, a single taste had caused instinct to propel Noelle over a ledge she couldn't see until too late. He was a drug to her, able to destroy any barrier, addicting her quickly, heating her inexorably, spinning her closer and closer to the bottom of what would either prove to be a deep, dark cavern of loneliness, or a bright, consuming bed of passion.

Hell, this time she hadn't even needed a taste. She'd fallen the moment he had approached her, and there had been no stopping her spiral to *splat*. Every cell she possessed had yearned to have his hands exploring her, his body pounding into hers.

Damn him and his irresistibility. Now she wanted more of him, more *from* him, and would have given him more of herself. Would have asked him to go home with her, where she would have given him all, everything.

Maybe. One-night stands weren't her thing, and never had been.

Maybe he would have wanted more than a one-night stand, though. Maybe he would have wanted to stay the night with her, see her again the next day, and the next. He craved her, after all.

Except he was already distancing himself from her. Regretting?

Hello loneliness.

With Corban, she'd known where they were headed before they ever hit the sheets. He'd wooed and won her, and then stuck around to polish his prize. With Hector, she'd never known, and it had never mattered.

With Hector, she still didn't know, and it still didn't matter. Damn him, she thought again.

"Hector," she began. She wasn't a coward. She would simply ask him what he expected from her. If he said they could give this thing, whatever it was, a try, she'd give the relationship everything she had. If he said this was the end—rejecting her for the third time in their acquaintance—she'd stab him in the jugular and hide his corpse.

Besides, this was her first murder investigation. Concentration was key. So after she found out where she stood with Hector, her mind would be clear, and then *boom*, she could solve the case and save the day. Easy as that.

"This was a mistake," he said before she could utter another word.

Just her luck, they reached their destination a moment later. The car parked in front of a line of police tape. Hector didn't push from the vehicle, but sat there, waiting for her response.

A mistake? A freaking mistake? Wow, that hurt. While she had luxuriated in what they could have done, could still do, he'd obviously been thinking of how to let her down without bloodshed.

*Do not react. You suspected.* She would paste a happy smile on her face, as always, and concentrate on the case.

The smile was a bit more difficult than usual to pull off, considering the emotional upheaval of the day. Needing a moment, she gazed outside, and yeah, she was highly aware she was acting like the very coward she'd denied being. The moon was full and golden. Other cars littered the area, official red and blue lights flashing. A wide, open field stretched in every direction, grass growing in patches, crisp leaves dancing in the gentle breeze.

Where was the slain human they were supposed to examine? She increased the periphery of her focus. About fifty yards of dirt had been sectioned off by that tape, but the handful of officers who were standing outside were talking rather than working.

"Noelle," Hector said. "Did you hear me?"

*Smile, damn you.* "Of course I heard you. I'm sitting

right beside you." She added, "I guess I should have told mother dearest yes. Her old biddie of a friend thinks I'd be perfect for her son the surgeon."

"No, you wouldn't," Hector growled, then caught himself. "But whatever you want to do is fine."

*Smile!* "And just so you know, this is gonna be Cherry Picking Barry all over again," she said before she could stop herself. *Cas, keep it cas.*

She didn't recognize any of the officers, none of them had attended the wedding, but that didn't change the facts. One look at her and Hector in their upscale attire, and it would be assumed they'd been out on a date, with plans to get hot and heavy afterward.

Had Hector wanted to get hot and heavy with her, she would have smirked. Now . . . she just wanted to hide. "People are going to think you're a god for possibly nailing me, while calling me all kinds of easy."

"I'm sorry, it's just that— Wait. What?" He turned in his seat to at last stare over at her. Those golden eyes were bright with an emotion she couldn't name. And maybe that was for the best. Just then, she could have removed his balls with the razor she had strapped to her thigh.

Why did no one want her for keeps?

"Who's Barry?" Hector demanded, and this time she could read the emotion. Fury, lethal in a way only a man on the very edge could be.

On her behalf? Sweet of him, but she wouldn't soften. "He's the guy I oh, so generously gave my virginity to." The rest spilled from her, her resentment no longer a living thing but sharper tonight because of the man beside her. "The next day, he told everyone what we'd done. All the guys slapped him on the back in a job well done, then tried to get into my pants as if they had a right to plant their flag, too, and all the girls but Ava treated me as if I had the plague. As if I would steal their boyfriends with my whoring ways."

"Tell me you hurt him."

"Me? No." A true grin kicked at the corners of her mouth. "But Ava wrecked his car. Slammed his pride and joy right into his parents' house." Now *that* was friendship.

A tense pause. Then, "I would have killed him for you," Hector said in a low, quiet voice that left no room for doubt. "I would have burned him and dumped the ashes in a pile of animal shit."

"Really?" Damn it. She was softening. *He doesn't want to continue seeing you, remember?*

His nostrils flared as if he could already smell the burning flesh. "Yeah, really."

"Well, you still can. He lives in the Lakeshore Apartments on Lake Shore Drive. Number eighteen B."

One of Hector's brows arched, the gold in his eyes frosting over in that way of his. He wasn't just on the edge of lethal—he'd already leapt and was falling. "You actually kept track of him. Why? Did you want to see him again?"

"Are you kidding? Hell, no, I don't want to see him again, but someone has to send his wife pictures of his illicit activities, and that someone is me. Yeah, I'm a giver like that."

A quicksilver blaze of amusement, gone before she could wonder at its source.

She waited, but Hector remained quiet and his expression never reverted back to . . . whatever. "I know what you're thinking," she said anyway. "Why'd I let him off with such a minor, lifelong punishment? Well, let me tell you a little something about me." *Something you might learn intimately, bubby.* "If anyone so much as drops a beer can on my lawn I pay for DNA testing. The very day the results come in, I have two tons of trash dumped in their yard. I don't get revenge, I teach valuable lessons. Barry's still learning his."

Hector massaged the back of his neck. "I'll remember that." His voice had dropped another octave, reminding her of when he'd pressed his erection between her legs. She shivered like the stupid girl she was. "Well, uh. Huh." He cleared his throat. "As I was saying. This was a mistake. Us messing around, not us showing up together."

*Smile—check.* "I know that, too. No need to drive home the point." Or rather, the dagger in her chest. "We're not going to see each other romantically. No big deal." Except, it was a big fucking deal!

*Maintain your happy face.*

His hand dropped from his nape to rest on the seat, his fingers digging into the upholstery with enough force to leave cracks. "It's not because I don't like you. It's that I'm dangerous, Noelle. Really, really dangerous."

"This is the AIR version of *it's not you it's me,* right?" she asked dryly. "If only you'd used it before, I would have known to use it on Dallas tonight."

"No, damn it!" Back up the hand went, scrubbing down his face, leaving red marks. "Well, yes, it is a version of that, but it really is me. I want you, so damn badly I ache all the damn time, but I can't do relationships. I just can't. Damn it!" So many *damns*.

Something in his tormented expression thrust its way past her defenses and clanged a warning. He wasn't just spouting nonsense to get rid of her. He believed what he said wholeheartedly. He wanted her—craved her, ached for her—but he couldn't let himself have her.

"Why can't you try with me? I wasn't picking out china patterns or anything." He'd like something bold. Scarlet, maybe, with ebony flecks and asymmetrical edges. "I save that for date two." She'd tried for a witty tone. She'd failed. She just sounded needy.

"You deserve something better," he said miserably. "I'm not just really dangerous, I'm *too* dangerous."

Dangerous. How many times had he tossed that word at her? As many times as he'd tossed out *damn*, she was sure. "Uh, have you met me, Agent Mean? I'm kinda dangerous, too." God. She was practically begging him to date her. How pathetic she was. She should stop, leave now while she still had a little dignity. He might want her, but if he wasn't willing to try, she couldn't force him.

"You're dangerous, yeah, there's no denying that. I saw you tackle a perp, then stab him in the leg when he ran away. But I'm on a whole different playing field, sweetheart."

This was the second time he'd called her sweetheart,

and her heart skipped a treacherous beat. When other guys used cute little nicknames with her, she wanted to strangle them with their own intestines. When Hector did it, she wanted to swoon like a Victorian maiden. Weird. "Let's pretend I believe that." She. Should. Stop. She should shut up. But then she recalled the handprints he'd left in that wall, the night he'd warned her away, and the way he always tugged on those gloves, time and time again, and some of her hurt vanished, leaving a hollow curiosity. "How? Make me understand."

A heavy pause. She thought he meant to deny her. Then, "I can . . . I hurt . . . People die when I touch . . ." He banged a fist into the dashboard, the skin boasting a slight glow—even though he still wore the gloves. There were several holes in the material. Tendrils of smoke wafted, curling up.

When he noticed, he trembled with abject fear, removed them, and fumbled for a new pair in his pocket. As he pulled those on, he said, "Look, it doesn't matter. I shouldn't have approached you. Shouldn't have promised you anything more. Nothing can ever happen." He turned away from her, facing his window, but hesitated. "All right? Okay?"

*I can*—kill? *I hurt*—women he touched? *People die*—because of his sometimes-radiant arms that could singe asbestos, or whatever material he wore, and burn through metal? Probably. He was so agitated, tension layered with more of that self-disgust vibrating off him.

So . . . say she was right. Say his hands really were hazardous, like weapons. Weapons he couldn't control.

Say he normally avoided women to prevent himself from burning them like he'd done the metal wall. Yet still he had kissed Noelle—three times. Still he had almost given her more. Because he hadn't been able to help himself. That meant he craved her, just as he'd claimed. As desperately as she craved him. Desire ruled him whenever he neared her. If only for a little while.

Could be wishful thinking on her part. Or she could be dead-on right. She needed to think, to figure out what she was willing to risk—like, say, her pride—to have this man in her life. Or if she was willing to risk anything at all. Right now everything she felt could stem from the lingering heat of his kiss, the fear of losing Ava, and the thrill of her first murder investigation.

"All right," she finally said. "I won't jump you." Not tonight, at least. "Now let's go solve this mystery so I can go home and call Ava."

Hector turned so quickly he would surely suffer from whiplash, his gaze narrowed and zeroed in on her, his lips pulled back in a scowl, his teeth a flash of white in the surrounding darkness. "What the hell, Noelle?"

Noelle glanced left, right, trying to figure out what had just pissed him off so badly. Nothing had changed, no one had approached the car. "What?"

"Why are you going to call her?"

"*That's* what twisted your panties? Jeez. This is the first night of her honeymoon, and I want to know how McKell performed."

A muscle ticked in Hector's jaw. "That's it? That's the only reason?"

"Yes. Why—" Finally, understanding dawned and she scowled. "What, you thought I planned to tell her about you and your speech?" She forced a chuckle. "Darling, if I told her about every man I came close to screwing, we'd never be able to discuss anything else." A lie, but he would never know that.

His eyes slitted further, but in the end, he emerged from the car without uttering another word.

# Nineteen

❧

SMILE IN PLACE, NOELLE exited her side of the vehicle, the length of her gown swishing down her legs and brushing the ground. The officers gave her a thorough once-over; some leered, the obviously blind ones shrugged and looked away, as if she were nothing special. Someone whistled, and someone else cackled out a, "Who's that? Red Carpet Barbie?"

"Nah, 'cause then we'd get to strip her and bend her however we wanted."

Snickers.

Had Ava been here, the man would already be on his knees, begging for forgiveness. Noelle would have cheered her on, content in the knowledge that she was loved unconditionally and protected fiercely.

Now she'd have to take care of herself. Something she could do, something she had done many times before, and something she would continue to do again and again, because—

"Shut the fuck up, or I'll rip out your throats and do it for you," Hector growled.

Silence. Absolute silence followed the threat. Or promise.

"Good boys." His tone gentled, though it was no less brutal. "Now tell me who called this in."

She wasn't going to point out that the men couldn't shut up *and* talk to him. She was too pleased by his defense of her.

Smile suddenly genuine, she walked to his side, clipping a few of the guys with an elbow to the gut as she did. They hunched over, wheezing for breath. "I'm so sorry," she said, so sincere she brought tears to her own eyes. "The dress . . . so long . . . I tripped . . ."

Hector coughed to cover a laugh. "So? Who called it?"

Hector . . . amused . . . the unveiling of his dimples . . . a shiver rocked her.

A young man with sandy hair and glasses stepped forward. He was average height, on the slim side, and just a little scared to find himself in Hector's sights. "Agent Dean, sir, uh, a witness called. Claimed he'd seen four men. Two were here, waiting. One in a suit. One dressed casually. Then two others just appeared. One was an Arcadian, so we think teleportation was used. The other was the victim. Alive at the time. Witness claims the guy in the suit said, 'Thinking you could blow the lid off my operation just got you killed' and pulled the trigger on a pyre-gun."

Hector had stiffened at the word *Arcadian,* then growled at the word *teleportation.* He must be thinking of the women he'd found, so long ago. The ones in the warehouse who had disappeared while in the .hospital. An Arcadian had been suspected then, too, but had never been found.

Noelle knew because she'd maybe kinda sorta peeked at some of his old case files.

"How'd the witness know it was a pyre?" he asked.

Pyres were made for AIR agents, and illegal for civilians to carry. Plus, they weren't the only weapons that lit up like firecrackers.

"Said there was a flash of bright light, but no booming sound. Said it was the same type of gun he saw agents carrying on that TV show, *As the Other World Turns.*"

Good show. *Gotta catch up on that.*

"Anything else?" Hector asked. "You check the tapes for alien voice?"

The officer gulped. "We did. There's nothing."

"I want to go over them myself."

"Of course. As for the rest, the vic was hit in the chest, his organs fried. That's when the witness screamed, and the three men realized they'd been spotted. They gave chase, but the witness hid and called us."

"Did he give you descriptions of the three?" Noelle asked, inserting herself into the conversation. *My investigation, too, big boy.*

Those spec-covered eyes flipped to her, softened. "No. He said it was too dark, and that he only knew one of the men was Arcadian because of the white hair and the instappear act. Which is why we called AIR."

"Where's the witness now?" Hector demanded.

A thumb hitched over his thin shoulder. "Back of my car, sir."

Noelle scanned each of the vehicles and spotted their guy in the back of the farthest, the inside light burning bright. A junkie, she thought. Human. Pasty, papery skin. Red, sunken eyes. Chapped lips. Dirt-streaked his face. He rocked back and forth and was muttering to himself.

"Put him in the back of mine," Hector instructed. "And post two guards at the doors. Eyes are to be on him at all times."

"Yes, sir."

Before the guy could rush off, Hector reached out and withdrew a pair of latex gloves from his uniform pocket. He pulled the latex over the gloves he still wore as he walked to the trunk of Mia's sedan. There, he grabbed a tool kit.

Expression blank, he ducked under the tape and strode away. All without a word to Noelle. Well, that wasn't going to stop her. She looked at the elegant length of her dress, then at the ground. With a shrug, she palmed the blade strapped to her thigh—earned a few more whistles—and stripped off the bottom half of the material, leaving herself bare from the top of her knees down. Risqué for a crime scene, sure, but she'd bared more skin at the last cocktail party she'd attended. This way, she wouldn't brush away any prints.

As the men gaped, she bummed a pair of gloves from one of the officers and followed the same path Hector had taken. All business, she thought. Her personal life would not get in the way.

He crouched beside a dark lump. Once there, she could smell the coppery scent of blood, the release of bowels. Could see . . . far more than she wanted. The man was on his stomach, his face turned to the side, away from her. She purposely didn't study that part of him too intently. Already she could see that his mouth was still open in a silent scream.

Hector rolled him to his back, careful, so careful. The vic wore dress slacks, and his button-down shirt had burned away. There was a gaping hole in his chest, the skin at the edges charred, the organs inside deep fried.

"Don't move," Hector said, digging through his now open toolbox. He stood before she could remind him that she wasn't stupid and returned to the tape. He walked the edges, stopping every so often to stake a halogen in the ground.

By the time he reclaimed his place at her side, those lights were bathing the scene with unforgiving purpose, chasing away every soothing shadow.

"What can you tell by glance alone?" Hector asked her. Lines of tension branched from his eyes, his skin losing a little color.

Still trying to teach her, even though she was now considered his equal? Fine. Whatever. "There are no tire tracks. No footprints, either. There's nothing to suggest the body was dragged. So, even though the witness is a drug addict, he was telling—"

Hector gave a start of surprise.

"Yeah, I noticed that, too. Anyway, he was telling the truth. Our vic was popped here and killed here."

"What makes you think he wasn't killed somewhere else and teleported in already dead?"

Was he serious? "Look at the burn marks where he's lying. He was still frying when he fell on his face, and charred the grass beneath him."

"Good. What else?"

"Judging by what the witness heard—'thinking you could blow the lid off my operation'—this was a premeditated crime. Our shooter wants to keep something hidden. And our vic was a good Samaritan trying to take him down. Which suggests he knew his attacker, or at least was connected to him in some way."

"Good," he repeated. "Really good observations, Noelle."

She was used to being patted on the head, told what she needed to do to be better—at everything. His praise, so easily offered, floored her. "Thank you."

"You're welcome. Now what else can you tell about him?"

Suddenly she was desperate to impress him. "Well, he had money." A soft breeze danced between them, lifting strands of her hair and caressing them over her cheeks.

Hector's gaze sharpened, as if she'd astounded him. "Explain how you deduced that."

"His pants. They're fitted for his frame specifically and not off the rack. Plus, the material is genuine silk rather than a synthetic blend. And look at his shoes. They're Burbans and go for three thousand dollars a pop."

A pause, as if he were processing what she'd said. "Good eye."

The praise lit her up inside. *Careful.* He could addict

her to his compliments as surely as he'd addicted her to his kisses.

"Let's find out who we're dealing with." Hector pressed his lips together, pulled a small ID scan from the box, and gently pressed the man's thumb into the screen. A blue light appeared, roving from the top of his print to the bottom.

With more care than a man as muscled as Hector should possess, he placed the victim's hand in the same position he'd found it. Then he read the screen. "Bobby Marks. Five feet eleven, one hundred and eight-five pounds. Dark hair. Dark eyes. Caucasian."

The name rattled through her mind until she felt as if she'd been punched in the temple over and over again. Now, more than before, she wanted to avoid looking at the guy's face, but her gaze strayed there anyway.

Familiar brown hair, rumpled and in disarray. Familiar brown eyes stared at nothing, still glassed with pain and terror. Those lips had once pressed kisses onto the top of her hand.

"You knew him," Hector said, a confident observation.

She must have gasped. "Yes," she croaked. "I do. Did."

Shock caused the words to leave her with the same inflection an automaton would have used. Zero. "He was a gambler. Built himself up from nothing. Won stock in several different companies. Sold some, bought more in others. Those with old money hated him."

As Hector dug around in his toolbox, he said, "Your family is old money." He took several samples from the body—blood, tissue, clothing, under the nails.

"Yes. My dad never met him. Died before Bobby's time. But my mother hates—hated him. She made no secret about that. No one did. So if you want a list of families who could have wanted him dead, it'll be a long one."

The witness had claimed the shooter had worn a suit. Could he have been a businessman Bobby had taken down?

"Yeah, I'll want a list. Did you?" Hector sorted the vials before placing them in their proper locations in the box. "Hate him, I mean?"

Surely he hadn't intended for that to sound like an accusation. As if she were a suspect, just because she'd had an association. "I thought he was charming. Ruthless in getting what he wanted, but charming." So charming, now dead. Gone. "But then, I'm a trust fund baby and my wealth never depended on my business. I could afford to like him."

And now he was dead, she thought again. Such a startling realization. She remembered his laughter. He'd laughed at her jokes, genuinely amused. He'd fetched her single malt when she'd asked, and had even danced with her a time or two. But he'd never laugh again. Never share a drink with her. Never dance with anyone else.

Though she hurt for what Bobby had surely endured, she forced herself to compartmentalize. Focus, drive. She couldn't save him, but she could avenge him.

Hector paused, and for a moment, she doubted he was even breathing. "Were you one of the things he wanted?"

In his mind, he'd just dumped her on her ass. Again. He had no right to the answer.

"Maybe at one time." She told herself she replied for the case, but deep down she knew better. "He loved having arm candy, and I played that role for him every once in a while. Then, a few months ago, he stopped dating. He still went to all the parties, but he never showed up with a woman. Always went solo. Always left the same way."

A whoosh of air, the click of a lid, the cinch of a lock. "Okay," Hector said, standing. His expression never changed. He gave nothing away. "Do me a favor and call Dallas. Ask him to get out here, and to keep it on the DL. I'll process the rest of the scene and see what we've got."

So. Hector didn't think Noelle was a good enough partner for this job. He wanted Dallas. Insulting, embarrassing . . . devastating. *Never good enough.* But okay. She'd call the guy. Then they could *both* be shocked and impressed with her skills.

'Cause yeah, she would solve this thing. No matter what she had to do, she would solve it. Bobby deserved vengeance. Bobby deserved peace.

And maybe then Hector would consider being with her worth any risk.

When the thought registered, she had to cover her mouth to cut off her cry of alarm. She was doing it again, reverting to her childhood ways, becoming a girl willing to do anything to prove herself, and when that failed, acting out for attention.

And though she'd successfully smothered the cry, Hector caught her distress and pinned her in place with the intensity of his gaze. "What's wrong?"

How did he do that? How did he always know? "Nothing," she said, lowering her hands. Shame coated her, a film on her skin. "Nothing." She would solve this case, but she wouldn't do it to impress a man or to prove she was worthy. She would do it for Bobby. Only Bobby.

Hector frowned. "You're lying." His gaze roved over her, perhaps searching for injuries. He must not have seen the condition of her gown until that very moment, because his jaw dropped. Heat melted his eyes into liquid gold, a frothing cauldron of . . . desire? "You're also almost naked."

Fighting the urge to snuggle up to him, to encourage his arms to wrap around her and buffer her from the rest of the world, from herself, even from him, she lifted her chin. "Right now you're my coworker, nothing more. You don't have the right to pry into my feelings or even to comment on my lack of clothing. So back off."

He was the one to radiate shame this time. "You're right."

"Aren't I always?" A flippant reply when all she really wanted to do was sag in defeat.

# Twenty

***

THE LITTLE COFFEE SHOP reeked of caffeine (a given), sugar (a bonus), and cigarette smoke (a crime). As the only patrons were AIR agents, however, no arrests would be made tonight or any other.

Noelle had spent some time in juvenile detention for lighting up in junior high. Of course, she'd intended to piss her parents off, and—she hated to admit this next one—she had hoped to develop lung cancer. She'd prayed the disease would strike her down, she'd be hospitalized, and all of her family would rush to her side, squeezing her hand, crying, telling her how much they loved her, just as she was, and how sorry they were to have treated her so badly.

Then she'd met Ava. First day, they'd exchanged insults and actually gotten into a fist-fight. Second day, they'd kissed and made up, and the little tart had leaned into her and said, "Why do you smell like my mom?" Noelle had given up cigs from that day on.

God, she missed Ava already.

Ava should be here. Ava should partner her on this case.

Should, should, should. Sighing, Noelle slid into the booth at the back of the The Last Stop, a small, run-down, all-night diner, expecting Hector to slide in beside her. He did not. He sat across from her, and Dallas claimed the space beside him.

And of course Dallas was back to his moody, broody self, glaring at her.

As big and muscled as they both were, they consumed the entire bench. The tabletop pressed into the hard ropes of their stomachs. Their shoulders rubbed.

They'd rather be uncomfortable than touch her. Awesome. Well, she would rather they were uncomfortable *and* touching her. She dipped low in her seat, stretching out her legs, ensuring one of her knees wedged between Hector's legs and the other wedged between Dallas's.

They stiffened in unison, and she fought a smug grin.

"That's bad for your posture, you know," Hector said in that grumbling tone he just loved to use with her. "Sit up. Now."

How cute he was, issuing commands as if he were her boss. "I don't think I will. And if my back knots up," she replied with the sugar-sweet tone *she* loved to use with her enemies so they'd never suspect her strike, "I'll let you massage it better, so you can stop hinting that that's what you want to do."

He scowled at her. She smiled at him, a mere baring of her teeth—before flipping him off. Dallas watched the byplay through slitted lids. His mouth hovered between a fierce frown and a twist of abject terror.

What was his deal?

Well, she wouldn't worry about him. Only the case mattered, she reminded herself. They'd dropped the witness at AIR before coming here, hoping he'd sober up and hurry through withdrawal so they could talk to him.

A harried waitress approached, a computerized notepad in hand, shifting impatiently from one sneakered foot to the other. She was older, with frizzy salt-and-pepper hair and ink stains on her hands. But she wore a necklace made from macaroni noodles, and Noelle's heart gave a lurch.

She'd made a similar necklace for her mother long, *long* ago. Madame Tremain had pinched the thing between her fingers and grimaced. Grimaced, as if she were handling a rotting animal carcass.

"Mama wears diamonds, darling, not pasta," she'd said. "Besides, we don't want nasty insects getting into the house, now do we? No, we don't. So throw this thing away, and we'll go buy a real necklace."

Noelle shoved the memory deep inside her, where a thousand others just like it resided.

"I'll have coffee," Dallas said. "Black, strong. Fine, just go ahead and bring me motor oil." There was something wrong with his voice. Gone was the charmer entirely. In his place was a raging asshole. "Oh, and about a thousand painkillers, if you're serving them."

"Only with the eggs. You?" One graying brow winged up as she focused on Hector.

"Just coffee for me."

At long last, that stressed gaze landed on Noelle. She hadn't even glanced at the menu glowing on the side wall, but she'd been to places very similar to this one and knew what they served. Except for one tiny yet important detail. "Do you have real meat or do you only use the syns and clones?"

"For God's sake." Hector, grumbling.

"Are you kidding me with this?" Dallas, snarling.

Noelle never removed her gaze from the waitress. "Well?"

"Syns and clones. You want real, you'll have to go somewhere else."

She heaved another sigh. Yeah, she'd figured that was the case; she was disappointed nonetheless.

During the war, things like water, animals, and, well, anything delicious had been contaminated, ruined, or almost completely wiped out. Now, to get the real thing, you had to pay—and pay out the ass. Only a few shops in this district catered to people like Noelle, who were more than willing to bend over.

"Oh, come on," the waitress said, what little patience she'd had vanishing. "You want something or you don't. Which is it?"

The attitude could use a tune-up, but its rust and lack of shine wouldn't diminish her tip. In fact, she could mess up Noelle's entire order, spit in her food, whatever, but the macaroni guaranteed her a hefty tip.

"I'll have two eggs, over medium, with a side of hash browns, and don't skimp on the butter or whatever variation you use. I want four strips of bacon, two sausage patties, and four hotcakes. I don't care what kind of syrup you bring, just make sure it's warm. Also, I want two pieces of toast, but don't put any butter on those. And I want jelly, whatever you've got."

An astonished, "That's it?"

"For now."

A *hmph* sounded as the waitress finished typing. She wandered off, and Noelle noticed that both Hector and Dallas were staring at her with equal measures of bewilderment.

"What? I'm hungry. I didn't eat before, during, or after the wedding."

"Yeah, but you just came from a gruesome murder scene," Hector, Mr. Obvious, said.

"And that means I should starve for the rest of my life?"

"It means you shouldn't eat something that looks like the dead guy's chest," Dallas snapped. "Now can the two of you stop flirting with each other? It's annoying."

Seriously, what was wrong with him? "How about this," she told them both. "I'll worry about my appetite and potential digestive problems, and you two worry about shutting your fucking mouths. Sound good? As for the flirting thing, your radar must be malfunctioning, Dallas. If you consider *that* flirting, I feel sorry for your girlfriends."

No response was forthcoming, just more staring. Although Hector seemed to be battling a grin.

She snuggled deeper into her uncomfortable seat, the vinyl cracked and torn and catching in what was left of her savaged dress. She couldn't wait to shower and change. Alone. Without Hector.

*Avoid, avoid.* Any topic was safer than the man across from her.

She cast her gaze through the smoke-hazed room. There were about twenty booths, nearly all of them stuffed with AIR agents, some in uniforms, some in street clothes. Conversations were loud, and laughter, when it came, was gruff.

There were two TVs posted in the far corners of the room, both playing the same game. Football. And there was Corban Blue in all his Arcadian glory, tall, strong, as pale as a moonbeam, making an astonishing pass, the ball whizzing through the air so quickly the camera couldn't track it.

Lately, she just couldn't escape him.

"What are you looking at with such an amazed expression?" Hector asked. He turned, saw the television, and grunted like the caveman he truly was. "I didn't know you were into sports."

"I'm not. I'm into the men. Uniforms are hot."

Hector had removed his gloves on the drive over and hadn't replaced them. Now he curled his fingers around the edge of the table, his knuckles quickly bleaching of color. What? Had her reply pissed him off? Made him jealous? Well, good. He deserved to stew.

God knew she would relive their interaction tonight over and over again, and it'd be nice to know he had reacted to her, even in so small a way.

Dallas nudged him, and the two focused on each other. A conversation about sports ensued, followed by an exchange of wedding gossip. Hector relaxed, the fine lines around his eyes easing.

Since neither of them seemed keen to discuss the case, she whipped out her cell and texted Ava.

*R U a vamp yet?* Fingers crossed the text interrupted something important.

McKell's blood could turn anyone or thing—like, say, a dog named Hellina that Noelle used to own—into a vampire. And now that bloodsucking bastard was vamping up her Ava. Her sweet, baby-faced Ava. Would her tan fade? Probably. Would she sprout fangs? Definitely. Hellina had.

No worries, though. Noelle would ensure Ava always looked her best. She drafted a mental Christmas for her friend. Sunless tanner, bloodred lipstick that wouldn't smear, a car with UV-repellant shield armor, and a recipe for making Mr. Bloody Marys with McKell's blood. Because they were mated, Ava would be unable to drink from anyone but McKell without sickening. So no noshing on agents or targets who got on her nerves.

Noelle's phone vibrated, signaling the reply had just arrived.

Knowing Ava, her cell rested on the nightstand beside the bed. Just in case Noelle needed her. A darling gesture, and one of the many reasons Noelle adored her.

Screen name *Tits McGee* said: *Nope. We bargained. He has 2 last 30 mins before I let him turn me. 3 tries in, and no go.* Noelle had named her after a character in an old movie she and Ava loved to watch, but just then she seriously considered changing the name back to Pocket Rocket. That one always had a nice ring.

*2 excited about having U 4 eternity, I guess.*

*I know! He's so lucky!*

The waitress arrived with the coffees, sloshing them on the table before hurrying away. Noelle added a liberal amount of fake cream and fake sugar, wishing to God she'd thought to bring a purse full of the essentials.

After a few sips of the nasty concoction, she started typing again. *Thought: maybe I should become a vamp 2.* She tossed out the suggestion as a joke, but absolute, utter longing swept through her. Ava was going to age slowly. Noelle wasn't. Ava was going to live a long, long time. Noelle had another forty or fifty years. Maybe. And that just wasn't good enough.

So what if she would never again be able to venture out in the daylight. There were simulators and virtual reality programs available. So what if she would be as pale as milk. That's what cosmetics were for. As long as she had Ava, nothing else mattered. Right?

Tits McGee: *R U joking? U better not B joking! I will stab U in throat if U R joking!*

Her gaze strayed to Hector, who was still engaged in conversation with Dallas. Still ignoring her. If she vamped it up, he would age quickly and she would age slowly. *She* would have to watch *him* die.

Okay, so maybe something else mattered. Even though Hector currently occupied the top spot on her shit list, the thought of him dead and gone made her chest ache.

She typed: *Let me think about it.*

*I will do my best 2 help w/right decision. Luv U.*

*Luv U 2.*

A few seconds later, her phone gave another vibration, and she had to blink rapidly to see the screen clearly.

Tits McGee: *Food 4 thought. U will look so hawt w/ fangs & I will*

The text ended there. Without punctuation, without finishing. Then Noelle's cell was ringing, Ava's voice saying, "You better answer this, genius, or I'll kick your ass!"

Frowning, Dallas glanced around the diner. "Ava's here?"

"No." Hector pinched the bridge of his nose. "That's Noelle's ring tone you're hearing."

"Uh, yes, hello?" Noclle said into the piece, knowing exactly who it was. On her way here, she'd programmed her ringer to go off for everyone *but* her mother, who had tried calling again. "Noelle Tremain, master of the universe at your service. How may I help you?"

"Stop texting my wife," McKell growled from the other end. *Bingo.* "I need her full attention right now." *Click.*

A chuckle escaped Noelle as she put her phone away. Original mission accomplished.

Hector's golden eyes pierced her, becoming a spot-light on all the needy places inside her. "Who was that?"

To hide the fact that she was now quivering in-side—God, his intensity was arousing—she waved the question away with a flick of her wrist. "You have no right to the answer. Besides, we're here for business. Let's get to it, shall we? If you two are done cackling like hens, that is."

Dallas popped his jaw. "I do not cackle. I bitch like a he-man."

"We have that in common, then." She sipped at her coffee, grimaced at the thickness, and added more cream and sugar. "So why are you here when I'm sec-ondary on the case?" A fact she would not let either of them forget.

Hector answered for him. "He helped me a year ago, with the women found in the warehouse. A mysterious Arcadian popping in and out after our tipster comes out of hiding. It's suspicious."

So he'd jumped to that as well.

"And I'm so ready to nail whoever was responsible," Dallas said.

The fact that both men remembered that case, de-spite the hundreds of others they'd since worked, meant it had left a mark deep in their souls.

"Any luck on identifying the Arcadian who snatched the women out of the hospital?" she asked. Nothing had been in the file, but then, all details weren't always reported.

Dallas shook his head, dark hair falling over his forehead. He didn't brush the strands aside. Maybe he didn't notice them. He'd been silent and stiff at the crime scene, but after seeing the body, he'd become *deadly* silent, and *savagely* stiff. "First order of business is finding out who Marks was working with and if any recent dealings had gone sour."

"I'll search Marks's home and office in the morning," Hector said. "Talk to his employees, that kind of thing."

*With me, right?* she projected at him. *Partner.*

His expression remained blank.

She brought her mug to her lips, blew into the steam, gulped. The sugar had dissolved, sweetening the taste, and the cream had thinned the liquid. To make sure she had his full attention, she moaned her approval louder than necessary, as if she were having sex with her cup.

He rubbed at his arm, his jaw clenched. Not so blank any more. "Don't do that."

Innocent as the devil, she blinked over at him. "Don't do what?" *Arouse you? Make you crave more of me?*

"So what I'm trying to say is, we should consider using the witness as bait to draw out the Arcadian or whoever hired him." Dallas's snapped words stopped her from doing something stupid, like leaping over the table and devouring Hector. Uh, she meant, slapping some sense into Hector. "If the two cases are connected, the Arcadian will try to cover his tracks and tie up all loose ends. Right now, the witness is the only loose end we've got."

"That we know of," she replied. "But he'll never agree. He was scared as hell already."

"Well, we don't have to use him in the field," Hector

said. "Just his name and someone who kinda looks like him. I don't want to go that route, though. Not yet. Not until we have a few more answers."

For a long moment after he'd spoken, he watched her, silent, his intense expression somehow transporting her back to the reception hall, with his arms caging her, his lips pressed into hers. Hot, aching arousal pooled between her legs.

*Stop. You have to stop this.*

She cleared her throat, breaking the spell.

He looked away. "I've got agents scouring Whore's Corner, searching for other possible witnesses. Especially someone who isn't a user. They're texting me updates and so far no luck."

"They probably won't find anyone," she said. "Witness mentioned a foot chase. Our killer would have found anyone else in the vicinity and we would have found a trail of dead bodies."

"Maybe. Or, if our killer found someone else, he might have taken him to a secondary location, thinking everything was then under control. But there are no footprints anywhere. So either our witness was lying and there was never a chase or they were wiped."

"Wouldn't be difficult for a rich man to wipe the prints. With the right equipment, you can wipe anything. You need to have the agents search the field for a small pinlike device. It's small, thin, and will blend in, but when shoved into the ground and switched on, it disrupts the natural lay of the land, kind of like shaking dirt in a glass." Of course, if the device was used, the body could have been dragged there without leaving tracks.

"Never heard of something like that," Dallas said. "Wouldn't we have felt a quake or something?"

"Nope. And you've never heard of something like that because it's black market and new. I certainly don't know about it because Ava and I trashed a senator's prized backyard after he threw a tantrum when she wouldn't sleep with him. I just like to stay up to date on new inventions."

"Up to date?" Hector said. "That's the alibi you're going with?"

A shrug of one shoulder.

"I'll have the agents look. As for us, we need to notify Mr. Marks's family about his death before the press learns his identity. I tried to phone the mother, Brenda Marks, on the way over, but there was no answer." There was a dagger-like sharpness to his tone. Clearly he hated that part of the job. "When she finds out, there will be a public outcry for action and answers, and we'll have cameras on our every move."

"Probably. Brenda Marks is as cold and unfeeling as a woman can get. You don't have to worry about any tears or accusations that you should have done your job and saved Bobby. But she does like the limelight, and she will phone every newspaper in town the moment you leave her."

A tangle of scents wafted to Noelle a split second before the waitress arrived. Noelle's mouth watered. Steaming plate after steaming plate was skidded across the table. Her stomach twisted with eagerness.

Her favorite development? The men stared at her food with absolute longing.

"Don't ask, because I'm not sharing." Smug, she lifted a piece of extra crispy bacon, bit off the tip, and gave another of those moans, as if the cloned meat was the best thing she'd ever tasted. Maybe it was. The flavors exploded on her tongue as she chewed.

"Not nice," Hector growled, rubbing his arm more forcefully.

Dallas reached out to confiscate a piece of toast, but she stabbed his hand with her fork in a lightning-fast motion he couldn't dodge.

"Ow!"

"The fact that I'm not sharing means *I'm not sharing*." She signaled the waitress and said, "My friend would like a bowl of pretzels if you've got them. Oh, and a bandage for his hand."

"I'll see what I can find." Off the waitress went again, returning a few minutes later with a bowl of crackers and a clean rag.

Dallas ignored the rag and munched on the saltines, glaring at Noelle the entire time.

Hector waved his fingers at her sausage. "Give me the patties or walk home."

O-kay. Normally a guy making any kind of demand *after* semi-rejecting her—more than once—would have pissed her off. But . . . that husky voice, paired with those glittering eyes, and the stubborn tilt of his chin, was just flat-out sexy. Wouldn't do to give in gracefully, though.

Forcing a put-on expression, she scooted the plate of patties his way, and said, "Only because I've had my hand wrapped around your . . ." His eyes slitted and she smiled innocently . . . "tool kit."

Dallas looked between them.

Hector's pupils pulsed at that, but he said nothing else, just focused all of his intensity on the food.

"Mia will be ticked." Dallas worried two fingers over his stubbled jaw.

"That I didn't share my toast with you?" Noelle shook her head as she shoveled in a bite of eggs, swallowed. "Try again."

The worrying paused for a moment. "No, moron, if the media learns Marks's identity before the family is notified."

He was lucky Ava wasn't here. The namecalling would have sent her friend into a red-hazed rage and when Ava raged, people required hospitalization. Or coffins. "But you guys still want his name kept out of the papers?"

"Yes." Hector bit into the sausage with gusto.

"ME's report will hit our desks in the morning, and you can wait to notify Marks's mother until then," Dallas said, shifting the bowl of crackers back and forth between his hands. "But there'll be no keeping the details on lockdown after that."

Noelle noticed that while she called the victim by his first name, Hector and Dallas used his last. Their way of remaining distanced, she thought. Any other case, she probably would have done the same. But then, she'd known Bobby before his murder.

"We still risk a leak beforehand." Reporters would be all over a rich man's death. Just like the vultures they were. While she could ensure information was filtered in the media outlets her family owned, she couldn't do a damn thing about the ones they didn't. "I'm sure a press conference will even be called, and as the primary on this case, your face will be plastered on every TV screen in town," she said to Hector.

He cursed under his breath. "I'll just say no comment and leave it at that."

Clearly the man had never dealt with a reporter determined to stake a flag in the cutthroat world of news. "The only way to keep them from running one story is to give them another. Something better. Hotter."

She polished off the rest of her food. Or rather, the portion Hector and Dallas left behind. As she ate, her hands busy, they threw what they could into their mouths, successfully managing to avoid a forking.

All the while they discussed false stories they could feed the media, and she listened, doing her best not to roll her eyes. Alien abductions and probings weren't exactly news anymore—considering the aliens lived here.

"I'll take care of the story," she said. "No one will care about Bobby." And that was a shame. But an agent did whatever was necessary to solve her case. That had been drilled into her head since day one.

"How?" Hector demanded.

"Trust me. I know how to manipulate the press."

"How?" Dallas insisted.

She would have preferred to make this call in private, but whatever. She lifted her cell and dialed her contact at *What's Happening, New Chicago*. After three rings, a too-perky female voice answered.

"This is Noelle Tremain," she said, and both Hector

and Dallas leaned toward her, propping their elbows on the table. Dallas still looked a little shell-shocked and sickly, but Hector was all intent and emotionless again. That must be his default setting. "You know, the heiress. The adventurer. The YouTube sensation. You saw me smack that AIR agent around last year, right?"

Yep. Default. His expression didn't change.

She wished she were better at reading him.

"Oh, my God! Elle! How are you, darling? I haven't heard from you in so long, I thought you'd forgotten me." A pout. Faked, of course. Just like the news Marsha Tolle delivered.

Noelle and Ava had gone to high school with Marsha, and though the girl had thought her dreams of stardom made her better than everyone but Noelle, she'd never said an unkind word about dirt-poor Ava. That's why, when she'd phoned a few times last year hinting for invites to certain exclusive parties, Noelle had given them to her. Now Marsha owed her.

Time to collect.

"As if I could have forgotten you, sweetie." She used the bubble pop voice she usually reserved for the men in her family, all air, no substance. "Listen, I just found out the most amazing news, and I wanted my closest friends to be the first to know."

A gasp of pleasant surprise. "I'm so honored you thought of me."

"Of course I did." Noelle forced a giggle, her gaze locked on Hector. His lips were now twitching, and she decided she might not need an instruction manual to read him, after all. He enjoyed her grade A acting. "So get this. I still can't believe it myself, but oh, it's just so exciting, and I'm shaking."

"What? What's happened?" Marsha couldn't keep the greed out of her tone.

"I'm pregnant! And you know that football star, Corban Blue? He's the father!"

# Twenty-one

———⟨⟩———

*E*VERYTHING'S CLEAR."
Hector's voice drifted from the upstairs of Noelle's home. Her heart drummed erratically as she navi-
gated the foyer on shaky legs. She tried to concentrate
on her surroundings rather than the gorgeous warrior
she yearned to have in her bed. The floor was a lovely
gold-veined marble, the wall tables carved from rich
mahogany. Crystal vases and bowls rested on top and
cast colorful flecks of light in every direction.

Still shaking, she climbed the winding staircase and
walked the plush carpet of one of her many hallways,
and entered her private wing.

She found him standing in the doorway of her bedroom, peering inside, as though frozen. His back was
to her, but he sensed her and stiffened.

Brushing past him, she breathed in the scent of wild
sky and clean laundry. After she'd hung up with Marsha, he'd driven her home. She hadn't been ready to
part with him, so she'd played the *it's dark out, and I'm
afraid to go in alone* card.

Whether he'd believed her or not, he'd checked every shadow, every closet for the bogeyman.

As she'd waited for him to finish, her mind had replayed their earlier kiss and her blood had heated. He was here, in her home. They were utterly alone. The low simmer of arousal she'd experienced all evening had exploded, demanding its due. Demanding satisfaction, no matter what he'd said about being too dangerous, no matter that she'd decided to think things through first.

And he didn't appear ready to leave . . .

He leaned against the jamb, and stuffed his hands in his back pockets. He wasn't looking at her, was studying her bedroom. A single sweep of his gaze, and he had memorized every detail, she would bet.

What did he think of the large, canopied bed, with the ice-blue silk draping the sides? Too girly? What did he think of the matching curtains, the fabric so sheer, so delicate, the golden rays of the sun seeped through the window every morning, haloing every inch with rings of shimmering fire? Too romantic?

He probably liked the stone hearth, with two thickly cushioned chairs in front of it, a small, round table between them. And the books . . . maybe. They were the real thing, with paper pages, and colorful covers, not the electronic pads. The books were old, some of them brittle, but she couldn't, wouldn't, part with them. Before Ava, those books had been her favorite, and often only, companions.

Noelle pictured Hector standing on her balcony, her garden surrounding him as he smoked a cigar. She'd never seen him smoke a cigar before, but whatever. She pictured him bathing in her natural spring, even crooking his finger at her, silently demanding she join him.

The water remained warm year round, always bubbling, always whirling. Even now, steam curled from the surface, winding through the air like ivy, clinging to the ceiling. Beyond that was her bathroom, complete with an enzyme shower, as well as a real water shower, a vanity mirror and chair, and a black and gold granite countertop.

Was Hector surprised by the elegance? Had he envisioned something more hedonistic? Something more exclusive? This wasn't the choicest location in the city, but it was close to Ava. To Noelle, that made it the best.

"Well," she said, turning to face him, splaying her arms. "What do you think?"

"I think this is where God would move if he could afford it."

As tall and thickly muscled as Hector was, encircled by such delicate, expensive things, he should have looked out of place. Plus, his dress shirt was wrinkled, and there was a dirt smudge on his pants. Dried mud caked the bottom of his shoes. But out of place? No. He was wild and wicked, the dark knight willing to do anything to slay his damsel's dragons.

And those tattoos of his . . . How had she dismissed them so easily after their first meeting? How had she never considered such markings attractive until him? Because damn. They were little roadways for her tongue to follow, swirling and dipping, up and down, tempting, luring.

A shiver slid down her spine. "I'm glad you like it."

A shadow of amusement before those amber eyes frosted over, an ice storm churning inside them. The change was reminiscent of his last rejection of her, and she braced herself for another.

"I should go," he said, but didn't move.

"Or you could stay." She'd wondered what she would risk to be with him. Right now the word "anything" popped in her mind.

He drew in a breath. "What is it you want from me, Noelle?"

His secrets, his body, and his slavish devotion. For starters. Things he wasn't yet ready to hear. "I want you to have dinner with me tomorrow tonight." Innocent, easy.

"Why? I told you I was dangerous."

"I know, but I still want you." *Putting yourself out there again, girlie. Probably not wise.*

*I know.* And she would have backed off if he hadn't shown her that glimpse of jealousy earlier. If he hadn't looked at her as if he wanted to eat her rather than the food. If he hadn't searched her home so diligently and eyed her bed so hungrily.

Even though the frost melted, the storm remained, turbulent and troubled. "That's a very bad idea."

"Hello, all the fun things are."

"Noelle—"

"How about this? I promise not to fuck you on the table, and you promise to enjoy yourself anyway." Role reversal. A direct hit every time. Not to mention the fact that she'd just insulted his masculine pride.

"Fine," he snapped. "Dinner. Together. Tomorrow night."

"Your enthusiasm is heartwarming. Truly." She didn't change course, though. Dinner wasn't meant to romance him, wasn't even meant to relax him. Though that would happen, too. Hopefully. Dinner was simply her way of learning about him.

Why he used hookers—and when he'd last screwed one. Why he refused to date. Why he thought he was too dangerous for Noelle to kiss. What, exactly, he craved doing to her.

Hector scrubbed a hand through his hair, an action she figured was habit. From nerves? Or desire? *Please be desire*. She studied his face. The hard pinch of his lips, the slits of his eyes. Desire, yes, but he was still fighting it.

Noelle closed the distance between them. He straightened from the jamb, stiffened, but he didn't try to prolong the separation. Practically purring, she placed her hands on those wide, strong shoulders.

His nostrils flared as he breathed. Deeply, harshly. "What are you doing, Noelle?"

Another step closer brought her breasts into contact with his chest. Immediately her nipples budded, rasping against his shirt just the way she liked. "I'm having a very stimulating conversation with you."

His muscles twitched underneath her palms, heat radiating from him in a continuous stream. "Talk to me from across the room."

"Why? Do I bother you when I'm this close to you?"

"A little," he admitted.

"Why?"

He seemed to brace himself for . . . something. Rejection, perhaps. "I told you I only . . . mess around with hookers. You shouldn't want me."

"But I do."

A low growl rumbled from him. "I kissed you and told you we could never do anything like that again, that I'm too dangerous for you. You *really* shouldn't want me."

"But I do," she repeated. "And you want me. You were hard for me before, and you can't deny it." She arched forward, brushing against that delicious place between his legs. "You're hard for me now."

His nostrils flared. "I . . . I . . ."

"Don't lie to me, and don't run from me. You hurt my feelings when you do."

He softened, but only slightly. "I don't want to hurt you."

"Then tell me why you only mess around with hookers, and why you are too dangerous to be with me. And what does *mess around* mean?"

They stood like that, touching, but not doing what they both wanted—grinding—for several long, silent minutes. His scent thickened around her, enveloped her, became a part of her, the heat of him intensifying.

"I don't like to talk about it," he finally said.

"Do it anyway."

"Actually, I *never* talk about it."

And yet he had with her. Before, at camp, and then again today. "Do it anyway," she repeated. "You almost did at the church. You almost did in the car."

His teeth gnashed together. "Both times, I stopped myself. I don't trust you enough."

Ouch. There was no arguing with that. Still, male pride might once again come to her rescue. "Do you like to do kinky, embarrassing things, and that's why you won't be with a girl like me?" She'd meant to sound flippant, or even suggestive, but the pain just kind of seeped out of her.

*A girl like me. Never good enough.*

Sheer, absolute longing painted the harshness of his features. "Sweetheart, I'd be happy with straight-up missionary with you."

Her eyes widened with surprise. The way he'd said "missionary," as if he'd never wanted anything more, well, she nearly stripped then and there. Permission first, then the shedding of clothing.

"Then don't be a pussy," she said to goad him. "Do *something* with me."

He was the one to step closer this time, and there was so much menace in his eyes she found herself backing away, despite the intensity of her desire for him. But he kept coming, until her knees hit the back of the bed and she fell to the mattress. His legs imprisoned her knees, halting any retreat she might have made.

"Something?" he growled.

"Anything."

"Like what? Help . . . me."

With pleasure. She grabbed his hips and pulled. He fell forward as she fell the rest of the way back. He managed to catch himself before their bodies aligned, straddling her waist, glaring down at her. He was harder than before, his erection straining the fly of his pants.

Moisture pooled between her legs, making her desperate for his touch, his tongue. Something, anything. Little aches arced through her bloodstream, razing her cells, making them clamor for contact, too. She drew two fingers down the buttons of his shirt, popping them and causing the material to gape open.

"Noelle," he rasped, bracing his arms as if he meant to push away. "I remember when you told me that you'd called dibs on Dallas."

Bothered by the idea? God, she hoped so. "First, I might have called dibs, but I never actually wanted him. Second, I do want to sleep with you." *More than I've ever wanted anything.* "But you have to give me something, Hector. Please. Info or another kiss. Gentleman's choice."

She traced her fingers along the ridges of his stomach, then circled his nipples. He sucked in a breath—but didn't tell her to stop.

He leaned down, nipped at her lower lip. God, she loved when he did that.

"To save you," he said. "There. That's an answer, a bit of the information you demanded. I stopped kissing you to save you."

Just a nip, but she tasted him. Sweet, minty, drugging. She let her fingers fall . . . fall . . . and cup his erection, rubbing up and down, and sweet merciful heaven. He was the stuff of fantasies. "From?"

Growls began to erupt from his throat. His hips moved with her hand, jerky thrusts that deepened the contact.

"You picked information. You can't stop there," she

said. "*Trust me.* I won't betray you, and I'll even share a secret about myself."

He stilled. A moment passed while he caught his breath. "If I don't?"

"I'll think you decided to give me a kiss instead. I'll keep throwing myself at you. I'll even up my game. And if you think I was shameless before, get ready. Flashing? Old news. Innuendos? Nothing. I'll show up on your doorstep naked, and that'll just be the appetizer."

*Bargaining?*

Well, she knew how to buy and how to take. With Ava, she knew how to give. Time, affection, anything and everything, because Ava gave so freely to her. But this thing with Hector was uncharted territory. What she wanted couldn't be bought or taken. And she found that she didn't want him that way, anyway. She craved his willingness.

"I can't tell you. Not in a way you'll believe. I'll have to show you," he said, his timbre guttural, gravelly.

Triumphant heat shimmered through her.

Quickly, as if he feared talking himself out of his actions, he removed his shirt the rest of the way, then extended his arms above her. He was still without gloves, and she could see that the strange light glowed from his shoulders to fingertips. Brighter and brighter, until she could no longer see his skin. Or his muscles and bones. Just particles, floating in the air, like a thousand little sparks that conformed to the same shape as his limbs. A morbidly beautiful, hauntingly lovely sight.

She'd known he sometimes glowed, but hadn't figured out why or how and never would have guessed *this*. Dazed, she reached out to touch. He jerked both arms higher in the air, preventing contact. The glow faded . . . disappeared, his skin returning to its natural burnished tan, though some of his tattoos were now gone. Both arms fell to his sides.

Sweat beaded on his brow, and the mix of emotion in his eyes startled her. She saw fear, anger, hope, and grim expectation.

"Don't ever touch me when I'm like that," he said hoarsely. "I could burn you, scar you. I could punch through your body and rip out your heart in less than a second."

"Hector, I—" Didn't know what to say. She'd never seen anything like that. Never *heard* of anything like that. Not among humans, and not among the alien races.

The grim expectation won the fight for dominance and now painted each of his features. "Do you understand why I can't let myself have you? I can force my arms to atomize, yes, but sometimes, most times, they atomize on their own."

She gulped, experienced a wave of fear. Atomizing unbidden. Like the times they'd kissed, when he'd burned through metal.

At the time, she'd been in tremendous danger, just as he'd said, but she hadn't even suspected. He had, though. He had known and he had feared, and that's why he'd left her.

What would have happened if he'd accidentally touched her, even in the slightest way? She wouldn't have felt the pain, might have even prolonged the contact, and she would have been severely injured.

"When does it happen on its own?" she asked softly. "Why?"

"When I'm aroused. When I'm frustrated. When I'm pissed."

"And you've hurt people before?" she asked, gentle now, so gentle. "Unintentionally?"

A hard nod as he leaned his weight into her and carefully, oh, so carefully, braced his hands beside her temples. Close, though not daring to brush against her. "I won't lie to you. A few times, I did it on purpose."

She wondered who he'd harmed—killed?—and why, but she wouldn't ask. Not yet. She didn't want such lethal memories to intrude on this moment. He was finally opening up, sharing, giving her a chance to prove herself worthy of his trust. So push for too much too soon? No.

Her mind caught on three little words. *Prove herself worthy*. This time, though, she was glad to do so. This was difficult for him, a huge step. She owed him the best she had to give.

"Why are your arms like that?" she asked. "Do you know?"

Some of the stiffness melted from his shoulders. "I was born that way, I guess. First time I remember hurting someone with them, I was eight."

Eight. So young. So sweet and innocent. "I'm sorry." The price tag on such a lethal ability must be unbearable, and yet he soldiered on. The mental and emotional strength he must possess . . .

She thought back. She'd *never* seen him touch anyone casually. Sometimes he handled suspects, but never for long. For the most part, he kept to himself. Perhaps he was as lonely as she often was.

He nodded to acknowledge he'd heard her. "I . . . care about you, Noelle. I don't like the thought of you in pain."

"Well, that's good because I can't feel any. Pain, I mean. I don't have any working receptors," she said. "That's my secret. That my father paid to have them fried."

A burst of confusion in his eyes, then anger. "You were altered?" he demanded. "Surgically? Why?"

"In case I was kidnapped again."

A cold wash of horror. *"Again?"*

He'd trusted her; now she would trust him. As promised. "Yes. Again. For ransom. The kidnappers told my father they'd kill me if he went to the police or if the media found out, but that wasn't why he kept things quiet. If no one knew, no one would miss the men responsible."

"Go on," he gritted.

"My dad paid good money for my release, but by then, I'd been a captive for three days and two nights."

"How old were you?"

"I had just turned twelve. Anyway, to get their point across, the kidnappers hurt me, on camera, and sent the videos to my father. A new video each day. They made the mistake of thinking him a simple business-man. Truth was, he'd worked for the shadier side of the government most of his life, as only a rich man can. He had connections and resources and in the end was able to travel all over the world without suspicion and do terrible things with no one the wiser."

"Good."

After he'd gotten Noelle back, he'd savagely killed the men who'd held her.

Only then, in an effort to be proactive, had he had his doctors screw with her nerve endings. *That* had hurt far worse than any torturing the kidnappers had done. So no, nothing Hector could do would cause her a moment of pain.

"Your dad loved you," he said.

Sadness flickered in her chest. "He loved the *idea* of me."

"I don't understand."

"Doesn't matter." She wiggled against him, her hunger for him returning full force. "Let's get back to the good stuff."

His eyes narrowed. "You may not feel the pain, sweetheart, but I could still do some damage." Comprehension blazed with lightning sharpness. "And now I realize you wouldn't know if I was causing damage until it was too late. We should stop," he added. "Before this goes any further."

"No!" Like a dog that refused to relinquish her new chew toy, she dug her claws into his chest. "Stay."

"I want to, I do. I like spending time with you—when I'm not battling rampant lust for you. God knows, I want you all the damn time. And I care about you, like I said, but I will not hurt you. I won't let myself."

He more than craved her. He cared about her.

He liked spending time with her.

The knowledge *affected* her. Deeply. How strong he was, to resist his own needs. How sweet he was, to protect others from what he could do. But she felt the same about him—she cared, she liked—and she wasn't going to let him shove her aside and keep her at a distance. Even though she was now scared, too.

"What about tying you up?" she asked. Anything. She would try anything to be with him. And a little bondage? *Nice.*

Shock flared in his eyes, that she so easily accepted, but it quickly dissolved in the face of regret. "I burn through rope."

"Chains?"

"Melt them."

Ouch. "What do you do with the hookers?"

A blaze of shame. "You don't need to know."

Did he think her desire for him would wane? "Tell me anyway. You know I'll press until you do." His expression remained stubborn; so, once again she pricked at his pride. "Remove your tampon and tell me, Hector. I've pursued you, I've won you, and now I deserve to know."

He snapped his teeth at her, reminding her of the times he'd bitten her. "They get on their knees and blow me," he snarled. "Happy now? Last time was over a year ago. And before you ask, I'm not letting you do that to me."

Over a year ago. So telling, whether he meant it to be or not. Tenderness filled her. She thought for a moment. Then she said, "All right. So you won't let me blow you. What *will* you let me do to you, Hector? Because you're not leaving this room until we're both sated."

# Twenty-two

*H*ECTOR PEERED DOWN AT the woman splayed underneath him, the woman studying him with an intensity and longing that floored him. She was addictive in so many ways. Her ever-changing scent—now jasmine and honey. Her always decadent taste—sugar and spice. But this . . . this was where the true danger lay. The way she looked at him. As if he were beautiful. As if he were strong, valiant, sexy . . . worthy.

When compared to her, he was none of those things. Hell, when compared to a piece of lint, he was none of those things. The fact that he and Noelle were so damn different hadn't changed. She was energy, a kaleidoscope of colors. He was linear, a bold black and white.

Yet, throughout their sexually charged conversation, she hadn't seemed to notice, or maybe she just hadn't cared, that he belonged in a different world. Desire had—and did—thrum from her in sultry waves, increasing his own.

And now he knew they had something in common.

A shitty childhood. Once Hector had assumed she'd never known pain or suffering. Stupid of him. She'd been kidnapped, tortured, then tortured again when she returned home. This beautiful, sexy creature had been made to scream with something other than pleasure. Never fucking again, he vowed. He would guard her, from afar if necessary.

"Why do you want me?" he asked, truly confused. He was a bad bet, no matter from what angle she studied this. And he knew she wasn't just leading him on or hoping for a temporary distraction. She could find that anywhere, with anyone, with a lot more ease and zero threat. Example: Dallas.

The thought alone nearly caused Hector to rip the silk covers at her temples into shreds.

"You fascinate me," she admitted.

Slowly he relaxed. On that front, at least, they were even. No one had ever fascinated him more than this— what had he once called her?—slice of elegance.

"Your intensity . . . I wonder, all the time, what it will be like, having every bit of it focused on me."

Curiosity too, then. How disappointing. Enough to make him walk away, though? No. Just then, he doubted anything could. She was soft beneath him, and though only their legs were touching, he could feel the heat of her. Could she feel the heat of him?

"I never noticed this until today, but your face displays every emotion you're feeling, in the minutest degree," she said. "Disenchantment, anger, arousal. I don't know why you felt the first two a moment ago, but I want you to listen to me. I've only had one serious boyfriend in my life, and only two sexual partners. One of which doesn't count."

"Barry," he said, still offended on her behalf. How dare anyone treat her like that prick had? "I'm putting the guy in ICU as soon as tomorrow."

Her lids went to half-mast, the gray of her eyes softening to a smoky silvery-blue. "I think you're a better gift giver than Ava, and she's a master. But the point is, I'm choosy, and I don't screw around for fun. Wait. I do screw around for fun, but it's also for keeps."

Two men. At last those words sank in, and grew roots. Only two. And she wanted *him* to be number three. He was baffled, humbled. And yeah, aroused. So damn aroused. The length of her glossy hair spilled around her head, her seemingly delicate shoulders. Her cheeks were flushed a lovely rose, and her lips were plump and parted, her every breath shallow and laced with need.

No matter how strong and valid his fears, he couldn't, wouldn't, spit on *her* gift to him.

"I've, uh, never had sex," he admitted. "Never been with anyone."

Those exquisite eyes widened. "You're a virgin?"

A stiff nod, cheeks flushing.

"Because of your arms?"

Another nod.

"Oh, Hector." A moan of excitement. "I'm glad. I like that. Want to be the first."

He leaned down . . . down . . . until her nipples were pushed against his chest, needy little peaks that enthralled him. She wigged until her thighs were outside his, trembling, locking around his hips. Damn, but she felt good.

"I told you. I don't want to hurt you," he croaked out.

"Then you're going to have to give me everything you can."

That wasn't much, but damn if he wouldn't do everything in his power to make every second they spent in this bed the best of her life.

And there was the voice of temptation, luring him into danger.

*Can't resist.* "I'll make you come without using my hands." He'd never tried that with anyone, but with her . . . "Do you want me to make you come?"

White teeth nibbled on her bottom lip, plumping and reddening the luscious petal further. Undoing him. "Yes, please."

"You just tell me how, then, and it's done." Whatever she suggested, he would try. He had very little experience with a woman's pleasure, but damn it, he *would* try. He desired her, had dreamed of her too many nights, had fantasized so many times reality was now blurred.

If, at any point, the burning and itching flared up in his arms, he would stop.

Stopping would probably kill him, but he would do it.

"Let's start with something small, easy. Like a kiss. Yes. Kiss me," she pleaded, breathless. "We've done that before, and nothing bad happened. Right?"

His gaze dropped to her mouth. Her tongue swept over her lips, leaving a gloss of moisture. His cock twitched, a lance of need shooting through him. Any minute now, and his zipper would bust, he was so full and hard.

He scooted off her, off the bed, and stood at the edge. She remained splayed on the mattress, her hair spilled around her, and her dress bunched just under her waist, hiding her panties. Fucking gorgeous. "Sit up for me," he croaked. Things were less likely to fly out of control that way.

Still trembling, she pulled herself up, hair cascading into place. What he would have given to run his fingers through the strands. He knelt in front of her, placing himself a little lower than eye level.

"If I burn you, scare you, do anything you don't like, tell me."

"I will." A feverish sigh.

Whether she would actually do so or not, he didn't know. He wouldn't risk her safety, though, not in any way, so he would remain vigilant. He would fuel her passion without becoming lost in his own. Something he'd never done. But for her . . . anything.

"Hector." She leaned into him and pressed their lips together. Her tongue swept inside his mouth, her intoxicating flavor exploding through him. As sweet as before, with a splash of something darker, richer.

*Don't touch her. Don't you dare touch her.* Or explore her curves, or knead her breasts, or finger her deep and hard. *He'd* probably come if he did. He'd never dared to thrust his fingers inside a woman, but he knew this one would be hot and wet, clutching at him.

"I want to put my arms around you," she breathed. "Can I?"

"Yes." God, yes. He placed his hands on his thighs, his fingers hooked over the curves of his knees. "Around my neck, but don't touch below my shoulders."

She scooted closer, placing her ass at the edge of the mattress while framing his torso with her legs. She danced her fingers across the spikes of his growing hair before sliding down to ride the ridges of his spine.

"Now. Kiss me now, and don't ever stop," she commanded.

"Yes."

Their tongues met, mated, rolling together, darting apart, finding each other again, dueling. She moaned, and he swallowed the sound. Her nails bit into his shoulders, perhaps even making him bleed. He liked the thought.

In a snap, the burning and itching in his arms started up, but only slightly. He disengaged only long enough to check them out. There was a muted glow seeping from his pores, but nothing to worry about. Yet.

And for the first time, he didn't have to worry about the woman he was with seeing what happened to him. She'd already seen. She knew the truth. And she hadn't judged him. She hadn't screeched in fear, hadn't pushed him away or commanded him to leave her home. All the things he'd always nervously and angrily presumed. She'd simply questioned him, doing her best to find a way for them to be together.

"Hector, I want more. Please."

Please. As if she needed to beg him. But he realized he had stopped to stare up at her, wonder radiating from him. This strong, brave female with a taste for luxury wasn't afraid of him. Wasn't disgusted by him.

If things proved too treacherous and he couldn't allow himself to come, too, he would still do everything in his power to bring about *her* release. But what could he do to her that did not involve his hands? He could think of a few things . . .

His heated gaze skated over her, locked on her deliciously hard nipples. Moisture flooded his mouth. "Take off your dress."

Without protest, she whipped the material over her head. Her breasts were hugged by a crimson bra that sparkled in the light. She wore matching panties that hugged the sweetest female body in existence.

"Unhook the clasp." His tongue was so thick, he barely got the words out.

"Yes." Her trembling increased, making her clumsy.

When the bra at last sagged open, freeing those lush morsels from their prison, revealing her berry-pink nipples, he leaned forward, as if in a trance. He flicked one with his tongue, then fit his mouth around it and sucked. Her hands once again made their way around him, holding him close . . . closer.

There was no woman more perfect. Lust incarnate, that's what Noelle was, her groans swiftly becoming cries. He'd begun the day desperate to avoid her, yet now he was desperate to have her.

"I want to see you, too," she said. "All of you."

"Not yet." He switched his attention to her other nipple, paying it the same homage, worshipping with his tongue, his teeth. Twice he found himself reaching up, his hands curving to fit against the plump mounds of her breasts, but both times he caught himself in time.

"Want to touch you, too." A needy whimper from her.

"Not yet." A groan. The burning climbed another degree, and soon thin plumes of dark smoke were curling from them, wafting to his nose. Shit. Fuck. Not here, not now. He pulled away from Noelle, stood. Shit, he raged again, even as he pulled the gloves from his pocket and slid them in place.

Noelle's moan of disappointment echoed from the walls, and he had to brace herself against the bed to remain upright. "Are we . . . done?"

Never had a woman looked sexier while pouting. "No." *Please, no.* "Can you stand?" he asked, his voice so guttural and raw he was almost embarrassed.

"Let's see." She pushed to her feet, wavered as a tremor racked her entire body, but she didn't fall. "I'm good."

He wanted her better than *good*. "Take off your panties."

Her pupils gobbled up her irises as she obeyed. "So forceful. I like you this way."

"Weapons, too." She had blades strapped to her thighs. She also sported an ankle holster, and the weapon inside did not appear to be a regulation pyregun. What it was, though, he couldn't tell.

Within seconds, she was completely naked. And fuck. He could blow his load just looking at her. Those more-than-a-handful breasts, that slightly concave stomach, those wonderfully toned legs.

"I want to see you now," she whispered. "All of you. You promised."

"I thought I could . . . hoped . . . but I can't. If I take off my pants, I'll be inside you."

Her gaze zeroed in on his zipper, her tongue peeking out to lick her lips. "And that's a bad thing?"

In a lot of ways, yes, but rather than ruin the moment and explain, he said, "Lay down, Noelle. Please. And keep your ass at the edge of the mattress."

"Your kinkiness is a very nice surprise, too," she said as she complied. Her legs were closed and now dangled over the side of the bed, shielding her feminine core from his view.

Once again he fell to his knees. "Put your feet on my shoulders, as close to my face as you can get them."

A moment of silence, of inactivity. Then, "Wh— what are you going to do to me?"

"I'm going to eat you up." Exactly as he'd dreamed of doing for months. In fact, a few mornings he'd even woken up already seconds away from release, because he'd devoured her in his dreams.

"Oh, God," she gasped out, and he knew his crudeness had ramped up her arousal.

First one leg, then the other, and then her feet were in place, anchored on his shoulders, and her knees open, his gaze enraptured by the new center of his world. The sweetness of her feminine musk drifted to his nose, and he breathed deeply, savoring. She was pink and wet, and so pretty he wanted to move in and stay forever.

Only a thin strip of hair covered her, like a treasure

map to her core. And he'd thought her pout sexy. *This* was the sexiest fucking thing he'd ever seen. He leaned in . . . closer . . . closer still . . . He'd never done this before and didn't want to mess up. Wanted to do it right, make it good for her.

No, he reminded himself. Better than good.

The savageness of his instincts wouldn't allow him to hesitate for long. Desperate to taste her, he licked his way to the treasure in question, the sweetest honey filling his mouth. A scream tore from her throat as her hips shot off the mattress. She liked, then. Well, he loved. And with a groan of pleasure, he buried his face and did as he'd promised.

He licked and he sucked and he nibbled. He consumed. She writhed. She gasped his name. She begged. She pleaded. She cursed him. She prayed for mercy. He never stopped, could never have stopped. This was heaven, pure and simple.

Again he found himself reaching for her, his fingers wanting inside her so badly they ached with the same raging desire as his cock. Again he caught himself just in time. *Mine, mine, mine. All mine. Will protect, even from myself.*

"Hector!" Her legs fell from his shoulders, and she jerked upright, but her hands never stopped clutching his scalp, holding him to her, and he never stopped enjoying her.

He licked his way to her clit, and sucked. Hard. So hard. His name on her lips was as addictive as everything else about her, and he was determined to draw it out of her again and again.

"Hector, oh, God, Hector I'm so close. I'm almost there . . . I'm . . . oh, God! There!"

Another scream ripped from her, her body convulsing, her grip tightening on him, probably leaving bruises. Bruises he'd wear with pride. He'd done this. He'd pleasured her, given her this, made her lose control. Her inner walls clenched around his tongue, a tongue he darted in and out, in and out, fucking her that way since he couldn't fuck her the other. All that delicious honey flowed down his throat, burned him alive and created a new creature.

Her slave.

Panting, she collapsed against the mattress in a boneless heap. He pulled back, but only slightly, and licked at his mouth, wanting every drop of her he could get.

He slid the edge of both his gloves back. His arms were shaking, still glowing, a little more than before, and more of the ink had faded. There were a few holes singed into the material, and those holes still released thin curls of smoke.

*But.* He hadn't burned anything down, and he hadn't hurt Noelle. So he would consider this a success.

He stood, his knees practically giving out. "Where's your bathroom?" Ragged breath in, ragged breath out. He needed a moment—or ten—to himself. To calm, to cool down. To finish himself so that he was no longer a menace. For the moment, at least.

As quickly as she'd fallen, she sat back up. Her gaze found his, and despite the languid satisfaction of her expression, she still bore signs of arousal. Heavy lids, an inability to steady her oxygen intake. "No," she said.

"No?" He blinked down at her. "No, you won't tell me? Or no, I can't use it?"

"No, you're not leaving me and taking care of that on your own." At "that," she motioned to his straining cock.

*Torturing him* . . . "Safer that way." The urge to do more to her, to have more of her . . . *can't, you can't.*

Her lashes fused together, hiding the perilous glitter of her eyes. Without another word, she reached out, unbuttoned and unzipped him, then jerked his underwear out of the way. "You're not going to deny me this. And you're not going to give it to someone else, even if that someone is yourself. It's mine. I earned it."

Hers. Fuck, but he'd never heard a more arousing speech. His cock sprang free, the tip already weeping. He should have moved away from her. Instead, he whipped his arms behind his back. He didn't have to ask what she was doing. He knew, and he craved. He was ashamed of himself, but yeah, he craved.

She wrapped her fingers around the shaft, seeming to marvel that the tips couldn't close. "You said before that you won't let me blow you. Is your answer still no, even if I'm dying to do it?"

"Noelle," he gritted. To have a woman willingly taste him . . .

"I'll take that as a yes. Please do it."

Good, because that's how he'd meant it.

She turned them both so that he was the one propped against the mattress and dropped to her knees. Then she fit her lips around the head of his cock, the wet heat of her scorching him perfectly. Down, down she slid on him, her teeth scraping him, until his length hit the back of her throat.

So good, so damn good. The shame vanished, and no guilt pierced him. Just the sweetest pleasure.

*Never before like this.* Sweat broke out in beads over his skin, his veins expanding to contain the ferocity of his arousal.

The urge to hold her, to guide her, was almost too much for him. So he moved his hands up, curling his fingers behind his neck, forming claws and locking down. Careful, he had to be careful. Already his forearms were hot enough to blister. Still he didn't tell her to stop.

He'd already lost that battle.

Up and down, up and down, she ate at him, swallowing the pre-come still leaking from him, humming as if she loved the taste. One of her hands played with his testicles, tugged on them.

He was so used to forcing himself to come as quickly as possible, he currently lacked stamina. And the fact that it was Noelle between his legs, Noelle sucking his cock, Noelle driving him to the brink, Noelle's taste still in his mouth, down his throat, he wouldn't have lasted anyway.

He'd never in his life been so turned on.

"I'm going to . . . if you don't pull away . . . you'll . . ." No one had ever swallowed him. Always he'd come in a condom, or told the woman to move away so he could shoot on the floor.

Noelle increased the speed of her strokes, the ferociousness of her suction, until he forgot his hands, forgot his ability, the problems, complications, reasons they should stay away from each other and exploded, jetting into her mouth.

He roared like an animal, out of control, utterly lost, never wanting to be found. The pleasure . . . too much, soul-changing, everlasting. Every muscle he possessed clenched, knotted. And he just kept coming and coming, and she just kept swallowing every drop.

Afterward, as he lay there, fighting for breath, she crouched beside him, careful not to touch him, and met his gaze. Her cheeks were flushed. She was panting, licking her lips as if she'd enjoyed him with the same intensity he'd enjoyed her.

"Okay?" she asked him.

He nodded, unsure he could find his voice. His arms had stopped glowing, but though they had immediately cooled down with his release, they were still too hot to be handling her.

A slow smile spread across those swollen bedroom lips. "And we'll do this again?"

Another nod, a little wary, a lot shocked. She wanted more of him? After all the work she'd had to do, she hadn't decided he was just a one-time thing?

The smile grew, became dazzling, more wicked than sensual. There were so many facets to her personality, he thought. The playful little girl, the vicious revenge-hungry woman. The seductress, the innocent. The giver, the taker. The game-player.

He wanted to fuck them all.

"Good," she said, purring like a contented kitten. "Because now I know what we're having for dinner to-morrow night."

# Twenty-three

---

*H*E WAS A BASTARD, Hector thought the next morning.

He should have phoned Noelle. Picked her up. They should have driven to Bobby Marks's house together. Instead, he now climbed the steps to Marks's front door on his own.

Hector had ditched her.

After last night, he just wasn't ready to see her. Even the *thought* of her fired him up, distracting him. And now that he knew the honey that awaited him between her legs, how the hell was he supposed to work a case with her at his side and not toss her down and ravage her every other minute?

He'd call her later. Apologize. Maybe she'd forgive him, maybe she wouldn't.

If she decided to end this thing between them, he'd be better off. *She* would be better off.

His hands fisted, and rage sparked inside his chest. *Can't lose her.*

*You will eventually.*

Those sparks heated.

*Concentrate.* He jerked on his gloves and rang the doorbell. He'd once again tried calling Brenda Marks, Bobby's mother, who lived a few houses down. No luck. When he finished here, he planned to go there. So far, Noelle's pregnancy story had overshadowed everything else, as hoped.

Noelle . . . pregnant . . .

*Fucking concentrate.*

Hector waited, expecting a servant. No one came to the door, so he rang again. The sky was cloudy, gray, a storm brewing. He felt as if he were being watched, but found no evidence of cameras, no one peeking from slits in the blinds.

He waited a few more minutes, then looked around. A Mercedes meandered along the street. Across the way, a human male—tall, lean, dark hair, handsome, probably some rich woman's boy toy—walked a shaggy white dog, paying Hector no attention.

There were four other homes around this one, each one bigger than the last. Lots of white marble, luscious trees, and colorful arrays of flowers. Again, no one watched him from the windows.

An iron gate surrounded each as well. Even this one. Bypassing Marks's gate had been difficult—his was more advanced than most—but not impossible. As Hector's presence at the door had proven.

This was the kind of neighborhood Hector had assumed Noelle would live in. While she'd renovated her place, she wasn't situated in the best part of town. But then, she was only ten minutes away from Ava's apartment, so . . . there you go. He liked that about her. Her sense of loyalty.

That's why he'd finally decided to trust her, to tell her the truth about his arms. Once, he'd thought a man would never know where he stood with her. She enjoyed her storytelling a little too much. Not to mention her silly-girl façade. But Hector was beginning to understand her.

You could *always* tell with her. She'd said she had only just noticed that he carried his emotions in his eyes. Well, the same was true for him and her eyes. You looked deep enough, and you saw how much need and vulnerability those silver irises radiated. And when she smiled wickedly, you were in trouble. But when she smiled sweetly, something he'd only ever seen her do for Ava—and now him—her faithfulness had no boundaries.

*Shouldn't need another reminder to CONCEN-TRATE.* Mad at himself, Hector carried his tools to the garage door around the way and hacked through the security system. Living on the streets finally paying off, he mused.

The door lifted slowly but steadily, revealing a black BMW, the windows tinted so darkly no one would be able to see anyone inside at any time, and a silver Viper. There was also a golf cart and a four-wheeler.

*What were you trying to blow the lid on, Marks?* Hector wondered.

Inside the house, he found reinforced steel walls painted to look like stucco. The kitchen was clean, nothing out of place. The living room, also pristine.

The office, emptied out. There were no computers. No electronic files. There was a desk and a file cabinet, but nothing inside either of them.

Had Marks cleaned up—or had someone else? Someone wanting to keep that lid sealed on certain information? Hector did a print sweep, but found only Marks's. He was about to head out to search the rest of the home when he felt the tile beneath his boot give the slightest shake.

Loose, he thought. No way a man as wealthy as Marks would have let such an imperfection slide.

Hector bent down and pried at the tile. Took some finessing, and a few hard jerks, but he finally got the piece to lift. A cubby. With a small handheld resting in the center. *Hello, pretty lady.*

Excitement rushed through him as he carefully placed the device in his tool box.

Upstairs, he found the media room. With two rumpled blankets on the couch, the area looked like a favorite. And one Marks had recently used to entertain a guest. The TV hadn't been turned off, and a daytime soap played across the screen.

Marks had been single, and there were no reports of him dating anyone. Four guest bedrooms, empty and sparkling. Then he found the master bedroom. The king-size bed was unmade, both sides clearly well used, judging by the indentations in the mattress. But unassailable proof that Marks had entertained a woman? The clothes hanging in the closet alongside his.

Dresses, both formal and casual. Sparkly shirts, and jeans with swirling designs stitched up the sides. The wearer had been more than an overnight guest. She'd stayed. Often. Maybe even lived here, though he'd caught no other sign of her. Only one way to find out the identity of his mystery girl, then. Hector set his toolbox down, straightened. DNA testing on her dirty clothing.

Behind him, he heard the quietest rustle of footsteps.

Palming the pyre holstered under his arm in less than a second, Hector spun around and aimed. A female had been approaching him with a vase lifted over her head. She swung it at him, missed as he jumped out of the way. Gasping as her momentum twisted her, she tried to catch herself and launch at him a second time.

"Not another move or I shoot." Only his reflexes had saved her from being shot the first go-round.

She froze in place. He could have pulled the trigger anyway, but he didn't. He was too curious, wanted answers now rather than later.

She was a Rakan, he realized as he considered her. A rare species that hardly ever ventured to earth. She possessed long golden hair, golden eyes, golden skin, and besides Noelle, was the most beautiful woman he'd ever seen.

His mystery girl, he would guess.

"Put the vase down," he instructed calmly. She'd meant to brain him, no question.

Nervous, she licked her lips. Even her tongue was golden. Glittery tears filled her eyes as she stuttered out, "P—please, do not h—hurt. This is my home. Y—you must leave." Heavy accent. He'd bet she hadn't been here long.

"Put the vase down," he repeated, more harshly this time. "I don't want to shoot you, but I will. And if I shoot you, you'll be helpless. Do you understand what that means?" He could do anything he wanted to her.

Slowly she obeyed, sitting the "weapon" on the floor. When she straightened, a tremor shook her entire body and the tears broke free of the dam, cascading down her cheeks.

"Who are you?" he demanded.

"M—margarete. Wife."

He arched a brow. "To Bobby Marks?" There'd been no wife on file. But then, a marriage to an otherworlder wouldn't exactly be legal. And Margarete's claim explained why Marks had stopped dating. Also explained why he'd never taken Margarete out in public.

Not everyone was pro-otherworlder. And as Rakans were hunted, often de-skinned and cut into pieces for their gold, Marks wouldn't have wanted to put her continued health in jeopardy.

"Y—yes. Bobby." She nodded, her hair dancing around her delicate shoulders. Dressed in a flowing ice-blue sheath, she appeared as innocent and truthful as an angel.

Wouldn't take him long to learn whether the image was true or false. "I want you to walk over to the bed and sit down," he said, and a sob parted her lips. Damn it. He had to be more careful with his phrasing. Bed most often equated to rape in this situation. "I'm not going to hurt you unless you challenge me. I'm an AIR agent, and I'm going to ask you some questions. That's all. When you're sitting, I'll lower my gun."

Hesitantly she obeyed, the tears flowing continuously now. As promised, he lowered the gun. Surprise filled her golden eyes. Keeping his gaze on her, he crouched in front of the toolbox and flipped the voice recorder on. Then he straightened, squared his shoulders.

She watched him, nervously rocking back and forth.

First things first. The part of the job he most loathed. "I'm sorry to be the one to tell you this, Margarete, but Bobby Marks was murdered last night."

"What?" The surprise gradually mutated into horror. "No. No! I saw him only yesterday."

Hector remained quiet, giving her time to absorb the news. First she spouted a few more denials about how he couldn't possibly be dead, then she cried, then she settled as shock took hold and numbed her out. Reactions he knew very well. He'd done the same thing when he learned about his brother.

"When was the last time you saw him?" he asked.

"I . . . I . . . yesterday. Last night."

"What time exactly?"

"I don't know. Maybe . . ." She glanced at the clock resting on the nightstand, as if that would help. "Around nine p.m. I think."

Keeping his tone gentle, easy, he said, "What had he done before that?"

Teardrops caught in her lashes, and she had to blink rapidly to clear her line of vision. "Dinner with me and his mother. He finally introduced me to her."

Good. They were getting somewhere. "How did that go?"

Her chin trembled. "I do not want to talk about this."

Words he'd said to Noelle only yesterday. "I know, but you must. I need to find his killer, and you can help me."

Several minutes passed before she collected herself enough to say, "He always made me hide when someone came over, but that hurt me, and he knew it, so he invited his mother over. When he told her, she screamed. I have never heard words as vile as the ones she used. He told me to go to our room and wait for him to come and get me. I did, but he never came."

So. The mother had just gotten a bit of bad news. Well, bad news according to her. She'd been upset. Motive for murder? Maybe, but that didn't explain what the witness had seen and heard.

Still. Hector definitely needed to question Ms. Brenda Marks. She was now a suspect, plain and simple. With her money, she could have easily hired out.

"And then?" he prompted.

Margarete shook her head. "I do not know. That was the last time I saw him."

"You didn't call him? Talk to him on the phone?"

"No."

"You didn't call anyone? Not even to report him missing?"

"No," she shouted, suddenly angry. "I trust no one on this planet besides Bobby. He told me people would injure me if they discovered me."

"How did you meet him?"

She drew her arms around her middle, as if battling

an abrupt waft of cold. "Why do you want to know? How can that help you with his . . . with his . . . ?"

"You'd be surprised by what helps," was all he said.

Her gaze darted away. "He came to my planet. We fell in love. He brought me here."

She was lying, Hector thought. The words sounded rehearsed, as if she were repeating something she'd been told. Plus, Bobby would have had to gain permission to go off planet, and he hadn't. Hector had already checked, per standard procedure.

He could take her in, lock her up in AIR for his suspicion alone, but he didn't want her logged into the system. Wasn't that he lacked trust—although he did—but he hadn't forgotten how those girls had disappeared from the hospital last year, an Arcadian suspected of taking them. And with an Arcadian involved in Marks's murder . . . no chances.

Besides, taking her from her home, her familiar surroundings, would be unnecessarily cruel. Whatever had happened, she had loved Bobby Marks.

Wouldn't hurt to garner her trust, either. She'd tell him anything he wanted to know if he could just make her trust him. "We think your husband was trying to gather evidence for a crime someone committed. Did he tell you anything about that?"

The color faded from her face, leaving her with a sickly ashen pallor. "N—no. I know nothing about that."

Abject fear. Okay. Definitely the right path. "Nothing at all?" Men would tell a woman anything during pillow talk. At least, he supposed. Look at everything he'd revealed to Noelle. Deeply personal stuff he'd never shared with any other person in all the years of his life.

This time, Margarete's chin was trembling too intensely for her to reply. She violently shook her head.

*You'll tell me yet.* "I don't want you to leave New Chicago," he told her. "I might have more questions for you, and you need to be available. If you leave, I'll hunt you down, and you won't like the results."

Threatening a frightened female who'd just lost her husband was far worse than cruel. He couldn't let himself care about that, though. Results mattered right now. Nothing else. And she would learn to trust him despite his strong-arm tactics. She would have to.

"I will not leave," she whispered brokenly.

"Good. But just in case you're tempted . . ." He withdrew a syringe from the toolkit and closed the distance. She shrank back, but he grabbed her arm only long enough to inject the contents. "I'm sorry for the sting." He released her, stepped back. "That's an isotope tracker. A few clicks of a button, and I'll be able to find you."

Rather than snip at him, she nodded in understanding.

*Won't feel guilty.* He'd come back tomorrow. And the next day. Until she spilled. Asking her follow-up questions, little things to get her talking. She'd learn that he could be relied on to protect her. That he was dedicated to helping vindicate her husband and put his killer away.

And maybe . . . maybe he'd send Noelle over. Maybe

Margarete just needed another female. Although No-elle was a ball buster and likely to offend. And threaten. And shout.

A pang in his chest. A rush of sensation through his body. *You're doing it again. Thinking about her. Reacting to her.*

"I need to do a little work around this room," he said, "but I want you to remain where you are, okay?"

A soft "Yes."

He dusted the dresser drawers for prints, took a couple pictures of the closet, even one of Margarete, and she did as promised. She never moved from the bed. The thing with AIR, you didn't always need a warrant for stuff. Otherworlders did not have the same rights as humans.

When he finished, he placed a holocard on the nightstand. A small black button that she had only to press for a blue screen to crystallize overhead, his picture, name, and number glowing. "This has my cell number. You call me if you remember anything about that night that you haven't told me. Anything at all."

A nod as she just kind of folded into herself. The numbness must be wearing off, grief taking over.

Hector packed up and took off, leaving the same way he'd come.

# Twenty-four

RATHER THAN DRIVE BACK to AIR HQ and type up his thoughts, Hector picked up two coffees, black, downloaded a copy of every newspaper being offered that morning, and programmed his car to head to the business district.

There was something he had to do—something he shouldn't do. A cold, callous crime, but also a public service, and one he would relish.

Took him half an hour to complete the task, and when he settled back inside his car, his knuckles were cracked and bleeding inside his gloves, but he was smiling. Time to get back to work. He programmed Dallas's address into the console and was soon winding down the road, the scenery more dreary than before. Thick gray clouds concealed the sun. Mist rose from the ground, and acidic dew scented the air, seeping into the car through the vents.

The car's sensors took care of the slowing, stopping, and turning, allowing him to lean back in his seat and close his eyes. Finally he could give in to thoughts about Noelle, if only to at last exorcise her from his mind.

After he'd left her place, he'd gone home, but he hadn't gotten any sleep, had tossed and turned, his body on fire for more of her. For everything.

Of course, even now he hungered for her.

Temptation, man. He'd known it was more dangerous than his arms. Once you tasted the forbidden fruit, you would always crave more. Yet still he'd gone inside her house. Stopped in her bedroom, transfixed by her bed, wondering if she'd ever lain there and pleasured herself while thinking about him.

The way she'd looked at him while he'd hovered over her, as if he were a slab of ribs and she was dying of starvation, had melted any remaining resistance.

Yet now, even though Noelle's honey was branded into his every cell, even though he could still feel her nipples rasping against his chest as he ground his erection against her, could still see her face soften as he tongued her to orgasm, even though he would never forget the way she'd sucked him off so perfectly, she was free to date anyone she wanted.

He hadn't asked for exclusivity, and she hadn't either. Just a dinner date.

He'd never before been on a date. Not with Kira, not really. Not with anyone. Would he know how to make small talk? Hell, would Noelle even want to see him tonight?

Would she ask someone else out?

Great. Now Hector wanted to fucking murder any man who even *thought* about her.

He was a mess. This was one of the many reasons he's always avoided relationships. Already he was jealous and possessive. Like arousal, those emotions weren't good for him. He'd just . . . he'd never craved a woman like he craved Noelle.

He wanted her like he wanted air to breathe, and not having her now, now, damn it, now *hurt*.

Noelle would be embarrassed by his past, so even if they made something work, she would leave him later. He just couldn't find a way around that fact. And if he was this much of a mess now, how much more of a mess would he be if they actually made love? If he'd actually tried to share his life with her?

If he harmed her irrevocably?

*Can't believe you're even considering going for more. You're a menace.*

Hell, at this rate, he really would destroy her. He'd redone his tattoos before Ava's wedding, but after what had happened last night, he'd already burned through some of the ink. And yeah, okay, he'd redone the tattoos this morning, would redo them every morning if necessary, but he was still treacherous. That wouldn't change no matter what precautions he took.

Damn it, he had to break things off with her. Completely. He couldn't risk being with her again.

When Noelle had dragged him on top of her, he'd felt the first sizzle and pop. Only thoughts of marring her flawless skin had given him enough strength to keep his arms pinned at his sides. Hadn't stopped last night's dreams, though. Dreams of going all the way. Of having her, in a thousand different ways.

Yeah, he should have called her this morning. She was a good agent, and besides, that's what partners did. Worked together. That's what she had probably hoped for. Fifty-fifty, equals in everything. Sharing details, and talking things through. He hadn't. He still couldn't. If he saw her, spoke to her, his good intentions would vanish like vapor.

*Have to see her sometime.* Not yet. Not now.

The car slowed, stopped, and Hector opened his eyes to find himself parked in the underground garage of Dallas's apartment building. He gathered the coffees and his reader before striding to the elevator. A short ride later, he was walking down the long, narrow hallway that led to Dallas's den of iniquity.

This was a nice building, one of the more expensive units in New Chicago, with clean walls, clean floors, and shield armor on the windows. Hector had been here a few thousand times, but this time he looked at it as Noelle might, comparing it to his own. His place lacked personality, Dallas's did not. Soft scarlet carpet at his feet. Vibrant stone walls at his sides. Colorful portraits of flowers hanging in every direction.

Dallas and Noelle. They were a better match.

Scowling, Hector knocked on the door harder than he'd intended. A few seconds later, that door slid out of the way. No one stood in the entrance, but Hector knew the agent had a camera hidden out here, monitoring everyone who approached. He walked inside, the entrance automatically sealing shut behind him.

"We're back here," Dallas called.

We? Hector followed the sound of his voice. He found Dallas and Devyn in the living room, on the couch, watching as a naked human female dusted the coffee table. She was short, curved, and stacked in all the right places, and any man with a fully functioning penis would have reacted to her.

Hector didn't react to her. Only Noelle tempted him past his endurance. No one else compared.

He'd wanted to talk to Dallas in private. He should have guessed Dev's presence, though. The boys were inseparable, and you couldn't be friends with one and not the other. Kinda like with Noelle and Ava.

*Now* his body reacted, his shaft twitching, his arms heating, itching. Shit. "Your wife doesn't mind you watching other women . . . work?" Hector asked Devyn as he set the coffees on the table, careful not to initiate any contact with the maid.

The king of the Targons never removed his amber gaze from the girl. "Silly boy. Bride called the service and picked her out for me."

"You mean me," Dallas corrected. "Bride picked her out for me."

Hector studied him. Tension still radiated from him. Bruises were under his eyes, as if he hadn't slept, and there were sores chewed in his bottom lip. "Well, get rid of her. I'm here on official business."

"The room isn't clean. Besides, I'm here to cheer up my bestie. Bestie—isn't that what people call their best friend forever? I've heard Noelle Tremain use the term with little Ava."

More twitching.

"We've had this conversation before. That's what teenage girls call them," Dallas muttered.

Devyn smiled his most charming smile. "As our bromance will last the ages, that sounds pretty perfect to me."

Hector glanced around. Usually, the place was a disaster area, with clothes strewn about, empty beer bottles everywhere, and food wrappers stuffed between the couch cushions. Now there were three stacks of folded laundry in a basket. There wasn't a bottle in sight, and a soft swathe of material was draped over the arm of the couch.

"Ma'am," Hector said. "There's something you can do for me."

Her blond hair was pulled back in a ponytail, giving him a clear view of her pretty face—and the fear that filled her brown eyes when she looked him over. A common occurrence in his presence. Noelle was one of the only females to regard him unflinchingly from day one.

Twitch, twitch.

"Y—yes?" she stuttered.

"Get dressed and leave."

Relief replaced her fear. "Certainly."

Amid Devyn's protests, she tugged a black and white dress over her head. As the material fell into place, it conformed to her curves. She slid her feet into too-high heels, and they clicked and clacked as she hurried out of the apartment.

"Now, then." Hector pressed a few buttons on his

reader, sending the contents to both Dallas and Devyn's systems, and fell into the chair across from them. He told them what he'd learned about Bobby Marks's wife, the explosive dinner with the mother, and they decided to hunt Brenda Marks down after checking in at the AIR office in an hour.

Every reply from Dallas was harder and harsher than necessary.

"So . . . you want to tell me what's wrong with you?" he asked.

"No," Dallas replied tightly.

"He had a vision," Devyn said.

"Hey!" Dallas frowned at him. "When I tell you something's a secret, and you tell me that secret is locked in the vault, you aren't supposed to blab about it."

Devyn blew him a kiss. "How was I supposed to know Hector would have the key to my vault?"

"Yeah?" Dallas grumbled. "And what's the key?"

"Your happiness. God knows, nothing I've done has helped your pissy mood. So maybe, just maybe, talking about it with the other man involved will."

Motions jerky, Dallas grabbed one of the coffees and drank deeply. "Fine, whatever, but you tell him. I can't discuss it without vomiting blood."

Dread poured through Hector's veins. What the hell was going on?

"Dallas had an unchangeable vision," Devyn said, meeting Hector's gaze with steady determination. "He saw himself in bed with Noelle."

"What!" Hector exploded, on his feet, a pyre-gun palmed and aimed before he realized he'd moved. He knew all about Dallas's visions. Knew they were never wrong. Knew that predicting the future was one of his many half-alien abilities. Damn that ability!

A narrowed-eyed Devyn said, "Sit down. Now," in a cold and deadly voice.

Deadly, but at the moment Hector was a predator without any type of moral compass. *No one* was more lethal.

"Don't make me ask twice."

As if he'd asked the first time. The Targon would kill to protect his "bestie." And as he could control energy molecules with his mind, manipulating human bodies as if they were nothing more than puppets, he attempted to lower Hector's arm.

Hector felt mental fingers clamping around his wrist, pushing, and resisted until both men realized the depths of his strength. He even let his skin atomize just enough to glow above the edge of his gloves and heat. "That's right. You can't force me to do anything I don't want to do."

Devyn hissed, as if he'd felt the heat of Hector's skin even through the mental connection.

When Hector sat and sheathed his weapon, he did it under his own steam. He only had trouble forcing his arms to cool. Dallas. Noclle. In bed. Together.

He'd known it was a possibility, had even considered them a perfect match a few minutes ago, but this . . . fuck no!

Red glittered over his line of vision, and he once again curled his finger around his gun.

"—listening to me?" Devyn asked, exasperated.

"Fuck!" he snarled, throwing out the curse like a weapon. "Fuck. Fuck. Fuck."

"Told you he'd react that way," Dallas said, falling back against the couch and staring up at the ceiling.

"Well, he should have kept listening to me and we could have avoided the tantrum," Devyn said after tsking under his tongue. "Dallas also had a vision of *you* sleeping with her, Hector. And I gotta tell you, that shocked the piss right out of me. I thought you were gay."

"Fu—wait. What?" The red dissipated with a single blink.

"Oh, now I have your attention."

Hector. Noelle. In bed. Together. Again? "Did I have sex with her?" he asked Dallas in a rush. "Did I harm her?"

Dallas gulped. "You woke up next to her, and both of you were naked. No, she wasn't harmed."

Shock blasted him, realization quick on its heels. In the vision, Hector had slept with her, *next* to her and naked, and he hadn't hurt her. A miracle. His heart drummed against his chest with stinging precision.

He could have her, all of her. *Would* have her. Dallas was never wrong. Praise that ability!

"The problem is," Devyn went on. "Only one of the visions will come true."

"That's not a problem. I want her. She's mine." Words he'd never thought to utter, but now that he had, he meant them. She. Was. His. If he could have her without hurting her, he would have her. Period. No one would be able to stop him. Not even Noelle.

Shit. He had some serious backtracking to do with her. Probably some groveling, too. She'd demand an apology for his lack of contact. He'd give it—and anything else she wanted.

"Lost you again." Devyn sighed. "Let me finish before you start unzipping your mental pants, all right? If one vision comes true, Dallas will be saved. If the other vision comes true, Dallas will be ruined. I don't want my Dallas ruined," the Targon ended with toxic force.

Hector's excited burst of possessiveness drained, leaving an empty shell in its wake. "I don't understand. Save him from what? Ruin him how? Which vision will cause which?"

Despondent, Dallas toyed with the lid on the coffee. "I don't know. I had the visions a while ago, but I didn't know what the double thing meant until Kyrin explained it to me yesterday. I wish we could both avoid her, or both have her, but apparently, no matter what, one or the other is going to happen."

"Not necessarily. I could kill her," Devyn suggested.

Hector jumped back to his feet, the pyre-gun extended, his finger resting on the trigger. "You will not go near her."

The Targon's lips stretched into a languid smile. "How adorable. You actually sound like you believe you can stop me."

"Oh, I can stop you. I can destroy everything you hold dear." Hector had killed in cold blood before. Not since he was a child, fighting his way out of the slums. But for Noelle, to keep her safe, he *would* kill again. And again.

One side of Devyn's upper lip lifted over his teeth in a scowl that would have scared a ravenous grizzly. "I dare you to try."

"No one's going to kill her." Dallas waved his hand through the air, the kill-or-be-killed vibe dissipating. "Okay? All right?"

"All I was saying was that accidents happen." Devyn spread his arms innocently. "And for that, everyone nearly snaps my head off."

Tendrils of smoke rose from the seams of Hector's gloves, making him cough. He gritted his teeth and sheathed the gun before he could melt it.

Dallas reached behind his back and withdrew something black and floppy and tossed it Hector's way. "New pair of mitts. Knew you'd need them."

Hector caught them and exchanged the old for the new. "Thanks."

"So that's why you asked me to bring them," Devyn said with a nod. "I thought you were getting kinky on me."

"You wish."

"No, Bride wishes. She actually asked me why you didn't kiss me at my wedding like Noelle kissed Ava at hers."

Now was not the time to recall that tantalizing meeting of female mouths and tongues and—

Hector gripped his thighs, and even though he felt the burn all the way to the bone, he knew his legs wouldn't bear so much as a streak of pink. If only the same were true for Noelle. "So what are we going to do about Noelle?"

He didn't want his friend hurt. Ever. For any reason. And he especially didn't want to *be* the reason.

His fantasy of being with Noelle, totally and completely, began to wither and die as quickly as it had formed.

"I don't know," Dallas said, despondent again. "I know you want her. I want her, too, but I can share, and I can walk away. No problem. You can't. However, I keep thinking, what if sleeping with her is what will save me?"

*Eyesight . . . going red again.* "And what if sleeping with her ruins you?"

A lengthy pause, a heavy sigh. "Yeah, that's always my second thought."

"For the time being, why don't both of you stay away from her?" Devyn suggested. "In the meantime, Dallas might have another vision and that vision might provide the answers you need."

"We can try and avoid her," Dallas said with a hint of anger this time, "but it won't do us any good. One of us will be with her when the time is right." He glanced at Devyn, frowned. "Talking about it didn't help. We have to change the subject."

Good. Talking about it wasn't helping Hector, either. He felt raw, brutalized, unsure. Capable of any dark deed. He desired Noelle, but he also loved Dallas.

Yeah, he thought, he did indeed love the guy. He joked around with some of the other agents, but Dallas was the only one who knew him and accepted him anyway. *Can't hurt him.*

"I'll have to talk to Mia," Hector croaked out. "Get

her to take Noelle off our case." Noelle would feel rejected, and rightly so. She'd be humiliated. Hate him. Never forgive him for so public a denunciation. Sickness spilled straight into his stomach.

"Thanks, man," Dallas said in an equally abrasive voice.

"Speaking of the case, is that why you emailed me the morning news?" Devyn asked him, studying the screen of the device he'd just pulled out of his pocket. "Ah. I see." A rich chuckle. "Motherhood certainly agrees with Miss Tremain, doesn't it?"

His own device had fallen to the floor when he'd stood, he realized. Hector didn't dare reach for it, too afraid he'd melt the plastic, so he leaned over and drank in the image he'd left on the screen. Noelle in black and white, a grainy photo but lovely nonetheless. She stood beside Corban Blue, and the bastard had his arm wrapped around her waist.

Both were dressed formally, Noelle in a short, tight dress that managed to glitter, even from the tiny screen, and Corban in a tux. He was tall, leanly muscled, his white hair slicked back from his face. He was almost pretty. Fine, no almost about it. He totally was.

Was that the kind of guy Noelle usually went for? If so, Dallas was more than a better fit for her; he was her type. And Hector couldn't forget that she'd once called dibs on him. Even though only last night she'd claimed never to have wanted him.

*Red returning . . . sickness spreading . . .* Hector inhaled slowly, held, held, exhaled even more slowly.

*Can't have her.* He needed to get used to that. He had before, and he would again.

Yet still the questions formed. When had the photo been taken? How long had Noelle known the guy? Did they still talk?

The urge to murder the football star suddenly bombarded him. Hector never should have claimed Noelle as his. His mind and body weren't going to let him forget as easily as before, were both forging full speed ahead as if her seduction was still an option.

The story speculated about the very things Hector had. Were the two on or off? How far along was her pregnancy? Was she having a boy or a girl? How had Corban reacted to the news? There were a few smaller photos of Corban—each with a different woman. How were those women taking the reports of his impending fatherhood?

A hard knock echoed through the room.

Dallas glanced at the monitor resting on the table beside the couch and jerked upright. The bronze of his skin leached of color, every negative emotion he'd projected returning to his gaze in a frenzied flood.

"What?" Hector demanded, already reaching for his gun. He sensed a threat, a big one, and reacted accordingly.

"Noelle," the agent said, his voice as dead as the grave. "She's here."

# Twenty-five

❦

**N**OELLE STROLLED INTO DALLAS'S apartment as if she owned it. In a way, she did. The building belonged to her family. Hell, half the buildings in the city belonged to her family. A reason to gloat, sure, but she never cracked a smile.

She was in too volatile a mood.

When Hector hadn't called or swung by to pick her up, as she thought she remembered him promising to do before he left her place last night, she'd assumed they were supposed to meet at AIR. So, after dressing in a tantalizing ensemble sure to entice him, off she'd gone, arriving bright and early and eager to see the man who'd given her such a glorious orgasm. Only to wait. And wait.

He was a good agent, and an even stronger, more dangerous man, so when he failed to show there, she hadn't worried for his health. She'd simply assumed his own mind-blowing orgasm had made him lazy and he'd slept in.

Hoping to wake him, she phoned him—no answer.

No big deal, though. He'd probably turned off his ringer. She'd driven to his home, a middle-class house in the center of suburban paradise. She'd looked forward to seeing him surrounded by his things, getting a tour of the place. Maybe kissing each other hello. But he hadn't answered the door.

At that point, she'd begun to fume. Where was he? What was he doing?

She'd broken in.

His furniture was plain but well cared for, his bedroom neat and tidy. There'd been no personal touches anywhere, and that had surprised her. He really did keep himself distanced from everyone.

Last night he'd made an exception for her, but he must have changed his mind, because clearly he'd ditched her like yesterday's news. His badge, gone. His pyre, gone. Which meant they were with him. Which meant, he was on the job. Without Noelle.

Mia Snow was a smart woman, had known Bobby's identity before Hector and Noelle ever made it to the scene. After all, one of the cops would have IDed him before calling AIR. Dealing with the rich was often difficult, and Noelle could help in ways Hector hadn't realized. Yet he'd rather go it alone than deal with her.

Well, he would soon learn that wasn't even a possibility.

She'd headed back to AIR to hack into the GPS database and find his location, planning to show up and knock the shit out of him. Along the way, the PI she'd hired to document Cherry Picking Barry's every move for the rest of his unnatural life had emailed her a string of photos.

Hector had stopped by Barry's office. Hector had beaten the ever-loving hell out of him.

Hector had somewhat redeemed himself.

However, white knight or not, the beating hadn't earned him a free pass. He had a lot to answer for. Now, however, she'd use words rather than steel-toed boots.

Dallas, Hector, and hello, gorgeous Devyn Targon were on their feet, watching her with differing amounts of astonishment as she sailed inside the living room. Dallas was wearing a wrinkled T-shirt and jeans, his dark hair in complete disarray around his model-perfect face.

The sight of Devyn, warrior king of the Targons, had her sighing dreamily. As always, he was a walking fantasy. His hair was dark and glossy, while his skin possessed the radiant sheen of crushed diamonds. And his eyes, oh, his eyes were the color of the richest, most decadent brandy.

He wasn't ignorant of his appeal. He'd be the first to tell you exactly how magnificent he was. Actually, no. Not true. Anything female would be the first to tell you. He'd be a close second.

He wore a pinstriped suit tailored specifically for his spectacular body, not a wrinkle or flaw in sight. His silky brown hair was styled away from his face, ensuring his amber eyes were perfectly framed, and his crushed diamond skin on full display.

At one time, he would have made her mouth water.

Same with Dallas. Over the last year, she'd developed an obsession for raw intensity.

Finally, her gaze moved to Hector. His hair looked even longer today, a glossy jet, with the occasional strand of flax. He wore a black T-shirt, black slacks, and both paid his bad-boy muscles the proper homage. His dark brows were drawn low, his golden eyes narrowed. Thick lashes fused together and cast spiky shadows over cheeks flushed with growing . . . anger? Probably.

*Fuck you, Hector.* Back to his pissy, distant self, regretting what they'd done. Whatever. He'd made his bed, and now he could lie in it. Alone.

"Morning, boys. I'm happy to see you, too. Oh, goody. Coffee." She grabbed the cup resting on the table and sipped. Grimaced. "Gross! What is this crap? Because it's definitely *not* coffee."

"We took turns peeing in the cup," Hector snapped.

Non-deserved hostility was always a party in a box. "Well, your piss needs cream and sugar." Wishing she had a shot of bleach for her mouth, she placed the cup back on the table.

"Too good to drink what the rest of us drink?" Dallas muttered. A night apart hadn't improved his mood, either. Wonderful.

"Yes, actually, I am." Her taste buds were not snotty; they just knew the difference between good and nasty as hell.

Hector shoved his gloved hands in his pockets. "What are you doing here?"

"Now, now. Is that any way to talk to your *partner*?"

He blanched.

That's when she knew beyond any doubt that he wanted to do this without her, despite the passion they'd shared. Hurt bloomed. Rather than give in to it, she raised her chin. "Dallas offered to take me to sexual heaven, and since I wasn't busy, I decided to let him."

"Sexual . . . heaven . . ." Hector nearly popped a vessel in his forehead. His gaze swept over her body. The deep V of her thin white top, with a silver chain hanging seductively between her breasts, the tightness of her black leather pants.

Dallas gulped, paled.

Devyn had already lost interest in her and was playing some kind of game on his phone.

"He tell you boys the same thing and you're expecting all kinds of pleasure? Should we just get in line?" she asked, then strode to the couch, about to scoot herself between the two very hard D's. That way, she'd have a straight-shot view of Hector's face. And his emotions. "Or am I interrupting some kind of male bonding ritual?"

"Don't sit there!" Hector shouted.

She froze, her pulse points even skittering to a stop. He hadn't sounded angry or even jealous; he'd sounded frightened. "Uh, okay." Unsure, she straightened. "Why?"

He ignored the question and pointed to the chair adjacent to him. Miles from the D's, it seemed. "Sit there."

After the way he'd treated her, she should flip him off and throw herself across Dallas and Devyn's laps.

Only Hector's terror stopped her. That terror struck her and spread quickly. With forced casualness, she ambled to the chair he'd "reserved" for her and flopped down.

She peered over at him. He watched her as intensely as when he'd had his face between her legs, trying to judge her reaction. Heat slithered across her skin, and her belly quivered.

*Don't think about that magic tongue of his.* She'd only want more from him. Want everything. Like sex in the shower to ease his fears about burning her. Not that she'd been thinking of ways to do that all fucking night.

He'd made his intentions clear. Romantically, they were done. He'd opted to let his fears rule him and that was fine. *Whatever,* she told herself again. She refused to beg for every scrap of his attention and affection.

"You're going to learn to include me," she told him. "This is my job, too, and there's nothing you can do to get rid of me." *Try again, and I'll gut you.*

A play of emotions in those beautiful golden eyes. An increase of terror, a blend of relief, joy, even shame. "It'd be better if we worked separately."

*No mercy.* "That's not happening," she said, as soft as she was able. "So let me help you kick things off. Why don't you tell me what you found at Bobby's house?"

One of his hands emerged to tug at his shirt collar. "How'd you know I was there?"

"I know all kinds of things."

Several heartbeats of silence. "Did you know he was married?"

She frowned. "No. He was married?"

An abrupt nod.

"You're sure?" Bobby had never hinted about being part of a committed relationship. Although his lack of dating might have been hint enough.

Another nod from Hector. He glanced at Dallas before pinning her with a resolved stare. "Wife was there, hiding. I picked up a handheld from his office, talked to her. She seemed genuinely upset by his death, genuinely surprised."

"Genuine can be faked, I promise you." Her implication: just like I faked it last night.

He popped his jaw, shrugged as if he didn't care what she'd done. "Her name is Margarete. She's Rakan, and I don't know how they met. I—"

"Wait, wait, wait," Devyn said, suddenly interested in the conversation. "You told us the wife was an otherworlder, not that she was a Rakan."

Hector splayed his arms. "So?"

"So you're an idiot. Rakans are rare."

"I know that."

"Did you know that slavers everywhere have a jones for the gold, and that's the only way your Marks could have gotten her? Believe me, I once looked for one myself. For *years*. Their planet was in ruins, and the remaining people scattered—but not here. Marks bought her, I promise you."

"Slavers?" Noelle asked. Buying and selling *people*. She knew it happened, but wow, not so close to home.

Devyn pursed his lips. "Oh, yes. There's a bona fide sex market, auction houses, you name it, it's out there. I used to attend those kinds of events and frequent those places myself, so I know what I'm talking about."

"You really think Bobby bought her?" Hector asked, looking past the living room, into a place Noelle couldn't see.

"Actually, I'm sure of it," Devyn said, and he did sound confident. "I wouldn't be surprised if whoever did the selling wants her back the moment he learns of Marks's murder, if he didn't do the murdering himself. That's what I would have done, if I were rotten to the core, that is, but my evil is only skin-deep. I would have sold her, then killed to get her back. She'd make a damn fine profit, over and over again. You'd be smart to put a detail on her at all times."

An idea tumbled through Noelle's mind. Sex market. A rare Rakan. *Blow the lid off* . . .

She sat up straighter. All the women she'd seen in those photos had been pretty. Taken from their homes. Held captive. No ransom had been demanded. They hadn't been beaten. Starved, yes, but that could have been because the skinny ones fetched a better price. Who knew?

Maybe nothing had been done to them yet because they hadn't been sold. Maybe they were to have gone to a single buyer rather than seeing to hundreds in a single day. Slavery had to be a big business. Skeevy, disgusting, and to the one doing the selling, worth killing over, as Devyn had said.

They could be way off base, but . . . maybe they weren't. Right now they had no other leads.

"I'll put that detail on the Markses' house, and I've got Margarete injected with our isotope tracker," Hector said, fingers flying over the keyboard on his phone, already texting Mia, she was sure. Probably even checking Margarete's location. "While I was there, I noticed the walls were reinforced metal. Those shields will keep any otherworlders from teleporting inside."

"You still have contacts in the slaver world, Devyn?" Noelle asked.

Hector propped his elbows on his knees, leaning toward Devyn, riveted. He cared about the victims. Truly cared, wanted justice.

She liked that about him.

*You softening, girlie? Look where that got you the last three times.*

*I'm hard as stone!*

"Nope," Devyn said. "About a year ago, a promising up-and-comer went missing. Gerard Hendrick, gone in a puff of smoke. He would have done anything to make a sale, was practically going door to door, then suddenly stopped. I didn't care enough to check up on him. Then, before I started helping AIR out, I killed my last remaining foot in that door to save our very own Eden Black."

Too bad. Would have made things easy.

Hector cleared his throat. "This is adding up to some heavy shit. We need to keep any connection between Marks, Margarete, and the slave market quiet. Not just because we might be wrong, but because we don't want anyone going after our Rakan. Of course, that's moot if the killer is the slaver. He already knows she's there."

"And the detail will catch him trying to grab her." So, in a way, she was like bait.

They spent the next half hour tossing around other

ideas, but nothing else stuck or felt even partially right. Not even the info Noelle kept to herself—for the moment. If Hector wanted to ditch her again, he'd have to fly blind.

Soon conversation began to lag. Then, of course, awkward silence reigned, no one wanting to look in her direction. She was extra, unwanted baggage. Whatever. *I don't care.*

Noelle wasn't letting Hector out of her sight. For the case, of course.

"You better answer this, genius, or I'll kick your ass!" Ava's voice suddenly belted out.

"Ava's here?" Devyn frowned, searching the room for a sign of her.

"You explain it to him," Noelle told Hector. "I need to take this." Without leaving the room, and knowing she was rude as hell, she fit the cell against her ear. "Tremain here, goddess extraordinaire."

"You're pregnant." A flat statement, not a question, and crackling with so much rage Noelle was surprised her mother hadn't already combusted. "With an otherworlder's child, at that. An otherworlder who is also a football player person."

*Football player person* was said with the same disgust one might expect to hear *malignant cancer*. Her mother was the biggest freaking human elitist on this planet or any other. "Mother, how many times do I have to tell you? You can't believe what you read."

A hopeful pause. "You're not pregnant?" What her mother didn't say but implied: *Thank God.*

A laugh escaped her. "I do have a bun in the oven,

yes." And it had been glazed with honey and sugar, butter melted over the top. "I'm just not sure who the father is. And, to be honest, I'm in a meeting with three of the other candidates, so can we save this conversation for after the paternity test?"

Another pause, this one heavy, crackling again. "You don't know who the father is? That's disgusting and idiotic, Noelle, even for you. How *dare* you embarrass the family like this! Your brothers are flying home. I've had to cancel my cocktail party. How far along are you? Is it too late to—"

"Thanks, Mom," she said cheerily. "Knew you'd understand." *Click.*

Okay, that had felt good.

All three males were watching her, their moods somehow suddenly lightened.

"That was an interesting one-sided conversation," Hector said, a gleam entering those luscious ocher eyes and chasing away a few of the shadows that constantly seemed to swirl inside.

"Sucks for you that I won't give you a play-by-play." *You don't deserve it.*

"You better answer this, genius, or I'll kick your ass!"

Another call? Groaning, she flashed her middle finger in a bid for one sec of silence. Then she placed the phone to her ear and tuned everyone out. "Tremain here."

"You're pregnant?" Jaxon demanded without preamble.

"Of course not," she said with a roll of her eyes.

"Who's the—oh. What?"

"We just needed the press to keep their rabid hunger for a story away from our case." Bothered her that Jaxon hadn't known that right off the bat. Like her mother and brothers, he still saw her as that flaky little girl, yet he'd spent the past year hovering over her shoulder.

*Well, you still feed that image. Can you blame him?*

Yes! Hector had seen through it. Why couldn't anyone else?

*And I'm still not softening toward him.* "Just don't tell my mother. She'll alert the press en masse."

"All right." Jaxon's chuckle slithered over the line. "You want me to throw fuel on the fire? Maybe have Corban come in?"

"Actually, tell my brothers that Corban refused to marry me, and that they should really let him have it, defend my honor, that kind of thing. That'll keep the vultures happy for quite a while. Oh, and they should let Corban have it in person rather than on the phone so he'll forever understand how he's wronged the Tremain name." Call waiting beeped. Damn it. She was changing her number. "Listen, I've got to go."

"Don't worry. I'll take care of your brothers."

*Click.*

Tune-in. Dallas opened his mouth to say something.

*One sec.* Tune-out. "Tremain," she said into the mouthpiece. Maybe Jaxon wasn't such a bad cousin, after all.

"What's this bullshit about Corban Blue being the father of your fake baby?" Ava demanded.

See? Ava hadn't needed to be told. Ava just knew.

"I thought you were lusting after Hector Dean," her friend went on. "And don't try to deny it, because I noticed the way you eye-raped him at the wedding. Why didn't you pick him?"

"Oh my God, I have missed you and your slappable mouth so much!" Noelle's chest constricted tightly. They'd seen each other just yesterday, texted constantly, but still. "And to answer your question, hardly. He doesn't deserve me."

At that, Hector scowled. Oops. Her tuned-out had failed this go-round. Just to be irritating, she pinky waved at him with her free hand.

Smoke curled from the tops of the gloves. Smoke that did not contain the slightest trace of nicotine. His hands . . . flaring up . . .

*Dangerous,* she thought. To Ava, she said, "Hang on," and got a lot of sputtering in return. "You should probably take a breather, Hector." Hint, hint. "Maybe go outside, cool down."

He gave an abrupt shake of his head. "I'll be fine."

He would know best, but . . . She didn't like this. *Can't question him here and now.* "So have you done the deed yet?" she asked Ava, keeping her eye on Hector.

Silence.

"Hey, you. Tiny tot," she added so that only Ava could hear. She didn't want anyone else calling her friend by that nickname. Then she added more loudly, "I'm talking to you."

"Me?" Ava asked. "It's my turn now for your exalted notice?"

"Yes." Hector had mentioned strong emotion caused the flare-ups, but what had set him off and why? "You're so lucky."

"That's true. So here's the other reason I called. I'm happy to say that forty-three minutes ago, I drank McKell's blood."

"But?" Though panic immediately clawed at Noelle's skull—*losing Ava, officially losing Ava now*—she forced herself to remain outwardly calm.

"But I don't feel any different."

She caught a hint of concern in her friend's voice, something she didn't hear very often. She pushed to her feet. One last, lingering glance at Hector—he was watching her through narrowed lids—and she gave the guys her back.

"Sweetie, it'll happen," she said, striding into the kitchen for a little privacy. If Hector took off without her, fine, she'd deal. She knew where Brenda Marks would be in an hour, and she'd go it alone if necessary. "I promise. And you know I always keep my promises." As she spoke, she looked through Dallas's cabinets. Soup cans sat alongside fallen boxes of cereal. What a sloppy, disorganized man. Soup should be next to bread mixes, and cereal next to bags of chips. Everyone knew that.

"Yeah, but what if it doesn't?" Ava said. "I mean, this is one thing neither of us can control or force. And what if McKell stays young and I start aging, and then I become a wrinkled hagbag of bones?"

When Ava worried, Noelle worried. She twirled a lock of hair around her finger, daggers in her chest, determination in her veins. "Do you want the God's honest truth or a sweet, soothing lie?"

No hesitation. "Give me truth. Hardcore."

"Okay, here it is. You're an idiot."

Ava got her second round of sputtering on.

"Remember when he turned Hellina?" Noelle's *dog*. "He told us hours passed before she experienced even the slightest change. Besides, we're talking about grumpy, possessive McKell. If he could, he'd keep the world's supply of oxygen to himself. Like he'll really let time have you. Time he can manipulate, I might add."

The sputtering slowed, stopped. "You're right."

"Of course I am. I'm always right."

She heard banging in the background.

"McKell's trying to bust into the bathroom," Ava said with what sounded like a shiver of excitement. "I maybe might kinda sorta have told him that his inferior blood wasn't working and stomped off."

Oh, to have video feed of *that*. "Go soothe the savage beast and call me back when you have fangs. I want to make fun of your lisp."

"Done and done. And Noelle? Thanks."

"Anytime, tiger." Noelle returned to the living room and found the guys exactly as she'd left them. Scowling at her. She flopped back into her chair. "So—"

"Who the hell was that?" Hector demanded.

Him and his demands today. At least his arms had stopped smoking. "That was some random guy I once banged asking if I was sure Corban was my baby daddy. Oh, and I almost forgot." Her cell was still in her hand, so she quickly sent all three men the same email attachment. "Check your in boxes. You've now got a copy of Bobby's financials, as well as his daily planner for the last month, as well as his mother's schedule for the month."

Because Hector hadn't left her behind, he had earned a reward. Information.

Stunned silence met her pronouncement.

Hector palmed his phone, fiddled with the buttons. Then he gaped at her. "How did you get these so quickly?"

Was he kidding? "If you aren't cheating, you aren't trying. A few taps of my keyboard, and magic happened."

"So you hacked into his system?" he sputtered, reminding her of Ava.

"And his attorney's and his mother's. You're welcome. Now you don't have to wait for answers."

"AIR can skirt a lot of things, Noelle, but not the paperwork needed to obtain this kind of info from a rich human." Chastising words, but there'd been . . . dare she think it . . . pride in his voice.

"So arrest me." When he made no reply, she added, "Anyway. Guess who inherited everything?" She didn't give anyone a chance to answer. "The mother. Yeah, that means she had motive to pay for Bobby's eternal good-bye, but I'm still not buying it. We do need to talk to her, though, because she was the last person to see Bobby alive. They had dinner last night."

"The wife confirmed that dinner," Hector said, massaging the back of his neck. "He introduced them, and Margarete said she was pissed. But like you, I'm still not buying. She would have been more likely to kill the otherworlder, even with the payoff for her son's demise." He pushed to his feet, and faced the still somber-faced Dallas. "I can't make that call to Mia now. You understand that, right?"

Dallas gave a choked, "Yeah."

"Call me if you . . . envision anything else."

A nod as stiff and reluctant as Hector's had been.

What was going on between them? And what had Hector meant by "envision"?

He breezed over to her. "Up."

Only place she would have let him tell her what to do was in bed. Now? He could suck off! "Ask nicely."

He shrugged as if he didn't care what she did. "Stay behind, then."

Bastard, calling her bluff like that. She was on her feet in an instant, and he nudged her out the living room with his shoulder. His skin was warm, almost too warm, the heat seeping past his clothes and into her skin, but oh, it was delicious.

"Your technique for guiding a lady out of a room needs work," she told him.

"Just move your ass."

"Hector," Devyn called just before they reached the door.

Hector paused, stiffer than before, definitely angrier. "What?"

"Remember what you were told today, and don't do anything stupid. I'd hate to resort to Plan B."

# Twenty-six

NOELLE QUESTIONED HECTOR ABOUT "Plan B" the entire first half of the drive to the restaurant. He did his best to ignore her and succeeded, his thoughts in turmoil. No way in hell could he tell her the Targon's plan involved a disappearing act on her part.

Devyn would do it, too. Off her, without any hesitation. Anything to protect Dallas. Worse, the Targon king knew how to hide bodies. So if Devyn wanted Noelle's death to be a mystery, it would be a mystery. No one would be able to find her or prove Devyn had been involved.

Just the thought made Hector want to vomit.

He should be trying to distance himself from Noelle, but fuck it. She should have worn a bra. Instead, the thin swath of white she called a blouse did nothing to hide the hard outline of her nipples. Nipples that had been pointing at him, practically begging for his attention the entire time they'd been with Dallas.

Attention Hector could have given her without

(much) fear. If Dallas's vision was true, and they always were, Hector could have had her without hurting or killing her. How, he wasn't sure.

And okay, now that a little time had passed, he realized Dallas hadn't provided a timeline for when the sex would supposedly happen. A year from now? Two? Nor had a location been mentioned. His home? Hers? Or some shitty motel while they were on stakeout? Had Hector been drugged out, to keep himself mellow? Or had he and Noelle just fallen asleep on a bed together and never actually made love? Dallas claimed he'd seen them wake up naked together, but he hadn't expounded on the sex itself.

Whatever. Details didn't matter. He couldn't have her, and that was that. Because what if sleeping with Noelle brought about Dallas's ruin? Hector would hate himself. But then again, what if sleeping with Noelle *saved* Dallas?

Shit. No wonder Dallas was such a mess. A man could drive himself crazy trying to figure this kind of thing out, second-guessing himself, all while craving the woman in question.

Yeah, Hector wanted to have her so damn badly he ached. She was too damn gorgeous for her own good. Those leather pants hugged her ballerina legs. Legs he'd had wrapped around his shoulders. And the necklace hanging between her cleavage kept jiggling, drawing his gaze.

Sitting in Dallas's living room, as casually as if they were picking their fantasy football team, while Noelle was within striking distance of Devyn, kissing distance of Dallas, and caressing distance of Hector, had been tough. Now as they meandered down a crowded roadway, her sweet, sexy perfume enveloping him, his mouth watered. His hands itched, burned.

No, even without Dallas's thing, Hector couldn't have her. He just couldn't.

"Do you want to talk about last night?" he asked her, just to break the silence. "Ignoring her" wasn't working for him.

"No." She peered out the passenger-side window, at building after building built to look as if they were composed of chrome and glass. Some were towering, some wide, but all were lit up like Christmas trees in the gloomy haze of the day.

"What about this morning," he persisted, "and why I didn't include you in the investigation?"

"I'm a smart girl. I've already figured it out. You're too dangerous, blah blah blah even though you didn't hurt me."

So dismissive of something that tormented him daily. "I could have."

"But you didn't."

"One wrong move, that's all it takes. I won't risk you," he gritted.

"So you've said, over and over. But let me tell you something." Swinging around, she glared at him. Those eyes were stormy, liquid silver with flashes of lightning. "I've been a nuisance to my family my entire life. The next time you want to do something for my own good, grow a pair and tell me. They at least have never left me in the dark."

He deserved that. And he hated, utterly hated, that he'd treated her the same way he'd seen Jaxon treat her—or worse. As if she were a pest, to be easily swatted away. And suddenly her comment about her dad loving the "idea of" her made sense.

Jaxon wished she were different. Her dad had probably wished she were different, too.

Shame on them, because she was perfect just the way she was. "You have my word."

"Good." She relaxed, but only slightly. "Then what's Plan B?"

"Not my tale to tell."

"Argh! Well, then, tell me more about your arms. Have you seen a doctor, been examined?" She threw the words at him, each one a weapon.

He replied anyway, happy to assuage her curiosity in *some* way. "No. Who could I trust? I'd be put down, and you know it." How weird was this? He'd gone from never talking about what he could do, to telling a vengeful woman whatever she wanted to know.

"Have you tried—"

"Everything. Yes. And even if I were normal, you wouldn't want to date a guy like me, I promise you."

"Thank you *so much* for making my decision for me. Appreciate it. Really."

He cleared his throat, disregarded her sarcasm. "I'm going to tell you stuff about me, okay, and I want you to listen. Don't ask questions and don't look at me." He didn't wait for a response. Didn't wait for her to turn away. He had to do this, had to tell her and finally, officially quash the blaze between them.

"I was born in Whore's Corner, and my parents were, obviously, poor. So, to make money, to support their drug habits, they entered me and my older brother into human cockfights. Before each fight, all the kids were kept in cages for about a week. We were treated like animals. They decided what we ate and when, and it wasn't much and never nourishing. We had to use the bathroom in the cages, on ourselves. That way, we'd be feral when we got out."

He lowered his gaze to the seat. Her fingers were digging into the vinyl.

"We never had to fight each other," he said. "My brother and me, I mean. That was the only thing we refused to do. But then one day, during a fight, my brother was killed. By a kid just like us, sold, used. A girl. They dragged Dean's lifeless body to my cage. Told me that I'd be fighting the girl who'd killed him the very next day. I . . . went crazy. I killed her during the fight, and then I killed my parents. I burned the ring and everyone in it down. There was nothing but ash and the echo of screams when I was done."

His voice cracked there at the end.

And still he wasn't done. "I ran off. Hid. Was found by the authorities. I gave them a new name, Hector Dean, because Dean was my brother's name. I also gave them a fake past, and they put me in the foster care system. For several years, I was so numb inside that my arms never acted up. But then, one day, someone pushed me too far, and I accidentally killed him. I burned the body to ash, just like I'd done to everyone in the ring, so no one would ever know."

He drew in a shuddering breath, gathering more courage. "I tried to be careful after that, tried to keep my emotions under control from then on. And I did, until I met a girl. Kira. I was just a teenager and I wanted her, and she wanted me, so we started hanging out. Things were great at first, I was still careful, but I got a little too excited one night, when we were about to go all the way, and I killed her, too. But I told you that already."

Finally silence, such heavy silence.

"And there you have it. My entire life. Now do you understand a little about why I've pushed you away? Not just because of my arms, but because of *me*."

"Y—yes." Emotion clogged her voice, but he wasn't sure *which* emotion. "I would have wanted you, anyway," she whispered.

Would have, she'd said, and that hurt. Meant she didn't anymore. *Do not cave. More at stake than her life now.* "Now answer a question for me. Who were you talking to on the phone earlier, the one you missed and called sweetie?"

"Ava."

He shouldn't have been relieved—but he was. Stupid on his part. But then, he doubted he'd ever get over this woman. And hell, he'd just ensured she never got under him ever again, either.

# Twenty-seven

T EN MINUTES LATER, NOELLE hadn't stopped shaking. She'd been shaking since Hector had begun his confession. Oh, the pain he had endured.

She ached for the traumatized child he'd been, ached for the strong yet broken man he'd become. But. Yeah, but. He still wasn't willing to try with her, didn't want her *enough*. And that's what everything boiled down to.

The car eased to the side of the road, then stopped altogether and parked at the curb in front of Alfonzo's, a members-only snobfest.

"I can do this, because I can do anything," she whispered, a pep talk for herself as she emerged into cool, damp wind and dodged a honking car that swerved to miss her. Emotionally raw inside, she flipped off the driver.

*Can't think about Hector right now. Have to focus. For Bobby.*

Later, though . . . .

Hector moved in front of her to block the wind. He held the door open for her, rather than allowing the doorman to do his job. What the hell? Push her away, and then act the gentleman?

*Killing me.*

Inside she saw dark velvet draping the walls and flecks of ebony and ivory sparkling in the floor tiles. Small crystal chandeliers hung over every table, the lights dim, a soft tawny, all to promote intimacy.

Multiple perfumes fragranced the air, a clash of designers. Champagne, chocolate—made from real, rare cocoa beans rather than fake—and caviar also joined the scented fray. Noelle's mouth watered, but she soldiered on without stealing a morsel or six from any of the trays carried past her. *Starving!* she thought.

For which she blamed Hector. She hadn't eaten breakfast; she'd been too busy hunting for him, fuming.

As they maneuvered around the tables, conversations ceased, then murmurs of a different nature arose. Noelle wasn't sure if the patrons were now discussing her scandalous pregnancy, or if they were focusing on the huge biker dude in front of her, a man clearly packing an arsenal of weapons on his battlefield body. Maybe both.

She wasn't bothered by the attention they garnered. To her, every person in the room was a version of her mother. Disapproving, superior, and entitled. So, basically, they could all suck it. Her life was her life, and she did not have to explain her choices.

Her gaze landed on a very handsome man at a table all by his lonesome. He was somewhat familiar to her. Must have seen him at a party or something. He had olive-toned skin and dark hair. Pain filled his azure gaze, but he smiled a sinful smile when he realized she was staring at him.

She nodded in acknowledgment.

Hector stopped abruptly, and Noelle rammed into him. His gloved arm stretched backward. For one second, only one, he settled a hand on her hip to steady her. Of course, he then realized he'd broken one of his cardinal rules—contact with another living being— and severed the connection.

Didn't matter. The touch, quick as it'd been, electrified her, the heat of him bypassing her clothing, her skin, just as it had every time before, settling deep in her bones. She shivered at the deliciousness of it. What really got her, though, was the fact that she'd never seen him touch anyone else this casually, even by mistake.

*Can't soften. Have to focus,* she reminded herself.

"What do you think you're doing?" Brenda Marks snapped. "Move along."

Ah, there she was. Noelle stepped around her maybe-partner.

"I'm Agent Dean," Hector said. "And we need to talk to you about your son."

Brenda's back, already ramrod straight, stiffened beneath the thin cut of her I'm-almost-a-businesswoman dress. "He's dead. I know."

Interesting.

"How do you know?" Hector asked. "Did you kill him?"

A flash of too-white teeth. "How dare you accuse me of something like that. I'm in mourning."

Mourning? Really?

"I know because someone from AIR called me," she said with a false sniff, "and told me he'd been shot, then asked me a few questions."

Hardly. No one from AIR would have called her without permission from Hector. "What was his name? The one who called you?"

"Agent Smith."

There was no Agent Smith. Either she was lying, or . . . what? The bad guy had called her and pretended to be an agent?

Hector crossed his arms over his chest. "What did he ask you?"

"Do we have to do this here and now?" Brenda demanded, glancing around the restaurant with embarrassment.

"Yes," Noelle and Hector answered in unison.

"Well, then, if we're playing Q and A, here's one for you. How did you get in here?" Brenda didn't give either of them a chance to reply. "Waiter. Waiter! Escort these . . . people outside."

The waiter merely stood there, shifting from one foot to the other, gulping nervously.

"I'm a member," Noelle said, at last gaining Brenda's full attention. They'd never before interacted, never been introduced, but the old bitch had to know who she was. Everyone did. "Getting in wasn't a problem." Her gaze scanned the other three women seated at the table.

Each female was around the same age: mid fifties, or maybe pushing a hundred and fifty. The number of surgical procedures staring over at her made it hard to tell.

They wore so much jewelry they could have sunk the *Titanic* before it ever hit that iceberg. Not a single lock of hair was out of place, their similar bobs cut and sprayed to withstand even tornados and hurricanes. Manicured nails left far too long. Makeup more of a mask than an accessory.

Oh, yes. They were definitely versions of her mother.

"Beat it before I decide to make examples out of you and carve my name into your faces," she said, adding, "Now!" when they hesitated. And, yes, she flashed her switchblade. Never left home without it.

Two stood so swiftly their chairs skidded behind them. The third remained in her seat, her lips thinned in a mutinous line. "Our food hasn't yet arrived, and I'm not leaving until—"

"She said *now*." Hector tapped two fingers against the handle of the pyre-gun holstered under his arm, and the protestor joined the others. They lined up and marched away, most likely intending to call their husbands. Or attorneys.

Noelle stuffed her blade back in her pocket and claimed one of the vacant chairs, then motioned for Hector to do the same.

"I don't care if they're the law or not. Get rid of these miscreants," Brenda snarled to the waiter. "They offend me."

"Oh, good. Timmy," Noelle said, reading his name-tag. "I'm glad you're here. We'll have the eggs benedict, that plate of salmon, like the one over there, a bowl of lobster bisque, and some grapes. Do you have grapes today?"

"Yes, Miss Tremain."

"Excellent. And put a rush on my order." She rubbed at her (very flat) stomach. "The baby's hungry."

"Of course, Miss Tremain." Relieved, he rushed away.

"Waiter," Brenda called.

He ignored her, continuing on.

Noelle propped her elbows on the tabletop. "Perhaps you didn't know, but my family owns this place."

Scowling—or, she would have scowled if her features weren't frozen in a perpetual look of contempt—Brenda tossed her napkin on the table. She patted her too-pretty-to-be-her-natural-color silver bob. Her hazel eyes were more green than brown, her eyebrows thin and shaped into the perfect arch. "I'll leave, then."

As she made to rise, Noelle whipped out an arm and grabbed hold of her wrist, jerking her back down, unconcerned by any brittleness she might have in her bones. Or, you know, initiating contact with one of the undead. "You'll stay there, or I'll do more than carve my name in your face. I'll bend you over the table and carve it in your fucking ass," she said in a sweet tone of voice. She even smiled. "This is a murder investigation, and you *will* help us."

Plastic-looking skin became chalk white. But when Brenda spoke, her voice was strong, dripping with vinegar. "Do you talk to your own mother with that filthy mouth?"

"Don't be ridiculous. My mouth is a *lot* filthier when I talk to her."

Hector's lips quirked at the corners, his dimples revealed one moment, gone the next.

Noelle's heart skipped a beat. *Have to stop noticing things like that.*

With her free hand, Brenda grabbed her napkin and slammed the material back into her lap. "Fine." Fury must have been smoldering inside her, because her frail body vibrated like a volcano ready to erupt. "But this is the last time I shall *ever* visit this establishment."

"Oh, no. Hector, do you have a tissue to mop up my tears?" Noelle released the woman and reclined in her seat.

Chin lifting, Brenda snapped, "Your mother *will* hear about this."

"Please don't forget to tell her I dropped the F-bomb, abused my family's good name, and—I know this hasn't happened yet, but it will—danced on the tables. I can have Timmy write everything down if you think you'll forget."

"You're as reprehensible as I've heard."

Hector spoke up for the first time since sitting down. "Talk about her like that again, and I'll haul your ass into lockup on so many charges your attorney will be filing motions to dismiss for a year."

Noelle's eyes widened. He'd just defended her. Hardass Hector who let nothing and no one bother him had just defended her.

Damn it, he was giving her whiplash with his personality changes.

"Now then," she said after clearing her throat. "What did Agent Smith ask you? And what were your answers?"

"Shouldn't you know that already?" Brenda huffed.

"Enough lip. Talk."

A beat of silence, a shake of her silver head. "He asked if Bobby had mentioned what he'd been working on lately. I said no. He asked if Bobby was dating anyone. I said yes, a filthy piece of gold-digging trash. He asked if I knew where the girl was. I said yes, Bobby's home, since they were living together. And that was it, the entire conversation."

Details they'd already possessed, but now the murderer knew them, too. And Noelle was now confident the caller was the murderer, and edging toward confident that the sex ring was at the center of everything.

"You had dinner with Bobby the night of his murder," Hector stated. "What did the two of you discuss? Besides your new daughter-in-law."

"She is *not* my daughter-in-law." Brenda lifted her wineglass, sipped. "But if you must know . . ."

"I must."

"Nothing. First thing he did was introduce me to the girl, as if I would support his choice. As if I would accept her, an *alien*."

Prejudiced bitch. Though Noelle had spent some time with Bobby, she'd had no idea his family-life was as harsh and unforgiving as hers. She could just imagine what the old bat had put Bobby through in his too-short life. The negative comments, the conditional love. If there had been any love at all.

Perhaps their mothers had been separated at birth.

"Did Bobby mention where he met Margarete?" Hector asked.

"No." An uncaring shrug. "But then, I didn't care to know. I told him to marry that sweet Kerry Jones and finally give me a grandchild. He declined."

"A travesty. I'm sure you would have been as maternal a grandmother as you were a mother," Noelle said dryly.

"Yes," Brenda said, deadpan, clearly unused to sarcasm.

"Did you hate your son?" Maybe she was asking for the case, or maybe she was asking because Brenda's answer would mirror her own mother's, and she was curious.

Another shrug. "I hated what he was doing with his life."

Expected, but still disappointing. "Enough to kill him?"

"At times." Brenda finished off her wine. "Does my answer surprise you? Well, it shouldn't. He was an embarrassment, Miss Tremain, and he did the things he did just to strike at me."

Yeah. That was why.

"Her name is Agent Tremain," Hector snapped.

*I won't look at him. I won't be thrilled about his ferocity.*

Brenda paid him no heed. "I'm sure your own mother understands my predicament."

"Bobby was in love with an otherworlder, Miz Marks. He wasn't a murderer or a drug addict or a child molester." She purposely omitted the part about his as yet unproven participation in otherworlder slavery. "What did you have to be embarrassed about?"

Haughty chin lifted, Brenda said, "A child is a reflection of his parents. So what did I have to be embarrassed about? Everything. But *did* I kill him? No. He cut me a check every month, paid my bills, whatever they happened to be. If I were capable of murder, I would have gotten rid of the alien." As she spoke, a vein pulsed in her forehead.

*Bitch* was too kind a word for her.

"Now you have access to his entire fortune," Hector said. "He left everything to you."

A cruel smile flashed, the edges dripping with relish. "I know. And do you know the first thing I plan to do when his home is signed over to me? Take out the trash."

The direction of Noelle's thoughts changed. From forcing herself not to ponder Hector's appeal to forcing herself not to kill the woman in front of her. "Speaking of the house, what time did you leave the night of your dinner?"

"I don't know. Nine, maybe."

"And your home is within walking distance of Bobby's?" Hector asked.

"Yes. But I didn't walk, I drove."

Afraid of the dark? Or of the thousands of people who would have loved to gut her and leave her bleeding on a sidewalk? Either way, Noelle knew Hector planned to check the security feed from the neighborhood and see if the timelines added up.

The waiter arrived with the tray of food Noelle had ordered, but before he could place a single plate on the table, she said, "Box it up for us, Timmy, and have it carried to our car." No way she could spend another second with her mother's doppelganger. Their questions had been answered. Time to bail.

"Of course, Miss Tremain."

"Oh, and add a couple slices of cheesecake to the order before putting everything on Mrs. Marks's bill."

"Of course, Miss Tremain."

Brenda hissed, tried to protest, but Timmy had already hurried off, the delicious-smelling goodies disappearing with him.

Noelle's stomach rumbled as she pushed to her feet. Hector stood as well, and she moved to his side. Her four-inch heels made her taller than ever, but still he towered over her.

"Thanks for everything," she said. One little slice across the woman's throat wouldn't be so bad, would it? "We really appreciate the conversation and the meal."

The old bat was still floundering to form a protest as Noelle and Hector stalked away.

# Twenty-eight

*H*ECTOR HUNG UP THE phone and forked another bite of smoked salmon into his mouth. He chewed, all the while watching Noelle. Trying to pretend he wasn't aroused by her, that he wasn't remembering every detail he'd confessed about his past.

His desk created a barrier between them, the food she'd ordered stacked on top of his files, equipment, weapon case, weapon cleaning case, and spread out like a picnic.

"Who was that?" she asked. She looked around, clearly trying to decide what to pick, finally settled on the dessert, and lifted its box and a fork. She snuggled back in her chair, crossing her legs and revealing her shoes.

And hell, they were bondage lingerie for her feet. Open toed, with diamonds encrusted on the strap around her ankles. Her hair was unbound, flowing down her shoulders, and just a bit mussed.

That white blouse she wore V'd so deeply he was always surprised she didn't flash him when she moved.

He'd had her lithe body under him, had sucked on her pert little nipples.

"Hector," she prompted. "My breasts adore the attention, but if you don't stop staring, my ass will have to file a complaint. It deserves notice, too, you know."

A flippant tone, but he detected a note of sadness. His gaze snapped up to her face as his cheeks heated. *Can't have her. You fucking can't have her.* But oh, the things she said. Her mouth aroused him as much as her body.

Her mouth . . . which she'd once wrapped around his cock . . .

Shit. He buckled down and concentrated on the case before his arms started acting up. "That was Mia. A few new developments. First, the pin you mentioned before, the one that wipes footprints. They found it."

Triumph bathed her features, making her glow. "God, I'm smart."

His chest constricted. "Second, the witness is now detoxed and has been questioned. He says he never saw the Arcadian's face, that the otherworlder always had his back to him, but he helped with a sketch of the shooter and the guy who handed him the gun. Those are being emailed to us right now, as well as being run through the database." Every criminal ID was stored there.

Suddenly all business, Noelle whipped out her phone, pressed a few buttons, and frowned. "Are you kidding me? The sketch of the shooter is a cartoon superhero."

Hector pulled up the sketches on his computer screen. Shooter had blond, wind-blown hair, his face blurred out. And he wore a suit so embellished with muscle ridges and color, the witness had to have been smoking crack when he—

Yeah. Okay. He *had* been.

The second sketch showed a hard, harsh face. Dirty, grungy. Dark hair, high forehead. Narrow eyes. Nose with a bump in the center. Wide cheekbones, a square chin. The kind of face kids probably saw in their nightmares.

This one was usable, at least.

"Seems surreal, having evidence finally fall into our hands," Noelle said. "Should we give the non-cartoon sketch to the media? Someone might recognize him."

"I'd rather wait. I'm too afraid Shooter will cut and run. And if he runs, we won't find him. He's managed to hide this long without even trying. He puts any real effort into it, and our case is cold."

"You're thinking like a poor man. If Shooter is rich and powerful, and judging by those gold coin buttons on his superhero suit, I'd say he is, he won't want to start over. He's killed to protect his empire, or whatever it is, and he'll kill again rather than leave."

Hector didn't take offense to her "poor man" comment. To her, he *was* poor. And she was right. "If Shooter is willing to kill again, he might just kill Bruiser the moment the sketch goes live to keep us from finding and questioning him."

"True." A moment passed as she pondered their options, her face scrunching adorably. "What about leaking word that we've got the witness? We can use him as bait as we talked about with Dallas and catch whoever comes for him red-handed."

"I still think that should be our last resort. Shooter won't go for the kill himself. He'll send his Arcadian or Bruiser, and I'd rather not go against the Arcadian just yet. Not until we've got precautions in place to counteract any ability he might have. Good news is, we're close. That handheld I found at Marks's place? Our tech hacked through the security program and discovered info on the sex ring."

Her eyes widened. "We were right, then."

"Looks like." A flicker of rage, quickly contained. Sex crimes pissed him off. Hector had never been raped, but his will had been disregarded countless times. He knew the total devastation of feeling helplessness, the terror of being trapped in your body as other people hurt you. "Devyn was right. Someone will be after Margarete Marks. The guards watching her said there haven't been any disturbances yet, but Mia's adding a few more just to be safe."

"You know, this is bad of me to say, but I really hoped Brenda Marks did it. I would have loved to lock her away. But okay, she didn't do it. A flesh peddler did. How has he stayed in the shadows so long? Why hasn't someone talked? Like a resentful wife who's been cheated on? Or children who walked in on their dad banging the weird chick in chains in the basement?"

"Fear. Bobby was keeping a journal. He bought Margarete for a limited time. Fell in love with her. Time was running out, so he bought her for a little while longer. He never met with the seller directly, everything was online and by phone. But there's no website."

"If there's no website, how'd he learn where and how to buy her?"

"From a friend, but he didn't put the friend's name in his notes. Maybe to protect him."

So that was a dead end. For now. "How was Margarete delivered to him? She wouldn't have willingly walked to his door."

"Marks wrote that a tall guy with more muscles than should be legal delivered her. Again, he didn't mention a name. My guess is he didn't know it, that the guy was there as more than a deliveryman, but to intimidate the buyer into staying quiet."

"Makes sense."

"Also, there's a caveat to every buy. If you want to tell a friend so he can get a female—or male—of his own, you have to get permission. If you tell anyone without permission, or how or where you got your companion, you die. You tell anyone about the transaction, you die."

"So who's disappeared in the wealthier circles, like that up-and-comer Devyn mentioned? As quiet as this entire operation has been kept, there have to be more than two victims."

"I'll do a search."

"Meanwhile, let's deconstruct the night of the murder. No one could teleport into Bobby's house. So someone had to either come to his door," Noelle said after swallowing another bite of cheesecake, "or sneak in. Since there's no sign of a break-in, I'm guessing the door."

"I'm with you." Wrong words, he instantly realized. He gulped, trying to swallow back his sudden rise of renewed desire.

Oblivious, she licked her fork like it was a lollipop. Or his cock. At the sight of that gorgeous pink tongue, Hector experienced full-on arousal, no more of that almost/maybe/could be shit—and there was no stopping it. That tongue had given him those same kinds of so-delicious strokes, and he wanted to feel all that wet heat between his legs again. And again.

He shouldn't have messed around with her, he thought darkly. Resisting her had become a whole lot harder. In every way.

Heat sizzled along the veins in his arms, and he set his food aside.

"What's wrong?" she asked, reading his approaching panic before he did.

He shook his head. "Nothing. I'm fine." *Mind, out of gutter.* "So someone comes to Marks's door and, late as it was, Marks had to know him or he wouldn't have answered. The journal doesn't mention an Arcadian, so it had to be Bruiser."

"Maybe the Arcadian was with him, though."

"No, wait. Bruiser was waiting with the shooter, remember? So Bruiser couldn't have been the one to pick Marks up. The Arcadian appeared with Marks, so the Arcadian was the one to go and get him."

"Could this Arcadian be so powerful that he can teleport past Bobby's shields?"

He'd never heard of such a thing, but then, wasn't he living proof that the impossible was always possible? "I'll have our techs look into it."

A knock hammered at the door.

Interruptions were standard; someone had something to ask at least once an hour. Hector didn't bother checking his ID screen. Frowning, he punched the code to allow the intruder inside.

The block slid open, revealing a smoldering Dallas. The agent didn't enter. He took in the intimate scene and stiffened.

*Nothing's happened,* Hector tried to project.

"You've got a visitor," Dallas said. "And you're not going to believe who it is."

His frown deepened. "Who?" He wasn't expecting anyone.

"Not you," Dallas said, motioning to Noelle. "Her."

"Who is it?" she asked, confused.

"Me."

A tall otherworlder Hector recognized but had never met stepped beside Dallas. He was eerily handsome, with pale skin and violet eyes. Strength radiated from his leanly muscled body, an electric pulse seeming to waft from him. An Arcadian. A football star.

Corban Blue.

Noelle might have claimed to like a man in uniform, but there was no way she would scoff at the perfect lines of the perfect pinstriped suit the perfect bastard wore. *I will kill him.*

"If you're here to file a complaint about the rumors," he growled, "you can—"

"I'm not." That violet gaze remained on Noelle, probably memorizing every luscious detail.

"Oh . . . shit," she muttered, sitting up straighter.

Hector's hands curled into fists. Maybe Corban wasn't here to complain, but he wasn't here to thank her, either. One harsh word uttered in Noelle's direction, and Hector would lash out, no matter that he could lose his job. When it came to Noelle's protection, he was finding that there were no lines he wouldn't cross.

"Good to see you again, Elle." There was so much husky promise in the guy's voice, the air practically thickened with sensuality.

"Uh, you, too, Blue."

See her . . . *again*? When had they last gotten together? And who the fuck did the ball player think he was, using a nickname with her? They were broken up. And why the hell was she uncomfortable? Nothing made Noelle uncomfortable.

He opened his mouth to question the Arcadian, but when Corban shouldered Dallas aside to crouch just in front of Noelle, Hector's mouth snapped closed. His questions could wait. Rage blistered through him. He stood, intending to physically force the man to back off. *Mine, she's mine, and I do not share.*

Corban grinned, unconcerned by the animal he'd provoked. "So. I hear we're having twins."

# Twenty-nine

❧

*D*ALLAS PASSED HECTOR A few fingers of scotch before downing his own. They both needed the alcohol. For different reasons, yeah, but need was need.

The pair of them sat in a shadowed corner of Wonderland, Hector's favorite bar. The tables were made of metal, but they were painted to look like tree stumps. Evergreen-scented bubbles sometimes cascaded from the ceiling and floated through the air. Weird music always played in the background, the beat fast and erratic, and when you studied the walls hard enough, you could see little fairies peeping out from lush green bushes. Fairies with fangs, always a nice combo.

"So what do you think she's doing?" he asked, miserable in a way he'd never been. And he'd been pretty damn miserable throughout his entire life!

"Who knows?"

"Well, I can guess." Hector slammed his glass on the tabletop with enough strength to crack the iron. Noelle had left AIR with Corban Blue, oh, about six hours ago. No one had heard from her since.

A soft glow emitted from his bare arms, and the scowl he gave Dallas could have slain an army. "She better not still be with that Arcadian."

"Dude, calm down. I've never seen you act that way."

No one had. Except Noelle. She'd seen every side to him. Harsh, aroused, teasing, cruel. She'd liked him anyway. Until he'd pushed her away that last time. And now that he'd confessed about his past, she wouldn't want him no matter how hard he tried to win her back.

Not that he could try to win her back.

"Usually you're the guy with complete control of his emotions," Dallas said. "Now you're like Dragon Man, able to spew fire and burn an innocent man to ash."

Closer to the truth than he probably realized. Hector pulled gloves out of his back pocket and stuffed his hands inside them, hiding his skin, his tats.

"So have you slept with her yet?" Dallas asked.

His scowl returned. "Came close before you told me about . . . Anyway, there's hardly been the time since, has there? We've been working a case since the moment we left your place. More than that, I haven't forgotten Devyn's threat on her life. And most important, you'll die, remember?"

Dallas's shoulders sagged. "I'm sorry. I really am. I know you want her."

*Want.* Too tame a word for what he felt for Noelle.

"Was she any—"

"Do *not* go there, Dallas," Hector said after tossing back the rest of his scotch.

"You're right. Bad form."

Possessiveness was like a spiked collar around Hector's neck. He wanted to hold the memories of what he'd shared with Noelle close. Especially since there could never be a repeat.

"What about your arms?" Dallas asked. "How'd they react to the stimulation?"

"Poorly. Which is why I ditched her the morning after"—*this* morning, to be exact—"and told her we could never do anything like that again. So I'd ruined things with her even before your little announcement."

*I blew it.* Big time.

*For the best and you know it.*

"I'm sorry," his friend said again.

"Clearly, you're the better man for her." He'd thought that very thing before, but saying it aloud rankled. His throat clogged up with a mix of fiery rage and sorrow.

Dallas heaved a heavy sigh. "No, I'm not the better man for her. She never wanted me, and that's a fact. She even tried to set me up with a friend of hers."

It was stupid how much delight he took in that. "Really?"

"Yeah. Don't get me wrong, I want her, but not as intensely as you do. Besides, I've never had a relationship last more than a few weeks. Being with her might save my life, but it would ruin yours and probably hers."

Yeah, because if Dallas slept with her then tossed her aside, breaking her heart, Hector would probably flip out. Violently.

"I won't touch her," Dallas added. "You have my word. I just . . . I can't hurt you like that."

His head snapped up. "But your vision—"

Electric blues dulled. "If one vision has to happen, it's going to be the one of you and Noelle. Hell, maybe that's the one that will save me."

Or maybe not. Guilt ate at him, but he couldn't deny he experienced a flood of relief. "Thank you. I—"

"Nope. You don't have to go there. We're friends. And I'll take care of Devyn, don't worry. He won't go after her."

"Thank you," he couldn't help but say again. He should let the subject drop at that, but couldn't. "Tell me everything you saw in the vision. Before the waking-up-naked part. Please."

A shrug. "Nothing else to tell. You were naked, she was naked, and you were both asleep. She woke up, sat up, and said, 'Thank God. Not a dream.'"

Disappointment joined the relief. "That's it?"

"Yeah."

So . . . Dallas hadn't seen the act itself. Which meant, there was a chance the act had never even happened. Maybe, as Hector had previously suspected, he and Noelle had merely fallen asleep beside each other.

"Then I still can't be with her." He worked his jaw back and forth. "I can't risk harming her."

Dallas signaled the waitress for another round. A few minutes later, she delivered.

She wore a short skirt that stopped just under the curve of her ass and flared out at her hips like a ballerina's tutu. Her red hair was split down the center and swinging over her ears in pigtails, and there was a heart painted in the center of her lips.

"Anything else?" she asked Dallas with an eagerness

that had nothing to do with the tip she hoped to get. Well, not the cash one.

"How about your phone number?" the agent asked huskily, as if trying to prove to Hector that he wasn't going to pursue Noelle.

She grinned, the heart blooming like the petals of a morning rose. "Already ahead of you, gorgeous. Check your napkin." With a wink, she sauntered away.

"Way to get over your heartbreak," Hector groused.

"I know, right. But if everything goes according to plan, I'll be getting *under* it."

Hector downed one of the shots, emptying the contents in a single gulp.

"Listen," Dallas said. "I've been working with Kyrin, learning how to deal with my own abilities. He says it's all about control. Mind over matter, that kind of thing. Maybe that's all you need to do to keep yourself leveled out when you're with Noelle."

Mind over matter. As if he hadn't tried that. "The danger . . ." A flash of Kira, lying naked in his bed, a hole burned in the center of her chest. "If I were to fail . . ."

"Well, how badly do you want her?"

No need to think it through. "More than I can even say."

Dallas's expression was total *well, there you go.* "Start training. Get yourself hot and bothered and practice touching vegetables or something."

An intriguing—if disturbing—thought. "I will." And that was the God's honest truth. He'd practice. For however long was necessary.

Would Noelle want him, though?

Would she wait for him?

"I did some digging," he said. "She used to date him, you know. More than date him. Live with him."

"Who, the waitress? Who'd she date?"

Another lethal scowl pinned his friend in place. "Will you keep up? *Noelle*. She used to live with Corban Blue. For a year. Twelve goddamn months, and that's all that was documented. So they could have been seeing each other long before they were ever caught by the media. And they could be alone right now. Together. Talking about their baby."

"You mean their babies. Plural. Word is, now she's having twins."

Hector jumped up and pounded the tabletop, ratting glasses, steam rising from the gloves. *Calm down. Now.*

Dallas held up his hands, palms out. "My bad, dude. They're only having the one kid."

"Not his baby. Mine."

"Yeah, yeah. Sure. The imaginary baby is yours. Continue."

He did, just kind of falling back into his chair. "I'm nothing like him." Deep breath in, deep breath out. Gradually the steam dissipated. "I'm not polished, rich, or cuddly. I'll embarrass her, I know I will."

After tossing back two shots of his own, Dallas choked out, "Backtrack a minute. You think Corban Blue is *cuddly*? The guy's lean, true, but he's taller than you are. And I felt the energy kicking off him. *Powerful* energy. Stronger than Kyrin's, even."

There was no telling what kind of abilities Corban possessed. Because, if Kyrin could control humans with his mind, move faster than a determined vampire, and teleport, Corban could certainly do that and a whole lot more.

He'd be the perfect one to test the shields in Bobby Marks's house. If he was still alive in the morning.

"He can touch her without worry," Hector groused. "I think I'm going to break his throwing arm into four pieces. That way, he won't be able to touch her *or* a ball."

Hector couldn't have her—yet—but he wasn't going to let anyone else have her, either, he decided. Whether she still wanted him or not. Whether she would wait for him or not. He'd *make* her wait.

Maybe that was the alcohol talking. Then again, maybe it wasn't. *She's mine.*

Dallas tried to change the subject. "So any luck with the sketches? Any possible matches in the database?"

"She was supposed to have dinner with me tonight," he plowed on, anger morphing into irritation—with her. "But did she call to cancel? No. Is she answering my calls? No. She just stood me up without a fucking apology."

So what that he'd done the same thing to her this morning. So what that he'd told her they were done. She had better manners than he did.

"I did some digging of my own, just like you asked," Dallas continued, "and you'll be highly interested to know—"

"The fact that she just accepted my dismissal without a fight is telling, you know?" *Pound, pound, pound—*

*metal creaking as it bent.* "Does she think I know how to handle this kind of thing? A relationship, intimacy, acceptance, and rejection, all in one day? Well, I don't."

"—that a few months ago, a businessman went missing—"

"Maybe she doesn't want anything from me anymore. Maybe I was a good time, only good enough until someone better came along. Someone more suitable. And now that someone has. Corban Fucking Blue."

"—just up and disappeared, though he left a note behind. Something about taking off to find himself—"

Hector laughed, but it was an ugly sound. "If she's not going to wait for me, I need her to tell me so that I can start with the forcing. Think I'll begin by killing everyone with a penis."

"—but he's never written another letter, never contacted anyone else and there were also several businessmen who committed suicide supposedly, though their families—"

"Fuck this," Hector growled. He drained another shot, and then his beer. "I'm going to her house." He was on his feet a second later, the table teetering, falling with a crash. "We're going to chat. She's always telling me I need to trust her, I need to open up to her. Well, she's getting her wish and she better like it."

After grabbing for the napkin with the redhead's phone number, Dallas joined him. "I'll drive you. Noelle might decide to kick your ass, and after my huge sacrifice, I deserve a little entertainment."

To kick his ass, she'd have to put her hands on him. Hector was totally okay with that.

Dallas laughed. "I wonder if she had any idea what she'd signed up for when she'd picked you."

They strode outside, the cool night air wafting between them. Full parking lot. Vehicles in his damn way. "What does that mean? I'm a fine choice." Never mind that he'd said he wasn't.

"You're like a caged bear. A cage she's somehow opened. Now the bear is on the loose and hungry. If she isn't careful, she's going to be the meal."

*I want her to be the meal.*

"I realize now that you've always kept a part of yourself on a tight leash wrapped in an iron fist," Dallas said. "Noelle has done what no one else has been able and destroyed the leash. Poor girl."

When they reached their car, Hector claimed the driver's side. He punched the coordinates for Noelle's address, and the thing eased itself into motion, out of the parking lot and onto the road. More civilians than usual were out this time of night, and he felt like someone was watching him.

Ten minutes in, he was seventy-five percent sure that someone was following him. He disabled autopilot, a steering wheel rising from the car's front console. Pedals popped up on the floorboard.

"What's doing?" Dallas asked, confused.

"Think we've got a tail."

Yeah, he was quite possibly drunk, but other cars *were* on autopilot and wouldn't hit him no matter where he swerved. He purposely made some wrong turns, doubled back, circled a few other parking lots, and worked his way *behind* the vehicle in question. A dark sedan, windows tinted to black, like a thousand others he'd seen on the streets.

"Phone in the plates," he said.

Dallas made the call as the vehicle sped up, skidded around a minivan, tires squealing. "In pursuit," he said into the speaker, then rattled off his coordinates.

Hector couldn't believe the stupid driver was making him do this. A few seconds later, they were told the vehicle was stolen. Chase on.

They soared around corners as if they were on rails, sped through lights, nearly hit oncoming traffic. Thank God for sensors that did more than differentiate between green and red. All Hector had to do was stay on the sedan's tail until reinforcements found them and caged the bastard. Or managed to nail the hood of the guy's car with a handy little device that would shut off the engine.

Which happened in three minutes flat. AIR swooped in from every direction, until there was no place for the culprit to go. They also pegged the hood, just in case. Hector parked and stormed outside, pyregun already drawn. Dallas did the same, approaching from the other side.

"Open the fucking door," Hector demanded, barrel pointed at the darkened window, his finger on the trigger. Guy had picked the wrong night for this shit. The alcohol had destroyed the rest of Hector's restraint. "And keep your hands in the air."

"Now!" Dallas shouted.

A moment passed, then the metal was lifting and moving out of the way. A squat, fat balding man came into view, skin pasty and dotted with sweat. He had his shaky sausage hands in the air, palms out.

In a trembling voice, he begged, "Don't hurt me, please."

Hector spun him around and pressed him into the car, then patted him down. No weapons. "Where'd you get the car? It's not yours."

"From my ex-wife. She loaned it to me."

"Try again. She reported it stolen."

The guy attempted to lift his head from the metal. "That bitch is—"

A flick of his wrist sent the guy back into position. *Bang.* "Why were you following me?"

A thready pause, beady gaze angling to find Hector's gun. Then, "The story. The pregnant Tremain heiress . . . I saw her with you earlier, and I . . . here, take the cameras, take whatever you want, just don't hurt me."

A fucking reporter. He'd known this would happen if he hung out with Noelle. Even though they weren't together—shit!—his face still might be plastered over the news.

He'd counted on a bone-deep fear to hit him and make him do what needed doing. Instead, he felt numb. Noelle already knew everything about his past. And to be honest, the rest of the world didn't matter anymore. "Well, this just in," he said. "You're under arrest."

# *Thirty*

―――――――◆―――――――

*T*HE NEXT MORNING, HECTOR rooted through the
cabinets in Noelle's kitchen, nursing a killer hangover—and a raging temper he barely had under control. He should go home. His arms were burning and
itching, and steam was already rising from his gloves.

He wasn't going home.

Noelle had stayed out all night. He knew, because
he'd broken into her home. She hadn't answered his
knock. Concern had gotten the better of his drunken
mind—fine, jealousy had—so he'd busted in her door.
Set off her alarm. Disabled her alarm. And waited.

He was still waiting.

Dallas was asleep on the couch.

When the local PD had arrived to check out the
disturbance, he'd flashed his badge and an I'll-murder-
you vibe, so they'd quickly taken off. Noelle should
have been alerted; she should have raced back. Clearly
she needed better security.

And where the hell did she keep her painkillers? A
couple hundred should do the trick, but though ev-

erything from the dishware to the canned food had a place, and a weird one at that—the brownies were next to the peas—he couldn't find a single medicinal bottle.

He paused for a moment, stuck on the food placement. Was there a method to her madness? Like Noelle would eat the brownies, and then feel guilty for her lack of nutrition so she'd go for a vegetable next. Hence, the peas.

*Know her so well, do you?*

Well, yeah, he kinda did. In his almost stalkerish watching of her the past few months, he'd noticed she treated rich people the same way she treated poor people when they reached her tolerance for bullshit. She enjoyed comfort in every form. Clothes, food, as well as her living and work spaces. She wouldn't jog a mile if she could drive it, and she loved pretending the world revolved around her.

Hell, it probably did.

He heard a muted "What the hell?" and stiffened in relief, pleasure, and a renewal of fury.

Finally. Noelle had returned.

She had a shit-ton of explaining to do. "Back here," he called, careful to keep emotion out of his voice. He might scare her away before he'd had the chance to scream at her.

*As if anything would scare that woman.* Except Corban Blue.

Stomping footsteps, mumbled curses. A moment later, she entered the kitchen, pausing to glare over at him. His jaw nearly unhinged. She looked fucking *eatable*. Dark hair brushed to a glossy shine, face scrubbed free of makeup and all the more exquisite for it.

A short, skin-tight black dress molded to each of her curves, shoving those breasts of hers under her chin. Black ribbons wound down her calves, ending in killer five-inch heels.

Heart slamming against his ribs, Hector decided not to ask her where she'd been. Wasn't his place. They'd made no promises to each other. That didn't stop red from dotting his line of vision as he said, "Your security sucks. You had no idea anyone was here."

A flick of her wrist sent her hair flinging over one elegantly bared shoulder. "My system is great. I knew you were here all along."

All along? Hardly. "The PD phone you?"

She propped a fist on her hip. "My system is synced to my phone, so I had your name the second you stepped onto my porch. I figured you had re-wired the door. What I didn't know was that you'd ruined it!"

Wait. Back up. "So you knew I was here, but you didn't come back." Because she'd been in bed with the Arcadian? The red thickened, bleeding into everything he saw.

"Exactly," she said haughtily, unaware that she stood in the crosshairs of peril. "I was busy."

"Were you busy with Corban Blue?" The barely suppressed fury escaped, too big for even his body to contain. *You weren't supposed to ask her about that.* Speculating was bad. Having it confirmed was even worse—like the burning and itching in Hector's arms.

He needed to leave before he inadvertently torched Noelle's house.

"If you must know," she snipped with her chin in the air, "I went to a dinner party."

"For two?" *Stop.*

*Can't.*

"Did the party last all night?" *You* really *have to stop this.* "Did something happen between you and Corban?"

"Why do you care?" Anger sizzled in those liquid silver eyes. "You're too dangerous for me, remember? And I'm too flighty and irresponsible for you. Therefore, if I want to find my pleasure elsewhere, I will."

Oh, hell, no. He managed to grit out, "I never said you were flighty and irresponsible."

"Whatever. You thought it. You're all the same, after all. You think the same, act the same."

"Who, men? Did Corban call you those things?" He braced himself against the counter, suspecting he might need the support. Something was wrong with her. Yesterday, before Corban's arrival, she'd been in a decent mood. Had even teased Hector about staring at her breasts. Now she was easily pricked, defensive and snappy. "You can tell me. Whatever happened, I can help you." *And kill him.*

"Why would you help me?" she said, incredulous. "You and I aren't dating."

Damn it. He hadn't seen her this worked up, since . . . ever. "Stop throwing questions at me, and give it to me straight. What happened last night?"

"None of your goddamn business. How's that for a straight answer?"

"*I want it to be my business!*" The words exploded from him before he could consider the consequences, the thought of her with someone else *destroying* him. "I like you. I admire you. I fucking want you, all the damn time. So let me help you with this, Noelle."

Her breathing picked up and her cheeks flushed, but other than that she gave him no other sign that she cared. "Hector, you like, admire, and want me, as you've told me before, but you don't have any sticking power. We both know this. And I'm not going to be pushed aside again."

"Noelle, listen to—"

"No! *You* listen. I'm done with you, okay? We're done. You and Dallas can show yourselves out." She walked away from him. Not once did she glance back.

He stood there a moment, his anger rising. Thoughts flashed through his mind like bullet points.

He was no good for her.

He hadn't yet tried the mind-over-matter thing.

He'd pushed her away time and time again, and probably would again.

He'd rejected her after they'd pleasured each other.

He hadn't hurt her physically, but he'd hurt her mentally, emotionally.

She hadn't given him any true encouragement since.

He shouldn't have come here, and he shouldn't have asked her about her nocturnal activities.

He shouldn't climb those stairs and enter her bedroom, either. But after making sure Dallas was still okay with Hector bedding her, then getting rid of the guy, then resealing her broken door, that's exactly what he did.

No sticking power? Fuck that. Today he'd be on her like goddamn glue.

Steam drifted from a crack in the bathroom door, and he pushed his way in. There were two stalls, one for enzyme and one for water. Both had clear glass walls. Noelle occupied the one with water—and she was facing him. Sweet mercy.

The sight of her utterly undid him.

He'd drunk water, of course, had even washed his hands in it a few times, but never had he seen the expensive substance splattered over someone's naked body. His cock hardened instantly.

Wet hair was plastered to her neck and shoulders. Water droplets poured over her lush curves, curling around her hard pink nipples, sliding down her flushed skin, then catching in the dark triangle between her legs.

"What are you doing?" she snapped. No hiding behind a towel or her own hands. She stood straight and tall and glorious.

He'd come up here to yell at her, to goad her into yelling at him. Seeing her naked and wet, he lost every thought but one: getting inside her.

Hector whipped his shirt over his head, and she gasped, her gaze falling to his chest, where his pectorals jumped at the thought of her touch. "You want sticking power, I'll give you fucking sticking power. But here's how it's going to work. You do what I say, when I say."

"Just . . . get out of here, Hector." The tremor in her voice sucked any heat from her tone.

"You wanted me before I pushed you away and you want me now. Admit it." He tore off his boots, then unsnapped his pants and shoved the material to the floor, satisfied to note they now rested beside her discarded dress.

The water continued to cascade over her as she glared at him, those eyes silver with fury and arousal. "So? I want you. Big deal. Being with you now won't change anything. You'll still consider yourself too dangerous for me."

Maybe, maybe not. "Not being with you has been torture. The last few days, my arms have been acting up whether we're together or parted. That makes me dangerous to everyone, not just you. Coming calms me down. Maybe coming inside you will calm me down for good."

Hope in her eyes, quickly dashed. "Or maybe it won't."

Dallas's vision might not have shown Hector actually pumping inside Noelle, but it had shown him naked with her. "Well, we're going to find out. So move over, sweetheart. You wanted me, now you're gonna get me."

# Thirty-one

A VERY NAKED, VERY ON edge Hector climbed into the stall, and Noelle could only gape. This was . . . this was . . . a dream, surely. She'd spent one hour with Corban. Just one, and he'd undone years of hard-won confidence.

*Do you think about anything before you act? No, because you're too flighty. How could you drag me into this? Because you're irresponsible.*

After the way he'd smiled at her inside Hector's office, she'd thought he was amused by the whole situation. But just as before, he'd reeled her in *then* struck. Emotionally whipped, she'd wanted only to go home and crawl into bed. On the way, she'd gotten the alert about Hector. Seeing him, wanting him, and being rejected by him for the thousandth time had held no appeal, so she'd done the unthinkable. She'd gone to her mother's to receive a mental shredding she would actually survive.

Fast forward to Hector in her kitchen, looking sexy and savage and acting jealous. As raw as she'd felt, she hadn't wanted to see-saw with him. *I want you, but I can't have you. I want you, but we can't be together*. Crap she just couldn't deal with anymore. So she'd bailed. Shockingly enough, he'd followed her.

Now he was going to *take* her. That thrilled her to her soul, delighted her, excited her, telling her without words that he was in this, willing to risk anything to be with her, but, oh, was he furious that he'd been pushed to his point. That *didn't* thrill her.

His nostrils were flaring with the force of his breathing as he backed her into the cool tile. Golden eyes glittered with menace, making his harsh features predator-rough. So beautiful, her Hector. Bronzed skin, dark little nipples, a washboard stomach. Those tattooed arms, so deadly and strong. A huge cock, pointed straight at her, pre-come already seeping from the tip. His testicles were drawn up tight, his legs thick and corded.

Any thoughts of denying him drained. Despite his fury, he was taking a chance. Did she fear his arms? Yes. Already intense heat wafted from him. Would he end all association if he accidentally harmed her? Yes. But whatever happened, she would deal. They'd been building to this moment for a year. Finally, she would have him. *All* of him.

"Say you want me, damn it," he snarled.

Arousal slid down her spine and pooled between her legs. This forceful side of him electrified her. "I want you, damn it."

His pupils expanded, the air around him becoming charged. "I'll keep my hands behind my back. You will not forget where they are and reach around me. Do you understand?"

"Yes. Now kiss me, Hector, please." She cupped his cheeks, drawing his lips to hers, but he'd already been headed in that direction.

Their mouths slammed together with a desire so potent, she could only groan in surrender. He kissed her as if he was dying, and only she held the cure. His tongue thrust against hers, rolled, then thrust again.

Mindful of his shoulders, she tangled her hands in his hair, loving the silky texture. The water continued to fall, crashing into the porcelain and creating a sultry background music.

With a groan, Hector jerked from the kiss. Panting, he peered around the stall. When he spotted the large bench at the other end, stretching from one side to the other, he backtracked and sat down, his arms still locked behind him. That luscious blue glow rose from them, as seemingly delicate as angel wings. Dimly she noted that the water hadn't cooled him down in the slightest.

His expression was one of pain and pleasure, and she knew he balanced at the razor's edge of each. His erection stretched between his legs, long and thick and wide. "Come here."

Her legs nearly buckled as she obeyed.

"Straddle me, knees at my hips."

"Yes." Again she obeyed. His rock-solid length rubbed against her clitoris, and she moaned at the pleasure.

"Don't put me inside you yet."

A whimper. "Hector."

"Birth control?" he gritted out.

"I'm clean. Can't get pregnant. Annual injection."

He absorbed her spout of information and nodded. "I want to suck your nipples now. Let me have them."

"Yes." Putting her weight on her knees, she lifted until one of her nipples was poised at his mouth. Like a ravenous beast, he feasted on the tiny pink bud. The moment of contact, she cried out. Such an exquisite sensation, the heat of him decadent.

He sucked and he bit and then he licked away the sting, his mouth growing hotter by the second and all the more arousing because of that. With him, she *felt*. His intensity, his warmth, they were so all-consuming her long dead nerve endings woke up and took notice.

"Other one," she gasped out, kneading the plump flesh so desperate for his attention. "Please."

A popping sound echoed as he released the nipple and switched his focus to the other, laving and nibbling. She reached down, wrapped her fingers around his cock, and stroked.

He released a hoarse, broken moan, his breath coming harder, faster. "Don't. Baby, don't. Let go."

*Baby* rather than *sweetheart*, a prayer rather than a curse. He'd done that once before, when their hormones were getting the better of them. *Love that*. Made this particular term more than special. Made it sexual. "But I want—"

"I'll blow, and I want to be inside you when that happens."

His first time, she remembered. As if she could ever

forget. This proud, beautiful man was a virgin, and he was gifting that virginity to her. Reluctantly she pried her fingers loose. She couldn't help but trace a fingertip up the shaft, then swirl around the slit, capturing his taste and bringing it to her mouth, sucking as she would a favorite lollipop.

Her eyes closed and she gave another moan. "So good."

A growl. "You are going to be the death of me."

*I want to be the* life *of you*, she thought, astounding herself. She wanted more than a sexual relationship with him. She wanted everything he had to give. Now . . . and for a long time to come.

"Finger yourself, baby. Pretend its me doing you right."

Her eyelids cracked open to half-mast, and she watched his face as she glided her finger between her breasts, down her stomach, stopping to dabble at her navel, then swirl at her pubic bone.

"Now," he commanded on a rough, ragged breath.

His eyes were fever bright, his cheeks flushed. His lips were swollen, red from sucking her so forcefully. Knowing he was tortured, she at last slid a finger deep inside herself. Warm wet walls closed around her, and she arched her back to go even deeper.

"Yes," he hissed. "Fuck yes. That's the way."

That azure glow intensified, but she was too lost in the pleasure to care. In and out, in and out, the palm of her hand rubbing at her clit.

"Add another finger."

She added a second, stretching herself.

"God, baby. You're so beautiful. Nipples puffed up and pink, belly quivering with desire. I want to be in you so bad."

"Yes. Please."

"Need to see you come first. Add another finger."

The third was a tight fit, but she did it, grinding down on herself. The air surrounding her was slick with moisture, a caress against her skin. Up, down, in and out, the pressure building. Her nipples rasped against his chest in that way she adored, the friction cranking her higher . . . higher . . .

Higher still . . .

Until she erupted, crying out with the force of her release. Her inner walls clutched at her fingers, but she kept pumping, riding the waves crashing through her. And yet, even with the climax, she wasn't quite satisfied. Her arousal remained, a sickness in her blood, driving her, making her ache.

"Goddamn, you're hot."

"Want you, Hector."

"Put me in you," he demanded.

Yes, yes, that's what she needed. Hector. Deep, so deep. She slid her fingers free and once again wrapped them around Hector's cock. The tip found her drenched entrance, but she didn't press down. Not yet.

"Ready?" she whispered.

The glow pulsed now, causing beads of sweat to form over her flesh. Maybe he needed a moment to calm down, to get control of—

"Do it!"

Thank God. She pressed, sliding down . . . down . . .

taking him all the way to the root, impaling herself. Then his hips jerked in reflex, sending him even deeper.

A spew of dark curses left him, followed by a stream of praise. "Fuck, yeah. So good, so damn good, baby, never felt anything better."

"Mmm. I've never felt anything better, either." He was so big, he stretched her far more than her fingers, but the burn revved her right back up.

"Move on me."

She flattened her palms on his chest, felt the erratic pound of his heartbeat. A mimic of hers. Again using her knees as leverage, she rose all the way to the tip, then slid back down.

Another round of curses from him. "I want your fingers in my mouth."

"Yes." Except when she reached up to obey, he shook his head violently.

"Not those. The ones you had inside you."

*Oh.* He wanted her taste in his mouth. God, that aroused her to the point of pleasure/pain. He licked and sucked her wetness from each, moaning and groaning. And all the while, she rode him, slow, so slowly.

When there was nothing left on her hand, he popped the fingers out. "Faster," he snarled. "Harder."

*Not yet, darling.* Still moving with tortuous slowness, she worked him. Until he was babbling incoherently. Until he was grinding his hips against her, trying to force her into a swifter rhythm. Until *she* was practically sobbing from desperation.

He'd wanted her enough to push past his fears. He'd waited so long for this moment. She planned to make him come so hard he'd never regret what they'd done—whatever happened afterward.

"You feel so good. I'm so close. Can't wait to feel you come inside me. Never had that. Want that. Need that. Need you. Only you. You're so—"

A roar of satisfaction parted his lips, and he slapped his hands against the tiled walls at his sides, arching his hips so high he completely cleared the bench. Her, too. Her knees lost their anchor, and she balanced only on Hector, his cock so deep inside her she'd feel him for weeks.

As he jetted, a hot stream she could actually feel, she propelled over the edge of satisfaction herself. "Hector!" Her nails sank past skin and into muscle, beads of blood trickling down his chest.

White lights sparked behind her eyelids, and she nearly collapsed against him. Even in the furious haze of a pleasure so intense she'd never known its like, she remembered. *Dangerous. Have to be careful.*

Good thing, too, because as she floated down from the high, she smelled the smoke, and knew. He'd set her bathroom on fire.

# *Thirty-two*

H ECTOR SAT AT THE end of Noelle's bed, a towel
wrapped around his waist. She paced in front
of him, but he couldn't look at her. Not yet. He'd destroyed her bathroom. Would have burned her house
down if the fire had started anywhere but the shower.
A twist of the nozzle and they'd managed to douse the
flames before they could spread.

By then, the tiles were already charred and black.

His first time was probably going to be his last time,
he thought darkly. A fact that utterly slayed him.

What Noelle had made him feel . . .

His body had existed for her, and her alone. He'd
become her slave—more so than any time before.
Whatever she'd wanted, he would have given her.
Anything to sink inside that warm, wet sheath. And
when he had . . . god *damn*. He'd almost come that
very second. It had taken every bit of his will power
to hold back.

He wanted that again. Every day, every night. Now
he knew. There was nothing better than discovering

your woman was drenched with arousal. Because of you. Feeling her pulse with satisfaction. Because of you. Hearing her cry your name. Knowing she was as swept up by the moment as you were.

How was he supposed to resist her now?

And he had to resist her. Until he learned to control his ability, he couldn't let anything like this happen again.

*You're a goddamn broken record, you know that?*

Yes. Proof: Would she wait for him? he wondered.

Hell, no, he decided a heartbeat later. She wouldn't wait for him. One, he couldn't give her a guarantee that he'd ever learn to control himself. Two, she was a beautiful woman with needs. Three, she did not handle any type of rejection well and she would consider his backtracking another rejection.

*Fucking hate myself.*

"You're about to tell me we're going back to being friends and partners and nothing more, aren't you?" she demanded.

His stomach churned with sickness. "Noelle—"

"Don't you *Noelle* me. Ten minutes ago I was *baby*."

And he would have chopped off his arms to be there again. "Your bathroom is toast. I could have hurt you irreparably."

"Argh! This shit again? Really? The bathroom's no big deal. I can have another stall in place within the hour."

No big deal. Right. "That's not the point, and you know it." And he'd known better. Had known sex was too hazardous for him.

*Gotta stay strong this time. Can't cave.*

"You said coming inside me might calm your arms down, and guess what? It did. You aren't glowing, and you aren't radiating any heat."

"Doesn't mean the process won't start over again if you touch me." *Or if I touch you.* Just the thought had his cock twitching. *Down boy.*

"So okay. Fine. What happens next?" She stopped in front of him, her hands on her hips. The scent of soap and orchids wafted from her. She, too, wore a towel. The fluffy material was anchored just above her breasts and fell to just below her ass.

Gorgeous female. Even then, after the damage he'd caused, as tortured as he was, his body continued to respond to her, craving her. "What do you want to happen?" he asked, finally looking up and meeting her gaze.

Noelle's heart lurched in her chest. Hector's expression was one of pain, regret, and soul-wrenching sorrow. Not about the sex. That, she knew he'd enjoyed. But about the danger he'd put her in.

"I want you to follow me around like a puppy, doing everything I tell you to do," she said.

"What else?"

Her lips pursed. "Tell me what you like about me."

He blinked, clearly surprised by the topic switch. "Everything."

There was so much conviction in his tone that he left no room for doubt. "Even if I told you that twice in my life I've hacked off Ava's hair, just because I was mad at her?"

His brow furrowed. "What does that have to do with anything?"

"I'm confessing my sins so you can reevaluate what you like about me."

"I won't ever—"

"I've also done every drug out there except Onadyn," she interjected. "And the only reason I've never done Onadyn is because it turns your skin blue for several hours, and blue isn't my color. Also, I went through a pyre phase and torched a school, as well as my parents' summer home. Oh, and I once stole a twenty from a homeless man. 'Course, he deserved it for kicking a robo-dog. Machines have feelings too, you know, but I still kept him from eating for God knows how many days."

Hector's golden gaze no longer crackled with tension, had softened with wariness. "Interesting, but why do you think any of that would make me reevaluate what I like about you?"

"It doesn't?"

"No."

Her heart fluttered, a thousand tiny butterfly wings in flight. "All right, then. What would you change about me?"

Another round of confused blinking. "Not a damn thing."

More conviction. Much more. He meant that, liked her just the way she was. Wasn't judging her. Further proof: he'd never tried to change her. He'd only ever tried to protect her.

She would have him. Fight for him.

In her mind, they'd just proven they could be together intimately successfully, but okay. He required more evidence. Problem was, he planned to push her away. Again. For her own good. *Well, not this time.*

*She* would do the pushing. Not away from her, but toward a commitment. She would have him, and that was that.

"Just so you know," she said. "Nothing happened with Corban. I refused to let him inside my house, so he took me to a restaurant. We talked for an hour before I left his ass there. I went to my mother's, went to a cocktail party with her, thought briefly about committing a murder/suicide, then stayed the night with her. The reason I was still in a dress was because I refuse to keep clothes at her house and had to buy something for the party. That was all I had to wear home."

He listened, his shoulders sagging with relief. "Thank you for telling me."

"That's what people in a relationship do." There. She'd said it, and he could deal.

He flinched. "Well, now I have to tell you something."

*Annnd, here it comes.* The "it's not you, it's me" speech again.

"You know one of the reasons I pushed you away before. My arms. Here's another. Dallas had a vision of the two of us sleeping together, as well as a vision of the two of you sleeping together."

A searing flood of confusion. "A vision?"

"Yeah. He's psychic."

Psychic. "Okay." Once she might have snorted at such a claim. Having worked with otherworlders, having dated one, and seeing their abilities firsthand, she'd pretty much believe anything. "I guess he got it right because I just slept with you."

Hector's nostrils flared. A return of his arousal? "The problem is, Dallas will either be destroyed or saved."

"Destroyed or saved, because I *slept with you*?"

"Yes."

"*How* will Dallas be destroyed? Or saved?" she added before he could correct her. Just like that, she understood why Dallas and Devyn, Dally's best friend forever, had acted so strangely around her yesterday.

A muscle ticked in Hector's jaw. "We don't know."

"You just know it'll happen."

A stiff, grim nod.

"Because I slept with you," she reiterated.

"Don't worry. Dallas gave his permission for us to be together."

"Oh, well, if Dallas gave his permission, then by all means," she said dryly. "Let's get married and have a thousand babies."

His teeth flashed in a scowl. "Look, I just wanted you to know where my head was at."

So she'd back off and give him some space? *Not gonna happen, darling. I'm coming at you guns blazing.*

On her nightstand, her phone beeped, signaling a text had just come in. "Get dressed, and we'll head to work," she said, walking over and palming the device. "We don't have to decide anything about our definitely committed relationship right now."

"Noelle—"

"Don't even think about denying we are involved in a committed relationship, Hector. We are. Well, you are at least. I'm allowed to fool around with other people if I so choose."

Silence. Good. Maybe he'd learn he would live a much fuller, richer life if he just sucked it up and gave her what she wanted, when she wanted it.

"You are *not* fooling around with anyone else," he finally growled. "Not even Don Carlos."

"Fine. But it's on you if he kills himself over the sorrow of losing me."

"Word on the street is, he's already moved on and is dating someone else."

"He is not. He loves me!" When she reminded herself they were talking about her imaginary lover, she forced herself to utter a put-upon sigh. "Well, I hope you're proud of yourself. You just got exactly what *you* wanted. You and I are only seeing each other."

As he strode into the bathroom, muttering under his breath about naughty girls who fought dirty, she read what Tits McGee had to say. *Guess what? Fangs R in!*

Ava and McKell forever, she thought, a sudden pang in her chest. She replied: *Told U!* She was happy for the lovebirds, she really was. And she wouldn't feel sorry for herself, that Hector was intent on resisting her. She was better than that. Sometimes.

*I bet U look hot! U doing well?* she typed next.

*Do look hot, but tired w/ a raging thirst.*

*Take it out on McKell.*

*Already on it!*

Of course she was. Ava liked dishing revenge as much as Noelle did.

Tits McGee: *So . . . U think anymore bout turning?*

Took her a moment to decide on the proper response. *Not yet, got case, miss you tho.*

*Miss you 2. BTW, case would B solved already if I were there.*

*Brat.*

*Slacker.*

"Why are you grinning?" Hector asked as he exited the bathroom. His pants were in place, and he was tugging his shirt over his head. A shame to cover all that muscled perfection.

Better question: why wasn't she jumping all over Ava's offer? But then, she already knew the answer. Because of him, that's why. A man who was determined to knock her burgeoning faith in romance down a peg. But he wouldn't. Not this time.

"Ava just called me a slacker," she said.

"And that amuses you? If I called you a name like that, you'd knee me in the balls."

"Twice."

His phone rang and he whipped the thing from his pocket. "Agent Dean." A moment of quiet. His cheeks quickly paled, his gaze swinging to Noelle. "Margarete? Calm down. I can't understand you." Pause. "Stay there. I'm on my way."

# *Thirty-three*

H ECTOR WALKED THROUGH THE Markses' residence for the second time in two days. Once
pristine, the home was now a wreck. Knickknacks were
shattered on the floor. Furniture was overturned. There
was a splatter of something wet and golden in the living room. Rakan blood, most likely.

There was no sign of Margarete, but he knew she
was here.

On his way over, he'd had Noelle call the agents
guarding the outside. She'd told them Margarete
claimed someone had broken in, someone she'd managed to fight off to lock herself in the hidden safe-
room Bobby had built for her.

They hadn't seen anyone enter. So either the Arcadian had teleported in despite the wall shields or the
guy who'd gotten in was very good at remaining in the
shadows. Either way was bad news for the investigation.

"I'll do a sweep for prints," Noelle said. The moment
he'd explained what was going on, she'd gathered up a

shirt, jeans, and boots in record time—and dressed in the car. He'd gotten peek after peek at skin he'd only just licked, breasts he'd sucked on, and a portal to paradise that had welcomed him with wet, greedy heat.

*Mine.* And he was hers. She'd said so.

"Thanks," he said. They only needed one print, even a partial, and they'd have the guy's identity. *If* he was human. Some alien races—like the Arcadians—did not have fingerprints.

Hector dialed the number Margarete had used to call him. He'd wanted her to stay on the line the entire time, but she'd hung up on him when he'd first entered the house, as if she didn't want to hear any fight that broke out. She picked up after the third ring. "Whoever broke in is long gone. I've checked the entire house. Will you come out for me? You're safe now, I promise."

"Y—you're sure?"

"Absolutely."

"All r—right." *Click.*

A minute passed, then another. Finally she rounded the far corner. Her golden skin was pallid, and there was a bruise on her cheek. The pink dress she wore was torn at the collar and thigh. Tremors rocked her slight frame, and she clutched a black glove to her chest.

Shouldn't have left her here, he thought, pissed at himself. "Let's get your injuries checked."

"All right," she said again.

"Sit here." Noelle righted the couch, and clapped her hands in a job well done. "I'll get one of the medics in here." They were waiting outside, unable to enter without permission. Off she went. And she knew to threaten whoever she picked with bodily harm if they mentioned the Rakan.

Margarete padded over and eased down at the far corner. After everything she'd been through, Hector didn't want to intimidate her, so he claimed the cushion at the other end.

"Can you tell me what your attacker looked like?" he asked.

She gulped, glittery tears cascading down her cheeks. "He was human. Tall with a body like yours. A crooked nose. Dark hair, dark eyes."

Well, well. She'd just described Bruiser, the guy from the sketch. So the Arcadian hadn't come. Which most likely meant he couldn't teleport here. *So close. We're getting there. Going to solve this.*

"Did he say anything to you?"

Before she could reply, Noelle walked in with a twenty-something medic following her. He was on the short and pudgy side, yet still possessed a brisk, confident stride.

"We'll pick up where we left off when you're done with medical," he said.

The medic crouched in front of Margarete, looked her over, and pulled what he needed from his bag. "This might sting a bit."

When he dabbed antiseptic on the cut on her hand, she flinched. That was the only reaction she gave, remaining stoic and silent as he bandaged her up and took her vitals. Entire process only took about twenty minutes, but because Hector wouldn't discuss case details with someone other than an agent, even a medic, the wait was torturous.

Finally, though, he, Noelle, and Margarete were alone. "Did your attacker say anything?" he asked again.

"He said . . . he said I belonged to his boss. He tried to inject me with something, like you did, but I kicked him just like Bobby taught me and got away. He . . . wore gloves. I—I managed to rip one off."

"Where is the glove now?" he asked, even though he knew it was the one she'd placed in her lap.

Her arms shook as she extended the material in his direction. Hector motioned to Noelle, who had stayed close. She wore gloves of her own, and confiscated the evidence.

She'd scrape skin cells from inside and have an identity within the next five minutes, no print necessary now. Urgency rushed through him. *So damn close.*

"He came here before," Margarete admitted softly. "Before you. That time, I hid before he spotted me, though, and he left."

"Will you tell me now how you and Bobby met?" he asked. "The truth this time."

Her lips rolled in, and she gulped. "He . . . bought me. The man who came today, he was the one who brought me here."

Unnecessary verification, but damn, it felt good. "Why did you lie before?"

She looked down, ashamed. "Because Bobby told me never to tell. He said he would be killed and I would be sent away and given to someone else." Her chin trembled. "I don't want to be given to anyone else."

"You won't." A vow. "Never again. I'll make sure of it."

"Don't mean to interrupt," Noelle said, glee bubbling in her tone, "but we've got him. Ruppert Gordman. Thirty-three, human. Picked up a few times for violence. No known address. If he's got an appointment anywhere and it's been logged into a computer, I'll find it."

The sense of urgency amplified. "Does that name mean anything to you?" he asked Margarete.

A moment of thought, then she shook her head.

The fine hairs on the back of his neck rose. His brow furrowed as he visually searched a room he'd already physically searched. He felt as if someone were watching him. He found nothing out of place, though. No eyes staring from portraits, no cameras. "I want you to stay at AIR," Hector said.

When she gave another shake of her head and opened her mouth to issue a denial, he held up a hand to silence her. "There are two other women there, and they've gone through the same thing you have. They were picked up by the guys who abducted you, and drugged. They were going to be sold."

"I—no." The glittery tears sprang forth anew, tracking down her cheeks. "I want to stay here."

"You can't," he said, using a tougher voice. "Bobby didn't change his will. Which means you aren't in it. Sometime this week, his mother is going to take over the deed, and she's going to kick you out. You'll have no place to go. No protection. This way, you'll be able to take what you want with you, and we can help you find a place when the one who wants to sell you is locked away."

"You won't have to worry about anything," Noelle

added gently. "I know a girl, who knows a girl, yada yada, and you'd be doing her a favor, watching over her house while she's off planet. It's a very safe place. I've been there myself."

He seriously doubted she knew a girl who knew a girl off planet. Ava was her closest—and perhaps only—friend. Which meant Noelle was planning to pay for everything herself.

Sweet of her, and for most people, probably bewildering. Nearly everyone at AIR had called her spoiled at some point. Even when she was merely a trainee, she'd had food delivered to her desk—and she had only shared with Ava, no matter how much bitching people did. She went through cars like some men went through condoms. She drank champagne and ate expensive chocolate treats and sometimes left the office in a formal gown.

He thought back, some things about her finally adding up. No one had seemed to notice that when their computers broke down, they were somehow fixed the next day. Or when an agent's kid got sick, she suddenly didn't feel well so maybe her doctor should check them both out, make sure the brat hasn't—and couldn't—give her anything. The faker, saving everyone's pride by making herself seem silly.

Bottom line, when something mattered, she took care of it. He realized that now. She just didn't want anyone to know she'd helped.

*Why?* he wondered. Because people would expect more from her? Because they would realize she wasn't . . . what had she called herself? A flake. Irresponsible.

Yeah, he thought. That was it exactly. She strove so hard to project that kind of image, then hated that people couldn't see through it. But then, she also held most people at a distance; that way, they couldn't hurt her if they didn't like her.

He did the same thing. He kept people at a distance so that they wouldn't like him. So that *he* wouldn't hurt *them*.

*Remember that.*

"Gordman has an appointment at Cirque du Culotte tomorrow," Noelle said, her relish back full force. "Ten in the morning."

Circus of the Panties? Shit. Hector was ashamed to note he knew the place. Located in the center of Whore's Corner, the worst the city had to offer. "It's a . . . massage parlor that specializes in, uh, happy endings," he said, having heard the question in her tone.

Her lips curled in disgust. "Okay, that's just gross."

He ignored the sudden surge of bile rising up his chest. What would she say if she learned he'd been in that particular shop?

"Margarete?" he said, returning his attention to the Rakan. "What's it going to be?"

Her golden head bowed. "Yes," she whispered. "I'll go to AIR."

"Good." No reason to mention he would have had her carted there with or without her consent. He pushed to his feet. "Grab some things, and we'll escort you there now." He and Noelle had a thousand things to do—and only until ten tomorrow morning to do them.

# Thirty-four

*H*ECTOR DIDN'T SPEND THE night with Noelle, but he did pick her up the next morning, as promised. Sweet progress, she thought. *I'll have him bagged and tagged by week's end.*

He hadn't yet experienced the full measure of a Noelle Tremain seduction. No man had. Too potent. Of course. But Hector was about to be the first. He'd addicted her to the goods, and now he would supply her with more. It was as simple as that.

He'd nearly popped his zipper when he had first spotted her outfit. Another deeply V'd top—why mess with what worked?—paired with a tight black skirt. Both allowed for easy access to her fun zones. Not to mention, the skirt barely covered her underwear when she sat down. And they had a thirty-minute car ride to enjoy.

Which they did. At first. He continued to move his gaze up and down her legs, his lips parted as he struggled to draw in enough oxygen. Until fifteen minutes in, when his entire demeanor changed. He began shifting nervously in his seat, avoiding looking in her direction entirely.

Twenty minutes in, the silence was making her crazy and Hector looked ready to vomit. What the hell was going on with him? This was more than simply trying to keep her at a distance. This was abject terror.

Not knowing what else to do, she studied the area. For a moment, she felt as if someone other than Hector was watching her, her skin prickling with unease, but she didn't see any signs of a tailing car. The sky was overcast and gray, mist saturating the air so thickly their windshield appeared to be having an allergic reaction; clear little welts bubbled everywhere. The buildings lining both sides of the sidewalk were dilapidated and covered with graffiti. Some had huge front windows with naked otherworlder men and women dancing just beyond the transparent shield armor.

The dancers had to be drugged. Their faces were expressionless, their movements halting. Noelle wasn't sure how some of them remained on their feet. Not a one of them smiled or waved people inside. And when they brushed against each other sexually, they didn't seem to enjoy it. They just . . . tolerated it.

On the sidewalk, bums stumbled into the buildings, prostitutes shouted at drivers, and trash tumbled in every direction.

Last night Noelle had dug up Gordman's financials. He was paid very well for a job he hadn't yet listed in his employment file, but he was paid in cash, so there was no paper trail at any bank.

She'd also gone through the parlor's financials, and

wow. Despite its piss-poor location, the place was a money flood. People really liked having their, uh, backs loosened. Most paid in cash, but Gordman's sessions were always comped.

Made her wonder. Could Gordman's boss own the panty circus? Or rather, run the corporation that owned it and *that's* why Gordman got in and out so easily? More digging to do later.

Finally the car parked itself at the corner of Derelict Drive. Noelle's name for it, at least. The massage parlor was a building over, on the right. The bricks were streaked with dirt and the singe of acid rain.

"Gordman's appointment isn't for another thirty-eight minutes," she said after checking the clock. "Do we just sit out here and wait, hoping we're not shanked for our car?"

"Yes." Nothing more than a snarl.

O-kay. Hector was more pissy than before. "Well, I'm not touching anything outside. This is a Petri dish of STDs, I just know it."

"Why don't you toughen up, little girl?" he snapped. "This is where I grew up."

Ahh. A lightbulb switched on inside her head. He was ashamed, didn't want her to see his roots, even though he'd told her all about them. Well, news flash. Ava had grown up here, too. This only made Noelle like him *more*. He'd pulled himself out. Made something of himself.

Not that she'd tell him that right now. In his current mood, he'd rip everything she said to shreds.

Noelle twisted in her seat, facing him. He wore a

long-sleeved button-up shirt, white, his jacket tossed to the backseat. The cuffs were undone and rolled to just under his elbows, revealing that beautifully bronzed tattooed skin.

Darker ink today, with a slight azure glow. He was big-time worked up.

"You need gloves." She dug a pair out of the console and tossed them on his lap.

A scowl marred his face as he jerked them on.

"You also need to come," she said.

"You offering to suck me off?" He leered over at her, hatred in his eyes, but there was no doubt in her mind that the hatred was self-directed.

Without a word, she leaned over and pressed the series of buttons necessary for darkening the tint on the windows. A black film thickened over each one, until no one could see inside. They still had a view of the outside world. Not as clear, but Hector would soon be grateful for the privacy.

Full-on seduction would have to wait. He needed something else right now. Tough love. The same thing he'd given her the day of Ava's wedding. Knowing him better now, she was absolutely certain that's exactly what he'd done.

"I know you grew up here, but once a gutter rat always a gutter rat," she sneered. "As if perfect, amazing, and, it can't be denied, gorgeous Noelle Tremain would ever offer to suck you off again, now that she's seen where you used to live."

"I'm not a fucking gutter rat." He threw the words at her, each one like a baseball.

*That's it, darling.* "You sure? What would you call this place and the people who live in it, then?"

Golden eyes sizzled. "You better watch yourself."

"Or you'll what?" Pretending to ponder the answer, she tapped two nails against her chin. "Wait. I can guess. Nothing, that's what. Because you don't have the balls to take what you want. If you did, you would have grabbed me the moment I got into the car and screwed me brainless. You wanted to, I could tell, but you didn't. You just sat there stewing about where you used to live, condemning me for condemning you. You're a pussy, Hector Dean, and I do not suck on—"

His roar filled the interior as he slapped his big hands against her hips and dragged her onto his lap. For a moment, she had no anchor. Then his mouth was on hers, his tongue thrusting deep, and her blood thrilled with sensation.

The taste of mint hit her, and she moaned. His cock was a steel pipe between her legs, and the thought of taking him inside her made her instantly wet.

The vise grip on her hips tightened further, and he rammed her forward, against him, then shoved her back, then forward again. She loved every second, but if he accidentally hurt her, he would never forgive himself.

"Put your arms behind the back of the seat."

He froze. "Shit!" As he panted, his head fell back against the neck rest, his eyes simmering with horror. "My arms are hot, and I touched you. Are you—"

"Oh, no, you don't. Put your arms behind the seat. Now. I need this as much as you do."

Though his expression didn't change, he obeyed.

Noelle shoved aside the V of her blouse, letting the material catch on the sides of her bare breasts. "Flick your tongue over my nipples," she commanded.

"Yes." Hector fit his lips over her berry pink nipple and bit down, tugging the bud, making it swell with a rush of achy blood. Licking away the sting was one of his new favorite things to do.

He should stop this. He knew he should stop. He'd touched her with hands that could have blistered her. Only reason she wasn't injured was because he wore the gloves, and she wore that sinful skirt. Had she been naked . . .

Oh, God. He'd lost control, wanting her so desperately he throbbed, ashamed about who and what he was, who and what he'd been—who and what he would always be.

As she'd shouted at him for being a pussy, she'd razed him with the disgust he'd expected—but that disgust had been directed at his behavior, at his resistance to her. Not at his past. She'd goaded him, and he'd let her. Now he was on fire for her. Had to see this through. *Couldn't* stop.

When she reached between their bodies and unzipped his pants, he anticipated her next sinking down on him, taking him all the way inside. Instead, she let him go, licked the palm of her hand, wetting the skin, and oh, damn, he'd never seen anything sexier.

Silver eyes flashed brightly as she fisted his cock. A

heated breath whooshed from between clenched teeth. Up and down she caressed, his hips arching into the touch.

"I want this," she whispered raggedly. "Can I have it?"

"Please." A tortured cry.

She released him, and he groaned at the loss of contact. He didn't mourn for long, though. She shoved aside her panties, giving him the briefest glimpse of pink and wet, and set herself at his tip.

Fingers shifted through his hair, and she tilted his head back for a drugging kiss. Down . . . down . . . she slid, taking him all the way in, just as he'd longed for. She swallowed his every groan of passion.

"Love this," she panted.

"Love." His thoughts short-circuited. There was only here, now, this moment. This woman. Her intoxicating flavor in his mouth, a sweetness only Noelle possessed.

Her nipples rubbed at his shirt, but he wanted them on his skin.

"Lean back," he commanded.

At first she didn't seem to hear him, so he growled the words at her. Her eyelids blinked open, and she tilted, resting her back against the driver's console. The new angle gave his pleasure a sharper edge, and he gritted his teeth to stop himself from coming.

With shaky fingers, he ripped the buttons down his shirt, causing the fabric to gap open and revealing his chest. "Up," he commanded now.

This time there was no hesitation, and she pressed against him. Skin to heated skin, and hell, the most delicious torture. She rode him, slamming down, faster and faster, until she was clamping down tight, shouting his name, tugging at his hair.

Just like that, tingles of sensation sparked in his balls and shot up his length, and he jetted inside her. He had to grip the rim of the seat to stop himself from grabbing hold of her. Already he could smell smoke.

When she stilled, collapsing against his chest, his muscles tensed and he tried to buck her off. "Noelle, please."

"You want to go again?" she asked with a wicked smile.

"You have to—"

"Oh, all right. I know the drill." Frowning now, she wiggled to her seat, ending the connection.

He looked his arms over. Holes in the material, but smoke no longer wafted through them, and there was no longer any hint of the glow. "Are you hurt?"

"No."

Like she'd really admit the truth, though. "Let me see your hips."

"No." She fisted her hands over the waist of the skirt, but not before he spotted the charred waistline.

He *had* burned her. Had probably blistered her.

She must have read the horror on his face. "Hector, I can't feel them. It's fine. *I'm* fine."

No, it fucking wasn't. "We are *not* doing that again," he said. And he meant it this time.

An innocent smile. "Whatever you say, darling."

# Thirty-five

S IDE BY SIDE, HECTOR and Noelle entered the dirty
building.

He'd donned his jacket to hide his decimated shirt,
but a patch of skin was visible between the lapels. Gorgeous, Noelle thought, already hungry for him again.

*Eyes ahead.* "Are you sure you don't want to field this
one solo?" she asked with a shudder. Threadbare carpeting snagged on her boots. A different porno played
on each of the walls, moans and groans echoing from
speakers placed throughout the lobby.

"I'm sure."

Once again with the snappy answers. Fabulous.
"One hundred percent sure or is there a way I can talk
you into changing your mind? Because I'm pretty confident I came into contact with a flesh-eating bacteria
when I opened the door."

"Hundred percent."

Anyone else would have pretended not to notice the
grimness of their surroundings, thinking to spare his
feelings. But he would have seen through the pretence,

and that would have made everything worse. He didn't need coddling. He needed someone to prove he was better than the location of his birth. "Little tip for you. Now that you're blissed out," she said, "you should be nicer to me. Otherwise I might start to think you're serious about never again getting busy with me."

He scowled at her. She smiled.

Several men sat on well-used couches, each of them eyeing her like a slab of ribs as she passed. *Feel so special.*

"Since you're actually making me do my job," she said to Hector, pausing a moment to let him pipe in that yeah, okay, she could head back to the car. He didn't. "I'll handle this first part."

"Fine. Whatever."

*Don't laugh.* At the reception desk, Noelle propped her elbows on the counter, just in front of a girl who reminded her of the AIR agent, Kitten . . . whatever. A Teran, only this one was mocha everywhere but her hands. Those were white, as if she were wearing mittens. Her outfit consisted of an ill-fitting black bra, wrinkled black-and-white panties, and fishnet stockings with a run in the thigh.

"Can I help you?" Purring tone, probably seductive to most humans, but Noelle heard the boredom laced through it.

"You sure can. You can listen. One way or another me and my guy are getting back there. I'll let you pick the way we handle things. Easy way or the hard way?"

A flash of irritation in that feline face. "Fuck you, bitch. Only one rule here and that's customer privacy. Now if you wanna book a session, be my guest."

"Easy way, then." In less than a second, Noelle had her pyre-gun palmed, aimed, and the trigger squeezed. A blaze of blue, and the otherworlder was stunned, unable to move or speak.

Behind her, curses and footsteps resounded as the men on the couches beat feet outta there.

"*That's* the easy way?" Hector asked, incredulous.

"Of course. Now she can't fight us."

"Well, we need her print to open the back room doors. What the hell are we supposed to do?"

"Hello. Cut off her hand." Problem meet solution. Practically skipping, Noelle rounded the desk, pushed the girl out of the way, and did a little typing on the computer. "Our guy's in room six. With Olga. A very popular girl, our Olga. I wonder if she'd be willing to share trade secrets."

"Here's another idea. I'll just carry our key. Though this seems like the hard way." He did, hefting the Teran's body over his shoulder. He carted her to the side door, then motioned Noelle over. "Place her hand in the ID box and hold it there."

"I don't know if you've realized this yet, but had you not utilized my services in the car, you wouldn't have been able to handle her. Think about that and get back to me with an apology for your attitude, then a poem of your own creation about my amazing thoughtfulness." As she spoke, she did as commanded, and a flash of yellow light descended over the girl's palm.

*Beep.* The door slid open, and they strode into the hallway. Several otherworlders strode this way and that, hustling in and out of rooms. The moment Noelle and Hector were spotted, the "masseuses" took off running in the same direction. Outside.

"They're going to give me a complex," she sniffed.

"You'll get over it."

What do you know. His tenor had actually lightened.

At room six, they repeated the process with the Teran and that door slid open, too.

Hector eased his bundle to the floor and palmed a weapon.

Gordman was lying on a long table, face up, his clothes on but open, a naked Delesean giving him a blow job, while at the same time her six arms caressed his body. He had his hands in her hair, forcing her to take him deeper and harder than she probably wanted.

"Yeah, that's the way," he groaned. "You—"

"Might want to stop," Noelle said, her own gun aimed and set to kill this time.

Gasping, the otherworlder jerked upright.

Gordman's eyes popped open and his dark eyes flashed daggers. "Get out before I fucking gut you."

"Original," she muttered.

Ignoring her, Hector flashed his badge. "Threatening an agent. Not wise."

Noelle anticipated paling, stuttering, even the emptying of bowels. A nice way of saying Gordman should be shitting himself from fear. *I'm so classy!* But the big brute pushed the otherworlder toward the door and sat up to right his clothing. The moment the three of them were alone, Hector reached back and closed the door.

"So, agent, mind telling me what this is about?" Gordman asked, all smooth and suave now. "I'm human. You have no jurisdiction with me."

"Sure we do. But let's disarm you before we get to that, hmm." Hector closed the distance and flipped Gordman to his stomach, patting him down, tossing a pyre-gun and three blades to the floor. No protest from Gordman, no aggressive moves.

After toeing the blades as far away as possible—to be bagged and tagged later—Noelle used the hem of her shirt to pick up and shove the gun into the waist of her skirt. They couldn't match the crystal to the burn marks found in Bobby's chest, one of the disadvantages of using a pyre, but they could test to see how many times the weapon had been fired recently.

When Hector finished, he backtracked to her side and rapid-fired questions at their suspect.

"Who do you work for?"

One shoulder lifted in a negligent shrug. "Myself."

"What do you do?"

"This and that."

"What were you doing inside Bobby Marks's home yesterday evening?"

A flicker of surprise passed over Gordman's rough features, then anger, both swiftly masked with indifference. "We were friends. I was visiting. Paying respects to his family."

"Then why didn't you knock on the door?"

Gordman next unveiled a cocky grin. "Maybe he'd given me a key. Maybe he told me to enter any time I felt like it."

Noelle so wanted to squeeze the trigger of her gun. Smug bastard. "Let's see that key."

"Sorry. Lost it."

"Of course, you did."

"Is that all?" the stupid shit asked, brushing an invisible piece of lint off his shirt. "Because you've wasted enough of my time."

*Add arrogant to the list.* "You were spotted at a murder scene, so no, that isn't all. You're under arrest."

"You're kidding me."

"I never kid," Hector said. "Turn around and put your arms behind your head."

Finally, panic. Gordman erupted into motion, a blur Noelle couldn't lock on. Which was probably a good thing. They needed to question him further, and because humans couldn't be stunned, the only thing her pyre-gun would do was kill him.

He threw himself at Hector, and the pair crashed into the wall, a tangle of hammering fists and kicking legs. They'd both lived on the streets, and it showed. They went for the throat, the groin, nothing held back.

"I'm not going in!" Gordman shouted.

Because his boss would never trust him again? Because his boss would kill him to eliminate a potential witness to past crimes?

"The hell you aren't," Hector shouted back.

Noelle would have sat on the table and watched from there, but . . . ick. So she stood off to the side and allowed Hector to impress her with his savage skill. And oh, did he impress her.

Every time Gordman dove for one of the discarded

blades, Hector was there, kicking him in the head and sending him flying, blood spraying. Bastard always got right back up, though, barely winded, as if he had a steel plate in his head. Hell, maybe he did.

Then Hector palmed one of his own blades, and got down to business. How sexy he was, a bit battered, golden eyes glittering with purpose.

"Slice and dice him, baby!" Noelle cheered.

Hector threw out an arm, but Gordman blocked with an upraised knee. A fast spin, Hector going low, and he nailed his opponent in the thigh. Another howl from Gordman as Hector straightened and swung a fist into his cheek.

The impact sent Gordman flying to the side, the blade jerking out of his leg. Hector followed him, going lower still, and stabbing Gordman in the ankle before he could leap out of the way.

Gordman fell to his knees, no longer able to support his weight. Merciless Hector wasn't done. He barreled into Gordman, sending him propelling to his back. With barely a pause to gain his bearings, he turned the blade, hilt protruding from his fist, and slammed the hard, rounded surface into Gordman's temple.

Gordman's body sagged on the dirty floor.

Hector, being Hector, straightened and kicked him in the stomach. No gasp of pain, no flinching. Gordman was well and truly out.

Panting, sweating, Hector picked him up fireman style. Keeping his back to her, he said, "Well?"

"Well, your timing needs a little work, but your level of vicious is off the charts and highly—"

A low, rumbling growl erupted from his throat. "I wasn't asking for a critique. I was saying that now that I've done all the work, aren't you going to get the door?"

"Oh. No. I told you. I'm not touching anything, and that includes the ID panel. And your hands will need a through enzyme wash before they are allowed anywhere near me again."

He laughed, the sound rusty, and yet the tension drained out of him.

*I did that,* she marveled, utterly awed. *I amused him.* Pride swept through her.

"Spoiled," he muttered. With affection?

"I prefer the word intelligent." She was getting through to him. Despite his fears, she was cracking through his resistance. *I'll have you yet, Hector Dean.*


Outside, the storm had at last burst through the clouds. Rain had sent everyone scurrying for shelter and now beat against the concrete.

When Hector started to make a dash for their car, Noelle stopped him with a shouted, "Let's find out which car belongs to Gordman. I have an idea."

Without asking any questions, he pressed the bruiser's limp hand into every ID panel on every car parked on the street. Took ten minutes, and they were soaked to the bone, but finally their efforts paid off. The locks to a black BMW automatically unlatched.

"Thank you," Noelle said, sliding inside. Dirty water pooled around her, probably staining the seat, definitely leaving a ring. Hector couldn't say he was sorry. The stupid bastard had cracked one of his ribs. He deserved this and more. "You can lock him in our car now."

He did, with no finesse whatsoever, and returned to Noelle. "What are you doing?"

She'd already ripped the console apart, hooked her cell phone to the appropriate wire, and was currently scrolling through . . . something. "I'm checking his GPS. He has no known address, and I'll bet that means he's been living with his boss. Neither of them would have wanted that on the record, you know. Anyway, that's the address he would have visited the most."

A moment of silence as Hector absorbed her words. "Smart." And damned impressive.

"I know."

He grinned. Adrenaline still pumped through his veins, but his arms were chilled out, and that was good. Being worked over by Noelle before the fight had probably saved that building and everyone in it. Not that he could ever let something like that happen again.

His grin faded. "Can you record every address he's visited in the past year?" His voice was harsher than he'd intended. "Maybe we'll find where other women are being kept."

"Now who's the smart one? I'll send each one to Mia."

A few more minutes passed, the rain hammering at his bruised body. Damn, but Gordman had iron in his knuckles. Worth it, though. Had the guy gone for Noelle, Hector wasn't sure what he would have done or how he would have reacted. He'd had only one

thought: protect her. And he'd been willing to kill—
and die—to do so.

"Most visited place is indeed a residence," she said.
"Wealthy side of town, two streets over from my
mother."

One step closer to the truth, to closing this case successfully. Saving lives. "Check and find out who owns
the house—"

"Done!" Silver eyes sparkled with glee as she whistled. "We have a name. Xavier Phillips. I've never met
him, but I've seen him around and I know his reputa-
tion. He's respected, a real hardass in the import/export
business. Blond . . . like the superhero sketch."

And yet another step, because of Noelle. He couldn't
believe that he'd once thought she would ruin every
case she worked. Without her, he wouldn't have gotten
far. He owed her, in more ways than one.

# Thirty-six

"**X**AVIER PHILLIPS. SHIT."

Hector and Noelle sat in Mia's office. Biggest office in AIR HQ, but small nonetheless. The ceiling was painted to look like a bright morning sky. Her desk was cluttered with equipment and weapons. A holoboard consumed one entire wall, photos and notes from all ongoing cases like tiny neon signs throughout.

"He's as rich as I am," Noelle said, "and we won't be able to book an appointment to see him. Well, we will, we just won't *see* him. We'll flash our badges and his employees will pretend to cooperate. His attorneys will call us back—they're always on site, guaranteed—and inform us that Phillips is out of town. An emergency. We'll make another appointment, but there will always be something keeping him away."

"Plus, we don't exactly have any hard evidence against him," Hector said. And he doubted Gordman, who was currently in lockup, sealed tight and being kept unconscious—just in case he had a cyanide pill they hadn't found or had a way of contacting his boss—would give them anything.

The GPS from the car was considered circumstantial. Gordman could have been threatening Phillips, an attorney would say, visiting his property without permission. Or even that Gordman had been working on his own, without Phillips's knowledge.

"So what do you want me to do?" Mia leaned back in her chair and folded her arms over her middle. She'd pulled her hair into a high ponytail and looked as young and innocent as kindergartener, not at all like the stone-cold killer she was.

"There's a charity gala this weekend, and I'm betting he'll be there," Noelle said. "Tickets are two thousand a pop, and I have two."

The reminder of her status made him uncomfortable, but nothing like before. She'd made her feelings for him clear. Respect. Desire. She was, by far, the world's most amazing woman.

*Mine. I want her to be mine. Only, ever mine.*

He rubbed the back of his neck. "We can question him there. Try to trip him up, maybe get him to say something stupid that we can use against him later."

"He's too smart for that," Mia said.

"We have to try."

"Maybe. But around a crowd of rich people? I don't like it." The head of AIR frowned. "He's a ruthless murderer, and if he strikes there . . ."

"With Gordman under arrest, and our agents raiding his warehouses"—already eight otherworlder females had been found, drugged out and awaiting auction, but they still couldn't prove Phillips had anything to do with it yet—"he'll know we're hot on his trail," Hector said. "We have to strike now."

Heavy silence. A heavier sigh. "I had a holophoto of Phillips the moment you gave me his name. We showed it to each of tonight's girls. Nothing. Gordman, on the other hand . . . they went hysterical at the sight of him."

"Don't you want to nail the man who put such a tool in charge?" Noelle asked, sly, so sly. "The party will allow us to gift-wrap him for you. But, okay, fine. You'd rather wait, give him time to hide evidence and kidnap more girls, that way—"

"God, you're annoying." Mia waved a hand through the air. "Fine. Go to the charity thing. Talk to Phillips, but no casualities or I swear to God you're both fired."

Noelle blinked innocently, and Hector had to stifle a laugh. No one mentioned her taking someone else, and for that he was grateful. He knew Dallas would have been a better choice. Smoother, able to suck up with a smile. Hector would be prickly and out of place, but no way in hell would he let Noelle go in without him.

"By the way. My anonymous tipster contacted me again. He said he's helped us out so much, it's our turn to help him. He wants to know the name and description of every female we find. I think someone he knows was taken, and he's searching for her."

"And you have no idea who he is?" Hector asked. "Or how he knew what we'd found."

"No, but I'm working on it."

Another round of silence. Mia splayed her arms in a *what the hell are you waiting for* gesture. "That's it. Dismissed."


For Hector, the rest of the week ticked by torturously, every second agony. Not just because he foamed at the mouth to confront Phillips, a man he *knew* was responsible, but because of Noelle. Every day she grew bolder, said something naughtier, wore something more provocative. He'd thought resisting her before was tough.

*This* was tough; this was hell.

He would walk by, and she would make sure to brush against some part of him. He'd sit next to her, and she would play with a strand of his hair. He'd decide to snack, and she would decide to feed him by hand.

His resistance was crumbling. He yearned to take her up on her nightly offer and stay over. Quite simply, he wanted to be with her, whether he could touch her or not. He wanted to breathe her in, laugh at her smart-ass remarks. And they were funny as hell. A guy never knew what she'd say next.

Like the time he told her to stop dressing like she was asking for it, and she said, "Wait until you see the outfit that *begs* for it."

The next day she'd examined her red satin sandals and with a frown said, "I'm thinking about buying two snakes."

His *are you kidding me* "Why?" had caused her to shrug.

"I'd name them Leftie and Rightie and when they were big enough, they'd become Mamma's boots."

Dallas had heard Hector's laughter as he'd passed by his office. The agent had stopped, looked inside, and though he'd smiled at them both, there'd been fear in his eyes.

His vision hadn't yet happened. Hector hadn't woken up naked next to Noelle, but if this kept up . . .

He had used every spare moment of his time trying to control his ability. So far, no luck. He'd scorched dozens of vegetables and nearly burned his house down. Now sexual frustration was a constant knot in his gut. In fact, his arms were currently itching, and his fucking tux offered very little relief.

*None of that.* He stood in Noelle's foyer, waiting for her to come down. Tonight was the night they would nail the slaver's ass to the wall.

No other enslaved women had been found, but no one else had been abducted or killed, so, gold star on that front. As Hector had figured, Gordman had refused to talk. Now it was time to see if Phillips would slip up and—

Noelle glided down her staircase, and Hector's mind simply stopped working. His heart stopped beating. Her lips were plumped and glistening, color high in her cheeks. Her eyes were heavy-lidded, almost slumberous. Silky brown hair cascaded in luscious waves.

Her dress glimmered against her body like violets trapped in sunlight, one creamy shoulder left bare. The material flowed over her curves, molding to her like a second skin.

"I know what you're thinking. I do look good in a variation of blue."

A slit rode the length of her legs, revealing a mouth-watering glimpse of thigh with every step she made. But the best part? A studded amethyst choker wrapped around her neck. Bondage and seduction at once.

*I've tasted her. Been inside her.* "I thought you said this thing was black and white," he managed to croak. *Have to get inside her again. Soon.*

*Have to make it safe for her first.*

A wanton smile that started his heart back up, but it was jacked into an unsteady rhythm. "It is." That silver gaze swept over him when she paused on the last step. "You look . . . amazing." There was reverence in her tone.

He actually felt himself blush like some stupid kid. "I won't embarrass you?" He'd rather die.

"No, but I might embarrass *you.*" She closed the rest of the distance to trace her polished fingernails up the lapels of his jacket. The scent of jasmine and honeysuckle accompanied her, his favorite, as sultry and drugging as a moonlit night, and his stomach tightened. "I don't think I'll be able to keep my hands off you."

Then she stepped back, ending the connection. Her expression cleared, and he had to fight the urge to return her to where he wished she could stay forever. In his arms.


Noelle had known Hector would look amazing in a tailored tux, but nothing could have prepared her for *this*. He was perfection personified. Sexy and devilish and utterly irresistible. Jacket, vest, tie—no bowtie for him—in black Italian silk, and he wore every piece with confidence.

During the entire twenty-minute drive to the old Glassky mansion where the party was being held, she stared at him, craving. He hadn't bothered to style his hair, yet the results were stunning. Those dark strands were exquisitely disheveled, the locks of flax like moon-kissed highlights. The hard gleam in his eyes gave him a don't-mess-with-me vibe, especially since one of those eyes had been blackened during his fight with Gordman and had only just now begun to fade.

She wanted him in her bed. Wanted to fall asleep in his arms every night, and wake up to him every morning. There was nothing she wouldn't do to make that happen, either.

This past week, he'd managed to keep his distance. But every morning at the office, when he'd first spotted her, he'd looked a little more despondent for not having locked their relationship down, his temper sharpened another degree. Any day he would break. And when he did, she would make sure he never regretted it.

Their car stopped at the base of a hill. Just outside her passenger door was a pier of steps that led to the front doors of the home. A red carpet had been rolled out, and reporters consumed both sides, holocameras flashing bright lights in the darkness.

The mansion itself was red and white brick, with multiple rectangular windows. The sides stretched wide and wrapped backward, as if hugging the jewel-toned gardens just beyond. Steepled layer after steepled layer made up the roof, with eight different chimneys adding to the height.

"Are you ready—" She stopped. Hector had turned an unpleasant shade of green. She leaned over, making sure to brush her lips against his ear, and whispered, "I want you so much, it's like a fever in my blood. Now get out of the car and come get me. Also, I forgot to wear any panties."

He nearly tore the door of the hinges during his hasty exit, but when he reached her side of the vehicle and helped her out with a gloved hand, he was steady as a rock, his expression blank, even bored. *Good boy.*

The night was colder than usual, and he wrapped an arm around her waist to keep her warm. Voices called out to them. "Who are you wearing, Noelle?" "Are the two of you dating?" "How's the baby?" "What does Corban Blue think of you seeing another man?"

Without a word, Hector tossed his remote for the car to the valet. A remote that would bypass the voice and fingerprint controls, allowing someone who wasn't programmed in to operate the panels.

They ascended the steps, and Noelle tossed an easy smile this way and that. She made a mental note to download every newspaper in the city tomorrow morning. A little computer magic, and she'd replace Hector's tux with a bunny suit and her dress with skin, and tease him, make him laugh.

God, she adored his laugh. The undertones were still rusty, still gravelly, but much easier to evoke now than when she'd first met him.

When they entered the foyer, Noelle claimed a glass

of bubbly from the waiting waiter—a Mec whose skin pulsed with the happy glow of pink—uncaring what anyone thought about her feeding alcohol to her bun in the oven. She scanned, but caught no hint of Phillips.

The crowded ballroom was something out of a fairy tale. A domed ceiling seemingly carved from solid gold, with intricate symbols framing the sides. The chandelier in the center was tiered, each tier wider than the one above, thousands of crystal teardrops cascading into a shimmery waterfall.

Alabaster columns opened into separate rooms, some with tables of food, some with artwork on display, some with lush, fragrant gardens. No matter where you stepped, soft music played in the background, blending with the sound of idle chatter and clinking glasses.

"Ava's happy I dragged you to this rather than her," she said to Hector. "She always hated these things."

He snorted, relaxing into the conversation. "I more than hate it."

To be honest, Noelle would rather be at home with the man she adored, snuggled up, watching TV, making love. Would that stun Hector? Horrify him? Or actually tempt him? "So . . . what if our guy doesn't show?"

"He will. AIR hasn't approached him, so he's probably relaxed, thinking Gordman hasn't given us his name. And won't."

"True, but—" From the corner of her eye, she spotted her mother and brothers making a beeline for her. Damn it, they'd told her they weren't coming because they were too embarrassed by her disgraceful pregnancy.

"Will you excuse me, Hector?" Heart drumming, stomach clenching, she looked back and forth between her man and her family. "I'm going to run to the ladies' room."

He frowned at her, didn't appear to believe her, but all he said was, "Don't be long."

"So commanding," she tsked under her tongue and took off like her heels were on fire. After placing her empty glass on a passing tray, she made sure her family noticed her change of location and followed her.

As she prepared herself for war, she led them to the far end of the room. Double doors opened into a gorgeous marble statue garden. No one meandered about, the air perhaps too cold and damp. *Hadn't stopped the vultures out front*.

"You shouldn't be here."

The unfamiliar male voice came from behind her, and she whirled. Someone had shut the doors before her family had reached her. From the shadows of one of the statues stepped the handsome guy she'd seen in Alfonzo's, when she and Hector had interrogated Brenda Marks.

He wore an expensively cut tux, polished loafers. "You shouldn't be here," he said again.

"And why is that?" She didn't see a weapon on him, but she wasn't taking any chances. Her fingers reached past the side-slit in her dress and closed around the butt of her pyre.

The moment she touched the handle, he disappeared from view—only to materialize behind her and grab onto her wrist, shocking the hell out of her.

"I don't think so," he said. "No weapons."

*Threat!* Throwing her head back, she nailed him in the chin and he released her.

She spun, aimed—only to watch him disappear once again. "Coward," she growled. "You want to play, because I'll play. Prison rules."

"Damn it, woman. I'm not going to hurt you. Had I wanted to do so, I would have. I've had numerous opportunities."

He'd spoken from her left, but when she turned, he'd already moved on. "Who are you?" she demanded, still not seeing him.

"Mia Snow's informer. For now, you can call me Anonymous."

His voice had come from the right this time, but again, when she turned he was nowhere to be seen. Her heart thundered in her chest. "You're also an otherworlder."

"Part Arcadian, to be exact. Now, then. I'm going to appear in front of you, and if you fire at me, I'll dodge, *easily,* and take off. You won't get to hear the tidbit I've got for you."

Indecision battled with curiosity inside her, but in the end the curiosity won. She lowered her gun to her side. "Start talking. If I don't like what you're saying, bad things are going to happen to you."

A warm chuckle rose. As promised, he appeared in front of her. She studied him anew, noting details she'd missed at first glance. His eyes were the same electric blue as Mia's. In fact, Noelle thought, frowning, the two shared similar facial features, too. The same sloped nose, the same cut cheekbones, the same full lips. It was like looking at a taller, penis-toting version of the AIR captain.

Were they . . . could they be . . . related?

No way, she decided next. He'd said he was Arcadian. Had proven it with his abilities. Mia was human. Right?

"I'm emailing you an address," he said. "There you'll find another of Phillips's victims."

"And the vic is . . . ?"

"His competition. A year ago, he treated Gerard Hendrick to the same pyre-fire as Bobby Marks. I watched him."

Was that so? "And you never reported it, even though you've been helping us? Why would you omit a detail like that?" Their investigation would have gone a lot smoother and a lot faster.

"Because Phillips is mine." Hard tone, determined. "I don't like him, and I don't like what he's doing. When I see an opportunity to cut at him, I take it, as long as I know he won't be captured."

She recalled the theory she'd batted around with Hector. "He took a woman from you? Someone you love? You're searching for her."

The blue in his eyes darkened to black as he nodded. "If he's dead, I'll never find her."

"If he's locked up, you can talk to him any time you want."

The corners of his mouth lifted with condescension. "You'll never lock him up. Anyone who tries to take him in will die. But let's say a miracle happens, because I can practically hear your thoughts and know you think it's possible to catch him. He'd just escape. Believe me, I know. I've been watching and studying him for over a year."

"Well, *I* haven't yet had a crack at him."

"Wouldn't make a difference. He's always a few steps ahead of you, keeping tabs on your progress."

The words left him so easily, and yet each was like a rock slamming into her skull. "How? Do we have a mole in AIR?" If so . . .

"Not to my knowledge, but then, watching AIR isn't hard to do. Anyway, right now Phillips isn't sure whether you have his identity or not. He's content, still doing business as usual. You approach, and that ends. He'll want to know what you know, who you've told, and he'll do anything to find out."

"Even kill us all, yeah, yeah, you informed me of that already."

Her flippancy irritated him and he scowled. "Maybe he'll simply interfere with your investigation by getting rid of you and your partner and making everyone else too afraid to take on the case."

"Kinda like what he does with his customers, huh?" As if she and Hector couldn't handle themselves.

"Exactly." His eyes narrowed, his gaze lasering into her. "So listen up. I know you're planning to do something stupid tonight, like talk to him. Don't."

Trying to tie their hands, hold them back. "We're not afraid of him, Mr. Anonymous. Someone has to take him down."

"Yes, and that someone will be me."

"You've had a year," she reminded him. Merciless, like Hector. "Maybe longer. You haven't exactly succeeded, now have you?"

"I've done a better job than you."

"Ha!" Was she this annoying when telling people how much better *she* was? "We've had a week. Give us another, and Phillips will be behind bars and Big Daddy's bitch."

His fingers flexed before curling into fists. "You have no idea the shit storm you will unleash if you continue on this path."

Whatever. Nothing she couldn't handle. "Why not tell all of this to Mia? Why come to me directly?"

White teeth flashed in a sudden grin. "Big scary tattoo guy is more likely to listen to you than to her. And now, enough questions. I told you what I wanted to tell you. You tell Mia I want that list of names and descriptions of every female you've found." The smile faded, leaving an expression of pain. "And tell her . . . tell her that Dare is back."

# Thirty-seven

─────────────── ❧ ───────────────

*B*Y THE TIME NOELLE returned to Hector's side, the guy—Dare?—had indeed emailed her an address, which she forwarded to Mia with a note about what had been said. No reply had come in, but then, she hadn't expected one. Mia wouldn't contact her until she'd verified the information.

Frown fierce, Hector eyed her up and down. "I was about to start a search and rescue. Where were you?"

She grabbed another glass of champagne. "You'll never guess what just—"

"Noelle," her mother huffed from her left, cutting her off.

Damn it! Her family may not have followed her outside, but they'd sure as hell waited for her return, hadn't they. And they were about to pounce, fangs and claws probably bared.

A quick glance, and she spotted her mother decked out in a regal black dress, diamonds glittering at her neck and fingers, her hair upswept. All three of Noelle's brothers trailed behind her.

"Incoming," she muttered. "There will be bloodshed. There will be casualties." Before, she'd hoped to warn her brothers. Threaten or insult Hector and suffer. *Too late*. Her mother was a lost cause.

"Phillips?" he asked, on alert.

"Worse."

The Four Horsemen of the Apocalypse arrived, forming a half circle around her and Hector. Carter, Anthony, and Tyler were taller than she was, but not taller than Hector, and that made her grin.

All three possessed the same shade of milk chocolate hair, but only Carter, the oldest, had Noelle's gray eyes. Anthony and Tyler had brown. Like mud, she thought with a snicker.

"I'm surprised to see you out in public," her mother said, chin in the air. "In your condition and drinking alcohol no less."

Maybe this conversation wouldn't be such a trial after all. Fighting a grin, Noelle drained her glass. "This is my baby we're talking about. She's been ready to party since the moment of conception. Maybe even before."

Gasps of outrage, twitters of embarrassment.

"I should have put you over my knee a long time ago. Maybe then you wouldn't enjoy hurting others quite so much." Carter, the eldest and the Tremain heir, glared up at Hector. "Who are you?"

"The guy who will punch your fucking nose into your brain if you talk to her like that again." Hector spoke without any menace, and that made the threat all the more real.

Carter paled.

Noelle stopped fighting and grinned. *My man deserves a reward for that.*

She made the introductions, and her mother—the warden of the Tremain household—gave him a look that said she'd seen better things on the bottom of her shoes.

"I always have the people hanging around my daughter investigated, Mr. Dean. Your yearly income is laughable, and you spend most of it on . . . on . . ." Madam Tremain lowered her voice, whispered disgustedly, "*professionals.* Who do you think you are, bringing that kind of filth around someone of Noelle's pedigree?"

Going straight for the heart. Or groin. Wonderful. And the longer they hung around, the worse it would get.

"He's the best man I know," she interjected, praying Hector believed her. Because it was true! "Better than the bastards you raised." When her brothers sputtered in offense, she glared them into silence. "You know you are. And guess what, Mother. Hector's better than you. Now, if you'll excuse us . . . I see guests in need of a good flashing."

Noelle gave her glass to a slack-jawed Anthony and dragged Hector to the other side of the doorway. His gloves were still in place, so she didn't worry about being burned.

Concern for Hector's feelings nearly overwhelmed her as she whirled to face him. "I'm so sorry." Their differing social status had always bothered him. To be reminded so brutally, and in front of witlessness . . . "She's a snob and I meant what I said. You are my favorite man."

His expression remained blank. "Don't worry about it. She didn't tell you anything that wasn't true. Didn't say anything other people aren't saying."

"Hector—"

Every muscle in his body stiffened, stopping her. "Game face on," he said. Determination radiated from him. "Mr. Phillips just walked in."

Noelle paled. "Wait. Before we approach him, I have to tell you what happened when I left you."

The story she next told him made Hector's blood run cold. Noelle was a capable agent, and he hadn't been apprehensive about her safety. Much. Fine, he'd been apprehensive. But as her words played through his head, he realized she could have been shot, stabbed, abducted, and he wouldn't have known until too late.

That was a quandary for another night, though.

"What do you want to do?" she asked.

Hector took one look at Xavier Phillips and knew Dare— *tell Mia that Dare is back,* he'd said. Dare, Mia's missing younger brother?—had told the God's honest truth. Nothing Hector said would get Phillips to talk. Nothing would trip him up. Too much confidence radiated from him. He was too at ease. Too . . . perfect.

Phillips was tall and lean with coiffed blond hair and flawlessly tanned skin. Two Arcadians flanked his sides, guarding him as they would a national treasure.

He stopped to shake hands with people, conversed, laughed, but never stuck around, and the guards never allowed anyone to get too close. He made the rounds, socializing. Acting friendly, charming females, and it was clear almost everyone liked him.

Only a few men revealed their fear around him. Their laughter was forced, their expressions frozen. Clients, definitely, who knew a ruthless side to the man that the others did not. A man who had abducted and sold countless women, as if they were no more important that sweaters. Strange, though, that Phillips had shared his identity with them rather than use a middleman. Made Hector wonder if Phillips had had to threaten them a time or two.

Things had worked out for Margarete Marks, but Hector doubted many others had come to enjoy their circumstances. Fury rose inside him, sparking the heat and the itch in his arms.

"Noelle," he said, purposely not glancing at her. "I need you to do something for me."

"Anything."

So eager to please, he thought. She assumed her family had hurt him when, in fact, the opposite was true. She'd rushed to his defense. Had called him the best man she knew. Her favorite. For a moment, he'd felt like king of the world. He couldn't let her know, not while they were here. She'd stop being so eager to please. "Stay by my side and stay quiet."

Dare wanted him to walk away, but he couldn't do that. *Wouldn't* do that.

"Uh, okay. Why?"

"That's not staying quiet."

A pause. A clink of her teeth as she gnashed her jaw.

"Come on." He kicked into motion, and as promised, Noelle stayed by his side. Shockingly, she stayed quiet, too.

When they reached Phillips's crowd, Hector shoved his way to the front, earning a few grunts, groans, and several protests—at least until his determination and savagery were realized, then everyone quickly backed away.

The Arcadians stepped in front of Phillips to shield him, but the confident businessman waved them back and frowned at Hector. "I hope you have a reason for such a rude display."

"I do. My name is Hector Dean, and I'm with AIR. I know what you've done, what you're doing, and I'm coming after you with everything I've got."

Smiling, Hector stalked away, a gaping Noelle still at his side and still silent.

"You made yourself a target," Noelle seethed the second they were in the car and speeding along the highway. She hadn't known what to expect as she'd followed him through the ballroom, but that short and sweet conversation wouldn't have entered the realm of possibilities. "*After* that Dare guy told us to stay away from him." Not that she'd planned to do so, but still!

"Yes, I did. And Dare is the name of Mia's missing brother. I don't know if the guy you talked to is legit or not, but her brother was once under the influence of a very powerful Arcadian female. A very evil Arcadian female, and he can't be trusted. So I did what I thought was right."

Putting himself in danger, and Noelle out of it. Placing focus on him and him alone. *Such* a Hector thing to do and something she should have anticipated. Well, now he would just have to deal with the consequences.

"Does your home have shields to protect against teleportation?" she asked.

"No."

"Then you're staying with me."

"No," he repeated. "I *want* the Arcadians to come for me."

Of course he did. "So you can, what? Be hauled to Phillips's lair and burn everyone to ash?"

"Yes," he replied, his tone dripping with relish.

*Damn you, Hector Dean.* "What if they shoot you in the head rather than take you to Phillips?"

A heartbeat of silence, then a shake of his head. "That's not his MO. Phillips likes to make the kill himself. He likes to prove his power."

"That happened once, you idiot! Twice if Maybe Dare Maybe Not Dare can be believed. And twice does not a pattern make. Therefore, you're going to stay with me. But go ahead. Argue with me. See what it gets you."

"Noelle—"

"Hector."

That golden gaze flipped to her, tortured. "I'm too volatile right now."

Her voice dipped huskily when she said, "And I know exactly how to calm you down."

His nostrils flared with his sharp inhalation of breath. "No. I can't risk you. I won't."

*Think again.* "Phillips saw me with you, and I'm very well known. He might try to get to you through me." She wasn't above a little manipulation of her own.

F-bomb after f-bomb filled the car. "All right," he finally growled. "Okay. I'll stay."

*So gracious.*

As excited as she was by the thought of having her man in her house, in her bed, all night long, she was also scared for him. He already battled a ton of shame over his past, and the number of people he'd burned. Did she really think he would suffer no mental anguish this time around?

Afterward, he would remember the screams, the smells, and his fear for hurting *Noelle* would increase. All the progress she'd made with him would be defeated in a single night.

"Noelle," he said, suddenly grave.

Suspicion arose, and her heart skipped a beat. "Yes?"

"What if I can't ever touch you freely, as you need?"

Suspicion confirmed. He'd already jumped to that thought path. Mouth drying, she peered over at him. He'd successfully cleared his features of any emotion, and she couldn't read him. "Hector," she said softly. "I'd rather have a conversation with you than have sex with someone else." Truth.

His jaw clenched, as if he were biting down, but he didn't say another word and neither did she.

# Thirty-eight

HECTOR KNEW BETTER THAN to stay the night with Noelle. Did he have the will to resist her? Probably not. Knowing her, she'd come on strong. She always did, and that was just the way he liked her. Definitely not.

But then all she had to do was breathe and he'd grow hard for her. He craved her more than . . . hell, *anything*. And he loved her. Damn, did he love her.

His eyes widened. He did, he realized. He fucking loved her with every fiber of his being.

She was the loveliest woman he'd ever seen. She had a big heart, a smart mouth. She challenged him, lied to entertain herself, could be violent when the occasion called for it, but she was also fun, sparkling, and as vibrant as the summer sun.

The fact that she threw no judgment his way—for anything—still managed to baffle him. The fact that she sought to comfort and reassure him any time he panicked, more so.

He'd fallen for her, all the way, and knew she was

more than an obsession now. She was his life. Her body was a perfect fit to his. Soft, warm, and wet. Her taste and scent were aphrodisiacs, her cries of passion a siren's song. Uninhibited as she was, she would try anything he asked. And she would like it. Beg for more. And yet . . .

*I'm so bad for her. In every way.* So yes. He *would* resist her tonight. No matter how greatly his body suffered.

Come morning, she'd probably hate him. Another rejection would be more than she could endure. The way her family had spoken to her . . . When this case was closed, Hector would be paying her brothers a little visit, and they'd receive the same intensive care treatment Barry had. But no wonder Noelle was so insecure about how people viewed her.

Hector could deal with her hatred, though. He'd rather she loathed his very existence than feel the sting of his arms.

And if she hated him, she would avoid him. She would treat him like she treated most everyone else. As if he were unworthy of her time. Which he was. Wasn't that what he'd pushed for since the beginning?

Yeah, but he'd kinda gotten used to her showing up wherever he was, throwing out *come and get me* glances, wearing scanty clothing, seducing him, saying outrageous things, making him laugh, never judging him, always defending him.

*What if I never have that again?*

Sweat beaded on his brow, panic for an altogether different reason pummeling him. Shit, he had to get himself together. Had to stay focused. He'd crumble before they even reached her house.

He'd guard her tonight, and that was all. In the morning they would visit the crime scene Dare had mentioned. Hector might even show up at Phillips's office in a bid to spur the guy into action faster. That might earn him a bullet in the brain, as Noelle had suggested, but that was okay.

If Hector had to die taking Phillips down, so be it. No more abducted women. No more otherworlders sold into slavery. No more threats to Noelle.

The car eased to a stop, and Hector emerged but remained in his open doorway, performing a swift, visual perimeter check. Front door, shut. Porch lights, on. Windows, closed. No one hovered on the property, no suspicious shadows lurked about.

Noelle commanded her door to open, then exited, quiet and withdrawn. Why? He hadn't even told her—

A menacing growl rang through the night. Hector shifted his attention just fast enough to see one of the Arcadians from the party appear out of nowhere, still in his tux, already barreling toward Noelle, something silver in his hand. Silver and sharp, glinting in the light seeping from her porch.

Oh, fuck no. With a roar, Hector dove over the hood of the car, sliding . . . sliding . . . praying he was able to shove her out of harm's way, even if he had to take a killing blow himself.

The otherworlder reached her a split second before Hector did. Her instincts were well honed, and when the guy slammed into her, knocking her down, attempting to sink the blade into her kidney—a kill shot—she twisted and rolled, and Hector soared over them both.

He popped to his feet a heartbeat later, whipping around, rage red flickering in his line of vision. Rage red, and blood. Despite Noelle's maneuver, the tip of the blade must have slicked over her dress and into *her*, because there were splatters of blood soaking the material to her waist. She held her side with one hand as she unfolded to a stand. In the other, she clutched a dagger of her own. It, too, was bloody.

She'd managed to stab the guy, and maybe that was why he hadn't yet teleported away . . . why he was lumbering to a stand, stumbling from her, escaping the old-fashioned way.

"You okay?" Hector demanded, so damn furious he felt engulfed by flames. He hadn't gotten to his woman in time. If she hadn't reacted as she had, she would be dead. Could still die . . . that blood . . . his burning, itching hands began to singe through the material covering them.

"I'm good, I swear," she said with surprising force. "Now go get him."

Hector needed no other prompting. He propelled into motion, giving chase. *This man. Had hurt. Noelle.*

This man would die.

Didn't take Hector long to catch up. He dove a second time, made contact. Both of them were flung into the huge oak in Noelle's front yard before rolling to the ground.

Hector grabbed the guy by his jacket. Or tried to.

His hands destroyed the rest of the gloves and ghosted straight through the man's body, hitting the cold slab of dirt beneath him. The otherworlder spasmed once—then never moved again.

Against his forearm, Hector felt the sizzling of the guy's heart. Knew the organ was in the process of *cooking*. He jerked free, the guy burning to ashes and scattering in the wind. *That* quickly.

*Not sorry.* Anyone who hurt Noelle deserved what they got.

Noelle!

Fear and fury battled for supremacy as Hector straightened the rest of the way. At the same time, flames sparked in the grass, where the body had been, catching, growing, then reaching the flowers, catching, growing, then slithering toward Noelle's house. *Shit!*

Hector swung around, searching for any other threat against his woman. No one else stepped from the shadows. He focused on Noelle. She held a phone to her ear with one hand, was still clutching her side with the other.

Pale and shaky, she disconnected from the call and took a step toward him. "Whole crew is on the way. Firemen, medics, AIR."

"Stay back, sweetheart. I don't want you burned." He held out an arm to ward her off, saw a mist of crackling blue, glowing so brightly his eyes teared. His jacket, gone. His shirt, vaporized. Skin, muscle, bone, vanished. Only that mist remained.

He'd completely atomized. Anything he touched would be razed the very instant of contact.

Horror swept through him, but he didn't give in to that emotion, either. Behind him, the fire continued to grow and rage. He could hear the crackle of flames, feel the smoldering of the bricks.

"Let me help you," Noelle said, silver gaze on him rather than her ruined home.

"Listen to me, sweetheart." Smoke wafted around him, thick and black, and he coughed. "You can't get close to me. Not right now."

Though she looked like she wanted to argue, she leaned against the car, maintaining distance. Was his proud, strong girl trembling?

"How bad are you?" he demanded. *Stay calm. Don't make things worse.*

"Not very. A few stitches and I'll be fine."

Stitches, a needle being threaded through her precious skin. Another spark of anger caused the azure to pulse. He grit his molars.

Finally, the medics arrived and converged on Noelle to patch her up. When one of them tried to approach him, shock and terror in his eyes, Hector issued a harsh threat that kept him and everyone else at bay.

The firemen arrived next, bustling around to douse the flames with whatever enzyme spray they used. They even sprayed *him*, but the blue didn't dissipate in the slightest.

He could have run, could have tried to keep his identity under wraps, but he wasn't leaving until someone he trusted stood next to Noelle.

As if summoned from Hector's thoughts alone, Dallas arrived, sprinting onto the scene like the hero he was. He checked on Noelle, who erupted into a speech Hector couldn't hear over the chaos of the sirens.

Hector turned to view the charred remains of Noelle's home. Nothing would be salvaged, he realized, fucking hating himself. His chest hollowed out, his fears flooding him. He could have torched Noelle, could have done that to Noelle.

That easily, he made a decision. They were done. In every way. No waiting to see if he could learn to control himself. No working together. No back and forth seduction. No hoping he would change. He'd just proven to himself that he could *never* be trusted around her.

A frowning Dallas approached him slowly. "What can I do to help you?"

"Shoot me with the strongest damn tranq the medics have. Twice." Without his emotions to fuel him, his arms would go back to normal. "Then take me home and make sure no one—fucking *no one*—comes over."

# Thirty-nine

*F*UCKING DALLAS, HECTOR THOUGHT two days later
as he strode through AIR. Conversations tapered
off. Eyes of every color watched him warily. No one
said a word to him. He didn't care.

The tranq had worked, returning his arms to normal
and knocking him out all night and most of the next
day. Except the bastard hadn't taken Hector home.
He'd woken up in the hospital, tubes and electrodes
hooked to practically every inch of him.

He'd been utterly shocked that no government of-
ficials were waiting to bag and tag him. Shocked that
reporters hadn't swarmed the place.

Shocked that a bandaged Noelle lay in the bed next
to him, sleeping peacefully, lovely and alive, and breaking his goddamn heart because he couldn't hold her.
He'd checked her file—thirty-eight stitches in her side,
a small blood transfusion—and left her there.

A very worried—and very pale, befanged, and pissed
off—Ava had been in the hallway, talking to Dallas,
who'd been giving her the scoop. They'd tried to stop

him, launched questions at him, but he'd kept going, hadn't looked back.

Now . . .

*You know what you have to do.*

He found Mia in her office, the door open. She sat at her desk, her dark head bent over an electronic file. A soft rap of his knuckles against the frame, and her attention snapped up.

Astonishment filled her baby blues, followed by concern and resolve. "Didn't expect you in until to-morrow," she said. "But, okay, we can do this now. Sit down." She motioned to the chair in front of her desk with an imperial wave of her hand.

After closing the door with the press of a button, he plopped down. "Wanted to give you my report."

One brow arched as she studied him. Leaning back, she crossed her arms over her middle. Same pose she'd adapted when he and Noelle had been here last, re-questing permission to attend the party. *I don't like it*, she'd said then. Now he got, "Okay, then, let's hear it."

"I told Phillips I was coming after him. He sent an Arcadian assassin to Noelle's home. That Arcadian stabbed her, and I gave chase. I caught him and killed him with my hands."

"Hands that glowed a bright blue," she said.

A jerky nod. No reason to deny it. People had seen. People had to be talking.

"Those hands of yours also turned Tremain's house into a bonfire, without the use of a match."

Another nod. He didn't wait for the questions, just tossed out the answers. "Any time my emotions get too volatile, my arms react. They heat. They burn things. Anything. Anyone."

"Explains a lot," she said. "So . . . are you an otherworlder?"

"No. I'm human. A mistake." A mistake that had ruined Noelle's life.

She rolled her eyes. "That's a bit self-deprecating, don't you think? We all have things we have to deal with. Look at me. I'm half Arcadian."

Took a moment for her words to sink in. "Impossible." Half-breeds, hybrids, whatever scientist wanted to call them, were . . . entirely possible, he decided. In this day and age, anything was. He'd even suspected— hoped—that's what he was, though he now knew better. He *was* a mistake, plain and simple.

"Anyway, we aren't here to talk about me," she went on blithely. "You went too far the other night."

Understatement of the century, but okay. Like he'd really correct her. "Yes. I did."

She arched a brow, the picture of curiosity and pique. "Is that something you're going to do again?"

"No."

"Good. If you ever feel yourself nearing the danger zone, come to me. Talk to me, and we'll take measures to ensure you get back on track safely. And just so you know, everyone who was there that night thinks you were doused with a toxic chemical, and that's why you were glowing. It's a miracle you survived, yada yada. Only you, me, Dallas, and Tremain know the truth. Also, Tremain claimed the Arcadian started the fire. I only know the truth because Dallas filled me in."

Just before passing out, he remembered telling Dallas to talk to Mia, to explain. He should have said something to Noelle, too. He despised the fact that she'd been put in a position to lie for him. He appreciated what she'd done, yeah, but he just wished she hadn't been backed into that corner.

"Casewise, Dare was right. If the guy Noelle spoke to was indeed Dare." Mia's eyes glassed over, as if she were fighting a sudden bout of tears. A second later, the glassiness vanished and she continued, her tone brisk. "We found bones at the location he gave us. Another abandoned field. Gerard Hendrick. Buried there for a little over a year."

"Can you prove Phillips was responsible?"

"No. And we can't prove the Arcadian who attacked you was one of the ones with Phillips at the party, either."

"He was. I made a positive ID."

"But you can't prove it. He's been burned beyond recognition."

Anger had his hands fisting. *Calm.* "So Phillips gets away with having an agent stabbed?" My *agent.*

*No, not yours. Not anymore.*

"No. We'll get him. The problem is, humans, *wealthy* humans, surrounded him at the time of the stabbing. We're asking around, hoping someone heard him order the hit, or saw the Arcadian leave, but so far no luck. And it doesn't help that he acted so quickly against your threat, or that Arcadians can only teleport to places they've previously been. The one who stabbed Tremain couldn't have followed you, or known you were going to her place—in theory."

So the bastard had been to her place before.

"Dare told Tremain that Phillips had you guys looked into the moment you were assigned to the Marks case, that he was watching your progress."

So Noelle was still in danger. Would be in constant danger until this was done. Until Phillips was dead.

"I quit," he said. He'd thought about this since the moment he'd woken up, and had planned to quit after closing the case—if Mia hadn't fired him first. Even though Mia seemed to accept him, seemed to think he could do a decent job from now on, he wasn't taking a chance.

As soon as he took care of the Phillips problem, Hector was leaving New Chicago.

As long as he remained near Noelle, he was a hazard to her continued health. That's where the true danger lay with her—the temptation of being with her. He'd known it, had fought against it, but now there was no denying it. His desires were his downfall. He wanted her more than he'd ever wanted anyone else.

He couldn't control his passion, and he couldn't control his fury. So he was disappearing.

Several minutes passed in stunned silence. "No," Mia said, shaking her head to emphasize her denial. "Unacceptable."

"I'm a menace."

"We all are."

"I quit, Mia." He wasn't working with the law on this one. He was going to kill the bastard in cold blood and end this. Today. Nothing and no one would convince him otherwise.

He stood.

"I'm giving you a few days to think this through," Mia gritted out. She wasn't used to flat-out refusal.

"Don't need them. I quit, effective immediately." Next up: Phillips.

# *Forty*

❦

NOELLE LEANED AGAINST THE side of Hector's Jag, waiting for him. Since her arrival in the parking garage, several agents had checked in and several agents had checked out. Each had wanted to speak to her, but she'd waved them on their way, not willing to deal with any distractions.

Hector had bailed on her at the hospital, while she was too drugged to notice. Bastard! He should have considered the possibility that Ava would wake her up, they would hack into the AIR GPS, and drive to wherever he was.

Ava, who made one hell of a gorgeous vampiress. A little paler, but all the lovelier for it, with sharp, white fangs and adorable claw-tipped nails.

Upon seeing her, Noelle had groggily said, "You're so cute, I want to stuff you in my pocket and carry you around forever."

Ava had replied, "After the scare you just gave me, the only thing likely to be stuffed is your face—with my fist!" And miracle of miracles, she hadn't had a lisp.

Then they'd hugged and if they'd been emotional pansies, they would have cried. Noelle had had something in her eye, that was all. They'd talked about Noelle's decision not to turn into a vampire herself, and Ava had understood. That didn't mean she'd been gracious, but she had understood. Noelle's heart belonged to Hector. She had to remain human, no matter what happened between them.

Now Ava sat in Noelle's car at the other end of the parking garage. Shadows enveloped her. The sun shone through the open pockets of concrete, lighting up the area behind and beside her, but even if a stray ray of light managed to sneak all the way to the car, the windows were completely tinted, as capable of blocking UVA as curtains. Which was necessary. As the books stated, vampires possessed very sensitive skin, and blistered easily.

After busting Noelle out of the hospital, Ava had refused to leave her side, keeping guard, ensuring Noelle remained conscious. So she'd lost a little blood. Big deal. She was on the mend and steady on her feet. For the most part. And the cut in her side? Whatever. *Had worse.*

*Where are you, Hector?*

The conversation she and Ava had had just before she'd exited played through her mind.

"Sure you want to do this?" Ava had asked. "Because if you want to break up with him, I've got a wicked cool speech, only six words, and he'll leave you alone forever."

Breaking up wasn't on the menu, but she'd had

to hear her friend's guaranteed relationship ender. "Tell me."

"Just say: I will finance your penile enlargement."

Noelle had nearly choked on her own laughter. "I don't want to be without him. He's mine. My McKell. I have to try and win him." One last time, she had to try to convince him they belonged together. No matter what.

The look he'd given her just before Dallas pegged him with the tranq . . . hard, determined, unwavering. He meant to end things.

"I'd like to say I'm dismayed that you picked a human torch," Ava had said, "but honestly? I expected worse."

Yeah, Noelle had spilled about Hector's ability. He'd kinda let the rabbit out of the hat on that one, anyway. Although things really were contained, the truth buried.

"So what do you think your likelihood of success is?" Ava had asked next.

"Darling, this is in the bag." Bravado, pure and simple. She'd never been so unsure. With his spine of iron, Hector rarely backed down from a decision.

The parking garage's only elevator, the one that led to and from AIR offices, dinged, opened, and out he strode. She straightened. He stopped short when he spotted her, then squared his shoulders, pasted a scowl on his face, and kicked back into motion.

"What are you doing up?" he demanded.

"Chasing you. You should feel proud. I've never done this for anyone else, but you've made me do it for you over and over again."

"You should have stayed in bed, damn it."

Her heart drummed unsteadily. They were off to a bad start. He'd just ignored her confession. Well, she'd just have to up the stakes. "I came here to tell you that I want you. I love you, and you need to deal with it." There. Out in the open.

She loved him. All that he was, all that he would be. Every obstinate, protective inch of him. His power, his passion, his drive. *She loved him.*

Stunned disbelief, then a furious shake of his head. "No. I don't need to deal with anything. I quit AIR. I'm leaving New Chicago. I'm leaving *you*."

A move she hadn't predicted. Sickness churned in her stomach. "I don't care about the house. I don't care about what was in it. Don't do this because you feel guilty. Don't do this because you're scared."

He gave a bitter laugh as he scrubbed an ungloved hand over his face. He'd taken the time to tattoo himself, the symbols dark and glossy. "Scared doesn't even begin to describe what I feel, Noelle. If you had been near me, you would have died. Do you understand that?"

"We've been over this. You could have, but you didn't. I could have, but I didn't."

"That's not good enough for me."

Here she was, fighting for him, for *them*, and he oh, so casually dismissed her. She reached out to flatten her palms on his chest, needing contact with him, any kind of contact, but he stepped away, out of reach.

"Hector," she shouted, stomping her foot in frustration. "Don't do this."

"I could feed you some bullshit line about not thinking I'm enough for you, say I'm still concerned about my past, or even tell you all the things I want to change about you," he said, broken, "but I won't. Even though I know you'd haul ass and never look back. Thing is, I love you. I love you so goddamn much, I'm a mess. I'm leaving you anyway. Nothing will change that. *Nothing.* Do you hear me?"

He loved her. *He loved her.* Only that knowledge beat through her dread and rallied her. "Don't do this, Hector. Give us a chance. Please."

*You're begging?* Yes, and she didn't care. She just wanted him.

His jaw clenched, as if he were fighting with the need to accept. "Go back to the hospital, Noelle. There's nothing more for us to say to each other."

"Hector, please—"

"Stop!" he shouted, at last killing the distance and getting in her face. "Just stop. Do I need to feed you the bullshit? Is that what it's going to take? We are done. Do you understand? Done."

In and out she breathed, the air like fire in her lungs, scorching. As she'd feared, he wouldn't back down. He was ending things, and that was that. He wasn't going to try, wasn't going to give her a chance. Even though he loved her.

"All right," she said, tears falling freely. "Okay."

He'd never looked more upset, but he said, "Finally."

A shudder rippled along her vertebrae, vibrating through the rest of her. "I'm through chasing you. I'm through seducing you for your own good. I'm through!"

She gave another stomp of her foot, emotion giving her strength.

"Good," he croaked. "That's good."

Her chin lifted. *Don't cry anymore. Don't you dare fucking cry anymore.* "If you learn to control your ability, don't come back for me."

"I . . . won't."

Bastard! "You should have wanted me enough to fight for me. The way I was willing to fight for you. I mean, I convinced myself you were different than everyone else, that you really saw me, and maybe you really did, but that still wasn't enough, was it." A statement, not a question. "I was never enough."

He took a step closer to her now, as if her pain had reached him as nothing else could have. "Noelle, don't say that about yourself. You are—"

"No!" She flattened herself against the Jag, was shaking her head. Dizziness hit her, but she didn't shut up. "You had your chance. You wanted to push me away, well, congratulations. You've now succeeded."

"It's for your own good," he shouted, beside her and banging a fist into the metal, shaking the entire vehicle. "I'm always on edge with you. I can't lower my guard for a second. If I do, I could kill you, and I couldn't live with myself if that happened. You deserve better. You deserve a man who can touch you. A man who can give you everything you need."

*You were that man.* He would never think so, though. "You know what? One day I'll get over you and move on." A lie, such a terrible lie. "One day I'll find a man who actually enjoys spending time with me, who thinks

I'm worth any risk, even a risk to myself. But you . . . you'll never get over me. I'm it for you and without me, you might as well curl up and die."

Tears filled *his* eyes, the gold shimmering. "You're right. You *are* it for me. I know there will never be anyone else. And I don't want anyone—" Suddenly his mouth sagged open, strange sounds escaping, and then his knees buckled.

"Hector, what's—" That's when she saw the Arcadian standing behind him—the Arcadian who had teleported in, stabbing a needle into Hector's neck. And now hers. A sting of pain, a flood of warmth.

In the background, she heard Ava's scream of rage, heard the pound of booted footsteps, then her entire world went black.

# *Forty-one*

❧

*H*ECTOR FOUGHT HIS WAY through a thick, cloying fog. He'd been shouting at Noelle, desperate to make her understand, aching for her, wanting to soothe the pain in her eyes, knowing he couldn't, when . . . something happened.

A sharp tingle in his neck, a total wipeout of the mind. What the hell had happened?

He blinked open his eyes, and several moments passed before he was able to focus. He was sitting in a chair, upright though he couldn't support his own weight. He was shirtless. And his— *Oh, fuck no!*

His bare hands were taped around Noelle's neck, her skin warm and soft beneath his palms, her pulse racing.

Horror lit a match of understanding in his brain. Teleported out of AIR. Strapped to a chair, Noelle strapped to a chair in front of him. All of his fears manifested, right here, right now. He'd been so careful never to touch her. And now . . . now . . . He wanted to hack off both of his arms. Wished he had. They wouldn't be in this situation.

Her hands were cuffed to the arms of her chair, her ankles cuffed to its legs. His gaze met hers. Rather than fear or pain, he saw anger in those silver depths.

"Are you—"

"I'm fine," she said without any emotion.

"Oh, good. Everyone's awake." Xavier Phillips stepped into Hector's line of sight, his expression smug, gleeful, his pale hair smoothed into place. Every inch of his gray business suit proved flawless, not a single wrinkle. He looked as if he were attending a meeting with the board rather than an execution.

And that's what he had planned, no question. He'd watch as Hector burned his woman to death. Afterward, he'd shoot Hector in the head. Or maybe he'd just let Hector go, let him live with the awfulness of what he'd done.

"Pays to have Arcadians in your employ." Phillips dusted an invisible piece of lint from his shoulder. "Makes gathering your enemies so very, very easy."

From the corner of his eye, Hector stealthily catalogued his surroundings. They were in a warehouse of some sort, emptied out but for the chairs they were perched on. Besides Phillips, there were two other threats. The Arcadian who'd grabbed them and a dark-haired, blue-eyed man Hector had once seen . . . when? Where?

He slashed through the lingering mental fog, scenes forming, vanishing, and realized he'd seen the guy walking a dog outside of Bobby Marks's home. And then again at the restaurant with Brenda Marks, which he hadn't thought anything about at the time.

Rich people lived in the same neighborhoods and frequented the same places.

Now, up close like this, he realized exactly who he was dealing with, and wanted to curse. Dare Snow. Noelle had noticed him at the restaurant, too, had said he was the one who'd approached her at the ball, but Hector hadn't noticed the resemblance to Mia until now.

An interesting development, but not one that would help him. Dare, undercover with his own goal, wouldn't blow everything he'd worked for to save Hector and Noelle. In fact, the guy might kill them before Phillips could, simply to keep his secret.

"How'd you know we'd be there, in the garage?" Hector croaked to Phillips, desperate to buy time, to think. He had to keep his emotions under wraps. Had to remain numbed out. Meanwhile, he also had to come up with a way to get Noelle the fuck out of there!

"One of my Arcadians stayed at Bobby's crime scene and followed you home. The next day you switched cars with a female agent, the head of AIR, and he placed a tracker on yours. I knew where you were every minute of every day."

Hector had felt eyes watching him so many times, but he'd never thought . . . never known. Some agent he was.

"I was content to leave you alone as you played at your investigation because I didn't expect you to get very far. When you took Gordman"—the barest hint of anger—"I experienced a moment of panic, but you never came for me, never approached me, and I figured he had kept his mouth closed. Now I can only assume he gave you my name?" A question, rather than a statement.

Hector would not admit they'd stolen information from Gordman's car. He didn't want the guy forewarned for the future, taking precautions. Just in case Hector failed in his current mission. "Exactly right." Gordman was slime, but he was currently under AIR protection, so he'd—maybe—be okay. *No guilt.*

"My mistake, then." Phillips reached out, dug his fingers into Hector's scalp, and forced him to face Noelle. "When my prized Arcadian failed to return the night of the party, I knew something was wrong and sent another. I was told your arms glowed blue and burned everything they touched."

*I'm so sorry, sweetheart,* he tried to project.

She seemed to look past him. "So why are we here?" she snapped. "What do you want?"

"You've been a nuisance, and I'm tired of waiting for you to go away. Now you'll share information with me or you'll suffer. And I don't think I need to tell you that you're going to die today, no matter what. It's how you die that's up for negotiation."

"Like?" she prompted. "What do you want to know?"

"Like, how did you know where I kept some of those women? Not Gordman. You raided several warehouses *before* you captured him."

She didn't miss a beat. "And if we don't tell you?"

*Damn it! Don't poke the bear.*

Phillips smiled fondly. "I must say, I enjoy bantering with you, Miss Tremain. In fact, I've wanted to meet you for a while. You're very beautiful, elegant, if a bit of a wild card."

"Can't deny it. But if you'd bothered to check my dating profile—currently single," she added with a dignified sniff despite her bindings, "you would have found out that I think slavers are pretty much the scum of the earth."

Hector didn't mean to, but he squeezed her neck in a bid to quiet her.

Phillips laughed, the sound as chic as the man himself. "All right, enough pleasantries. Let's get this interrogation started." When he extended his arm, palm out, the white-haired Arcadian gave him a syringe. "This is adrenaline"—a dramatic pause to ensure he had their attention—"among other things. You see, I did a little research on you, Miss Tremain, and discovered interesting facts about your father and what was done to you. What?" he said when she balked. "You thought that was a secret? Sorry to disappoint you, but acquiring information is a hobby of mine. Anyway, I found the methods for keeping you awake during your surgery quite interesting."

Hector gulped, struggled in his chair, but all he managed to do was shake Noelle around, and he stilled. Sweat beaded on his forehead. He could guess where this was headed.

"Here's what is going to happen," Phillips said. "I'll ask a question. One of you will answer. When you don't, I will inject Agent Dean straight in the heart. And just so you know how serious I am, he'll get his first injection now."

"Don't you dare," Noelle growled in her first true surge of emotion. A potent mix of rage and fear Hector knew intimately.

"Oh, I'll dare."

Hector tried to scoot out of the way, and Noelle tried to shove him out of the way, but even with their joint efforts, Phillips reached between them and slammed the needle deep in his chest without any problems.

Instantly, Hector's blood heated and his heartbeat quickened. Tingles erupted in his shoulders and flowed down his arms, catching in his fingertips. A slight glow seeped through his pores, causing his fresh tattoos to crackle. All over, sweat began to pour from him.

"Fascinating," Phillips said, watching him closely.

Noelle didn't seem to notice. But then, her pain receptors were fried, so she wouldn't know if she were nearing decapitation.

Fear and more of the horror blended inside him, the adrenaline or whatever it was cranking them up, magnifying both until he could barely breathe. Shit, shit, shit! *Concentrate. Protect Noelle. Must protect Noelle.*

Dallas had said it was all about restraint. Mind over mind. Mind over fucking matter.

"You were about to tell me how you knew where my otherworlders were being kept," Phillips stated calmly.

Both guards flanked his side, glaring down at Hector. His skin itched, heated another degree. He closed his eyes. *Calm.* "Lucky guess, that's all." Keep the focus on himself, away from Noelle.

"Another injection already?" Phillips grinned, held out his hand. "Very well."

"Anonymous source," Noelle rushed out. "And no, we don't know who it is."

Truth mixed with a lie. Smart. How would Dare react? Hector looked the white-haired Arcadian over first, not wanting to be obvious, then Dare. Still glaring, no hint of fear. All the while, sweat continued to pour off Hector, his heart a maddened fist in his chest.

"Sorry, but you'll have to do better than that." Phillips curled his fingers around a new syringe but didn't use it. Yet. "AIR is a well-oiled machine. Inquiries would have been made. Calls and emails would have been traced. Anonymous would not have remained a mystery for long."

Silence. He and Noelle stared at each other, worried, unsure. So far, Hector had things under control. But—

"All right. You only have yourself to blame for this," Phillips said. A second needle jabbed into Hector's heart.

The flood of heat was instant, the organ hammering against his ribs so hard the beat soon became warped. His horror intensified. His fear intensified. The itching and burning in his arms intensified. The glow in his shoulders and forearms intensified.

Smoke curled from his skin, thickening with every second that passed.

No. *No!* Air hissed through his teeth. Couldn't burn Noelle. Must remain calm.

"Hector," Noelle said, her tone gentle. "Look at me. I'm fine. *I'm fine.*"

He couldn't hurt her. He couldn't. He would rather die. Mind over matter. MIND OVER MATTER.

The glow continued to brighten . . . brighten.

"I'm fine," she insisted.

"And I want a name," Phillips said smoothly.

Both voices were a blur of noise inside Hector's head. *Mind over matter.* He chanted the phrase over and over. He would not hurt Noelle. She was his love, his life. HE WOULD NOT HURT HER.

Every muscle he possessed bunched and strained. He would not hurt her. He would not fucking hurt her. More sweat poured from him, little rivers all over his body. Okay, okay. So he couldn't control his emotions or his body's reactions. But maybe he could *move* them. He attempted to channel all the heat into his chest, away from Noelle, imagining sucking it there like a vacuum.

To his amazement, the itching in his arms just . . . stopped. The heat even muted. His chest was a different story. The itching and the heating erupted there.

Noelle blinked in astonishment. She felt it, then; it wasn't just his imagination. She felt the ease from fire pit to over-warm bath.

Hector kept sucking on the heat, letting it pool around his heart, burning and crackling there. *I can do this,* he realized. And if he could redirect the burn . . .

Phillips said something else. When there was no reply, he held out his hand for another syringe. Frowning, saying something else, he slammed that third syringe home.

Hector released an animalistic roar—and channeled the heat into the needle, into the hand holding it. Shoving, shoving desperately, pushing every ember out of him, holding nothing inside.

Whether the act would work, he didn't—

Phillips released his own roar as the plastic syringe instantly melded to his hand. Eyes wide with pain, rasping shallowly, trembling, he stumbled away, fell to his ass. He issued commands, or tried to, his words jumbled. His guards scrambled to him, trying to help him rather than ensuring the captives remained in place.

A new tidal wave of adrenaline filled Hector. His sweating increased yet again, and so did the burn. But so did his strength. A side effect Phillips probably hadn't considered. As he drew the heat into his chest, he gritted his teeth and ripped at the thick adhesive holding him to Noelle. Weakened from the extreme temperatures, the tape split apart, and suddenly Hector was free.

He allowed himself a brief look at Noelle's neck— red, blistered, but otherwise fine—before he shoved the guards out of the way and leapt on top of Phillips, grabbing *him* by the neck. Hector released the mental bonds on the fury and the heat, and his arms lit up, two inextinguishable bonfires.

Phillips struggled against him, mouth flailing open and closed, eyes tearing—until his head detached from his body. Both his head and his body erupted into flames a second later. Burning . . . burning . . .

Dare punted Hector in the side, trying to force him off the bastard, but it was too late. Satisfaction washed through Hector. Phillips would never abduct or sell another female, and Noelle would be safe now. Even from him. Hector hadn't hurt her, even while jacked up on emotion. Even with his hands shackled around her neck.

Suddenly the side door burst open and armed AIR agents flooded inside. People were shouting commands, but Hector still couldn't make out individual words.

He couldn't quite catch his breath and his arms were still blue and glowing. He scooted back, out of Noelle's path so that the agents could get to her. The white-haired Arcadian vanished in one blink, and Dare in the next. Now that Phillips was dead, the Arcadian would be Dare's only link to whomever he searched for.

Concentrating with everything he had, Hector willed his arms back to normal, channeling the heat through his entire being, spreading it out, letting it seep through his pores like mist. Took several minutes, but the glow finally began to fade, the burn to subside.

Even though he'd been controlling the ability for several minutes, an eternity surely, his success still managed to shock him. He'd never dreamed . . . had always hoped . . . yet had always found disappointment. Now . . . he could trust himself around Noelle. Beyond a doubt, he could be with her safely.

Joy ripped through him, as unstoppable as an avalanche.

Whatever she wanted from him, he would give her. An apology? Begging? Whatever she needed, he would supply. They would be together. Yes, she'd told him they were done if he pushed her away. But that was before this, before he'd proven himself. And she loved him. Just as he was, she loved him. Noelle was not a woman to love lightly.

He dragged himself to his feet. His clothes were singed and still smoking. His muscles twitched with energy, his heart beating so swiftly and with such force he feared it would burst through his chest at any second. "Noelle." Where was—

There. She had her back to him and her arms around Ava.

"Noelle."

Twisting, she met his gaze. Her expression was blank, and he experienced a kernel of unease. "Yes?"

"Are you okay?" He closed the distance between them, so desperate to touch her, to finally hold her as he'd always fantasized about, he could barely contain himself.

"I'm fine. And hey, thanks for not killing me," she said with a bland smile. Then she returned her attention to Ava and the pair strutted out of the warehouse.

# Forty-two

❦

NO MATTER WHAT HECTOR did or said the next few weeks, Noelle wanted nothing to do with him. She never gave him anything more than that bland smile. Once, she'd even patted him on the top of his head and pinched his cheek like she'd done to Dallas that first day of camp.

A lesser man would have given up. There was stubborn, and then there was *I'd rather die*. Noelle bypassed even that. But Hector wasn't a lesser man. Noelle had chased him, and now he was chasing her. That was only fair.

For too long, he'd just accepted the fact that he couldn't be with anyone. Then she'd come along and screwed with his head, his body (thank God for that!), and his heart. Now she had to live with the consequences. Because bottom line? He wouldn't live without her.

He was from the streets, something he'd once considered a stumbling block between them. Well, no more. Over the years he'd learned how to break the rules, and that's exactly what he planned to do with her.

Noelle spent all of her time furnishing her new home, as well as recovering from the stitches in her side and minor burns on her neck. Though she'd told only Ava her new address, Hector had found her and had showed up the very day she'd moved in.

After discovering out how he'd done it—AIR had pegged them both with the isotope tracker while they were laid flat in the hospital, which was how they'd come to the "rescue" that day in the warehouse—she'd shut the door in his face.

Same thing the next night, and the next. Seeing him hurt her soul-deep. So talk to him? Hell, no.

She had warned him. Let her go again, and lose her forever. At the time, he'd been okay with that. Just because he'd changed his mind didn't mean she would change hers.

He'd proven to himself that he wouldn't hurt her. So what. He could touch her without fear now. So what, she thought as longing swept through her. He'd pushed her away one too many times. Had broken her heart into a thousand pieces he could never hope to patch up.

And any time she thought she would cave, she just reminded herself that he could change his mind yet again. He could decide he was still too dangerous and leave her. *Not going through this again.*

She climbed the steps of her new porch, used the ID pad to let herself in. Night had fallen, and she'd forgotten to program the lights to switch on automatically. She'd spent the day with Ava, who'd kicked McKell out of their apartment and to his man cave so that Noelle could be pampered in peace.

In her living room, she patted the walls until she found the light switch. Took her forever, because she hadn't yet learned the layout of the place. Hadn't had voice recognition software installed, either, so that she would only have to speak a command for things to happen. Finally, her finger caught on the switch and light chased all the shadows away.

Hector sat on her new couch, gorgeous as always. Black hair unkempt, shirt wrinkled and rolled up to his elbows, his pants dirt-stained. His arms were bared, without gloves. His tattoos were dark, freshly applied—but those tattoos weren't symbols for peace. Her name was scripted on every inch of visible skin, from fingertips to elbow. Her heart gave a leap. *Stay strong.* "What the hell are you doing here?"

Golden eyes pierced her. "Forcing you to listen to me. I'm sorry. I am so sorry for nearly leaving you."

Another leap. "Nearly leaving me? Ha! You did. Your apology is too late. I've moved on."

He flinched, then quickly rallied. Determination wafted from him.

"I heard you quit AIR," she said, trying for a breezy tone. When she returned to work, she and Ava would be partners. They would work the night shift. Together, as they'd always dreamed.

As thrilled as Noelle was, she hated the thought of working without Hector.

"Mia hired me back," he said. "Paired me with Dallas. We'll be working the night shift, too."

So he'd checked up on her. *I will stay strong, damn it.* "That's cool. Whatever. I'm sure Ava and me will be kicking so much ass, we'll never be in the office."

"Predators should be afraid." His features softened. "I also came to tell you that I love you. With everything that I am, I love you. Just the way you are. I don't want you to change. I just want you to be with me."

And yet another leap in her chest. *Strong.* "Like I said, you're too late."

"Noelle—"

"Look, you really need to go." Before she broke down in front of him.

Hands fisted, he stood. "You were always enough for me, but I was never enough for you, and I know that. I'm not talking about my past, either. Because I'm the best man you know. You said so."

"I changed my mind."

"That just means I have the chance to change it back. Just give me a chance. Please."

*Strong, strong, strong.* "I told you nothing you said would make a difference, that if you pushed me away you'd lose me. You pushed me away. We're done, that's what *you* said."

Shame fell over his face, a curtain. "I will never forgive myself for that. I was stupid and afraid, thinking to protect you."

"Instead, you broke my heart. Hurt me worse than anyone ever has." Tears burned the back of her eyes. "And one day you'll be stupid and afraid again. You'll accidentally burn me and the risk will be too much for you." She spun around, facing the foyer before those damn tears started falling. She'd cried in front of him once; she wouldn't do it a second time. "Good-bye, Hector. You can see yourself out."

Just as she'd done in the warehouse, she walked away from him without ever looking back. She pounded up the stairs, her heart breaking all over again. He'd just offered her the world, everything she'd ever wanted, and she'd basically said no thanks.

*Had to be this way.*

A tear at last fell, followed quickly by another.

When she reached her bedroom, she flipped on the light. There was her new bed, an oversize king with the softest cotton sheets. Red, one of her best colors. Hector would never enjoy her there. *She* would never enjoy *him* there. Never—

A pound of furious footsteps behind her. A gasp catching in her throat, she swung around. A scowling Hector rounded the corner. Without a word, he increased his speed, picked her up and launched her backward. She bounced on the mattress. Before she could right herself, he had her pinned.

"I love you," he snarled down at her, "and I'm not letting you go again. Ever. For any reason. Not even your reasons. I should have listened to you, and you can forever hold that over my head. You can remind me at every holiday and every time I leave my socks on the floor. I'll deserve it. I should have stuck around, rather than giving in to my fears. But now you're doing the same thing. Cutting and running because you're afraid. I understand, I do, but you better listen up, baby. You once had to chase and seduce me. Now I'm chasing and seducing you. That's what I've been doing, but clearly I need to step up my game the way you stepped up yours."

His lips smashed into hers, and his tongue swept inside her mouth. He tasted of mint, just like before, and she moaned as desire began to burn through her sorrow.

His hands . . . his hands stripped her, stripped himself, and then caressed her everywhere. He left no place untouched, was *worshipping* her. His fingertips learned her face. Kneaded her breasts. Traced over her stomach, her legs, even her feet.

"I've wanted to do this since the moment I met you," he whispered fiercely. "You're so soft, so warm. So sweet. Spread for me, baby. Please. I need to put my fingers in you."

Passion fogged her brain, and she obeyed without thought, needing him, loving him.

One thick finger slid inside her. "Oh, damn, baby. You feel so good. Better than I imagined. And I imagined doing this to you every damn night." Another thick finger entered her.

Groaning at the erotic sensation, she arched her hips, sending him deeper. A third finger joined the others. His skin was hotter than a normal man's, but that's what she needed. She felt him there, so wonderfully deep, arousing her in the most beautiful way.

"I want to do this to you every night, want to wake you up this way every morning. And if not with my fingers, with my mouth. I want you all over me, in me. You were right, baby. You're it for me. There's no one else. There's never been anyone else and there will never be anyone else. Just you. Only you."

As he spoke, he rocked those wanton fingers inside her, surging in, pulling out, until she was sobbing, desperate for relief. Then he scissored them, stretching her, and the sensation was so strong, so amazing, she had to grip his shoulders to keep herself from flying off the bed.

"I want to feel you this way," he rasped, "coming on my fingers."

"Yes."

In, out, slow, so slow, then faster, faster. Then his thumb brushed over her clit, and she shot off like a rocket, spasming around those fingers still pumping in her, sending her over a second time. She cried out at the bliss, the utter rightness.

"Hector! More, give me more."

"Always." He moved on top of her, his cock sinking inside her, his chest pressing against hers. Her legs wrapped around his waist. His mouth returned to hers, his kiss now slow and drugging. He tangled his fingers in her hair, angling her head. Touching her, always touching her.

He made love to her as if he needed to savor her. As if he didn't want to move too quickly for fear of scaring her away or ending things before he'd gotten enough. As if she were *everything* to him.

One of his hands moved down, down, plucked at her nipple, making her shiver, then slid between their bodies and found her most sensitive place. He rubbed as he continued stroking in and out, finally picking up the pace, just a little faster . . . faster.

Her muscles clenched, readying for another release. He pressed harder, and she shot off again, this climax so intense she left claw marks in his back. "Hector!"

"Noelle, my Noelle." Just like that, he erupted, her name roaring from his mouth, his hot seed shooting inside her.

When he collapsed on top of her, he immediately rolled to the side so that she could breathe, but he didn't allow any separation between their bodies. He held her tightly, panting, sweat sheening them both.

"Baby, please. Tell me you still love me." He cupped her cheek, his thumb tracing the rise of the bone. "Tell me you'll give me another chance, just one more, and I'll do everything in my power to make you happy. I swear I will. And I will never leave you, never change my mind," he added in a rush before she could reply. "I know what it's like to be without you. I can deal with anything but that."

She felt his heart beating against her ear, pounding in an uncontrolled rhythm.

He wasn't done. "I've been working with my arms, and I've got control. It's all about channeling the heat. I can atomize my entire body now, keeping the flames inside. I can also release the heat in continuous, manageable streams, all the time, so that I never overheat and catch fire if I don't want. Am I still a little scared I'll hurt you? Yes. And if I accidentally burn you, I'll be even more scared, but we'll work through it together."

Silence.

She traced her fingertip along the letters of her

name, the one on the top of his palm. "I meant what I said. You really hurt me, Hector."

"I know," he said sadly. "Of all the things I've done in my life, that's the one I would change first. You are *everything* to me." When she remained quiet, he added, "I will never try to change you. I love you exactly how you are. You're perfect."

"That's true," she said, her heart singing. She could forgive him and have this, she thought, weighing her options. Could have him and his body and his intensity now and forever. Or, she could send him away, unable to get past what he'd done, and go to bed cold and alone. Again, forever.

He wouldn't run if things got bad with his arms; she believed him about that. He'd always told her the truth; even when he'd broken things off, he'd told her the real reason, refusing to "feed her bullshit." So . . . was there really a need to think things through?

"How about this?" he said, clearly about to do a little manipulating. "Be with me, if only to convince everyone at AIR that I'm not gay. Did you know everyone thought that? The other day, Phoenix tried to set me up with one of her boyfriend's friends. Also, you took my virginity. If you dump me, I'll have to tell everyone you're a skeevy user."

Holding in her giggles proved to be a struggle. "All right. But only to convince everyone of your straightness. And you'll have to marry me," she said. "I want a legal right to boss you around. And you'll sign an agreement stating that if you ever want to end things, I get custody of your soul. That is nonnegotiable. Actually, go ahead and just hand over your soul right now. I get it no matter what."

He jerked upright and peered down at her, hope making him radiant. "You mean it?"

"Yes." A wave of tenderness swept through her. He'd never looked so happy, so relaxed. "I am going to boss you around, no question."

His lips quirked at the corners. "Not about that. I know that. About marriage."

Trembling, she reached up and cupped his jaw. "Yes. I think Hector Tremain has a nice ring to it, don't you? Besides, it's time you made an honest woman of me and supported your fake kid."

A bark of laughter as he swooped down for another kiss. "Twins, baby. We're having twins. And I *knew* those kids were mine. By the way, there's a ring in my pants pocket."

Rusty as his laughter was, it delighted her. Noelle didn't think she'd ever been this happy before. She was loved, cherished, accepted, adored. But the best part? She was understood. "Really?"

"I told you I was going to chase you around like a puppy until you caved."

"Let me see it."

Another kiss, one that turned so heated they began grinding together, making love again, his hands all over her, relearning her, worshipping her as she had always deserved—Hector would be the first to declare how true that was, she was just sure of it—and finally climaxing together.

Afterward, she wondered if, when she and Hector

woke up the next morning, because he was staying the night, damn it, and he was going to snuggle the hell out of her, if that would mean Dallas's vision had finally come true. If the countdown to his salvation—or damnation—would begin.

They'd soon find out.

Hector finally made it to his pants and grabbed the ring. When he returned to the bed, watching her with such loving adoration and longing that her chest ached in the best way possible, she couldn't keep her hands off him and had to climb into his lap.

"Show me!" she demanded greedily.

He rested against the headboard, the ring enclosed in his fist. "If you don't like it, I can always exchange it."

Slowly he opened his fingers. A skull and crossbones with diamonds for eyes rested in his palm, and she utterly melted. "Oh, Hector. My mother is going to have a heart attack when she sees this."

"Like I said, I can exchange—"

"Don't you dare! *I love it!* It's the most perfect ring ever. Put it on me right now, now, now!"

"So the bossiness has begun." Grinning, he slid the ring into place and she admired it in the light. What other man would have given her such an exquisite piece? He knew her. He really knew her, saw the true Noelle, and he loved her anyway. "I wanted to buy you other things, too, but I wasn't sure what to get the girl who has everything."

"You," she whispered, those silly tears returning for an altogether different reason. "I only ever want you."

"You've got me." He squeezed her tight. "Now and always."

"I love you," she said, twisting and throwing her arms around his neck. "Now let's have sex again!"

He was laughing as he tossed her down on the mattress, and Noelle knew they were *both* happier than they'd ever been or had known they could ever be. No matter what happened next, they were together. They would always be together.

And now, if she and Ava ever got into trouble—let's face it, they totally would—Hector could burn away the evidence. No need to mention that would be one of his husbandly duties, though. Not yet.

"I love that you aren't afraid to speak your mind," he said, kissing his way down her body.

"You love everything about me."

"True. So very true."

Coming soon from #1 *New York Times*
bestselling author

# KRESLEY COLE

# LOTHAIRE

An Immortals After Dark Novel

Centuries ago, Lothaire the Enemy of Old rose to
power, becoming the most feared vampire in the
immortal world. Still driven by a past filled with blood
vows and vendettas, the lethal warrior will not rest until
he captures the vampire Horde's crown for himself.

But the woman destined to be his Bride—a vulnerable
female whose blood stokes his desires to a fever pitch—
is the only one who can derail his quest for absolute
power. When forced to choose, will Lothaire succumb
to the torments of his past, or seize a future with her?

**COMING IN HARDCOVER JANUARY 2012.**

GALLERY BOOKS
A Division of Simon & Schuster
A CBS COMPANY

www.simonandschuster.com